KING *of the* MIDDLE MARCH

KEVIN CROSSLEY~HOLLAND

KING of the MIDDLE MARCH

Arthur

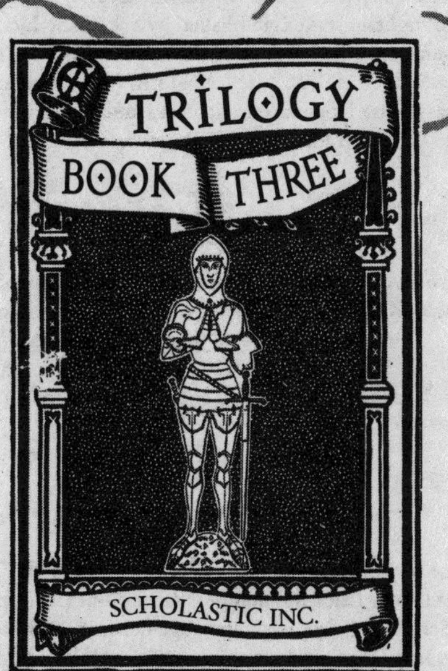

New York Toronto London Auckland Sydney
Mexico City New Delhi Hong Kong Buenos Aires

ISBN 0-439-26601-7

Arthur A. Levine Books hardcover edition designed by Marijka Kostiw, published by Arthur A. Levine Books, an imprint of Scholastic Inc., October 2004

12 11 10 9 8 7 6 5 4 3 2 1 6 7 8 9 10/0

Printed in the U.S.A. 40

First paperback printing, March 2006

The text of this book was set in 11-point Hoefler Text, with chapter titles and numbers in 14-point Callifonts C26 PostScript. The drop caps and page decorations were based upon thirteenth-century ornamental lettering.

for
judith elliott —
with love

the characters

ON CRUSADE

ARTHUR DE CALDICOT, aged 16, author of this book

LORD STEPHEN DE HOLT

TUROLD, the armorer

RHYS, the stableman

SIR WILLIAM DE GORTANORE, Arthur's father

LADY CÉCILE, Sir William's mistress

SIR SERLE DE CALDICOT, Arthur's foster brother, aged 19

TANWEN, a chamber-servant

KESTER, her two-year-old son

MILON DE PROVINS

BERTRAND (BERTIE) DE SULLY, aged 13, Milon's nephew and squire

GENNARO, a Venetian councillor

ENRICO DANDOLO, the Doge of Venice

SILVANO, the Master Shipwright

SIMONA, his daughter, a translator, aged 21

WIDO, Milon's armorer

GIFF, one of Milon's foot soldiers

GODARD, one of Milon's foot soldiers

SARACEN TRADERS FROM ALEXANDRIA

PAGAN, Milon's priest

CARDINAL CAPUANO

GEOFFREY DE VILLEHARDOUIN, sometime Marshal of Champagne

MARQUIS BONIFACE DE MONTFERRAT, leader of the crusade

ODD, a Venetian crusader

PIERO, a steersman

COUNT SIMON DE MONTFORT, a French leader

ENGUERRAND DE BOVES, a French nobleman

ROBERT DE BOVES, his brother

TADDEO, the Doge's surgeon

ABBOT GUY DE VAUX

A SHOEMAKER FROM MILAN

A ZARAN BOY

CHRÉTIEN, a miner from Provins

GISCARD, a miner from Provins

A FRENCH SERGEANT

NASIR, a Saracen singing teacher

NASIR'S TWO WIVES AND HIS DAUGHTER

ZANGI, Nasir's assistant

SISTER CIKA, a Benedictine nun

HAMADAT, captain of a merchant ship

A WANDERING SCHOLAR

A LOMBARDIAN KNIGHT

A TRADER IN PIACENZA

IN THE MARCH

SIR WALTER DE VERDON

LADY ANNE DE VERDON, his wife

WINNIE DE VERDON, their daughter, aged 14

LADY JUDITH DE HOLT

IZZIE, a chamber-servant at Holt

RAHERE, the musician and jester at Holt

SIR JOHN DE CALDICOT

LADY HELEN DE CALDICOT, his wife

SIAN, their daughter, aged 11

OLIVER, the priest at Caldicot

GATTY, Hum the reeve's daughter, aged 15

SLIM, the cook at Caldicot

RUTH, the kitchen-girl at Caldicot

ROBBIE, the kitchen-boy at Caldicot

LADY ALICE DE GORTANORE

TOM DE GORTANORE, aged 17

GRACE DE GORTANORE, his sister, aged 15

THOMAS, a freeman and messenger at Gortanore

MAGGOT, Thomas's wife

MAIR, Arthur de Caldicot's mother

MERLIN

IN THE STONE

KING ARTHUR

QUEEN GUINEVERE

SIR LANCELOT

KING PELLAM, Guardian of the Holy Grail

THE LADY OF THE LAKE, Sir Lancelot's foster-mother

LADY GISÈLE

SIR KAY

SIR GAUTER

SIR GILMERE

SIR ARNOLD

SIR SAGRAMOUR

SIR ECTOR DE MARIS

SIR UWAIN LE BLANCHEMAINS

SIR GAWAIN

SIR PERCEVAL

NASCIEN, a hermit

SIR MADOR

SIR BORS

SIR AGRAVAIN

SIR MORDRED

SIR URRY OF THE MOUNT

AGATHA, Sir Urry's mother

FYLELOLY, Sir Urry's sister

SIR TOR

SIR GAHERIS

SIR GARETH

THE BISHOP OF ROCHESTER

SIR LIONEL

THE ARCHBISHOP OF CANTERBURY

SIR GALAHAD

SIR LUCAN

SIR BEDIVERE

YGERNA, King Arthur's mother

ANIMALS

BONAMY, Arthur de Caldicot's warhorse

SHORTNECK, Sir Serle's warhorse

STUPENDOUS, Lord Stephen's warhorse

PIP, Arthur de Caldicot's horse in England

KINCALED, Sir Gawain's horse

A LEOPARD, in a Croatian church

A LEOPARD, belonging to a Lombardian knight

STORM AND TEMPEST, two running-hounds (or beagles)

Author's Note and Acknowledgments

ONCE MORE, I HAVE BEEN GIVEN A GREAT DEAL OF HELP. Hemesh Alles has drawn and redrawn attractive maps, as well as provided additional artwork based on medieval sources; Gillian Crossley-Holland lent me books on beekeeping and the stars; Maryann Johnson corrected my sketchy Italian; Ann Jones enlightened me about "hiraeth" and matters Welsh; Mike Tapper unearthed valuable information on early medieval galleys; and the Tree Advice Trust taught me about olives and apricots.

I've used "The Heart-in-Waiting" and lines from "Swarm and Honeycomb" from my *Selected Poems* (Enitharmon Press, 2001), and two short passages from my translation of *Beowulf* (Oxford University Press, 1999). I'm grateful to the BBC for inviting me to review the problems and pleasures of writing this trilogy in its admirable and regretted Radio 3 series, *Work in Progress.*

My heart leaped when, last summer, Rodney Slatford most generously offered me a silent house in which to write when interruptions on my own doorstep threatened to overwhelm me. Richard Barber, Arthurian scholar and medievalist, not only lent me absorbing research material, but he and his wife, Helen, accompanied me and my wife to the Dalmatian coast to see Zara (Zadar) and discover how to lay siege to it. In typing and correcting very many drafts of this book, Claire Conway has been unfailingly patient and blessedly good-humored, even when confronted with literally thousands of revisions. I am so grateful to her.

My wife, Linda, has made a quite extraordinary contribution — discussing the issues, suggesting provocative ways of fictionalizing them, fine-tuning the text, choosing the illustrations, and emboldening me with her tolerance, unwavering support, and love. This trilogy has engaged us, side by side, for almost five years.

Many of my foreign publishers and translators have become friends and heartened me with their hospitality and regular encouragement: especially, perhaps, Joukje Akveld at Lemniscaat and Asfrid Hegdal at N.W. Damm. I owe particular thanks to Arthur Levine for his rapid and generous response to a draft of this book, and his incisive comments on it.

The success of any book, let alone a trilogy, depends on a team effort. So I thank in particular the children's books department at Orion: Judith Elliott, Fiona Kennedy, Alex Webb, Jane Hughes, Rowan Stanfield, and Iona Campbell. Judith has given this text the benefit of repeated close readings and made very many helpful suggestions, as well as known how to urge me on, and when not to. I first wrote for her thirty years ago, and she is a dear friend and a great editor. This book is dedicated to her.

And finally: All the names in the Middle March are taken from Ordnance Survey maps with the exception of Caldicot, Holt, Verdon, Gortanore, and Catmole. But these are no more than my names for five stunning early medieval sites. Maybe some of my readers will be tempted to go and find them.

BURNHAM MARKET

JUNE 16, 2003

CONTENTS

KING
of the
MIDDLE MARCH

SWORD AND SCIMITAR

AWAY EAST OVER THE THOUSAND-TONGUED SEA, WITH ALL its sweet promises, its stabs and sudden rushes, one silver-gold blade of light.

A sword. No! A scimitar. That's what I saw when I lifted the salt-sticky flap of our tent.

Lord Stephen and I reached Venice at noon yesterday with Turold, our armorer, and our stableman, Rhys. Saint John's Eve. The day when Winnie kissed me right on the mouth, two years ago, long before we were betrothed.

We weren't allowed into Venice herself. All the crusaders are billeted out here on the island of Saint Nicholas. But we've been invited to a sea-feast in the city, and so have Milon de Provins and his squire, Bertie, who is only thirteen.

Frenchmen wearing red crosses, Germans and Italians, Flemings with their green crosses: There are thousands and thousands of crusaders on this island, but we haven't met any other Englishmen yet.

All night I slept and stirred and slept to the sounds of water. They washed away our seven-week journey.

The sun rose; I was newborn.

GOD'S ARMY

IT WAS ONLY WHEN I RODE BONAMY DOWN THE SPINE OF this island today that I understood what an army really amounts to.

And I'm part of it!

Saint Nicholas is very long but no more than half a mile wide, and Lord Stephen and I and Rhys and Turold have a very small camp right at the northern end. About a quarter of a mile away there are fifty men from Provins, led by Milon, and beyond them I came to the encampment of hundreds of Italians. As I rode in, a trumpeter played. His trumpet caught fire in the sunlight, and I stood up in my saddle and shouted.

Then I saw a monk standing in the middle of a crowd of sitting men.

"Lei!" he called out. *"La Francia? La Germania?"*

"English," I said.

"Inglese," the monk shouted. *"L'Inghilterra!"*

He put his staff between his legs and waddled round, with a waggling tail, and everyone laughed. I've heard that the Sicilians and Greeks think all the English have tails, but I didn't know the Italians do as well.

I dismounted and the monk forefingered me. "I say crusade is a new kind of warfare," he called out. "A holy fight. Here are soldiers like monks."

The Italian soldiers didn't look like monks at all. Greasy. Half-shaven. They looked like bandits.

"They say no like San Niccolo," the monk told me. "No much women. No much wine. I say, put on the armor of God."

"The whole armor of God," I replied. "The belt of truth, the sword of the spirit, the helmet of salvation!"

"Bravo!" exclaimed the monk. He reached into the pocket of his gown and pulled out a little wooden box. Then he stepped towards me, and opened it.

Inside, there was a leathery brown stick of a thing with a black tip, lying on a pad of scarlet silk.

"Finger," said the monk. "Finger of San Runcimano. Kiss!"

He closed the box again, and held it up. I closed my eyes and held my breath. I kissed the lid.

Next, I rode into the encampment of some soldiers from Picardy. They were all yelling and jeering. When I came close, I could see two men having a swordfight. One was on his knees and gasping. His left arm was dangling beside him and blood was dripping from his hand.

Then I recognized Milon's squire, Bertie, standing just a few steps away.

"Bertie!" I called out. "What are you doing here?"

Bertie jerked his head, but his eyes never left the fighting men. "Look at them!"

"Does Milon know?"

"I don't care."

"Why are they fighting?"

"It's a test. He won't surrender."

"How can we beat the Saracens if we start shedding each other's blood?"

"You can't have a test without a winner and a loser," Bertie said. "He's lost two fingers. So far. Look!"

I didn't want to look, and I don't know why the man on his knees didn't surrender. I wheeled away fiercely and Bonamy snorted.

"Where are you going?" Bertie shouted. "Arthur!"

All the way down the island there were encampments — conical tents and pyramids, marquees and flapping makeshifts that looked as if they'd blow away as soon as the sea wind opened its mouth. And milling around each encampment there were knights and squires and soldiers, and a few women and children.

I saw pairs of squires wrestling and practicing at quarterstaff, I saw little groups running races and trying out sword strokes against the pel, and suddenly I heard in my head the voice of Alan, Lord Stephen's first armorer: "You won't last long on a crusade. You'll get mulched!"

But I've grown three inches since then, and I've practiced hard, even when I didn't want to; even when Lord Stephen was away. I'm much stronger than I was before.

I saw some men praying, some sharpening their weapons, shaving each other with cutthroats, watering their horses, singing raucous songs; I saw a chain of men unloading dead chickens and thousands of loaves from a Venetian galley. Two whole mounds of them, side by side on the beach! I saw a Flemish falconer loose his bird, and watched the falcon climb and stoop on a seabird. Turold says gulls are stringy and taste fishy, and even more salty than our salted pork at the end of winter.

I'd just left the German camp when the devil whispered in Bonamy's right ear.

Bonamy snorted. He almost screeched. He reared up on his hind legs. Then he leaped forward, and it was all I could do to stay in the saddle.

"Bonamy!" I yelled. "God's gristle! Stop!"

It was no use.

Bonamy charged straight through the Angevin encampment. He uprooted one of the kitchen-tent pegs, and dragged the guy rope behind him. The whole thing collapsed.

I could hear people yelling and dogs snarling and cooking pots clanging, but I couldn't stop Bonamy. He kicked off the rope and galloped back up the spine of the island past the Flemish and Norman encampments before I was able to pull him up.

One of the Angevin cooks screamed oaths and shook his ladle at me. God help me! I'm not riding anywhere near that camp again.

When we got back, Bonamy looked at me with his damson eyes as if absolutely nothing had happened. He gave me a friendly neigh.

I inspected his hooves, and then his genitals. I looked into his mouth, his left ear, his right . . . It was puffy and almost closed. A wasp, maybe, or a hornet. Anyhow, a devil's sting!

I could tell something was worrying Lord Stephen. "What's wrong, sir?" I asked.

"Two knights from the Île-de-France have just arrived. They've told Milon that five other knights have broken their oaths."

"But how can they?" I asked. "They've taken the Cross."

"Exactly," said Lord Stephen. "They say they're going to make their own way from the port of Marseilles."

"Well, that's not too bad then," I said.

"It is very bad," Lord Stephen replied. "We asked the Venetians to build ships for thirty-three thousand men. But nothing like that number have arrived, and Saint John's Eve has already come and gone. If many more knights are going to make their own choices instead of bringing their men and money here, we'll be unable to pay the Venetians for their ships."

"What would happen then?" I asked.

"There would be no crusade," Lord Stephen said bluntly.

"No crusade!"

"We can't launch the crusade without ships," Lord Stephen said, "and the Doge won't provide us with ships unless we pay him."

"But after taking the Cross," I cried, "and all our preparations, and all our journeys, surely, sir . . ."

"All for nothing," said Lord Stephen. "Anyhow, how are we to achieve the land oversea? Tell me that. By the front door? Or should we try to cut off the Saracens' supplies?"

"What do you mean, sir? Are you saying we wouldn't go straight to the Holy Land?"

Lord Stephen gave me a watery smile. "How many miles to Bethlehem?" he asked me.

"That's what Gatty asked me," I said.

"Who?"

"Gatty. At Caldicot."

"Ah!" said Lord Stephen, half-smiling. "Yes. She walked all the way to Holt, didn't she. Love-dumb for you!"

"No, sir," I said. "Anyhow, she told me once — "

"Another time!" Lord Stephen said briskly. "Come on! You've been out all day, and you haven't even told me what you've seen and heard. And after that, Turold has some job for you and Rhys wants you to wash down Bonamy."

"Seawater dries sticky," I said.

"It can't be helped," Lord Stephen replied.

When I rode down Saint Nicholas today, I thought there must be more than thirty-three thousand men. Not fewer, as Lord Stephen says, but many, many more! Three times thirty-three.

Surely there are enough knights here to raise the money for the Venetian boats.

hover, then swoop

IT IS DIFFICULT TO WRITE IN THIS TENT.

At Holt, almost no one came into my room, and I could leave my parchment on the window ledge. And at Caldicot, I could sit in my window seat with my ink-perch at my elbow.

I had beetles and spiders for company there, and sometimes a slug or a squirm — that's what my foster sister Sian used to call them. But here there are hordes of flies, whining and buzzing, and they bite the back of my neck, and the backs of my knees, and my knuckles.

There's no table here and no window ledge. So sometimes I prop myself up against my saddlebag and stuff a cushion between my knees and use that as a table; and sometimes I stretch right out, and kick up my heels, and write lying on my stomach. But each time, I have to pack my parchment away again as soon as the ink is dry and I've polished the page. I know I'm meant to use a boar's tooth, but before I left, Winnie gave me one of her teeth and that works almost as well.

I've brought plenty of oak-apples, and acacia sap, and green vitriol in a glazed bottle, but it's not easy to make ink here because there's no fresh rainwater and also, if I'm not careful, grains of sand get into the mixture.

On the way here, most of my quills were wrecked. Turold bent them in half when he jammed his hammer into my saddlebag. When I went to the scriptorium at Wenlock, Brother Austin told me the outer pinions of geese and swans make the best quills, but the only feathers here are those of herring gulls. Their insides are furry, but at least they're strong and shave easily.

Lord Stephen and I had so much to do before leaving that, although I've often looked into my stone and stepped into Camelot, I haven't been able to write anything at all for months. There wasn't even time to write about my betrothal to Winnie. But I do want to write down everything now.

When we embark on our galley, and sail south, slicing through the water, my pen will hover, then swoop, and mew, and scream.

Sea-feast

I WAS ACROSS THE TABLE FROM MILON AND BERTIE. HIS FULL name is Bertrand de Sully, and he's Milon's nephew as well as his squire. He's as stocky as his uncle, but small as a shrimp.

"Arthur!" exclaimed Milon.

I bowed to him.

Milon pursed his lips. "I forget, you think," he said.

"No," I replied carefully.

"Yes," said Milon, "I not forget I knight you." Milon turned to our Venetian hosts. "Arthur bravee!" he said in a loud voice.

Milon had just begun to explain to the Venetians how in Soissons I stopped a man from knifing a woman, when the first course arrived.

On my platter were three creatures that looked like very juicy white worms, white tinged with pink; they wore plate armor and had long whiskers.

Lord Stephen's eyes gleamed. "No time for faint hearts," he said under his breath.

Milon and Bertie were tucking their napkins under their chins, and the four Venetians laid theirs over their right arms, and then they all munched their worms as though they hadn't eaten since last week.

One of the Venetian councillors, Gennaro, raised his glass goblet. "Welcome back!" he said. "Our friends in God. Our partners!"

Then we all tapped the table with our knuckles, and raised our goblets.

I'd scarcely eaten a mouthful before a servant brought in a platter piled with strange black and yellow and green gobs and nuggets, like the nose-pickings of giants.

"Oh dear!" said Lord Stephen. "You're spoiling us."

But that didn't fool the Venetian sitting next to me. "Sea snails," he said. "Out of their shells! You like?"

They tasted disgusting, but it didn't matter. I felt charged with such excitement.

When I entered service with Lord Stephen as his squire, I supposed we would be joining the crusade at once. But that was two and a half years ago, and since then I've chosen Bonamy and trained him; I've been fitted out with a suit of armor and practiced my fighting skills; I've learned to speak French; I took the Cross from our young leader, Count Thibaud, before he suddenly died.

We met the old Doge when we traveled here before, sixteen months ago. He's at least eighty-four, the same age Saint Luke lived to. His eyes are bright and clear, but he's stone blind. He waves his arms like a baby, and never stops talking.

Milon and the other envoys told him there's no sea power to compare with the Republic of Venice, and asked the Doge to build the ships to carry the crusaders and their horses.

"You are asking a great deal of us," the Doge said, but in the end he agreed to build ships for more than four thousand knights and the same number of horses and nine thousand squires and twenty thousand foot soldiers, so every able-bodied man in the city has been boat-building for the last fifteen months. Not only that. The Venetians promised to feed us and our horses for the first nine months as well.

I managed to wash down one of the worms and three of the nose-pickings with more wine, and then the servants brought in the next course. Alive!

"Magnifique!" exclaimed Milon.

"Bellissimi!" exclaimed the four Venetians.

"What are they?" I asked.

"Lobsters!" said Gennaro, laughing.

The eight lobsters were blowing out vile sea-spittle, and they peered at me in a kind of sunken way.

The servants carried the lobsters away to be boiled, and brought us blobs of matted blood and glossy brown balls on a silver platter.

"Oh!" gasped Lord Stephen.

"Cows' eyes," I said. "I'm sure they are."

"Ceriglie e cipolle!" said one of the councillors. "Cherries. Onions! *Marinati!*" They all shook their heads and laughed.

Milon and the other French envoys agreed on a price of five marks for each horse and two for each man, and then they borrowed five thousand marks from Venetian moneylenders, and gave them straight back to the Doge so that work in the shipyards could begin. They swore to make full payment as soon as we've all mustered here, while the Doge promised all the ships would be ready to sail by the Feast of Saint Peter and Saint Paul. That's the day after tomorrow.

I had to eat my lobster with a long metal pick and crackers.

"This enemy you must defeat with weapons," said one of the Venetians. "First the lobsters, then the Saracens, yes?"

It tasted quite sweet. More like meat than fish, really.

Next, the servants came back with white wine and a huge bowl of fruit: pomegranates, grapes, cucumbers, lemons. There were oranges as well, and dates, which look like a badger's droppings and have stones in them.

"From Egypt," said Gennaro.

"Saracen fruit!" I exclaimed. "Like the fruit Saladin sent to Coeur-de-Lion when he caught the red fever."

The councillor smiled. "Trade," he said.

"So then," said Lord Stephen, "the Saracens have numbers in their heads and dates in their mouths."

"And stars in their eyes," I added. "Sir William told me the Saracens have written books about astronomy."

"We are ready now," Gennaro said, "but are you?"

Milon nodded. He picked a piece of something from between his teeth and flicked it onto the floor. "I am ready," he said, and he shrugged. "But everyone not here. Everyone bring money."

The councillor leaned back in his seat. "We wait," he said.

"Men from all over Europe," Lord Stephen added. "Provins and Picardy and Champagne, Anjou and Burgundy and Germany and Italy. Even a few from England! All in this one place and all at one time. It's not easy."

"Not easy to build ships," said Gennaro. "Galleys. Horse transports. Two hundred ships in five hundred days."

"Incroyable!" exclaimed Milon.

"We wait," said the Venetian coolly. "You give us money, we give you ships."

"Our new leader is on his way," Lord Stephen added. "Marquis Boniface."

Chin-pie and a miserable wood louse

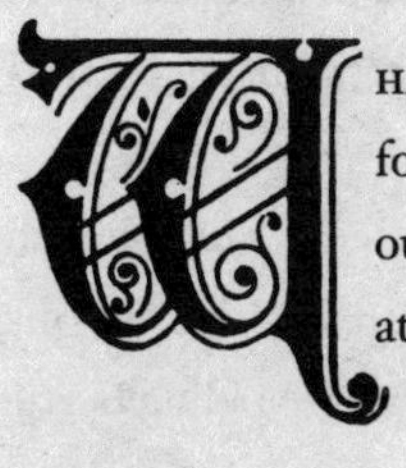

HAT I HAD MEANT TO DO WAS SAY SUNSET PRAYERS for my mother. But as the soft light filtered into our tent, I began to think about Oliver, our priest at Caldicot. And then I heard us arguing.

"No, Arthur. You're wrong. Suffering scarcely matters."

"It matters if you've got nothing to eat," I exclaimed. "How do you think Gatty likes going to bed hungry? And with every bone in her body aching?"

"My dear boy," Oliver said patiently, "you're a foolish child of God. I've told you before: Poverty is part of God's will."

"How can it be?" I demanded.

Oliver drew in his breath sharply. No! It was the wind sucking the cheeks of our tent. And then I heard someone calling me. Far off, and repeated, and high-pitched.

"Arthur! Help! Arthur!"

I picked up my jackknife and dived out of the tent. Bertie was in the water up to his chest, and four squires were poking him with quarterstaffs and laughing.

I ran across the beach as fast as I could, but two of the squires saw me coming and waded out of the water to meet me.

They jeered at me, and one grabbed my right arm; the other made a dive for my right leg.

"Watch it!" I yelled. "I've got this knife!"

I waved the knife; I kicked my left leg. But the two of them dragged me into the water, and one of them put his foot on my chest and held me under until I was choking.

The water rushed around me, and right into me. My ears were blocked and bubbling, but I could still hear them laughing. I kicked. I twisted. I was drowning.

They let go of me then. I got onto my knees, retching, and coughed the salt water out of my nose, my throat. I rubbed my stinging eyes. Then I saw the other two squires were holding Bertie under as well.

Still kneeling in the water, I raised my left hand. I drew back my knife.

The squires jeered. They taunted us. Then they made off, hooting.

Bertie struggled to his feet. He too was fully clothed.

"What were they saying?" I croaked.

"Water rats!" said Bertie. "Lily-livers!"

"What happened?" I asked.

"Nothing."

"You said something."

"They gave me a chin-pie."

I looked at Bertie's red chin. "Why? What did you say?"

"Only what they are. Sausage bladders! German slime!"

"Bertie," I said, "you shouldn't pick fights. You know what my father said when I was thirteen and told him I wanted to go crusading?"

"What?"

"'Shrimps don't last long when they get washed out to sea.'"

"I'm not a shrimp," Bertie said angrily.

My father. Sir William de Gortanore. I give thanks to merciful God each day that he decided not to come on this crusade. He does believe Christians and Saracens are equal in God's eyes, and that's more than Oliver does, but he's sixty-seven now, and completely blind in his itching left eye, and half the time he's in a rage.

I hate my father. He has stopped me from finding my mother. And he murdered her husband, Emrys — either that or he had him murdered — and he beats his wife, Lady Alice. The first time I talked to him as my own blood-father, he warned me, "When people start digging, they may find their own bones." His right eye glittered.

I know it's dangerous to go behind my father's back, but the strange thing is I think he's somehow nervous of me. Maybe he's worried because he's not sure exactly how much I've found out.

Bertie and I waded out of the water. "What about your father, then?" I asked him. "Milon told me he's half-English."

"He is."

"Where is he?"

"At home. His whole body's shaking, and his hair has fallen out. He can't even hold a knife or a spoon."

"What about your mother?"

Bertie flopped down onto the wet sand. It was quite hard, and rippled like the clouds above us. He splayed the fingers of his right hand and stabbed the sand, and then he just bunched himself up like a miserable wood louse.

"Is she dead?" I asked.

Bertie didn't reply; he just nodded, and I squatted down beside him.

"My mother had to give me away when I was two days old," I said. "I still can't bring her to life again."

Bertie went on staring at the sand. "What do you mean?"

"You're shivering," I said. "Go and get some dry clothes on. I'll tell you sometime."

I stood up and tramped back across the foreshore to our tent. No one was there, so I delved to the bottom of my saddlebag, and checked my seeing stone was safe, and then I pulled out the little screw of grey cotton. I unwound it and the inner wrapping of floppy cream silk. I took out my mother's glowing gold ring. The tiny engraving of baby Jesus in his mother's arms. I slipped it on.

When Thomas, my father's servant, gave it to me, I promised I wouldn't tell anyone about it, but I'm hundreds and hundreds of miles away from England and Sir William now.

I'm going to tell Lord Stephen how my mother secretly sent it to me, and ask him whether it is all right to wear it.

My mother's ring on my right hand. My betrothal ring on my left. I'll be well armed!

I got down on my knees. In the tent's quiet vestry-light, I said sunset prayers for my mother and Winnie. . . .

Which is what I was going to do before Oliver interrupted me.

Galleys and Transports

THEY'RE SO PURPOSEFUL. EACH GAZING ACROSS THE water, openmouthed; each tethered by its stern.

Soaring maypoles with rigging gently chittering; yards festooned with sagging sails; giddy sky-cages like rooks' nests in a dry year; chains and iron beaks; an array of swaying sea-castles; a whole kingdom of quiet hulls and squeaky decks and booming holds and chambers and walkways and ladders and oarsmen's benches: I don't know exactly how to describe the ships, but I couldn't take my eyes off them.

Silvano, the Master Shipwright at the Arsenale, showed us around the dockyard. He told us the biggest ship is almost two hundred feet long and will hold one thousand crusaders. She's called *Violetta*. I thought it would be better to call her *Sunflower*, or even *Gog* or *Blunderbore* or something like that, but Silvano shook his head and gave me a wink.

"My wife!" he said. "Violetta."

The oak hull of each galley is made of two hundred and forty different wooden parts, but they're all set on just two huge frames. So complicated. So simple. No wonder everyone says the Venetians are the most skillful boatbuilders in the world.

"Where does all the wood come from?" I asked.

"Not Dalmatia!" said Silvano, and he stuck out his lower lip. "City of Zara people rebel for twenty years." He waved his arms.

"Foresta Umbra," he said. "Forest of Shadows in far south Italy. Very difficult. Very expensive."

"So everything's ready!" Lord Stephen said. "Down to the last shaving."

"Pronto," Silvano replied. "Two hundred ships." He rubbed his right thumb and forefinger. "Now money!" he said.

Lord Stephen smiled that wistful smile that just flickers around the corners of his little mouth. "Well, all these ships are young and impatient, aren't they, Arthur? We mustn't keep them waiting."

"When you pay?" demanded the shipwright. "We Venetians keep our promise. You crusaders break yours."

Before we left the dockyard for Saint Nicholas, one of our boatmen lit a torch and set it up in the stern. The water around us soon caught fire, and turned itself into flashing daggers and stars.

Glass Venetians

AT HOLT, THREE OF THE CASTLE WINDOWS HAVE BEEN leaded and glassed, and Lord Stephen has an azure Venetian glass goblet with a twisted stem.

Here, glass is used in all kinds of ways. For jugs, tureens, drinking glasses. And for jigsaw pictures of Mary and Jesus. I've seen women wearing necklaces strung with little glass balls, pale green and violet and misty blue. They're like sea-eyes.

If you half-close your eyes, Venice might be wholly glass. Windows flashing, domes shining, water jigging and leaping as if it were plucked by sky-puppeteers with invisible silk strings.

Venetians have sallow skins. The men are golden ruffians. Even when they shave, they look unshaven, and wiry hair grows all over their bodies. The women are beautiful lionesses, with hair of two or even three different colors — tawny and bronze and copper. They're always laughing, and most of them have singed, husky voices; they speak very fast, with much more to say than time to say it in.

Their eyes are so large and liquid that at first I supposed Venetians must be gentle or even breakable. But actually, they're tough too, and self-interested and calculating.

however hard we try

AMB-CLOUDS, AND THE SKY'S BLUE PASSAGES; AND then my own face, rather blurred. My big ears. My eyes, wide and alert. That's all I could see to begin with.

And then, when I held up my seeing stone to the sun, this last day of June, I thought I could actually see through it. Like staring into a pond, down through the layers of water, beyond the spawn and the wrigglers.

But my stone is much, much more than a mirror or a pond. It is a world. I still keep it in the dirty old saffron cloth in which Merlin gave it to me, only now it's even dirtier, and each time I look into it I see my namesake, King Arthur, or the knights of the Round Table. His fair fellowship.

Once upon a time I thought I was Arthur-in-the-stone. Sometimes what happens to King Arthur seems to copy what happens to me, but sometimes it's the other way round. He and Ygerna, his blood-mother, have found each other, and I believe that in the end I will find mine. I've hoped the same hopes as Arthur, and feared the same fears. I've seen Arthur's knights ride out, north and south, east and west, questing for the Holy Grail, and I've seen Sir Lancelot and Queen Guinevere naked to one another, joyful and sorrowful, and I keep wondering what will happen if the king finds out.

My stone is telling me something, if only I can work out what.

Duty and sacrifice and honor and passion, insult and treachery: I've seen all those in my stone, and I see more all the time. From the day Merlin gave it to me, I've never gone anywhere without it.

When I stepped into our tent and looked into my stone again, the king was there. Sitting alone at the huge Round Table and staring into it.

A huge hunk of rock crystal. A hemisphere. It's too heavy for even one hundred men to lift, so Merlin, the Hooded Man, must have spirited it to Camelot. Within the crystal there are nodules and black warts, cracks, splits. There are stars and dark holes. And there's a mass of tiny threads, silver and shining, like gossamer on a misty autumn morning. It makes me think how everything in the world turns out to be connected, even if we don't realize it is at first.

King Arthur stares, and then he gives a sudden start, and looks around. He can hear a voice, but he doesn't know where it's coming from.

"Where are your knights, Arthur? Where are they all?"

A man's voice, dark with pain.

"Arthur! Your fair fellowship. Gone with the four winds. Is there no knight worthy to see the Holy Grail?"

I knew who it was the moment I heard him. King Pellam, Guardian of the Holy Grail, who was wounded by Sir Balin, pierced with the same lance that pierced Jesus through the ribs.

"Not one knight of the Round Table?" the voice demands, sorrowful and angry. "Can no man ride from here to Corbenic through this wailing world, and redeem the sin of Judas? Can no one ask the right question?"

King Arthur clenches both his fists. "What question?" he growls.

“The words that will heal me and save me from this agony,” the voice replies. “The words that will heal the suffering wasteland, and allow it to grow green again.”

Then King Pellam fell silent; my stone went blind.

I waited. I wrapped both hands around it. I stared so deeply into it that nothing else in the world existed.

The wasteland . . . All at once, I thought of Haket, Lord Stephen’s priest. He told me all Christendom is a wasteland, a wilderness of the spirit. He said people are taking the law into their own hands and behaving not as Christians but animals.

“Until we’re Christian not only in word but in deed,” he said, “how can we ever enter Jerusalem?”

But how can humans be perfect? We can’t, however hard we try. So it can’t be only through our own efforts that we will reach the Holy City, but also through God’s grace, because He wants us to chase all the Saracens out.

Nothing is easy

"Do you really think I want to be cooped up in this stuffy tent, teaching you the ten categories?" I demanded. "I could be galloping Bonamy, or collecting clams, or oiling my armor and talking to Turold. I have to brush Lord Stephen's clothes. I could be writing."

"I'm not stopping you," said Bertie.

I shook my head. "You know perfectly well what Milon and Lord Stephen have told us. Four classes each week. Two for my French. Two for your learning."

"What's the point? Milon doesn't know about quantities and qualities and all that."

"The more you learn, the more you understand. I like learning French. I like the sound of it. One moment throaty, the next like bright birdsong."

"You can't learn prowess," Bertie said, bright-eyed. "Let's go outside."

"No," I said. "You won't work outside."

Bertie grinned. He's got a gap between his two upper teeth. "I don't need to understand how you say something to know what it means," he said.

"Which category stands on its own?" I asked.

"The substance," said Bertie, screwing up his face as if he'd tasted something awful.

"Tell me a substance."

"A sword."

"What else?"

"I don't know. A horse. A finger."

"Good," I said. "What about two?"

"Two what?"

"Two fingers."

Bertie looked at me as if I were trying to trick him. "That's a substance and a quantity," he said cautiously.

"At last!" I exclaimed. "So what are the other categories? All the ones that can never exist on their own but must always belong to a substance."

"I can't remember," said Bertie. "This is so boring!"

"Then let's get it over with. Come on! Times. Activities."

"There's no point," said Bertie. "I'm not going to." He stood up and tousled his hair as if he were trying to get rid of every category and judgment and substance and accident in his buzzing head. "You can't teach me anyhow. You're not a priest."

Nothing is easy when it's new. How can I talk to the Venetians who can't speak English? How should you pitch a tent in soft sand? How do you crack a lobster? From the moment we got here, we have been faced at each turn with new difficulties.

I do like challenges, but what I haven't found out yet is how to teach Bertie. If I were Serle, I'd just shout at him. But I'm not like that. Anyhow, he's much younger than I am, and we've got to live side by side for weeks and months.

◆ ◆ ◆

This evening, I told Lord Stephen about my mother's ring and how she secretly sent it to me. I explained how I promised Thomas, Sir William's servant, that I wouldn't tell anyone about it.

"And you kept your promise," Lord Stephen said. "Which is more than Thomas did. He failed you. He said he'd arranged for you to meet your mother, but she never came."

"Perhaps she doesn't want to meet me," I said.

"Of course she does."

"That's what I think sometimes," I said.

"Anyhow," said Lord Stephen, "you're quite right to tell me everything now."

Then I showed Lord Stephen my ring.

He had to hold it very close to his eyes so he could see baby Jesus reaching out and giving His mother something . . . what it is, I still don't know.

"Yes," Lord Stephen said. "Wear it, and keep it warm. Your mother cares for you. You will find her."

Fighting Fear

HAT'S IT LIKE?" I ASKED. "FIGHTING? IN A BATTLE?

Wido, Milon's armorer, sniffed. Then he looked round the ring of Milon's foot soldiers sitting under the sun and narrowed his eyes. "Go on then, Giff! Tell Arthur."

Giff got to his feet and stared down at me. He smiled slightly; I think he did. He has a scar running from one corner of his mouth across his cheek and under his right ear, so it's difficult to tell.

"You've been afraid?" he inquired.

"Yes," I said. "Sometimes."

" 'Course you have," said Giff. "We all have. When?"

"When I had to belly out across the ice and rescue Sian. She's my sister. Well . . . she was."

"Dead," said Giff.

"No! No, it's too difficult to explain."

"That all, then?" asked Giff. First he looked at Wido, then round the group, and I saw him wink. Suddenly everyone leaped up and howled and stepped towards me, and I gasped and put up my fists, but when I looked round again, they were just laughing.

Giff drew back his lips so I could see his teeth. "You was saying?"

"Across the ice," I said, and I realized I was out of breath, "and once I was afraid when Alan the armorer pressed his quarterstaff down on my windpipe. And when I wrestled with Jehan. You know, Milon's farrier."

"Jehan," repeated Wido. "We knew Jehan, didn't we, boys?"

"He wounded me," I said, and I held up my left arm and showed them the long scar.

"Mad as a monkey," said Wido.

"What happened to him?"

Wido clutched his throat with his hands, and then jerked back his head. "But you, Arthur," he said. "You bravee!"

"Bravee!" repeated the ring of foot soldiers, and they all laughed again.

"You knight," said Wido.

"Not yet," I replied. "That depends on Milon."

Wido caught the eye of another man. "Godard! I thought you'd swallowed your tongue."

Godard advanced on me. He's not all that big, but tough and sinewy. "Fighting-fear is different," he began, and he rubbed his right hand across his mouth. "Soon as you know there's going to be fighting, it's like a fever. Makes your skin crawl. You get the squits. Then you start trembling and it don't stop. Isn't that right, boys?"

All Milon's men were nodding. One of them looked the same age as I am. His Adam's apple was bobbing up and down.

"Your mouth's fig-dry," Wido said.

"And the Night Hag, she tramples you," said Giff.

Godard rubbed his hand across his mouth again. "And your fear gallops with you into the fight. You're alive! Your blood's on fire. You're afraid. Everyone's afraid. Some people show it, some don't."

"And some are brave," added Wido, "and some aren't."

"Milon says you can't learn to be brave," I said. "It's just instinct."

"You can learn loyalty," said Wido. "And duty. You can stick it out."

"But when a Saracen runs at you, and he's howling?" I asked.

"That's when it counts," Wido replied. "In the thick of it."

"Cowards!" said Godard in disgust. "They're worse than grass snakes."

"They should be skinned," said Wido.

"Remember bloody Gotiller?" asked Godard.

"He did for us, all right," said Wido. "We lost five men because of him. So after the battle we opened up his stomach and drew out his gut and wound it round a pole."

"The Saracens are worst," said Giff. "I've fought the Germans and the Angevins, but the Saracens are worst. Howling and wailing. Ghastly wailing."

Godard wrapped his arms around his chest. "Saracens know about loyalty and duty, all right. Bloody infidels! They're cruel as fishhooks, and they think God is on their side."

"Want to know what they did to a mate of mine?" Giff asked me.

The hot sun beat down, and I realized I was shivering. "What?" I asked.

"He'll find out soon enough," Wido said.

What I'll find out is whether I'm good enough. Whether everything I know to be right — duty and loyalty and grit — is stronger than my fear once I'm actually in battle.

Not just fear. Worse than that. Yellow seizure. Battle-terror.

I've trained hard, and I trust Bonamy, and I know what I should do, but I'm still afraid.

Enemies of God

HEY'RE KILLERS, MILON'S MEN! WIDO AND GODARD and Giff."

"Killers of evil," said Lord Stephen. "That's what Saint Bernard said."

"No, sir, you don't understand. They murdered one of their own men because he was a coward and let them down."

Lord Stephen blinked several times. "Or because his fear made them afraid," he said.

"I wish I hadn't talked to them."

"Sit down!" Lord Stephen said. "Standing there like that, first on one leg, then on the other."

"I'm sorry, sir."

"This sun's bad enough without my having to stare right into it. Now then, Arthur! What is our crusade?"

"An act of devotion," I replied. "A quest that requires fighting skills and can win us great honor. A war against the enemies of God."

"Yes, all those things," said Lord Stephen. "We're only fighting because keeping the peace would be wrong — we're not killing for the sake of it."

"Milon's men are," I said.

"Look at it from their point of view," said Lord Stephen. "They didn't choose to come. And what's in it for them? Company. Adventure. A woman or two. That's all."

"Yes, sir."

"As I told you at Soissons," Lord Stephen said, "there are many reasons why men take the Cross, some noble, some not, and leaders have to make do with all sorts and conditions of men. But when we stand before God, each of us must answer for himself."

Lord Stephen swatted away a noisy fly.

"Do you remember Salman?" I asked him.

"Of course," said Lord Stephen. "The dying Saracen trader."

"The way he smiled at me, and then thanked us and blessed us. I think he was ready to stand before God."

"Not God," Lord Stephen corrected me. "A false prophet."

"What I can't understand is why the Saracens are such enemies of God. Oliver says they are. Count Thibaud said they are."

"I say they are," said Lord Stephen in a quiet, firm voice. "If I didn't believe that, I wouldn't be sitting here. However, that doesn't mean we have to howl and rant and rail against them."

"The Saracens write books about astronomy and algebra and singing," I said. "Fustian cloth was first made in Egypt. The Venetians trade with the Saracens! And the one I met was a sweet-tempered man. So why are the Saracens enemies of God?"

"Because they deny Christ," said Lord Stephen. "Because they worship Allah instead of the true God. Because they bow down to a false prophet. Because they sully the holy places in Bethlehem and Jerusalem. Is that enough?"

"Yes, sir."

"Of course, there are some good Saracens, just as there are some bad Christians."

"My father told me about Saladin."

"There you are. A great leader and a fine man. Now if he were here, your father would say —"

"I'm glad he's not!" I exclaimed.

"Yes," said Lord Stephen, and he smiled gently. "Well! So am I!"

"Is it true that Saladin was a better man than King John?" I asked.

Lord Stephen closed his eyes. "Very probably," he replied.

"The king tried to unthrone his own brother!"

Lord Stephen sighed. "Leaders often have to look in two directions at the same time," he said.

"What do the Saracens say about us?" I asked. "Sir John told me they believe they're fighting a holy war too. A *jihad*!"

"We have much in common," Lord Stephen said, "but far more that separates us. They believe Jesus will come down from heaven and call on the quick and the dead to follow their religion. Islam."

"When?"

"They believe the sun will set in the east during the Last Days. I don't know exactly what they say about us. But all your questions . . . I've got some good news for you."

Then Lord Stephen told me Milon rode in while I was collecting our consignment of cheese and bread and fruit from the morning barge, and announced that if I'm ready, he will make me a knight three weeks from today. The twenty-seventh day of July.

I wish I were being knighted on the ninth day, because nine is my number. But at least twenty-seven is three times nine, and Oliver would say that's even better. I can hear his voice now. "My dear boy! It's obvious. Three times nine! One nine for the Father, one for the Son, and one for the Holy Ghost."

If only I could spirit Tom here and we could be knighted together. My half-brother; my best friend. If I were in battle, I'd rather have Tom alongside me than anyone else. He could beat Serle at swordplay when he was only fourteen.

But I wish he hadn't said what he did on the day Winnie and I were betrothed. About how he'll gladly marry Winnie if I don't come back from the crusade.

Of the Body, of the Heart

12

I couldn't sleep, so I looked into my obsidian, and at once I saw them. Queen Guinevere standing at the window of her room, pressing her cheeks against the cold bars, and Sir Lancelot standing in the garden below, with a long ladder under his left arm, and a sword in his right hand in case anyone is lying in wait for him.

The moon is creamy and soft, and the jewels on the queen's dress wink; Sir Lancelot's sword flashes.

"I will!" says Sir Lancelot under his breath. "I can!"

Guinevere draws in her breath. "You cannot!" she says in a low voice. "I wish you could, just as much as you do."

"How much? How much do you wish I could?"

"With my heart."

"Then I will!" Sir Lancelot says hoarsely. "I'll show you how strong your love makes me."

Now Sir Lancelot sets up the ladder under the queen's window. And now he sheathes his sword and climbs the ladder.

"No!" says the queen.

Sir Lancelot grabs two of the thick iron window bars. With all his strength he pulls. I can see his nostrils flaring. He wrenches the bars right out of the stone walls.

"You're cut!" cries the queen. "Let me see." She reaches out and takes Lancelot's left hand. "To the bone," she whispers.

"To the heart, my lady," Sir Lancelot replies.

Now Sir Lancelot grasps the third bar with his right hand, and stands on the topmost rung. With a yelp, he half-springs, half-hauls himself into the queen's candlelit chamber.

Queen Guinevere and King Arthur's most trusted knight step into each other's arms.

"Let me bind your wound," murmurs the queen.

"I've known worse," Sir Lancelot says. "Men who fight expect to get wounded."

He brings the queen close again.

"No knight is as strong as you," the queen whispers. "And you know how a strong man excites a woman's love. Sit here, and I will dress your wound."

Now Guinevere finds a white silk shift so fine you could crumple it up and conceal it in your fist. She puts the hem between her teeth, and tears a strip to wrap round Lancelot's left hand.

"When I was a boy," Sir Lancelot says, "I was brought up by the Lady of the Lake, and I longed to be a knight.

"'Are you so sure?' she asked me. 'Do you know what being a knight means?'

"'I know some men are worthy because of the qualities of the body and some because of the qualities of the heart,' I replied.

"'What's the difference?' the Lady of the Lake asked me.

"'Some people come out of their mother's wombs big-boned or energetic or handsome, and some do not,' I told her. 'If a man is slight or lacks stamina, he can't do anything about it. But any man can acquire the qualities of the heart.'

"'And what are they?' the Lady of the Lake asked me.

"'Manners. Tact. Restraint. Loyalty and generosity.'"

Queen Guinevere wraps both arms round Sir Lancelot. "Of the body . . . ," she whispers. "Of the heart . . . You have both, my lord. How did the Lady of the Lake answer you?"

"She said just wanting to be a knight didn't mean it was right. She told me that a knight has responsibilities. He must be open-minded and open-handed, and generous to people in his care, especially the needy; he must give thieves and murderers no quarter; a knight must protect Holy Church against evildoers and infidels."

"Has there ever been a man with such qualities?" asks Guinevere, smiling.

"That's what I asked the Lady of the Lake, and she told me a good many names. She said that so long as these responsibilities were my true aims, I would be worthy to be a knight. And she said a knight must never by his own actions dishonor the order of knighthood. A knight should fear shame more than death."

Sir Lancelot and Queen Guinevere gaze at one another.

"There is no shame between us," Sir Lancelot says, "in what we say or what we do. Our love is pure."

"For as long as it is ours and ours alone," the queen replies, "and we do not hurt or dishonor the king."

"For as long," says Sir Lancelot, "as no one poisons it with jealousy or with malice."

"I love you, Lancelot," Guinevere says. "But I am Arthur's queen."

"My nightingale!" Sir Lancelot says hoarsely.

The queen says nothing. Her heart is hammering. It is hammering.

Something Very Nasty

OMETHING VERY NASTY HAPPENED THIS AFTERNOON.

Instead of the food-barge, a messenger sailed over from Venice with a gift for Lord Stephen. A wooden box the size of a nosebag, tied up with ribbons of many colors.

When Lord Stephen opened his box, it was stuffed with rotten stinking fish guts, goggle-eyed and gaping-mouthed. Fish guts, fish tails, and a mess of bones.

Lord Stephen recoiled, and the messenger held out an octavo of parchment.

"Read it!" Lord Stephen snapped at me.

Grand Councillors of Venice to Lord Stephen de Holt and Milon de Provins on the Feast of Saint Andrew of Jerusalem

We sign and seal agreement with you. We make two hundred ships ready for Feast of Saint Peter and Saint Paul. We feast you with your squires.

You? You sign and seal agreement with us. You promise pay us eighty-five thousand silver marks. More, you eat our food, you drink wine ale each day.

You are no good partners, we have no faith in you. Your words are worth fish heads!

When you pay us?
Written on Rialto

BY FOUR GRAND COUNCILLORS

Lord Stephen clapped his hands. “Saddle Stupendous!” he told me. “I’m riding over to see Milon.”

Catching Fever

I HAVE MADE UP A SONG.

To begin with, I wasn't sure what it would be about, but the words "catching fever" kept coming back into my head. I started to think about Winnie, and what Wido and Milon's men told me about fighting; and that's when I sharpened this quill.

Blazing hair and tawny eye! Freckle-face!
Winnie, no sooner do I think of you
Than I burn, I freeze, my heart starts to race.

That first day we met, that first hour, we both knew.
You've plighted your troth, and I'm your true believer,
So why am I anxious that you'll be true?

Men say fighting is like catching fever.
You shiver and sweat, you glory, you curse,
And beg for mercy from God, our Fate-Weaver.

That's just to begin with. It all gets worse.
You get the squits, your smile's a grimace,
And yet you're more alive than anywhere else.

Love-sickness and battle-fear: Are they the same?
Both painful joy, and both such joyful pain.

I would like Winnie to see my song, but I don't know whether there will ever be a chance to send it to her.

15 A Mother to Find

"W HAT ARE YOU SINGING?" I ASKED RHYS.

"Nothing," said Rhys.

"Names?"

"The colors of horses."

"Go on, then."

So Rhys whistled-and-sang:

"What are you called?
Piebald!

What's your name, squire?
Chestnut-on-Fire!

Hey you! Misfitten?
Me? I'm Flea-Bitten!"

"Chestnut-on-Fire," I said. "I like that. The first time I saw Bonamy, his coat flashed like a horse chestnut breaking out of its shell. Anyhow, what are you doing?"

"What does it look like?" Rhys replied. "Stupendous's bridle has come to bits."

"And, by the look of it, his bit's come to rollers and keys and rings and cheek-pieces!"

Rhys grinned.

"What about Bonamy's wart — just above his left fetlock?"

"Nothing serious," said Rhys. "I'm keeping an eye on it, see." He looked up at the swirling sky. "Rain!" he said. "The first spot."

When I went back to our tent, Lord Stephen had still not come back from Milon's camp — his second visit there in two days — and it was too damp to air his clothes, so I lay on my back and began to think about Queen Guinevere and Sir Lancelot.

Can it be true that their love is blameless?

Guinevere is married to King Arthur.

The truth always rises to the surface. People will find out, and then there will be a great deal of bitterness and pain.

Overhead, the canvas darkened and gulped, and I remembered how the king felt when he first saw Guinevere, shaken and yet strong, the same as I feel when I look at Winnie.

Merlin told Arthur that he was love-blind. "Don't say I haven't warned you," he said. "If you were not so deeply in love, I could find you a wife both beautiful and loyal."

I think the king still needs Merlin, and I do too. The last time I saw him was one day in May, when he appeared at Holt and I told him how I was between my squire-self and my knight-self. At the crossing-places . . .

"On a quest," Merlin replied, "is there anywhere else to be?"

But then he disappeared. That's just like Merlin.

I still don't completely believe he has left this world. He knows magic. He leaped the salmon-leap. Forty-seven feet! And once he just vanished on the top of Tumber Hill. I half-believe I will see Merlin again.

It's only two weeks now until Milon knights me, and before that I want to think more about what it really means, and how things will change when I'm a knight. I'd just started when Bertie stuck his head through the tent flap.

"Come on!" he exclaimed.

"Where?"

"The Rialto. We can go on the food-barge."

"I can't."

"You can!"

"Not without asking Lord Stephen."

"Come on!" said Bertie enthusiastically.

I don't know why — maybe it was Bertie's grin; in any case, I jumped up, though I knew it was wrong. "Come on then!" I said.

"Really?" shouted Bertie.

The two of us ran down to the empty food-barge, which was just about to go back to Venice.

As soon as the oarsmen pulled us out from the dock, Bertie stood up and yelled, "Saint Nicholas is a prison, and we've escaped!"

"What happens to prisoners when they're recaptured?" I asked.

"I don't care!" said Bertie, and he stuck out his jaw. "Now tell me about your mother!"

So I did. I told Bertie her name is Mair and I still haven't been able to meet her.

"Is that what you meant when you said you couldn't bring her back to life again?" he asked.

"Yes! She's a poor village woman, and she was married, and my father used her. But it's even worse than that. I've found out that

Emrys, my mother's husband, openly accused my father in church, and soon after that, Emrys disappeared."

Bertie gave a sharp whistle.

"I was taken away from my mother, and sent to foster parents," I told him.

"So you could be a page?"

"No, I was just two days old. To get me out of the way, so my father could behave as if nothing had happened. He must have been afraid my mother would tell me."

"But you did find out," Bertie said.

"Not until two years ago," I said, "and Sir William has warned me against trying to meet my mother. He's dangerous. I think he murdered Emrys — and he knows what would happen if the truth comes out. He would go to the gallows."

"I'd try to meet her anyhow," Bertie said.

"I have tried," I said, "and Lord Stephen has been helping me. My mother entrusted this ring to two of my father's servants, Thomas and Maggot, to give to me. Then, when I promised them favors, they told me they'd actually arranged for me to meet her."

"But you said you hadn't."

"I woke up so excited on the day we were going to meet. I did a handstand and called out the whole alphabet backwards while I kicked my legs in the air."

"What happened?"

"Lord Stephen and I rode to the meeting place. The Green Trunk. A huge old fallen elm, wrapped in dusty ivy. We waited and waited. All afternoon. We waited. . . ."

Bertie screwed up his eyes and shook his head.

"Maggot said my mother was ill, but she and Thomas are untrustworthy. They're in my father's pay, and they probably never even told my mother about meeting me, and how it matters more to me than anything in the world. But sometimes I'm afraid she doesn't want to meet me."

"But she sent you the ring," said Bertie. "She must love you. Can't you just go and find her yourself?"

"That's what I asked Lord Stephen, and he said he dreaded to think what would happen if Sir William found out we were going behind his back."

"Why? What could he do?"

"I don't know. Something to my mother. I don't want to put her in any danger," I said. "I never thought it would be this difficult."

"You're lucky, all the same," Bertie said. "At least you've got a mother to find. I won't see my mother until I die."

SARACEN TRADERS

HEN WE REACHED VENICE, BERTIE WAS MORE like a hound than a human. He ran to and fro, put his nose into this and that, yelped with excitement; it wouldn't have surprised me if he'd lifted a leg.

"Come on!" I said.

"Which way?"

"I don't know. Let's head north."

"Why?"

"Because then we can head south later on, and find our way back to the boat."

"You're always working things out," Bertie said.

But walking north in Venice isn't as easy as all that. The streets and passages keep swerving and turning to avoid all the canals that lace the city the way our bodies are tangled with veins and arteries. Some come to dead ends, some cross stone bridges, and some are so narrow, people can reach out from second- and third-story windows on either side and touch fingertips. In them, it's gloomy and impossible to tell whether one is heading north or east or west or even back south again.

After a while, though, Bertie and I came to a *campo* — a kind of square space surrounded by buildings — where there's a market.

In the back streets, it's so quiet you can hear the echoes of voices and footsteps, the swishing of water. But the *campo* was noisy and packed with people.

One stall was like a small open-sided tent made of rugs decorated with crimson-and-sepia dragons and turquoise peacocks, and a phoenix perched above swirling orange flames, and all kinds of other beasts. Three dark-skinned traders were sitting on stools inside it.

Bertie and I were staring at this stall when someone clamped his hand on my right shoulder.

When I turned round, I found myself looking up into the tanned face of Silvano, the Master Shipwright.

"Artù?" he said. "Yes. You Artù."

"Yes. I am."

"Where is Lord Stephen?"

"Not here," I said nervously.

"Ah!" said Silvano. "Money! He get money?"

"I don't know," I replied. "Soon. Very soon."

"Who he?" the shipwright asked.

"Bertie," I said. "Bertrand de Sully. Milon de Provins's squire."

"How old?"

"Thirteen," said Bertie.

"Not!" said Silvano, laughing. "Nine-thirteen. Ten-thirteen."

Bertie scowled. "I said thirteen," he repeated.

"This stall," I said. "It's wonderful."

"Sì!" said Silvano. "Saracen carpets."

"Saracens!" squeaked Bertie. "You mean . . . like we're going to fight?"

Silvano shook his head. "Traders! Not fighting men."

The three traders stood up and stepped out of the stall. Hot as it was, they were all wearing gowns that came down to their wrists and ankles, and their faces were even darker than the darkest Venetians'. Their watchful eyes reminded me of the gentle trader I talked to in Coucy. But they weren't wearing skullcaps, and the woman's hair was covered with a kind of wimple.

"But they're Saracens," said Bertie.

"Man and wifeman and brother," said the shipwright. "Old friends! Saracens trade in Venice with no trouble. . . ."

"And in Champagne," I added.

"I didn't know that," said Bertie.

"And Venetians trade in Damascus," Silvano added. "In Aleppo and Amman. We pay tax for full security. Venetians trade much in Egypt. Very important." Then he stepped forward and greeted the traders — giving each man a handclasp, and bowing slightly to the woman.

"They ask where you come from," the shipwright said.

"England," I said.

"L'Inghilterra," Silvano translated, and one of the traders clutched his neck, and all four of them laughed.

"He says he has seen a map," the shipwright said. "A map of your country across the Sea of Darkness, and it looks like an ostrich's head."

"What's an ostrich?" Bertie and I asked at the same time.

The Saracen woman put her hand over her mouth in surprise; then she pointed to an absurd-looking bird decorating one of the rugs, and the four of them laughed again.

I'd never seen a map of England. I didn't know what to say.

"I'm French and English," Bertie announced. "Tell them that."

Hearing this, the traders laughed again and pointed out an animal on another rug that was half-bird and half-beast.

"They say your skin is so white, it is almost blue," Silvano told Bertie.

"It's not," Bertie protested. "It's they who look strange, not us."

"Where do they come from," I asked, "and what are they selling?"

"Alexandria," replied the shipwright. And then, seeing my blank face, "Egypt! They sell many. Pepper and ginger, cinnamon and mace. Sponges. Perfumes." Silvano smiled. "Perfumes for my daughter! They sell gold."

"Gold!" exclaimed Bertie. "Let's see."

"Traders say they tell your fortune," Silvano told me.

"How?"

"Your hand."

"No thanks," I said. "I mean, I want to find out for myself."

"I will!" said Bertie, sticking out his right hand. "Tell mine!"

One of the traders held Bertie's little wrist. He stared at his palm, and suddenly I was aware of his silence, the quiet gaze of the others, and the hubbub of the market around us.

"What does it say?" asked Bertie.

"Nothing," Silvano said. "He says it tells nothing."

"What do you mean — nothing? Why won't he tell me?"

The Saracen shrugged.

"Does it say I'll die?"

"We all die," Silvano replied.

"I mean . . . ," Bertie began, but then he faltered. "You know what I mean."

The trader looked levelly at Bertie, but then his expression softened, and for a moment I thought he was going to embrace him. But instead he said something very quietly.

"Bertie," Silvano said, "he says he can tell you nothing you do not know yourself."

In one corner of the *campo,* someone began to bang a drum. Thump. Double-thump. Thump. Double-thump.

Then I saw four monks, carrying a roughly hewn cross, and a fifth swinging an incense burner; whenever they paused, the stall-holders rushed forward to kiss the cross, and the monks were advancing towards us.

"*Baciate! Baciate il crocifisso!* Kiss the cross."

The traders screwed up their faces, and so did I, at the stink of the incense; the people around us yelled, and the traders yelled back at them.

"They say incense is made from excrement," the shipwright told us. "Excrement of Patriarch in Constantinople, and excrement of other Christian priests. All Saracens know that!"

"They can't say that!" I exclaimed. "Why do you let them?"

But after yelling and jeering at the Saracen traders, the crowd moved on, following the priests, shouting, *"Baciate! Baciate il crocifisso!"* The traders shrugged, then grinned at the shipwright.

"Each day!" Silvano told us. "They say same thing happen each day. Christians never learn."

"Why should they think they're superior?" I protested. "They worship a false prophet."

Silvano smiled and put his large hand on my right shoulder again. "For traders," he said, "trade is most important."

"But that's wrong," said Bertie.

One of the traders stepped forward and gave me a handclasp.

"He says the prophet Muhammad . . . he says was a trader," Silvano told me. "Oversea."

And when I looked into the trader's dark eyes, I saw they were dancing.

"He says, glory to God! May the Lord of the Universe protect you both," the shipwright said.

On our way back, I asked Bertie about his palm, and why he was afraid.

"I'm not afraid."

"No, but . . . you asked about dying."

Bertie reached over the side of the barge and trailed his hand in the water.

"Everyone's afraid of dying," I said. "I am."

Bertie rinsed his hand; he purified it. "This is the third time my fortune has been told," he said in a flat voice. "The first man said I would never live to grow old. The woman at Soissons Fair told me I would die before I was a man."

MY SHINING PROMISE

17

OUR ARMORER WAS WAITING FOR ME. AS I RODE BACK after exercising Bonamy, he met me a full furlong outside camp.

"What's wrong?" I asked.

Turold's face looked more cracked and crumpled than ever. Like a piece of pigskin parchment that hasn't been properly stretched or scraped.

"Lord Stephen's upset. Very angry."

"He's not," I replied. "He understands. Bertie got beaten, but Lord Stephen said I was spreading my wings because I was about to be knighted; he said when I'm a knight I'll have to be responsible all the time, not just some of the time."

Patient Turold listened to me. Then he opened his eyes wide, and his forehead was crisscrossed with wrinkles. "Not that," he said. "Visitors!" He jammed his right fist into the socket of his left hand, and then twisted it.

"Who?"

But the armorer just turned his broad back and started to trudge down the track towards our camp.

"Tell me!" I called out.

Turold looked over his shoulder without breaking his step. "That's not my place," he said gruffly. "You'll see."

The moment I lifted our tent flap, I did see.

Sir William. My father.

And my foster brother Serle. Lounging on my bed.

And a woman, a lady, whom I've never seen before. The three of them, and Lord Stephen sitting on his stool, blinking and almost as blind as a mole.

How long did I stare at them before I stepped in? No longer than it takes to breathe in and out again. But it seemed as long as half my life.

"S-ss-sir," I stammered, and I got down on my right knee.

"Where have you been?" boomed Sir William.

"Nowhere."

"Sowing your wild oats, I suppose."

"Yes, sir. I mean: No, sir."

"Make up your mind!"

"Yes, sir."

"Only fools open their mouths before they know what to say."

"I didn't know you were coming, sir."

"Of course you didn't!" my father said. "We scarcely knew ourselves, did we, Serle? Come on! Get up!" My father reached out, but instead of giving me a helping hand, he gave me a push, and I staggered sideways and fell right over Serle.

"Mind yourself!" shouted Serle.

Sir William roared with laughter. "Got you!" he said. "Keep your wits about you, Arthur."

When I scrambled to my feet, I looked at Lord Stephen. Blinking furiously, he stood up and knitted his stubby fingers over his stomach, as he always does when he is trying to compose himself.

"Arthur," he said in a level voice, "this is Lady Cécile."

Sir William grunted.

I bowed to Lady Cécile. She has bright blue eyes, and very fair skin, and the way she looks and moves is quite stately, like a queen almost.

"Is Tom here as well, sir?" I asked.

My father wiped his nose with the back of his hand, and shook his head.

"I thought . . ."

"You thought wrong," said Sir William. "I need him at home to manage Gortanore and Catmole with Lady Alice."

He stared at me with his glittering right eye. He looked down. I followed his gaze and then I realized.

"What," he barked, "is that ring?"

I covered my right hand with my left hand. I went hot. I went cold. I felt breathless.

"Show me."

"No, sir."

"You heard me."

"It's mine."

"Show me, I said." Sir William lurched towards me and grabbed me by the wrists and wrenched my hands apart. Then he seized my ring finger and bent it back and glared at the ring.

A mother, sweet and mild, with her baby son in her arms, reaching out, offering her something. Her son, safe from all the suffering in this world. My ring! My mother's ring!

"I know that ring!" Sir William growled. "It's mine!"

"No, sir. It was a gift."

"How dare you?" stormed Sir William.

Then he dragged the ring off my fourth finger.

"Please, sir! Please!" I panted. "No! Please!"

I could hear Lord Stephen calling, "Sir William! No!" and Lady Cécile crying, "William! William!"

It was no use.

He strode out of the tent, and down across the beach, and Lord Stephen and I followed him.

"Man!" called Lord Stephen, and he was having to trot to keep up. "Come to your senses! This is your son. Your son."

"Sir! Please, sir!" I kept clutching Sir William's arm, but he took no notice, and it made no difference.

"Your son!" Lord Stephen shouted. "Stop!"

But Sir William stepped right into the water. He drew back his arm. He hurled my ring as far out into the waves as he could.

My shining promise. My ring that warmed to my mother's blood, and warmed to mine. She sent it to me, and it has been my hope. Leading me. Leading me towards her. My father has thrown it away.

A Little March Miracle

HREE TIMES SINCE THEY ARRIVED, THE SUN HAS snarled and stained the western sky with blood, and still Sir William is behaving as if nothing has happened.

In the half-dark, each wave looks like the Green Trunk. The salt water gathers, it breaks, it sobs. In the half-dark and the dark I have stood where Sir William threw away my ring.

My mother! Each time I close my eyes I can see her, but she will not show me her face.

Before, I hated my father for what he has done to my mother, and the foul way he treats Lady Alice. Now, I hope the earth will open under him and close over him; I hope the sea will swallow him.

Lord Stephen knows how I feel.

"Bitterness is like poison," he warned me. "Your feelings won't harm Sir William. But they will harm you."

"Yes, sir."

"Now, remember! In only ten days, Milon is going to knight you."

All the same, I know Lord Stephen is very troubled too.

What I didn't know to begin with is that Serle has brought Tanwen and their son, Kester, with him. They were down at the food-barge when I rode back to camp yesterday.

I'm pleased for Tanwen because she loves Serle, and for us

because he's not so mean and sharp-tongued in her company. I like her, anyhow. But all the same, Serle shouldn't have brought her. She is Lady Judith's chamber-servant, and she didn't dare tell Lady Judith she was leaving. She just hurried out of Holt early one morning carrying Kester on her back.

Lord Stephen is very upset about this, and Sir John will be angry as well because Tanwen and Serle can never marry. She's only a servant and has no parents or property.

Kester was born on the ninth day of May. So he's two years and two months and two weeks old. With his dark hair and dark eyes and funny, pointed chin, he looks much more like Tanwen than Serle, and that's a good thing. When he laughs, it's a mixture of chuckles and snorts.

Tanwen has told me much more news than Serle, and what's most important is the news about Gatty. I mean, about her father, Hum, and about Lankin.

Soon after we rode out of the March, Hum had pains in his stomach and lost his appetite, and then he died. Lankin came to his funeral.

"It was the first time he'd come out of his hut all year," Tanwen told me, "and his hair had grown down to his shoulders. The stump of his right wrist was all purple and puffy. In the middle of the service, Lankin bawled out: 'Scum! The filthy liar! He'll rot in hell for ten thousand years.'"

"That's terrible!"

"Well! Hum lied about him in the manor court, didn't he?" Tanwen said. "Anyhow, Gatty can never be betrothed to Jankin now. Not now his father has dishonored hers."

Later, I asked Serle what would happen to Gatty, with her mother and her father both dead, and only her grandmother left, lying like a corpse in their cottage.

Serle stared at me, and his thin lips curled. "Well, Arthur, seeing as you're not there to look after her yourself . . ."

Two years ago, I would have been provoked. But not now.

". . . Sir John's asked Oliver to keep an eye on her. The strange thing is that, since Hum died, Gatty has started to sing."

"What do you mean?"

"She sings all day long. Sad songs. Happy songs. No one has taught them to her. Oliver says it's a little March miracle."

Another thing I've found out is that Lady Cécile is Sir William's mistress.

I remember Sir John did tell me Sir William was away from home half the time, visiting his manor in Champagne; and I think he said he also visited a lady there. But it was all so far away then.

Lady Cécile is French, and firm and kind, and treats everyone as if they were her children, even Sir William. She's rather top-heavy, and the way she gathers Kester to her, you'd think he might suffocate. But he crows and chortles, and seems to like it, and evidently Sir William does too.

I can't understand why Lady Cécile is fond of my father. How can she be? I quite like her, but seeing her and Sir William together makes me think of Lady Alice.

Her curl dancing out from under her wimple. Her orange cloak. Our weekly French lessons and laughter. And the way she's helped me try to meet my mother.

"Sir William shouts at Lady Alice," Tom told me once, "and sometimes he thrashes her, but he still worships her."

Grace told me Lady Alice often cries when Sir William is away in Champagne. She has to do all the lady's work and half the lord's as well, figuring the accounts and managing the duties on the two manors. She goes to bed tired and wakes up tired, and that makes her cry again.

Sir William and Lady Cécile have pitched their tent on the other side of the one Rhys and Turold share. I think they dishonor Lady Alice in the way that Queen Guinevere and Sir Lancelot dishonor King Arthur.

Sir William is a one-eyed, silvery, bristling wild boar. He may be a murderer. He used my mother and then he threw her away.

My ring! Our unending ring . . .

Winnie's Letter

NOW! FIVE FULL DAYS AFTER HE RODE IN, MY FATHER has given me a letter from Winnie.

Or rather, he left the letter with Lord Stephen before he and Serle rode out of camp to have a proper look at Saint Nicholas. He's already impatient at the delay in launching the crusade, and keeps grumbling.

As I unrolled Winnie's letter, I began to tremble.

Winnie to Arthur
this fifth day of June

To my betrothed

It is five weeks since you gave me my ring but it seems more like five months, and Sir William says it will be at least ten weeks longer before he hands you this letter.

A singer came to Verdon. He sang:

"God, help the pilgrim!
I tremble for him
For the Saracens are treacherous."

I am not in the *least* content that you will be away for two years, or worse.

When Sir William rode over to talk to my father again about terms for our marriage, he brought Tom with him, and we went hunting with my father's hawks. My father says Sir William is very difficult and bad-tempered. He says now we can't settle all the terms until Sir William comes home from the crusade.

It has taken me all morning to write this letter.

My mother sends you *une fleur de souvenance* — and so do I.

Hurry up!

I do not know whether any saints protect crusaders against the Saracens, but may Saint Boniface save you from Germans and Flemings, and Saint Clotilda save you from the murderous French. Do you think about me?

BY YOUR LOVING AND IMPATIENT WINNIE

When Sir William returned, I told him I had read Winnie's letter, and he sniffed loudly.

"Sir Walter may seem like a decent man, but he's a devil. If he doesn't agree to my terms, he can stick his sweet daughter in a nunnery."

"We're betrothed, sir," I said.

"I told you," Sir William barked, "I only agreed to your betrothal because you were going on this bloody crusade. But that doesn't mean you'll marry her. Not unless Sir Walter and I agree to terms."

"I love her, sir."

Sir William snorted. "Quite frankly, it would be better if you married Sian."

"Sian!" I yelped. "She's my sister."

"Your cousin!"

"Well, my foster sister."

"Don't argue with me!" Sir William said. He rubbed his blind eye. "Love her! What do you know about love?"

I looked at the ground. I thought of my mother.

"Now then!" said Sir William. "Are you ready?"

"What for, sir?"

"What do you think?" Sir William bellowed. "The crusade! If we're not on our way soon, the French will fry the Flemings or the Germans will juice the Italians. Mark my words! There are squabbles and fistfights all the way down the island."

"The Marquis de Montferrat still hasn't arrived, sir," I said.

"I know that," Sir William replied.

"And Lord Stephen says we can't pay the Venetians. We haven't got anything like eighty-five thousand marks."

"The Venetians will make a deal," my father said. "They'll have to."

"They sent reminders to Lord Stephen and Milon," I said. "Nasty ones."

"Milon," Sir William said. "I've met this Milon at last. Good man. Strong as a mule."

"Yes, sir."

"He says I've arrived just in time."

"Sir?"

"He's knighting you next Friday."

"Yes, sir."

"You didn't even tell me."

"I was going to, sir."

"And you a knight before Tom!"

"I wish he were here, sir."

"I'm glad he's not," Sir William barked. "Tom's exactly where he should be. But you, Arthur, you're glad I've arrived in time to see you dubbed a knight. Aren't you?"

The Greatest Name of Any Knight

20

MY STONE.

"From this moment, here on Tumber Hill, until the day you die, you will never own anything as precious as this." That's what Merlin told me. "No one must know you own it."

If Sir William knew about it, he'd probably throw my stone away too.

Sir Lancelot is sitting on one side of a blazing fire and a lady is sitting on the other. They're in a hall with a gallery like ours at Caldicot. Two servants are standing at the foot of the stone staircase.

"To think Sir Lancelot has chosen to stay under my roof," the lady says. "Well, as you can see, this is only a modest place, and even so I can scarcely afford its upkeep. A swarm of wild bees have taken over the tower room. I shall have to put you in the garret over the gate."

"Lady Gisèle," says Sir Lancelot. "You've reminded me of a song my foster mother used to sing:

> "A swarm of wild bees swirled around this tower.
> They fizzed through the openings, and nested
> In the chamber. They made honey here . . .

"I'm more than happy to stay in a house of such sweetness!"

Lady Gisèle smiles. "And you, Sir Lancelot, have honey on

your tongue," she says. "All I hope is that, when he is old enough, you will be so generous as to knight my young son."

"A knight who dubs a squire has a duty to him," Sir Lancelot says very seriously. "To guide him. To support him."

"But I don't know whether he'll be strong enough," Lady Gisèle says.

"There are good and bad knights of the body," Sir Lancelot replies, "but no bad knights of the heart."

Late into the night they talk, and then they stand and embrace. A servant carrying two candles leads Sir Lancelot away to his chamber.

But then my stone began to sparkle and all I could see in it were tiny pins of light. I started to think about being knighted the day after tomorrow, and whether Milon has a duty to me, and then, when I could see into the stone once more, the full moon was already riding high and Sir Lancelot was leaping out of bed.

He looks down from his window and sees a knight pounding on the great oak door with both gauntlets.

"Help!" shouts the knight. "Is no one there? Save me!"

Now I can hear the sound of hooves, and three more knights gallop up. Without a word, they draw their swords, and brandish them and slash at the knight.

Sir Lancelot quickly arms himself, ties his two sheets together, and knots one end to a window bar.

"Three against one!" he shouts. "You shame yourselves."

Now Sir Lancelot clambers out of the window, slides down the sheets, and lands with a clank.

"Leave them to me!" he yells. "An early breakfast!"

One . . . two . . . three . . . after just six of Sir Lancelot's strokes, all three knights are lying on the earth. Not one of them even tries to stand up again.

"I yield to you . . . and I . . . we yield to you."

"No!" says Sir Lancelot, turning to the man he has just saved. "Yield to him!"

Now the man raises his visor, and to his astonishment Sir Lancelot recognizes him. It is Sir Kay.

One of the three knights struggles, and creaks terribly, and sits up.

"Sir," he says to Sir Lancelot, "whoever you may be, I will not yield to Sir Kay. But for you he would be a dead man."

"Have you no shame?" Sir Lancelot retorts. "Three against one. If any one of you had fought against Sir Kay, he would have worsted you."

"Sir Kay! He's all bluster."

"And blunder."

"And he's foul-mouthed."

"Listen to me!" Sir Lancelot growls. "Either you submit to Sir Kay, or you die."

"We submit," the three knights mumble.

"To Sir Kay," says Sir Lancelot.

"To Sir Kay."

"Very well," says Sir Lancelot. "Ride from here straight to Camelot, in time for the Pentecost Feast. Tell Queen Guinevere that Sir Kay has sent you, and she is to do with you as she wishes. Swear it!"

"We swear it," say the three men.

"On your swords," says Sir Lancelot.

"On our swords."

Sir Kay and Sir Lancelot stand and watch as the three groaning knights get to their feet, remount, and quietly walk their horses into the night.

Now Sir Lancelot turns to the oak door, and a servant swings it open, and leads them to the hall.

Lady Gisèle is waiting for them, and Sir Lancelot lifts off his helmet.

"Sir Lancelot!" exclaims the lady.

"It's you!" exclaims Sir Kay.

"I thought you were asleep," says Lady Gisèle.

"Lady, I was, but I had to get up to help an old friend."

Lady Gisèle shakes her head and smiles. "Out of the sweet-tongued came forth strength," she says.

"Lady," says Sir Lancelot, "this is Sir Kay."

"You are welcome," says the lady.

"May I take him to my garret, to unarm and wash and sleep?"

"It's the only room I have."

"And it's more than enough," Sir Lancelot replies.

As soon as they are on their own, the two knights talk.

"Who were they?" asks Sir Lancelot. "Those three knights."

"Bad, worse, and worst," Sir Kay says. "A man who betrays his wife. A man who betrays his son. And a murderer. You saved my life."

"Any knight would have done the same," Sir Lancelot replies.

"If only that were true," says Sir Kay.

"I hope," Sir Lancelot replies, "I always hope a knight will fight for another man if he's in danger, and so win honor. Let me help you unarm."

Sir Lancelot unties Sir Kay's mittens and holds his mail-shirt while Kay steps out of it. And now Sir Kay unstraps his chausses and loosens his quilted cuisses. He looks around the garret, and yawns.

"What a shabby place this is!" he says.

"Be grateful!" says Sir Lancelot.

"Shabby and dingy."

"Mind your tongue," says Sir Lancelot. "Lady Gisèle has given me all she has."

"Really?" says Sir Kay, and he raises an eyebrow. "Out of the sweet-tongued came forth strength! Now what did she mean by that?"

"Not what you think," says Sir Lancelot.

As soon as Sir Kay is undressed and wearing nothing but his braies and shirt, he gets into bed, leaving Sir Lancelot to unarm himself.

"You're worn out," says Sir Lancelot. "You sleep."

"I am asleep," Sir Kay replies, and he yawns again.

Within a few moments, Sir Kay really is asleep. He doesn't even stir when Sir Lancelot gets into bed beside him.

But Sir Lancelot doesn't blow out the candle. He lies with his head propped up, thinking. And now he has a quick look at his companion, and quietly gets up again. Quietly, as quietly as anyone can put on creaking, squeaking, whingeing armor, Sir Lancelot puts on Kay's cuisses and chausses, his aketon and mail-shirt. Now, he glances at Kay again, but Kay wouldn't wake if Lancelot leaned right over him and clapped his hands.

"Well," says Lancelot to himself, "I think Kay will see the joke. And other knights will find out whether I'm worthy of my name."

Sir Lancelot tucks Sir Kay's shield under his left arm, picks up Kay's helmet and the burning candle, and leaves the room.

But as soon as Sir Lancelot steps out into the passage, a draught blows out his candle. He's left in the dark.

And my stone lay dark in my right hand.

Tom looks quite like Sir Lancelot. They both have generous, broad brows, and the brightest, unflecked blue eyes. Not as pale as this Venetian sky; not as dark as sapphire. Forget-me-not blue.

Sometimes I think I'm almost at war with myself because I'm anxious and in a hurry, but Sir Lancelot and Tom are both easygoing. I've seen how ladies, old as well as young, quicken to Sir Lancelot and hope he'll dally with them, and it's the same with Tom. Lady Anne is always spirited when Tom's around; and Nain peers at him, and blinks, and grins her toothless grin.

If I could choose anyone to be here when I'm knighted, it would be Tom. If only Sir William had brought him, and not Serle.

On Saint Nicholas, the whole of the night sky sometimes seems to jolt and flash, and that's what happened inside my stone as well. Then at once I could see deep into it again, and I was at court. At Camelot.

King Arthur and Queen Guinevere are sitting on their raised seats, Sir Mordred is standing nearby, and the great hall is packed with knights, squires, ladies, maidens, musicians, servants. Looking into the hall is like looking into fallowfield at Caldicot in July: a mass of poppies and speedwell, cornflowers and fritillaries, greenweed and red clover; one hundred different kinds of long grasses, all of them slightly swaying.

"I am Sir Gauter," says one, "and my brothers and I recognized Sir Kay. By his shield — azure with two keys argent. We've all been on the sharp end of Kay's tongue, and so we decided to teach him a lesson. With the sharp ends of our spears."

There's a gentle rustle in the hall. A light wind from nowhere that no sooner breathes than it's gone again.

"When he rode past our pavilion," Sir Gauter says, "I challenged him. But Sir Kay threw me, and my horse broke his neck."

"I'm Sir Gilmere," says the second brother, "and I knew that knight couldn't have been Sir Kay. He could never have thrown my brother. He can't aim straight! We think this knight killed Sir Kay and stole his armor and shield."

"I'm Sir Arnold," the third brother says, "and Sir Gilmere and I rode after the knight, but he flattened us both."

"I ran after them," says Sir Gauter, "and then the knight told us he knew we were good knights. 'Knights of the heart as well as the body.' We knew he couldn't be Sir Kay.

"'Yield to Queen Guinevere.' That's what the knight said. 'Tell her Sir Kay has sent you to her.'"

"It was the same for us!" shouts a knight at the back of the hall, and I recognize one of the three knights who chased Sir Kay to Lady Gisèle's manor.

All the flowers in the field of many colors, all the leaves and long grasses, are whispering.

Sir Sagramour and Sir Ector de Maris, Sir Uwain and Sir Gawain: Four knights at the Round Table get to their feet.

"We were dozing under an oak tree," Sir Sagramour says, "when we saw a knight ride past, and because of his shield we thought it was Sir Kay. We thought we'd find out if he was made of anything but hot air. So I challenged him, and at the first end he threw me."

"And you can see what he did to me," says Sir Ector, Sir Lancelot's own brother. "He drove his spear right through this shoulder."

"When he smacked his spear against my helmet," says Sir Uwain, "I was so dizzy, my head spun like a top."

Sir Gawain slowly shakes his head. "This knight turned me and my horse arsy-versy. And you know what? He never said a word, but I could see him smiling through his mouthpiece."

"Who is he?" demands Sir Sagramour.

"He comes from the devil," Sir Ector replies, clasping his shoulder.

"And he can go to the devil," adds Sir Uwain.

"That's what we thought," Sir Gawain tells King Arthur and Guinevere. "And I said, 'It's Sir Lancelot. I know it is. The way he sits in his saddle! I'll lay my life on it.'"

Whispers, murmurs, gusts of laughter. Which all die away as a single trumpeter blows three blasts and Arthur-in-the-stone stands up.

"What have we heard?" he calls out. "Story upon story, and pieces of one story. Word-wonders to sharpen our appetites for this Pentecost Feast. Many knights of my Round Table are still away in the wilderness, questing for the Holy Grail, but we have waited long enough. Let the feast begin!"

Now the golden trumpeter is joined by three pipers and three drummers.

And now a hammering! A hammering and then a screeching, and the hall doors are forced open.

Two knights clatter in, and as soon as they enter court, they take off their helmets.

Everyone in the great hall begins to shout — shout and then laugh. Without breaking their step, Sir Lancelot, wearing Sir Kay's armor, and Kay, in Lancelot's armor, pass through the fair field of folk, and up to King Arthur and Queen Guinevere.

"Greetings!" says the king.

"I've ridden here from Cornwall," Sir Kay says, "and not one knight has challenged me."

"And I've ridden here through a gauntlet of taunts," Sir Lancelot says. "Insults and challenges, gibes and jousts."

"So we have heard," says Arthur, smiling.

"My path was a smooth one," says Sir Kay.

"And mine," says Sir Lancelot, "was sharp and pointed."

"Welcome to the feast," Guinevere says.

"There is more to tell," says Sir Lancelot. "Morgan le Fay put me under a spell while I lay asleep under an apple tree, and the daughter of Sir Bagdemagus saved me. I killed two giants and rescued their prisoners, sixty ladies and maidens. And then there's Sir Turquine!"

"Tomorrow and tomorrow we will hear all of your story," King Arthur says. "And you, Kay. You never need a second invitation."

Kay's scornful lips tighten into a kind of smile, and he bites on his tongue.

"Sir Lancelot!" says the king. "Little more than a year ago, you were still a squire. But scarcely a week has passed without our hearing about you."

Queen Guinevere gazes at Sir Lancelot, and her eyes are on fire.

"Little more than a year since you were still a squire," the king says again, "and you've won yourself such honor. Yes, the greatest name of any knight in the world."

21 WAX AND DIAMOND

OU KNOW MY WALL HANGING?" LORD STEPHEN asked me.

"The story of your life, sir?"

"So far."

"Lady Judith showed me, sir — the panel when you were seven and fell out of a tree, and your betrothal, and when you met Queen Eleanor."

"Do you remember the one with two hearts?"

"Side by side on a shield? One was gules and one argent."

"Exactly. Well, on the day before I was knighted — "

"Who knighted you, sir?"

"Will you let me finish? You're as bad as an untrained terrier." Lord Stephen glared at me. "Sir William's father . . . he knighted me, if you must know. Now on the day before, my own father told me a knight should have two hearts: one adamantine as a diamond — "

"Adamantine, sir?"

"Unbreakable. And the other heart, he said, should be soft as hot wax. A knight should be hard and cutting when he's dealing with cruel men. He should give them no quarter. But he should allow himself to be shaped and molded by considerate and gentle people. A knight must be careful not to allow cruel men anywhere near his heart of wax, because any kindness extended to them would be wasted. But he should never be harsh or unforgiving to women and men who need care or mercy."

"Whatever we do to others we do also to God Himself," I said.

"Very good, Arthur. You should have been a priest."

"Sir!"

"Just a joke."

"You do think . . ."

"Yes, Arthur, I do. I am proud of you. Proud of you and proud for you. Now, have I said that before?"

"No, sir."

"No, well, once is enough! You've served me well as a squire and given your utmost, and you'll continue to serve me well as a young knight."

"Yes, sir."

"Tomorrow's a great day for you."

"The most important day of my life."

"Tomorrow, yes," Lord Stephen said, "but it's the next day and the day after that really matter."

"Sir?"

"Certain events in our lives mark our passage through this world. Baptism, confirmation, betrothal, and marriage . . . But what matters is how we make use of these crossing-places. How we apply them to the rest of our lives. Isn't that right?"

Lord Stephen told me that Milon's priest will come and shave a tonsure on the top of my head early tomorrow morning, and explain the ceremony, and tell me the order of the words. After that I am to wear white, and Milon will give me a white surcoat, and a new sword.

I am writing all this quite calmly as if it were happening to someone else, but it is happening to me, Arthur.

I know I'm still young to be knighted. Tom's seventeen, and he hasn't been knighted yet, and Serle wasn't until last year, while Lord Stephen and I were away.

Although I've never actually seen the ceremony, I saw in my stone how Sir Kay was knighted, so I know what it's like. The great church of Saint Paul picked up and echoed all of Kay's words. Even though my ceremony will not be in a church, I think it will be the same for me. My vows will echo and travel with me all the days of my life.

Merlin, Questioning

22

I HAVE SEEN MERLIN AGAIN.

I was asleep, curled up in a dune. At first the sea was all glitter, but then I saw a misty shape hanging over the water, and the shape grew towards me.

"Merlin!" I shouted.

He was riding Sorry, his poor old rounsey, and wearing his dark hood, and when he looked at me, his grey eyes were like shale the tide has just washed.

"What did I ask you?"

"Ask me?"

"What did I ask you?" he demanded in his deep voice. He smiled and unsmiled, and at once he began to blur again.

"Merlin!" I cried.

But he faded. In front of me, he dissolved into air.

Ask me? The truth is, Merlin asked me questions the whole time. Well, Arthur? Is that what you think? Is that what you mean, Arthur? What will your quest be?

Merlin said knowledge is dry as dead leaves unless you're ready for it, and the only true way to understand is to keep asking the right questions.

So in a way, Merlin is here even though he's not. He's still helping me to help myself. Because of what he's taught me.

Isn't that what my dream means? Isn't Merlin asking me to go on asking?

SIR ARTHUR

23

HIS TWENTY-SEVENTH DAY OF JULY IN THE YEAR OF Our Lord 1202: It may have been the feast day of the Seven Sleepers, but I wasn't one of them. I didn't want to miss anything; and all my life, I will remember everything. Even the little things: how Rhys trimmed Bonamy's feathering and wound strips of white linen above his fetlocks; the way Serle's right stirrup broke, and his foul curses; Milon saying Turold's face is like a map, the kind the Saracens make; the golden buttons on Cardinal Capuano's tunic blazing in the sunlight; yes, and Bertie punching the air with both fists after Milon dubbed me.

For a while I lay on my bed. I listened to the sea breathing for me. I watched our tent suck in its cheeks and blow them out again. I heard a distant trumpeter, like a hidden longing, summoning me. Then I leaped up.

Before Lord Stephen and I had broken our fast, Milon's priest, Pagan, rode into camp; and as soon as he'd tossed back a tumbler of ale, he shaved a round spot on the top of my head.

"When you took the Cross at Soissons," he said, "you enlisted in God's army. And now, with this tonsure, you prepare yourself to become one of God's knights."

"Why are you called Pagan?" I asked him. "A heathen Christian. That's very odd."

Pagan smiled a weary smile. "Words sometimes change," he said. "'Pagan' once meant 'villager'; now it means 'heathen.'"

Pagan told me I should feel honored because Cardinal Capuano had agreed to lead me through the responses. He's only just arrived here from Rome.

And then, when I'd got dressed in my new white clothing, nothing but white, Pagan led us all down to Milon's encampment.

The sun took one look at me, and drove her golden lance into my skull. Straight down through my poor bald fontanel! All day my brains seethed, and Serle says my tonsure looks like one of those eggs that come out of the shell streaked and spotted scarlet.

As we rode in — Lord Stephen and I, followed by Sir William and Serle, with Lady Cécile behind them, then Rhys and Turold, and then Tanwen with Kester — Milon's trumpeter raised his shining trumpet. Quick and keen as the blasts of the huntsman. I could see Bertie, grinning at me, and Wido, and Godard and Giff, and at least a dozen other men.

Milon stepped towards me and held Bonamy's bridle while I dismounted.

"You ready?" he asked me.

"I don't know, sir."

"Not?" demanded Milon, frowning.

"I mean, I'm trying to be. I've thought, and I've prayed. I've tried to understand what a knight should — "

"Bon!" said Milon, and he clumped me on the back and led me over to Cardinal Capuano, then leaned on my shoulders until I dropped to my knees.

The cardinal is very still and watchful, but somehow his body has collapsed into itself. He's quite a big man who looks rather small — the opposite of Lord Stephen, who's a small man who looks quite big.

"God be with you! *Saluti!*" said Cardinal Capuano. He put his head slightly to one side, then held out his pectoral cross for me to kiss.

Seeing this, everyone else got onto their knees — everyone except my father. He tried to, but couldn't manage it.

"Dratted joints!" he growled.

Everyone stood in a circle around me and Milon and the cardinal.

Wido and Giff and Godard: What were they thinking? That I'm raw as an unripe greengage? That I'll fail myself and fail everyone else as soon as I actually come face-to-face with howling Saracens?

And Lady Cécile: She stood next to Sir William with her eyes closed, her pink-and-pale-blue eyelids trembling like butterflies on the bough.

And Bertie: the way he stood, legs well planted, shoulders pulled back, chest thrust out. Compact and intent and excited.

The day grew still under the weight of the sun, and all around me I could hear bright splashes of sound. Man-shout and hoof-thud, bell-clang and shingle-screech, bagpipe-wheedle, drum-thump: all the noises of an army making ready. . . .

I closed my eyes and began to expel the old air inside me. All my old life. I pushed it out, all out, with little coughs, until my lungs were flat as folded parchment. Then slowly I breathed in again, new air, fresh salty air. I opened my eyes and looked at the cardinal.

"Arthur de Gortanore!" the cardinal began.

De Gortanore? Is that who I am?

"Why do you wish to become a knight?"

Why? I've always and always wanted to be a knight. Since before I can remember. But I wasn't sure whether Sir John wanted me to be, or whether my Yard-skills would ever be good enough.

"To get rich?" the cardinal demanded. "To lay your hands on Saracen treasure? Gold, jewels, armor, horses? Is that why?"

No. No, that's not why at all.

"Arthur de Gortanore, is that why?"

"No, sir."

"Then why?"

"I wish to become a knight so I may serve Our Lord Jesus Christ. Pure in heart, strong in body."

"A knight is a guardian," the cardinal continued. "Whom will you guard?"

"I will do all I can to defend and care for people less fortunate than I am," I replied.

As I said these words, I thought at once of Gatty. I could see her hoeing her croft, and singing. I thought of Jankin and Howell, and all the villagers at Caldicot. I thought of Tanwen, and Kester.

"In the kingdom of Britain," I said, "many people suffer. Many go to bed hungry. It's not just."

Cardinal Capuano looked down at me and rubbed his chin. I knew this wasn't quite what he had expected me to say.

"My child," he said, "all of us are equal in the eyes of God."

That's what Oliver told me. And he told me poverty is part of God's will. I don't believe that. I think a knight is bound to do everything he can to look after the people in his manor.

"Arthur de Gortanore," said the cardinal, "do you undertake to defend widows and orphans?"

Gatty! She's an orphan now. And my mother's a widow.

"I do."

"And will you oppose evil wherever you find it?"

"I will."

"It is said and well said," the cardinal continued. "The Saracens are evil. Never doubt that for one moment. They desecrate the holy places in Jerusalem; they defecate on them. War is violent, war is cruel, war is bloody, but it is natural. It is natural, and peace is unnatural. Love God, and win honor by destroying His enemies."

Is that true? I thought. Is war really natural?

Then Cardinal Capuano slowly proceeded round the circle. Everyone kissed his cross except Lady Cécile and Tanwen. He rudely walked past them, I don't know why.

The cardinal turned to Milon and nodded, and at once Milon drew his sword and stepped up to me. I bowed my head, but I could still see the tip of the blade trembling above my right shoulder.

As the first ray of sunlight at Caldicot touches and sets light to Tumber Hill . . .

Three times and lightly Milon tapped me on the shoulder.

"In name of God and all His saints," Milon said, "I dub you knight. Sir Arthur! *Le chevalier* Arthur! *Courage! Courtoisie! Loyauté!*"

At once everyone in the circle shouted, "Sir Arthur! Sir Arthur!" ten times. One hundred times! Then they all scrambled to their feet, and began to grab my arms and hands, and hug me and tousle my hair — well, what's left of it.

After this, Milon himself fastened a new sword to my belt.

When I unsheathed it, everyone covered their eyes because it was so dazzling.

"Bravee!" cried Milon. "Sir Arthur bravee!" And then he showed me what his armorer had engraved on my sword, just below the hilt.

A ring. My ring! How did Milon know about it? The same square, flat top. A mother and her child. Wouldn't my mother be proud for me now? She would, wouldn't she?

I looked at Milon. His expression didn't alter, but his eyes simmered. Mine began to sting.

"Ring of hope, ring of patience," Milon said quietly. "Ring without end."

I didn't dare look at my father; I didn't want to. And I mustn't let him see the ring. I lowered my head and my eyes filled with tears.

"Come on!" said Bertie enthusiastically. He helped me dress in a new white surcoat, embroidered with a bloodred cross on the front and back, and then Serle gave me a length of sacking taller than I am.

"Here!" he said. "From Sir John."

"Sir John!" I exclaimed.

I unrolled the sacking and inside it was the most beautiful bow, made of yew.

"He says he knows it's scarcely the right gift for a knight," Serle said, "and yew's against the law anyhow because you're not yet seventeen."

"He gave you yours when you were sixteen," I protested.

"But seeing as he promised you . . ."

"It's wonderful!" I cried. "It's wonderful. And you brought it all the way from Caldicot? Look! The stave's exactly right." I fingered the ancient yew, and for a moment I remembered the bow made of shining elm that Will made for me and Sir John gave me almost three years ago. "I've stopped growing now," I said. "I think I have, and the stave's just half a fingerspan taller than I am."

At noon we feasted and after that we all rode down to the strand. I showed a trick Rhys has taught me, leaning right down out of my saddle at full gallop, and grabbing a jackknife stuck into the sand. I missed it the first time but got it twice after that. Then, in honor of Sir John, I displayed my bowmanship, shooting a full furlong. I've never been best at Yard-skills, but I've always been able to notch fast and shoot straight, and it was the same today.

After this, Serle and Bertie and I tilted at the quintain, and then I fought them at quarterstaff and swordplay.

"You, Arthur," said Milon approvingly. "Sharp as a Venetian's tongue."

"Not really, sir. I wish I were."

"I invite sea-feast councillors," Milon said. "But they not come. Shipwright not come."

"I'm not surprised," Lord Stephen said. "The Venetians are extremely impatient and angry."

"Sir Arthur! Sir Arthur!" my father mumbled. "Well! The bloody Saracens had better watch out." I looked at him, and then I had to look again to be sure. He was nodding at me, and smiling. "As for the Venetians," he boomed, "people around here accord them far too much respect."

Away east, out over the sea, it looked very murky, and before long I heard a low growl. An old sea-god, yawning. A gruff warning.

Still Burning

24

"You remember those Saracens," I said, "telling your fortune?"

"What about it?" Bertie replied.

"You don't have to believe them, you know. It's not like believing the Gospel."

"Who says I do?" said Bertie, and he swiped at the long grass with his stick.

"But —"

"I told you!" Bertie said angrily. "I don't want to talk about it."

"I swore oaths when I became a knight," I said, "but I don't actually believe all Saracens are evil. I hope it's not wrong to take a vow you don't completely believe in."

For a while, Bertie and I walked down towards the food-barge in silence. The quartermaster recognizes us now, and sometimes gives us extra food.

There was a horseman ambling towards us and I could tell by his sword he was a knight. When we drew closer, I saw his forehead was marked with a cross.

The cross wasn't made of parchment or linen or anything like that, and it wasn't a paint or a dye. It was a scar. It had been branded into him with a burning stick or a knife. A suppurating, purplish-brown cross that stretched from the roots of his hair to the bridge of his nose, and from the top of one ear across to the other.

"God be with you!" said the knight.

"And with you," we replied.

The knight's face was so disfigured, I could scarcely look at him, but his manner was courteous and gentle.

"Good luck with the quartermaster, Bertie," the knight said. "Good luck to you and your friend."

"Sir Arthur," Bertie said rather proudly. "Sir Arthur de Gortanore."

The knight smiled and inclined his head, and then rode on.

"I've met him before," Bertie explained. "He comes from Provins and once he gave me two quails' eggs."

"He looks horrible," I said.

"I know," said Bertie, "and he said the cross is still burning. He told me this crusade is a penance and the more we suffer, the more certain we are to reach paradise."

"By wounding ourselves?" I asked.

"I don't know," Bertie said.

"Some people are disfigured because their parents had pleasurable thoughts whilst conceiving them," I said. "That's what I've been taught. And some are disfigured because they're conceived in sin. But I'm not. And Kester's not."

"Why?" demanded Bertie. "Who's his father?"

"Serle," I said. "Didn't you know?"

Bertie whistled under his breath.

"Some are disfigured because of their parents," I repeated, "and some because they get wounded. But how can it be God's wish that we should damage ourselves?"

"Serle?" said Bertie, grinning. "Kester's father?"

Once, Gatty painted the sign of the cross on my forehead; she said I was like a crusader and Serle was a Saracen.

I wish . . . there's so much that I wish. I wish I could find out more about Gatty and her singing.

What I hope is Oliver will arrange for Lord Stephen's musician, Rahere, to teach her. He knows more about singing than anyone. He told me about the Saracen singing master, Ziryab, and breathing exercises.

"Come on!" he'll say in his squeaky voice, "*Ut, re, mi* . . . A voice is a human instrument, Gatty. *Fa, sol, la* . . . You must put yourself, everything you are, into the sound you make."

25 At the Stork

A YOUNG KNIGHT IS STANDING AT HIS PLACE AT THE Round Table, and I recognize him. Perceval. I haven't seen him since he stole Blanchefleur's emerald ring, and eight kisses. He wasn't knighted then.

"Sir Perceval," King Arthur says. "Tell us a wonder, and then we can feast."

Perceval opens his eyes wide. "This world is a wonder," he replies.

"Spare us!" says Queen Guinevere.

"Just whet our appetites!" the king says.

Sir Perceval scratches the back of his right ear. "Well, I did hear something last night. I was staying at a new monastery, and after supper the abbot took me to his lodgings. We drank sweet yellow wine and that unloosed our tongues all right.

"'Not far from here,' the abbot told me, 'there's an inn called the Stork because once a guest stood on a table and chalked a stork high up on the wall. It had a long beak and huge wings and stiff legs.'

"'What's so strange about that?' I asked. 'When I was a boy and lived in a cottage with my mother, we drew birds and animals all over our walls.'

"The abbot sipped some more yellow wine, and swilled it around his mouth.

"'Next morning,' he said, 'the guest went on his way. But that same evening the stork flew down from the wall! It flapped its huge wings, and flew out of the door and three times round the inn. Then it came back in, and flapped up into the wall.'

"'You mean . . .'

"'I do,' said the abbot. 'The stork became nothing but a chalk drawing again. Well, word of this wonder flew like the wind, and people were soon flocking to the inn. The stork never disappointed them. Each evening it came down from the wall and flew round the inn three times. And the innkeeper sold so much food and drink that he soon became extremely rich.'

"'Who was this guest who chalked the stork on the wall?' I asked the abbot.

"'Ah! I was coming to that. One day he returned to the inn, and as you can imagine, the innkeeper treated him like a king. The guest smiled, and he told the innkeeper to honor God by always showing generosity to each of his visitors. Then he snapped his fingers at his chalk drawing, and the stork came down from the wall and the guest mounted it. Away they flew, and neither of them was ever seen again.'"

Queen Guinevere claps her hands.

"A wonder!" King Arthur calls out.

"Was he a holy man?" asks Sir Perceval. "A saint? An angel? No one knows who the guest at the inn was. Anyhow, the abbot told me that the innkeeper was always generous to his visitors. And not only that. With all the money he'd made, he founded a new monastery — the monastery where I stayed last night. He paid for every stick and stone of it."

"Amen," says King Arthur, and he points at his trumpeter. "Let the feast begin!"

lifeblood

26

ODAY A MESSENGER BROUGHT A LETTER FROM THE Doge to Lord Geoffrey de Villehardouin and Milon and our other leaders.

Doge Enrico Dandolo of Venice to Lord Geoffrey de Villehardouin and the French envoys on the Feast of Saint Lawrence the Martyr

You break solemn agreement, you bleed us. You do not pay for two hundred ships. You eat our bread meat fish fruit, each day you drink our wine ale water. You ignore letters from Grand Councillors.

Now you envoys choose. In next seven days you pay eighty-five thousand silver marks of Cologne, or we cut off all supplies. No barges. No food. No water.

This is last warning.

Written on the Rialto, with Venice lifeblood

BY DOGE ENRICO DANDOLO

This letter was like a spark that set light to all the impatience and frustration that has been building up during the past seven weeks.

I was washing Bonamy in the sea, and Serle was nearby, jumping

Kester over the waves. Then I heard shouting and saw nine men running along the ridge. I mounted Bonamy and rode him bareback across the strand.

The men were charging down to the food-barge, and one man rushed at the quartermaster and held a knife to his throat while the others loaded themselves with as much food as they could carry. Dead chickens shoved inside their bulging tunics! Loaves of bread stuffed into their sleeves! Strings of sausages knotted round their waists!

Away they waddled. The quartermaster was unable to do anything about it.

So was I. I know I'm a knight and I've sworn to oppose evil and defend the helpless, but what could I do? I'm not like Sir Erec or Sir Lancelot. I wasn't even armed, and I can't fight nine men at the same time.

Serle came in after riding halfway down the island, and he says there has been trouble in almost every camp.

"Everyone's trying to save their own skins," he said.

"They won't save themselves by looting the food-barge," I said.

"No," said Serle. "The two ringleaders have lost their left hands as examples to their camps."

I screwed up my eyes, and thought of Lankin at Caldicot, and how he lost his right hand. "Why left?" I asked.

"So they can still fight the Saracens."

Serle and I were interrupted by Lord Stephen and Sir William, and before long the four of us walked out across the strand and along the water's edge in the moonlight. Four knights!

"It's the Doge's fault for threatening us," said Serle.

"He has waited a long time," Lord Stephen said. "Seven weeks."

"Why can't he wait a week or two longer?"

Sir William sighed noisily. "He knows he'll have to, and he knows in the end he'll have to make a bargain. He's playing a hard game, that's all. Quite right too!"

"But when people start to take the law into their own hands," I said, "and riot and thieve . . ."

"The Doge has probably counted on all that," Lord Stephen replied. "It increases the pressure on our leaders."

"Bloody fools!" Sir William exclaimed. "The lot of them! Acting as if the world's coming to an end. Dandolo doesn't mean it. If he starves us all to death, who's going to pay him?"

"I thought the Venetians were meant to be our friends," said Serle.

Sir William sniffed, and spat into the sand.

"They're our partners," Lord Stephen replied patiently. "We have our aims, and they have theirs."

At Last

27

GOOD FORTUNE AT LAST! GOD BE PRAISED!

For seven days our army has been tearing itself apart. All over the island there were fistfights and cudgelings, insults flying, petty thefts. A few men went off on their own, wandering along the foreshore; some got down on their knees, praying and singing.

No wonder the Doge doesn't want us on the Rialto. This ragged army of twelve thousand men, short of food and drink, starved of women, miles from home.

But this afternoon, on this fifteenth day of August, our new leader Marquis Boniface de Montferrat arrived in Venice at last.

His boat was awash with flowers and he was escorted by four Venetian councillors. Like us, they believe the marquis is the answer to their prayers.

A huge crowd gathered to greet him, and as soon as he stepped ashore, the marquis spoke to us.

"I am very glad to be here," he said. "At last! Thank you for being so patient!"

We all laughed. And something, something anxious, dissolved inside me.

Marquis Boniface glanced to left and right, smiling and nodding, and for a moment I thought he was looking me in the eye. He has quite long black hair, and a well-trimmed moustache and beard.

"I will meet the Doge tomorrow," the marquis announced, and his eyes flashed. "And I promise you, you men — God's knights! God's squires! God's men! — I will make a deal with him."

At this, many people clapped and cheered, and I saw Serle holding Kester right up so that he could see the marquis.

"In the name of God, and the name of good sense, I will make a deal," the marquis repeated. "An army can't fight on an empty stomach. An army must have ships."

Around me, everyone growled in approval.

"Tomorrow," the marquis called out, "I will take our six envoys to press our case. At my second meeting with the Doge, I will have with me not only Cardinal Capuano but the oldest knight and youngest knight in this entire army. I've instructed my squires to ride into each camp and seek them out. I will strike the best possible bargain." The marquis tightened his right hand into a fist and punched his breastbone. "In the meantime," he called out, "let it be clear I will accept no indiscipline. None whatsoever. You know the punishments." The marquis raised his other hand and clasped them both above his head. "God wills this crusade!" he shouted. "*Deus lo volt!* God wills it!"

All around me, people began to call out, "God be praised! God wills it! God with us!"

After this, the marquis mounted a Barb stallion and rode down to his camp, a mile south from ours.

Sometimes, after a thunderstorm, the face of the exhausted earth is tear-stained but fresh and fragrant, full of hope. That's how it felt this evening on Saint Nicholas.

instruments of the devil 28

NOW I UNDERSTAND WHY CARDINAL CAPUANO WAS SO rude to Lady Cécile and Tanwen.

I heard him preach a sermon on the strand this morning.

"These are Christ's words," he began. "My brothers, Christ speaks this sermon. I'm simply His mouthpiece." The cardinal crossed himself. "You've taken the Cross, and when you exterminate the Saracens, when you wash the streets of Jerusalem with their blood, you'll receive great rewards here and in heaven: the rich spoils of war; pardon without penance for all your foul sins; eternal life."

The cardinal looked up at the sun, and then squinted at us. "But some of you are fools!" he called out. "Would you put this at risk? You pander to your desires by keeping with you your wives, your mistresses, your wenches. Women are depraved witches. They're instruments of the devil!"

Instruments of the devil? How can they possibly be?

"Every woman," the cardinal called out, "is to leave this island within five days."

There was one long moment of silence, and then everyone started grumbling, jeering, whistling. Cardinal Capuano showed us the palms of his hands, but that was as useless as telling the salt-waves to stop breaking. He was still speaking, but no one could hear a word.

Witches! Winnie and Grace, my half-sister, aren't witches, and Gatty isn't. And what about all the women who are nuns? What about the Virgin Mary?

Lady Alice and Lady Judith and Lady Anne: They're not depraved. They're loving and generous.

I wish Oliver were here. I know the serpent persuaded Eve to tempt Adam, and it's true that women are sometimes more fickle than men — I think Winnie quite likes to tease me about her feelings for Tom — but that doesn't mean they're evil.

Sir William is furious about Capuano's ruling, and his face is the color of a cooked lobster. The hairs sticking out of his nose are just about as long as a lobster's whiskers too!

"It's God's will," said Lady Cécile.

"Nothing of the kind!" barked Sir William. "It's the whim of a Roman busybody. A lily-white bastard!"

Lady Cécile says we must all bow to God's will, but Tanwen is inconsolable. She wept and couldn't stop, and now she and Serle have been out walking for hours. They left Kester with me, and it took him a very long time to fall asleep.

We could cut off Tanwen's hair and dress her as a boy — some of the Picardian women are disguising themselves like that. But what about Kester? Poor Tanwen!

Only a few days ago, Saint Nicholas was discouraged and desperate. Then the marquis arrived, and everyone shouted and cheered. But now Cardinal Capuano has thrown us all down again. . . .

YOUR TRUE BELIEVER

BUT MY RING," I PROTESTED.

"I know," said Lady Cécile. "That was wrong."

"Wrong?" I said, more loudly than I meant to. "It was terrible."

"But you should never have taken it. That's just as wrong."

"It was a gift," I said, as calmly as I could. "From my mother."

Lady Cécile laid a hand on my wrist. "I see," she said very quietly. "You mustn't judge him too harshly. I've seen more of the world than you, and believe me, sons often regret their fathers, fathers often deplore their sons. But he's proud of you, you know."

"Proud?"

"Yes, and all the more so now you've been knighted! He's proud of Tom and Grace too."

I don't think Lady Cécile can know anything. If Sir William cared at all, he wouldn't stop me from meeting my mother. Does she even know who my mother is?

"And remember," said Lady Cécile, "he's sixty-seven, almost sixty-eight, and blind in one eye; all his bones ache." Lady Cécile sighed. "I do doubt whether I'll see him again. I know he's always blustering and berating you, but look after him, Arthur." She laid her hand on my wrist again. "You need him, and he needs you."

I can't understand how Lady Cécile can love my father. What is it that I cannot see?

I like Lady Cécile. It's just that I wish she didn't dishonor Lady Alice. If we'd talked earlier, I think she could have told me more about my father, and I could have told her things too. Why do we only discover the true value of something when we're about to lose it?

Before Lady Cécile and Tanwen and Kester left camp, I copied out my poem for Winnie: "Blazing hair and tawny eye! Freckle-face! . . ."

Sir Arthur to Winnie, my betrothed
this twenty-first day of August

I hope you like my song.

What your father says about Sir William may be true, but he does not really mean half of what he says, and in the end he will reach an agreement with your father so that we may marry.

Turold has punched a hole in my half of our pledge-coin, and I have threaded a leather lace through it and wear it around my neck. Is your half safe?

Please greet Sir Walter and Lady Anne. I think about you each day, and Tanwen will tell you about our lives here.
Copied on Saint Nicholas

BY YOUR KNIGHT AND CRUSADER

I asked Tanwen to give these words to Winnie and tell her everything — about my being knighted and Saint Nicholas and our camp and the looting and about Sir William and my ring and the waiting and meeting Saracen traders and about Bertie and . . .

And, somehow, it all seemed rather useless. Winnie and I are half this wide world apart. I can do nothing but wait.

Then I asked Tanwen to take a message to Gatty.

"How can I remember all this?" Tanwen complained.

"Just a short one."

"Well, then?" said Tanwen, smiling her elfin smile. "What is it?"

"Tell Gatty to put herself, everything she is . . . no, not that! Tell her, tell her I can hear a little lark singing, and best things don't never get lost."

"You can hear a lark singing . . . ," Tanwen repeated.

"A little one."

". . . and best things don't never get lost."

"That's it," I said.

"What's that supposed to mean, then?" Tanwen asked.

"Gatty will understand," I said.

the wheel of fortune

I FELT LONELY AFTER TANWEN AND KESTER AND LADY CÉCILE were rowed away. They left with at least one hundred other women, and the whole island has been strangely quiet: as if we have waved farewell to half of our own energy and spirit.

So much has happened since I was knighted. But actually, all my duties to Lord Stephen are the same as before, because I'm still in service to him. I have to brush his clothes and ensure they're well aired, and that's not easy because the sea air is very damp; I have to lay them out each morning, and help him to dress, and lace his boots, and hold up the basin so he can wash; I have to check Rhys is grooming Stupendous each day; I have to carve for Lord Stephen and Sir William and Serle at our little trestle table, and serve them. Yes, I spoil the chicken and unlace the rabbit and chin the salmon and tame the crab. . . .

But all the same, being a knight does feel different. Bertie is quite impressed, and I felt very proud when he told the branded knight that I was a knight too. Sometimes Rhys and Turold call me "sir" now, and Lady Cécile told me my father's proud of me.

Turold says he has never seen a finer sword than mine. I keep unsheathing it when I'm alone, and fingering the blade, and the ring engraved on it.

"Sir Arthur!" Lord Stephen said late last night, when we were both lying on our mattresses.

"Yes, sir?"

"Nothing!"

"Sir?"

"Sir Arthur, Sir Arthur, Sir Arthur . . . I'm just sounding it out! It sounds good, doesn't it."

"Yes, sir."

I want to see knights! I want to hear knights! So as soon as I was sure Lord Stephen was asleep, I burrowed to the bottom of my saddlebag and pulled out my obsidian. My companion-stone.

Arthur-in-the-stone is sitting under an elm tree, talking to his three wise men.

"I had this dream," he says, "and I've never been so afraid. I woke up shaking."

"We will explain it," replies one of the wise men.

"First I was in a forest, surrounded by wild beasts. Wolves. Wild boar. Lions licking their chops. I ran away from them, into a valley surrounded by high hills. The valley floor was green with the most succulent new grass, sprinkled with clover. Above me the clouds opened, and a lady came down. A duchess. She was holding a large wheel in one hand and turning it with the other."

"A duchess?"

"What was it like, this wheel?"

"Turning or whirling?"

"She was wearing damask lined with otter fur; she had a train that was trimmed with gold. Her wheel was made of Welsh gold inlaid with rubies; each spoke was as long as a spear, and splintered with silver.

"There were nine chairs fixed to the outside of the rim, and eight kings were sitting in them. When the duchess spun the wheel, six of them were turned upside down. They clung to the rim, yelling, gabbling, confessing:

"'I was cruel, I know . . . I had men tortured . . . I was extortionate . . . I abused women . . . I was the greatest and now I'm the least . . . king of the wheel . . . damned, damned . . .'"

King Arthur sighs. "Then one by one they lost their grip and fell off. Only two men were left sitting in their chairs, but neither was content with that. They tried to claw their way up to the very top. One was dressed in royal blue, decorated with fleur-de-lys; the other wore a silver coat and, around his neck, a magnificent gold cross."

"Did they get to the top?" one wise man asks.

"I was coming to that," King Arthur replies. "The duchess smiled at me, and I greeted her.

"'Welcome!' she said. 'If anyone on earth should honor me, it's you, Arthur, son of Uther Pendragon and Queen Ygerna. All that you are is because of me. I have been your friend. You will sit in the topmost chair. I choose you to be the greatest leader and king on God's earth.'

"Then the duchess picked me up with long white fingers and set me down in the ninth chair. She combed my hair. She gave me a scepter and an orb incised with a map of the world, the continents and oceans. Then she slipped a sword into my right hand.

"After this," King Arthur tells his wise men, "the duchess strolled over to an orchard, still carrying the gold wheel, and I was sitting in the topmost chair. She offered me plums, pears, pomegranates; she gave me white wine that fizzed out of a well.

"But then, at midday, her mood completely changed. It darkened like a sky that suddenly swarms with thunder-clouds.

"'You fool!' she said. 'You're as bad as the others.'

"'Lady!' I protested.

"'Silence!' she shouted. 'Don't waste words. Everything you've won, you'll lose. Then you'll lose life itself. You've enjoyed your kingdom and the pleasures of power for quite long enough!'

"The duchess glared at me with the eyes of a terrible wildcat. She whirled the wheel, and the two climbing kings fell off. Then I fell off! I couldn't move. I knew I'd broken every bone in my body. That's when I woke up."

"Arthur," says the first wise man, "the meaning of your dream is obvious. Lady Fortune gives and Lady Fortune takes away. She was your friend, and now she's your enemy."

"You reached the height of your powers," the second man says. "From now on, whatever you attempt will fail."

"You and only you are responsible for your actions," says the third man, "and as you well know, there's no power without abuse of it. The greater a man's power, the greater his sins. Confess your guilt. Found abbeys. Before long, you'll fall headlong."

"Who were the six kings?" asks Arthur.

"Alexander and Hector of Troy and Julius Caesar," the first wise man replies.

"Sir Judas the Maccabee, Joshua who flattened the walls of Jericho, and David who slew the giant Goliath and first sang the psalms," says the second man.

"And who were the climbing kings?" the third man asks. "One was Charlemagne and the other Godfrey of Bouillon, keeper of the Holy Cross, conqueror of Jerusalem. But no warlord is a saint. Charlemagne and Godfrey may have been Christian, but they were no better than the first six kings."

"And now Lady Fortune has named you as the ninth," says the first wise man. "The nine noblest men ever to have walked on middle-earth."

"Men will talk about you."

"And sing your praises."

"They'll write poems and stories and chronicles about you."

"The wolves and the wild boar and the lions," the first man says, "are evil men. Your enemies. And some of them, Arthur, are inside Camelot, smiling at you, pretending to be your friends."

"Who?" asks the king.

"Mend your ways!" says the first man.

"On bended knees beg God for His mercy."

"Save your soul."

31 The Youngest and the Oldest

"BERTIE SAYS WE MAY SAIL TO EGYPT," I TOLD LORD Stephen.

"Who told him that?" Lord Stephen demanded, blinking like an indignant owl.

"Milon's men."

"And why should they know?"

"Are we, sir?" I asked.

Lord Stephen dug his elbows into his mattress and sat up. "Rumors," he said, "are nothing but rumors. But I did warn you that we might be ill-advised to head straight for Jerusalem. That's what the Saracens expect. And where they're best prepared."

"But why Egypt, sir?"

In my head I could see Gatty standing in the little armory at Caldicot holding a pair of fustian breeches, and my telling her they came from El-Fustat in Egypt, and her asking me, "What's Egypt?"

"Why Egypt?" Lord Stephen repeated. "Because it's the storehouse of the Saracen world. Rich in grain and fruit and spices. Rich in gold. Do you know what the city of Alexandria's called?"

"No, sir."

"The market between the two worlds: between the land oversea and North Africa. If we can take control of the Saracens' storehouse and cut their lines of communication . . ."

"The Venetians won't like that," I said. "The shipwright told me about all the trade between Venice and Egypt, and Bertie and I met three traders from Alexandria. One of them told me that Muhammad was a trader."

Lord Stephen harrumphed.

"There's another thing I wanted to ask you, sir."

"There always is," Lord Stephen replied.

But before I could ask why Cardinal Capuano attacked women, almost as if he were afraid of them, a horseman rode in to our camp.

I brought the man back into our tent.

"A message from the Marquis Boniface, sir," the man told us. "He says twelve thousand men have assembled here on Saint Nicholas but we signed an agreement with the Venetians to build ships for thirty-three thousand men, and are obliged to pay for them. There is no alternative."

"We are well aware of that," Lord Stephen said very drily. "We've been reminded of it each day since we arrived."

"In the name of suffering Christ," the messenger said, "the marquis calls on each earl and lord in this army, each knight, each squire, each foot soldier, armorer, and stableman, to give money or valuables to help. Let each man consider what he can give."

Lord Stephen blinked at the marquis's messenger. "I will consider it," he said. "And you, Sir Arthur. You will, won't you?"

"Yes, sir."

"I know!" said Lord Stephen, his eyes gleaming. "You could give that silver pledge-penny."

I put my hands to my neck.

"Well, halfpenny!" Lord Stephen said.

"Sir," said the messenger. "I don't think the marquis means . . ."

"I should hope not!" Lord Stephen said, smiling. "What's the use of honoring one commitment by dishonoring another?"

"Within three days," the messenger said, "one of the marquis's envoys will visit you to discuss this matter further." He bowed, and left the tent, and almost immediately another man rode in. A second messenger from the marquis.

"Dear Lord!" said Lord Stephen. "What next? Do you remember mornings like this at Holt?"

"You are Sir Arthur de Gortanore?" the messenger asked me.

Am I? De Caldicot? De Gortanore? How long will it take me to get used to my name?

"When Marquis Boniface arrived on Saint Nicholas," said the messenger, "he began a search for the youngest and oldest knights in this army to accompany him to meet the Doge. We have visited each camp. You are sixteen years old, and not yet six months?"

"Yes. Yes, I am."

"Then you, Sir Arthur, are the youngest knight on this island."

I gasped.

Lord Stephen clapped a hand on my shoulder. Then he turned to the messenger. "What about the oldest knight?" he said. "Who is he?"

"He's sixty-seven, almost sixty-eight," the messenger said. "Sir William de Gortanore!"

SEEING EYE TO EYE

AROUND US THE WATER YAPPED AND PAWED OUR BOAT.

"It's a good thing the cardinal's not here," Marquis Boniface said. "This would have finished him off."

"Why didn't he come, sir?" I asked.

"A bad mussel, or an oyster," replied the marquis. "He's so sick, he wishes he'd never been born."

The boat lurched and I looked anxiously at our two oarsmen, but they were laughing, and didn't notice me.

"We'll make do without him," said the marquis. "So! Sir William and Sir Arthur. Father and son! Most surprising."

"Nothing surprises me," my father said. "Not any longer."

"Don't say that!" said the marquis, and he smiled at me. "I'm sure your son will. And what could be better? Our children's achievements warm our blood."

My father said nothing. He sniffed and looked into the distance. And then, as our boat lurched again, he grabbed at the gunwale, missed it, and fell over backwards.

The marquis and I each took one of my father's hands and pulled him up onto the crossbench again.

"Leg!" gasped my father. "Bloody leg! Massage it, boy! Go on!"

So I rubbed my father's right leg, and as I did I looked at his right hand. The back of it is covered with brown spots. The half-moons on his nails have almost completely disappeared, so maybe he won't live much longer.

"That's enough!" my father said. "I can do it better myself."

"Cramp?" asked the marquis.

My father fished into an inside pocket of his surcoat, pulled out two small furry feet, and glared at them. "No good at all," he said. "Mole!"

"You need eelskin," said the marquis.

"Useless!" exclaimed my father. And he tossed them over the gunwale.

"Eelskin," the marquis said again.

"Lady Alice," I began, "she says . . ."

"Your mother?" the marquis inquired.

"My second wife," Sir William explained.

"Yes, she says hare's foot is the best, sir," I said.

"For stiff joints, not for cramp," my father said curtly. "That's enough from you, Arthur."

"Ah!" said the marquis. His gaze flicked between us. "Well, my family swears by eelskin garters," he said. "I'll have my squire ride over a pair for you."

My father grunted. Then he turned and glittered at me. "Surprises!" he muttered. "I'll surprise you."

Just before we reached the quay where the Doge's servants were waiting to greet us, the marquis glanced round at us and rubbed his moustache. "Now to work!" he said.

Up one flight of echoing steps. Down another. Through half a dozen staterooms. Stopping to listen to a fanfare. I could climb to the top of Tumber Hill and down again in the time it takes before you actually meet the Doge.

Then in trips a little old man, with a servant at his elbow to guide him and catch him if he stumbles.

The Doge's joints are not at all stiff. He gestures all the time, and his voice is light and quick. And his blind eyes are so bright, you'd suppose he had just seen paradise — not like my father's eye, which has turned the color of congealed blood.

The Doge and Marquis Boniface greeted one another very warmly, first embracing and then talking for a while. Then the marquis told the Doge about us.

"I've brought with me two men," he said, "the oldest and the youngest of all the knights, just two representatives of my huge army encamped on Saint Nicholas. One is sixty-seven, the other sixteen. More than fifty years divide them."

"You are both welcome," said the Doge.

"But they are united in their purpose," the marquis continued, "as are we all. Not only that. They're father and son!"

"Padre e figlio!" the Doge repeated, and he waved his arms.

"Most extraordinary!" said the marquis. "We searched the whole island and found them side by side in the little English camp. Sir William de Gortanore. Sir Arthur de Gortanore."

"One family, yes," my father blared. "And what is more important than family?"

Is that what my father said? What is more important than family?

"We're here to represent all Christian families," my father went on. "All the families in Christendom. Indeed, sir, we represent the Holy Family, suffering now because of the Saracens."

The Doge listened patiently, then gave my father a faint smile.

"Bravo!" he said.

When I took the Doge's hand, it was crumpled and brittle. Dry as a dead beech leaf.

"England," he said. "Coeur-de-Lion."

"Yes, sir."

"I fought with him," my father boomed. "At Acre. Now there's a leader for you!"

"King John?" the Doge inquired mildly.

"Lesser metal," my father replied.

"One thousand marks," Marquis Boniface added. "That's his entire contribution to this crusade."

"Poco," said the Doge, and he pursed his lips.

We were shown to a bench while the marquis and the Doge sat down in chairs, and they soon began a serious discussion about the treaty. Even after everyone has made a contribution, we can't raise anything like as much as eighty-five thousand marks. But the Doge says the Venetians can't accept less. On the other hand, it would be unthinkable to tear up the contract and send everyone home, because the Venetians would be left with two hundred ships they do not need, and everyone in Christendom would spit at their name for allowing the crusade to fail.

"The price for each man and horse is too high," the marquis complained.

"It's the right price and you know it," replied the Doge. "What's wrong was your envoys' estimate of how many men would take the Cross."

Although the marquis and the Doge kept disagreeing, they both kept smiling.

"Words, words, words," my father grumbled. He got up and headed for the door. "I need a piss," he announced in a loud voice, and a servant led him out.

I felt blood rush to my cheeks. Can't my father tell the difference between a camp and a palace?

The Doge snapped his fingers — at least, he tried to — and before long a servant brought a platter of black olives and little squares of hard, pungent cheese, and a pitcher of red wine.

"What are we to do?" he asked, as much to himself as to Marquis Boniface. "Christendom is watching us. Our children's children will judge us. What would be most wise?"

The Doge tilted back his head and lifted his hands, beseeching God; then he gazed blindly at the marquis, and frowned as if he were trying to find the right words. But I had the feeling he knew exactly what he was going to say.

"I have one idea . . . one proposal. For twenty years the city of Zara has rebelled against the Republic of Venice. The people there have broken their oaths; they rebel against us; they dishonor their debts to us. It was all we could do to find enough oak to build your ships without supplies from their forests." The Doge gritted his teeth — the few teeth he has left — and shook his head angrily.

At this moment, Sir William blundered back into the room. "The needs of nature!" he announced. "No compromise!"

"If you agree . . . ," the Doge began, "if you agree to help us recover Zara . . ."

The marquis didn't move a muscle.

". . . as is our right," the Doge added. "We have every right to reclaim our own territory before joining this crusade. Didn't Coeur-de-Lion do the same? If you agree," the Doge repeated, "my councillors might agree to postpone payment."

"I see," the marquis said quietly.

"We will divide the spoils," said the Doge, "and you can pay us out of your share. Then we'll set sail for Egypt."

Egypt! Bertie was right.

"But," said the marquis, "the people of Zara: They're Christians."

Christians! My head felt as if it were bursting. We're meant to be fighting Saracens, not fighting ourselves. If Cardinal Capuano were here, surely he would be angry at the Doge's suggestion.

"True!" said the Doge in a matter-of-fact way.

There was a long silence.

"Well!" said Marquis Boniface. "I see I must consider it. I will discuss it with my envoys."

"And I with my Grand Council," the Doge said. "I think we see . . . eye to eye." He laughed gently. "In a matter of speaking," he added.

Then the Doge stood up. When he took my hand, he smiled slightly.

"Signor Artù," he said.

"Sir?"

"Compromise!"

Deep Waters

I WAS ON MY WAY TO THE FOOD-BARGE THIS AFTERNOON when I noticed a knot of people much farther along the shore. Then I heard distant shouting.

As I ran along the ridge towards them, I made out a little rowing boat halfway over to the marshy islet that lies right opposite Milon's camp. There was no one in it, though. Then I spotted two people splashing in the water.

I ran down to the shore and saw Pagan, Milon's priest, standing on a slimy rock.

"What's happened?" I asked.

"Bertie!" said Pagan. "Again!"

"What?"

"Trying to swim out to the little islet."

"He can't swim. Not that far."

"Exactly! I told him not to."

"Look!" I exclaimed. "That man's almost reached him!"

"A fisherman," said Pagan. "Saving Bertie and losing his boat."

Pagan and I and a group of Milon's men all watched as the fisherman grabbed Bertie and then, swimming on his back like an upsidedown frog with Bertie in his arms, propelled himself towards us.

I went down to the water's edge. I waded into the water up to my waist, and as soon as I could, grabbed Bertie and helped to haul him out of the water.

Bertie collapsed onto his hands and knees, and choked and coughed; he vomited; and then he lay on a heap of seaweed with his eyes closed. He looked like a stranded starfish.

"What were you doing?" I asked him.

Bertie didn't reply.

"Bertie!"

"Sir Laurent challenged me."

"You can't even swim. Not properly."

Bertie opened one eye. "He said I wouldn't dare."

"You're mad!" I said. "You almost drowned."

"I don't care."

"You do."

Bertie tried to sit up, then flopped back onto the seaweed again. "You know what I told you," he said, and his voice was hoarse.

"But that doesn't mean you have to . . . You don't want to die, do you?"

"Of course not!" said Bertie indignantly, and he propped himself up on his elbows. "Of course I don't. I was being alive. You'd be the same if you were me. You'd want to be fierce and alive the whole time."

34

To Lead You and Look After You

IT IS ALL AGREED!

Seven days of consultations, seven days of gallopings up and down the island and crossings between Saint Nicholas and the Rialto. Then at noon today Marquis Boniface and our envoys met the Doge and his councillors in the basilica of Saint Mark's to solemnize our new understanding, and Lord Stephen and I accompanied them.

The Grand Council even provided us with a translator. She's called Simona, and she's twenty-one. She told me she quite often translates for English merchants visiting Venice. When she was seventeen, she got betrothed to an English cloth-trader from Norfolk and learned English from him, but before they could marry he and his companions were attacked and killed by bandits near Verona.

Not only was Saint Mark's packed, but the huge garden in front of it was swarming with people as well. So many people were sitting or standing up in the olive trees that I thought the branches might break.

"No, no!" said Simona. "Olives seldom break. *Gli albicocchi* . . . apricots! They break."

Simona looks rather like an apricot herself: Her skin's sandy-pink and slightly furry, and she's small and smiling and round.

"In our garden," she told us, "we have *albicocchi*. Last year the fruit was so heavy, two branches broke."

Saint Mark's must be the most beautiful church in the world because the walls and the cupola and the roof are covered in burnt gold and you walk on mosaics. Thousands and thousands of tiny colored stone squares, no bigger than my fingernails. Patterned in squares and semicircles and triangles. Bishop's purple and cornflower blue and olive green and rust and orange.

Before high mass, the Doge tripped while climbing the steps to the lectern, and almost fell.

What if he had? What if he'd quickly wasted and died? And what if Cardinal Capuano hadn't eaten a bad oyster, but had come with us to meet the Doge? Sometimes it seems that great decisions are the result not of careful intention but of sheer accident.

The Doge stood at the lectern. "My people!" he called out in his reedy voice. "I nearly fell! I nearly fell, and our crusade nearly failed. The greatest undertaking ever undertaken by Christian men. But we have grasped it with both hands!"

To emphasize his point, the Doge grasped the lectern, and the Venetians in the basilica laughed.

The Doge waited until he could be heard again, and that was good because he was speaking in Venetian, and Simona had to translate for us. "My people!" he called out. "These crusaders are the best, bravest men in the world. Venice is proud to be part of this crusade." The Doge paused. "I am old," he said, "and my health is failing. Like a cat, I often doze . . ." The Doge rapped the lectern. "And I'm instantly awake! I've been your leader for longer than most of you have been alive. Will you allow me to take the Cross? To lead you and look after you on our pilgrimage?"

Now the whole basilica waved and roared like the sea.

I looked at Marquis Boniface. He didn't look troubled; he just looked thoughtful.

"Will you allow me to live or die with you?"

There were tears in Simona's eyes. "He is blind and sees. He is old and always young," she said. She took Lord Stephen's right hand and squeezed it.

Lord Stephen bent towards me. "And he's wily!" he said. "Extremely wily!"

The Doge proceeded to the altar, flanked by priests. Then one priest sewed the scarlet cross onto the front of his cotton cap, and around me everyone was cheering.

"Why his cap?" I asked Simona. "Why not his tunic?"

"So everyone can see it," Simona replied.

After this, the priests rang handbells; they swung incense burners, and many other Venetians came forward and took the Cross.

"I swear . . . I swear . . . I swear by Almighty God that I will serve Doge Enrico Dandolo of Venice, and be loyal to him in Zara and wheresoever he leads me."

Most of the Venetians seemed to know we're going to Zara before we fight the Saracens, and they were glad about it, but what will all the crusaders do when they find out? And what will Cardinal Capuano say?

"I swear . . . I swear . . . I swear and acknowledge Enrico Dandolo as my true and only lord. Let everyone bear witness!"

The Venetians did bear witness! Each time a knight completed his vows, he was greeted with a shout, and around me many faces were shining with tears.

And then the Doge held up his thin hands. "Release the ships!" he called out. "Untether them! Point their prows east!"

There was such cheering and crying and stamping of feet that you might have thought the whole world was breaking into bits.

"So now our crusade has two leaders," I said.

"A recipe for disaster!" Lord Stephen replied grimly.

Tonight, bonfires blazed in each camp on Saint Nicholas.

Lord Stephen and my father both chose to sleep, so Serle and I walked down to Milon's camp with Rhys and Turold.

As far as we know, we are still the only Englishmen to have joined this crusade. That's very surprising and disappointing because when Fulk came to the March and preached the crusade, it seemed certain many people would take the Cross. Sir Josquin des Bois said he would come, and so did hundreds from other parts of England.

"You can blame King John for that," said Lord Stephen. "If he'd chosen to come himself, or even encouraged others, many would have followed."

Milon's men had tied torches to the ends of their lances. They ran around in the dark, waving them and giving strange, short little shouts. Crossing and quartering the Provins camp. Beating its bounds.

Then we all gathered in a fire-circle. Pagan gave thanks that our crusade can sail at last, and we prayed for our own safety, for our families and everyone at home. . . .

The wind was from the west, and as it blew over the camp, it snatched sparks from the torches, and tossed them; it carried them off, so fleeting, down to the dark sea.

35 Cheeks and Strutting Peacocks

ON CLEAR DAYS, THE MOUNTAINS NORTH FROM HERE look quite close, but Simona says they're more than fifty miles away. Their peaks and valleys are like a long line of open, ravening beaks.

Before we left Saint Mark's yesterday, Simona showed us two mosaic peacocks, even more beautiful than the woven ones decorating the tent of the Saracen traders in the *campo*.

"They promise life everlasting," Simona said, "because peacocks never, never die." Her breasts heaved and her dark eyes flashed, and then she pinched Lord Stephen's pink cheeks!

Lord Stephen harrumphed and smiled rather nervously.

"Well, then! Yes! Well, then!" he exclaimed. "With all Lady Judith's peacocks at Holt . . . Holt! England! With all her peacocks, I do believe we could lay a path of feathers from earth to heaven."

"Ah!" groaned Simona. *"Paradiso!"*

She took Lord Stephen's arm and nestled against him, and her painted eyelids fluttered.

"Whatever next!" Lord Stephen said.

I could see he was smiling, though. And very nearly strutting.

NOT ASKING THE QUESTION

WHEN I LOOKED INTO MY SEEING STONE, I COULD see King Arthur and Queen Guinevere and a young woman mounted on a mule in the great hall at Camelot.

"People say your court is the finest on middle-earth," the young woman begins. "They say it compares with the courts of Alexander and Julius Caesar."

"Dismount!" says King Arthur.

"I will not," the young woman replies.

"Fresh rushes on the floor," Queen Guinevere says, "strewn with marigolds and wild mint. No one's allowed to ride into this hall. Not even on a mule!"

"And everyone dismounts when the king is dismounted," Arthur tells her.

"Forgive me," says the woman, "but I will not dismount until a knight comes to the castle of Corbenic and wins the Grail. Is there no knight at your Round Table who can do that?"

She is wearing a white wimple and has a shield hanging from her neck: a scarlet cross on a snow-white background. Her mule, he's white as well, and a hound is following them.

"Many knights have tried and many have failed," the king says.

"They have all failed," says the young woman. "Even Sir Gawain failed to ask the question, so the Guardian of the Grail still writhes in agony. His wounds bleed day and night, men fight, kingdoms crumble, this whole world is a wasteland. I was there when Sir Gawain spoke to Nascien, the hermit . . ."

Then my seeing stone led me out of the hall, and into the dark cave itself. I could see nothing at first, then nothing but sparks, torches. After that, three shadowy figures: the woman on her mule, Sir Gawain, and the hermit.

"Everyone knows about you," Nascien begins. "How you dared face the Green Knight. Everyone's got a story to tell about you. Your prowess. Your endurance. Your honor. So is that the end of your story?"

Sir Gawain doesn't reply.

"You're not a soldier of God," Nascien tells Gawain. "Your fame is written in other men's blood."

"I have opposed evil. I've defended the weak."

"You beheaded an innocent woman, Lady Saraide, Sir Blamoure's wife. You're a spiritual beggar!"

Now Sir Gawain leaves the cave, and mounts Kincaled. I can see him cantering up to the gates of a great castle. It's made of marble, like the Doge's palace.

Two boys take off Sir Gawain's armor; two young women dressed in cloth of gold wash him. And now two knights lead Gawain to an inner courtyard. The ground is parched yellow grass, and in the shade of an arbor covered with vines, a man is lying on a bed. Its four posts are glowing: They're made of red gold.

The vines are shriveled; the grapes are wrinkled grey pebbles.

Sir Gawain walks softly up to the man. King Pellam, Guardian of the Grail. I saw Sir Balin wound him with the lance Longinus used to pierce Jesus.

"Gawain," says the king, and his voice is little more than a whisper, "you have come to Corbenic and I cannot even raise myself to greet you."

"That is why I have come," Sir Gawain says.

He looks at the wounded king: his ivory skin; his eyes dark with pain; his scarlet hat emblazoned with a gold cross; the blood oozing from the gash in his ribs.

Now the arbor fills with yellow light brighter than that of the rising sun.

"Gawain," says the king, "this light is the sign of God's great love for you. You are one of the bravest, the most honorable knights on earth.

"Once before, a knight reached Corbenic, and this same light shone. But he failed to ask the question, and that is why his quest failed."

"Whom does the Grail serve?" Sir Gawain says, and he closes his eyes.

"Whom does the Grail serve?" the king repeats. "That is the question."

Gawain gazes at King Pellam. "I will not fail you," he says.

Now the same two knights lead Sir Gawain away to a gloomy hall where twelve white-haired knights are sitting and about to eat. Who are they? Are they Jesus's disciples?

A door opens. Two young women glide in and the room fills with light. One woman is carrying the Holy Grail, covered with thick white silk, and a dazzling sunbeam rises from it. I can scarcely look at it. The other woman is carrying Longinus's lance. Its tip is dripping with blood.

The Grail . . . the Holy Grail. It is covered, but within it I can see a shape. A boychild.

The two young women pause in front of Sir Gawain.

"Now!" say the knights. "Gawain! The question!"

But Sir Gawain just gazes at the Grail, transfixed, the Grail and the lance, and he keeps reaching out towards them. Three drops of blood fall at his feet. Gawain keeps reaching out, but the young women float the Grail and lance away from him.

"The question! The question!" the old knights urge Sir Gawain, but Sir Gawain is dazed.

"At once!"

"Now or never!"

It is no good. Sir Gawain sees the lips of the old knights moving, but all he can hear is the whirlwind of his own sins and shortcomings.

Now the young women leave the hall and the old knights stand up and follow them. Sir Gawain stands alone in the gloom. He is utterly worn out. He cannot stay awake. He lies on a couch and sleeps. . . .

A horn blast echoes through Corbenic, and at once Sir Gawain scrambles to his feet. As it dies away, he can hear through one wall King Pellam moaning, and through another a choir of angels singing. . . .

Now in comes the woman wearing a white wimple who rode right into Camelot on a white mule.

"Sir Gawain," she says, "you've committed many sins, but so has every man. Your greatest failing lies in what you've left undone. You did not ask the question."

"I could not!" Sir Gawain cries. "I wasn't able to."

The horn sounds again, and a voice without a body booms through the hall. "The man who does not belong here: Let him be gone."

Now the young woman leads Sir Gawain to his loyal Kincaled, and he rides away.

Hoots of wind! Stinging rain, and the hammer of thunder!

"I have failed King Pellam," Sir Gawain says to himself. "I've failed King Arthur and the fellowship of the Round Table. I've failed myself."

The thunder becomes a distant rumor. The spattering rain softens into a blur. Like a feeding butterfly, the air trembles and faintly flutters.

Now I can see the court at Camelot again, packed with knights and ladies, and the young woman in a white wimple, still mounted on her mule.

"You see?" says the young woman.

"But I believe a knight will achieve this quest," King Arthur replies.

"My shield once belonged to Joseph of Arimathea," the young woman tells them. "He painted this cross on it with blood. I will leave it with you, hanging on this pillar, and only a knight who can achieve the Grail will be able to remove it. I'll leave my hound too. He'll recognize the knight and lick his hand." The young woman pauses. "Look at me, Arthur!" she said in a loud voice.

She reaches up and sweeps off her wimple and everyone gasps. She is completely bald.

"Once, I had honey tresses," she calls out, "but now not a hair will grow on my head. Blame all the knights who have failed. Pellam's kingdom is a wasteland. Children starve; babies are bloated with hunger. Nothing can grow until a knight comes to Corbenic and asks the question."

the lesser of two evils

LORD STEPHEN PROPPED HIMSELF UP AGAINST HIS saddlebag, but Sir William preferred to stand because he finds it difficult to sit. I knelt on my mattress, and Serle lay on his stomach with his chin in his hands.

"What I don't understand is how we can attack other Christians if we're soldiers of God," I said.

"No one's said anything about attacking them," replied Lord Stephen.

"One day, Arthur," said Serle, "you're going to trip up on your own conscience."

"Either your conscience or your tongue," added Sir William. "One or the other, they'll do for you."

"No," said Lord Stephen. "Arthur has a point. I've heard today that several knights are talking of breaking their vows and turning for home."

"Well, then," Serle said nastily, "Arthur can go with them."

"Take your choice!" Sir William said. "Either we sail to Zara or this whole bloody crusade disbands."

"The Doge did say it was his right to recapture Zara before we sailed against the Saracens," I said.

"That may be true," Lord Stephen replied. "But recruiting us all to help him? I don't know about that. In any case, he wasn't even coming with us until the day before yesterday."

"Are the Venetians just out for themselves, then?" Serle asked.

"Everyone is!" my father retorted. "Let's get on with it. All the foot soldiers, and Turold and Rhys, do you think they give an owl's hoot about where we're going or whom we're fighting?"

"It's a job for them," I replied. "It's a cause for us."

"What I think," said Serle, "is all this talking makes things worse."

"No!" I said. "It makes things clearer." I turned to Lord Stephen. "Do you accept the agreement, sir?"

Lord Stephen screwed up his face and sighed. "What I think is that not being able to pay for the ships, and our great quest, together justify this . . . this solution. I don't like it, but I can accept it."

"Where is Zara?" asked Serle.

"Across the Adriatic," Lord Stephen said. "Away down the coast."

"What will happen when we get there?" I asked.

Lord Stephen gave me a thin smile. "And before we get there," he said. "I hear we'll be stopping at the port of Pirano to exercise our horses and to replenish our supply of fresh water."

"What if the people of Zara resist?" I asked.

"Believe me, boy!" my father said. "When they see the size of our fleet, they'll speak at both ends!"

Lord Stephen licked his lips and rubbed his mouth with the back of his right hand. "This sand!" he said irritably. "It's getting into everything. The wind's in our face again."

"And God's behind us!" Sir William barked. "Sweet Jesus! Cheer up!"

love and lemon

IMONA'S FRAGRANCE MADE ME ACHE. SO COOL AND clean. Like an early morning pool of creamy rose petals, just fallen. It reminded me of dawn at Caldicot, dew on the grass, muzzy patches of gossamer, the first beech leaves still soft . . .

Here, everything is sticky and salty. Saint Nicholas reeks of sweat and rot and manure, and we scarcely notice it.

"Where have you come from?" I asked.

Simona stuck her thumb over her right shoulder. "That galley."

"From the Rialto?"

"Sì."

"Who said you could?"

Simona looked at me as if I were an idiot. "My father."

"Your father?"

"Silvano," Simona said. "The Master Shipwright."

"I didn't know that," I exclaimed. "Silvano's your father?"

Simona smiled. A dawdling smile. "What are you doing?" she asked me.

"Oiling Bonamy's saddle. These flaps should be supple and soft."

"Supple and soft," Simona murmured. "I like these words."

"And they're sodden and sour," I said.

Simona sat down beside me.

"Sir Arthur!" she said.

"Yes?"

"I call you Arthur?"

"Yes, of course."

"Do you love?"

"What do you mean?"

"A girl."

I'm not sure why, maybe it was the way she asked, maybe because I haven't talked about them for so long, except to myself, but I began to tell Simona about Grace and Gatty and then about Winnie and our betrothal.

"Her father's a Marcher knight," I said.

"Marcher?"

"From the borderland," I said. "Between England and Wales."

"What is she like?"

"Herself!" I exclaimed. "Her hair's red-gold. Burning. And her eyes are tawny. She's very bold and always laughing, and she has a hot temper. On our betrothal day she was wearing a white silk dress and opal ear-jewels, and they flashed and swung on their stalks each time she moved."

"My dress was green," Simona said.

"My father only agreed to our betrothal," I told Simona, "because I was leaving on this crusade, and he warned me that he and Winnie's father haven't settled all the terms yet. I remember exactly what he said: 'Young women are ten a penny. There are plenty more Little Miss Winifreds, believe you me.'"

"No!" exclaimed Simona. "You love Winnie; she loves you."

"That's right," I said.

"Did you swear?"

"Both our families joined hands around us," I said. "Everyone! Simona, what's wrong?"

"We couldn't do that," she said, "not when I was betrothed."

"To an Englishman."

"Yes, and his family was all in England." Simona shook her head. "But my family is big. Six brothers. Many, many cousins and nephews and nieces. They all joined hands around us."

"You exchanged gold rings," I said.

Simona held up her left hand.

"Yours is like a gold knot," I said. "Look at mine!"

"Bello!" said Simona.

"Winnie complained hers was too tight," I said, "and her mother told her young women always say that, and she'd get used to it."

Simona reached over and touched the cord around my neck.

"My half of our pledge-penny," I said. "I pledged to protect Winnie according to God's law, and pay for the rearing of our children, and share my property with her. Then I broke the coin and gave her one half."

"Same," said Simona.

"And Sian made everyone laugh," I said. "My foster sister. She's eleven, and she called out, 'I love you, Arthur. I wish I could marry you!'"

Then I remembered Tom saying that if I didn't come home from the crusade, he'd gladly marry Winnie for me, and Serle saying in that case he stood a very good chance; but I didn't tell Simona that.

"I knew," she said. "Women know."

"What?"

"You, and love. Love and a cough cannot be hidden! I think you love to be in love."

"And you love to talk about it," I replied.

Simona closed her eyes, and took a deep breath. "He was called Aylmer," she said. "Aylmer de Burnham."

"Tell me about him."

Simona looked up. "Here's Lord Stephen."

I jumped up and gave Simona my hand.

"Simona!" said Lord Stephen, smiling, and he gave her a small bow.

"You both," said Simona, "I've brought you a sailing gift!" She slipped her fingers into the bag tied to her belt.

"A gift!" said Lord Stephen, smiling sardonically. "From a Venetian?"

Simona frowned at him, then gave him a playful push. She pulled out of the bag two small flasks.

"What are they?" I asked.

Simona drew out one of the stoppers. "Hair soap," she said.

I sniffed it. Cool and clean and sharp.

"Lemon with curds," Simona told us. "Wash your hair with it. It will dissolve the salt. All the stickiness."

I stooped and picked a pretty violet periwinkle. "Here's a present for you too," I said.

Simona smiled. She fixed the flower in her hair.

Embarkation

OU REALLY WANT TO KNOW?" ASKED GIFF, AND HE leered at me. He was sitting on the mangonel, facing the cup, which is as large as a rainwater barrel.

"Stones?" I asked.

"And stuff," said Godard.

"Like what?"

Giff fingered the rope. "We chuck whatever there is."

"Once, we chucked a corpse," Godard said. "One of their own men. He'd fallen off the wall, so we threw him back up again."

"I did fifty loads of dung," said Giff, and both of them laughed coarsely. "I buried them in it. You can't wait, can you, Arthur?"

"Sir Arthur!" Godard corrected him, and they both laughed again.

Giff and Godard and Milon's men have loaded all kinds of Venetian siege engines onto the transport ship: mangonels, tormenta, ballistae.

"And these are just the little creatures," Giff said. "The manglers and crushers. Once we get there, we'll make the scaling ladders and the towers and cats."

"What are they?" I asked.

"You'll see," said Godard, and then he chuckled at Giff. "You remember when we hurled back that head?"

All day the quay was packed with knights and squires, priests, armorers, stablemen, foot soldiers, servants, carpenters, sawyers, caulkers, sailmakers, ropemakers, oarsmen, and despite the cardinal's orders, dozens of women, all loading our transport ships with open crates of salted mackerel and cod, smoked mullet and tuna, creels of herring, pails of mussels and whelks, oysters and cockles, limpets and barnacles, leaking prawns, knots of eels, flitches of ham, legs and sides and haunches of beef and mutton, dozens of rabbits and hares hanging on hooks, baskets full of unplucked chickens, white loaves, black loaves, trencher loaves, tubs of oats and barley, barrels of groats, eggs, small bins of grey salt, rounds of cheese, olive oil and walnut oil, jars of ginger and cinnamon and saffron and cloves, mace and galingale and grain of paradise, strings of shallots and garlic and onions, leeks, horseradish, spinach and parsnips and cabbages, broad beans, red carrots, mushrooms, and fruit of all kinds — peaches, apples, pears, plums, medlars and cherries, dried raisins, dates and sweet figs from Egypt, pots of honey, reed baskets of pistachios, pine nuts and almonds and hazelnuts, kegs of ale, casks of verjuice and red Venetian wine, pouring pitchers, pepper mills, ewers and linen napkins, clay ovens, pewter mugs and leather tankards, sacks of charcoal, tinderboxes, tripods, hooks, iron cauldrons, long-handled pans, stirring sticks and flesh hooks, clattering platters, pottage bowls, porringers, bundles of skewers, trays, serving dishes, shaggy towels, chopping boards and knives, ladles and wooden spoons, leather bottles, ashwood pails, costrels and flasks, mousetraps, swords in their scabbards, circular shields and shields shaped like hearts and hunchback moons, lances, war hammers, axes and daggers, longbows and crossbows, quivers of arrows, bracers, caltrops, staves, helmets, chausses and cuisses and coats of mail, aketons and fustian breeches, whetstones, spades and shovels, sledgehammers, chisels and claws, saws and pickaxes, augers, props, sheets of tin, iron-tipped rams, ladders, coils of stout rope, set-squares and planes, mallets, breast-drills, scalpels and saws and pincers, leech-jars and rolls of bandaging, pots of oil-and-ash soap, Milon's wooden bathtub, large basins, cutthroats and polished steel mirrors, combs, bags of wormwood and lemon balm and marjoram, crocks of ointments, sacks and saddlebags stuffed with all kinds of clothing, tunics and doublets, hoses and belts, surcoats, caps, needles and waxed thread, a fool's cap and bells, boots and rolls of hide, lasts, pissing pots, Bible boxes, psalters, ampullae full of holy water, reliquaries, crosses and altar cloths, patens, pyxes, incense burners, candles and vats of wax, prayer beads and holy oil, pairs of cymbals, handbells, lutes and citoles and nakers and tabors, rebecs and lutes, bagpipes and crumhorns and shawms, winding sheets and sacks, a hideous mask on a stick, parchment and quills and inkhorns and oak-galls and pumice-bread, a sundial with the four winds puffing their cheeks, rolls of canvas, barrels of tar, backgammon and checkers and chess boards, little boxes of dice, squares of leather, sheepskins, mattresses, woollen blankets, marten and squirrel and rabbitskin bed-covers, bolsters, pillows, as well as all the siege engines . . . and one or two things I can't remember.

Yelling and whistling and milling and elbowing, shouldering and cursing, foul-mouthing and bawling, staggering, tripping: As I looked down from the deck of our transport ship, it was like looking down at an anthill. The crusaders were just as busy as ants, and like ants, they got in each other's way.

I was waiting on the quay with Bonamy this afternoon when Shortneck suddenly neighed and bucked while Turold was leading him along the plank to the door in the side of our horse carrier. Maybe another devil-hornet!

They both plunged off the plank into the water between the ship and the quay.

Shortneck swam to the end of the quay and scrambled ashore, and I picked up a grappling pole and lowered it for Turold.

The first time I did so, I clopped him on the head by mistake, and he opened his mouth to yell at me and swallowed a gallon of water. But then, choking, he grabbed the end of the pole and I pulled him along to the landing stage.

Poor Bonamy! When he saw what had happened to Shortneck, he wasn't at all eager. I tried to walk him to the bottom of the plank, but he dug in his front hooves and lowered his head.

"Ride him roundabout, sir," Rhys told me. "He'll calm down."

At least the door in the side of our ship is level with the stalls. In some of the transports, the horses lose their footing on the steep ramps inside the ship, and slither and slide down them.

Bonamy's stall is only a little wider than he is. There are leather straps hanging from a beam, and the stablemen belted two pairs of them under Bonamy so that he's half-suspended and his hooves barely touch the deck. In stormy weather, when the ship begins to roll, he should swing with her, and be safe. But all the same, he's not very happy.

Tomorrow we sail for Pirano and then Zara. So these are the last words I will write on Saint Nicholas, on the hundredth day since Lord Stephen and I left Holt.

the vermilion galley

AS THERE EVER BEEN SUCH A SIGHT IN THIS WORLD?

The Doge's oarsmen rowed his vermilion galley from the Rialto, and a huge crowd gathered on the quay. We raised our arms and cheered as they anchored.

The prow of the Doge's galley is made of iron and shaped like a dragon's head with a gaping mouth, and the banner of Saint Mark tugs and cracks above it, and the bulwarks are plated with colorful shields painted with all seven tinctures.

The moment I saw them, I thought of the huge press of knights when Arthur pulled the sword from the stone . . . the shields on their surcoats, stitched with such a gamut of colors and devices.

The entire galley is painted vermilion — the ribs, the sterncastle, the landing skiffs and the oarsmen's benches, even the oars, everything except the rudder and the mast and tackle.

Next to the mainmast there was a vermilion awning, made of samite, and under it I could see the Doge. He was wearing his white cotton cap stitched with the scarlet cross, and standing quite motionless, both arms outstretched. Like a victor. Like the crucified Christ.

There were priests in the middle story of the sterncastle, ten of them, maybe more, and they began to chant:

"Come, Holy Ghost, Creator come,
From Thy bright heavenly throne!
Come, take possession of our souls,
And make them all Thine Own!"

How can Marquis Boniface turn away from all this? After all these preparations, and all this time.

He has decided he must go to Rome, but even if the Holy Father does object to our sailing to Zara, what can he do? He can't stop us now. Anyhow, we need the marquis with us. He's our leader.

A hundred trumpeters stood up along the bulwarks. They raised their silver instruments and, behind them, dozens of musicians beat their tabors and drums.

We yelled, we roared, we howled!

Someone grabbed my right arm and started pulling me backwards. It was Bertie.

"Quick!" he panted. "Come on! I've been looking for you everywhere."

"Why? What is it?"

"Quick!"

We barged and plunged our way through the cheering crowd, until we reached our galley.

"You've held everyone up," Bertie gasped. "Milon says you're to come aboard at once, or he'll sail without you."

heaven's messengers

41

WITHOUT BREAKING MY STEP, I STOOPED AND picked a periwinkle growing amongst a scruff of weeds, and then I ran up the ramp.

"Are you mad?" Sir William shouted. "Throw that bloody flower overboard! Do you want to drown us all?"

"What do you mean?" I panted.

"Periwinkle!" Sir William snapped. "*Violette des sorciers.* The flower of death."

"Death!" I yelped.

I stared at the blue star and twirled the stalk between my left thumb and forefinger. Then I sent it spinning over the gunwale.

As the Venetian oarsmen rowed us out from the quay, the priests began to ring bells. And from all the galleys around us, bells answered. What a clangor! Contrary and spirited, quicksilver, gruff, they held their own water court: heaven's messengers, riding with us, washing over the little marshy islets, appealing to the four dark corners of the world.

But the seawater slapping our prow was sharp. Tart. Abrupt. Short sounds without memories.

Then the sailors hoisted the lateen sail. Canvas snapped, rigging whipped, the mast screeched. We turned to face the open sea.

For a moment, I thought of Oliver and one of the old poems he recited to me:

> Then those warriors stowed gleaming war-gear
> deep within the galley; they launched
> the well-built boat and began their journey.
> Foaming at the prow and most like a seabird,
> The boat sped over the waves, urged on by the wind . . .

A maelstrom of gulls whirled above us, silver-white and screaming. I stood on the prow and hurrahed to high heaven.

DISASTER

THIS IS WHAT HAPPENED.

As soon as we sailed out to sea, leaving Saint Nicholas over our right shoulders, the wind picked up. At once our oarsmen began to mutter and curse.

"Bora!"

"God against us."

"God's teeth!"

"Worse wind, sir," one of the sailors told me, and he compressed his leathery face. "Bora is bad worse wind."

Ahead and aft and all around us, our great fleet began to dance. Gaping galleys strained their graceful necks and reared up; the horse carrier nearest to us jerked and lifted and dipped through the water, foaming at the prow, and I thought of poor Bonamy and all the other horses tethered and swinging in their stalls; and the giant transport ships, the ones seventy paces long that hold a thousand men, *Violetta* and *Eagle, Pilgrim* and *Paradise* — the waves parted for them, frothing and gnashing.

Then the bora really opened its mouth, and the sailors scaled the mast ladders and pulled down the sails. Lord Stephen and my father and Milon took refuge in the sterncastle with the captain, and almost everyone else except the sailors and oarsmen went below deck because the saltspray kept flying into our faces, but Bertie and I sheltered behind a landing skiff.

That was when I saw it. The *Violetta,* the biggest ship of all, the one Silvano named after his wife, was in terrible trouble.

She was listing, and scarcely moving. Hundreds of men packed the deck, white hands waving. They must have been shouting for help but, because of the noise of the wind and waves, they could have been dumb men.

Bertie and I waved and yelled, and our oarsmen began to swing our galley round, but she was so heavy, and the fierce wind kept barging her back.

The *Violetta* was sinking. It seemed to happen so slowly, it happened so fast. Water began to break over the leeward gunwale, and it must have gushed down through the hatchways, and the huge ship settled, darker and deeper, and all her pale sails panicked.

Then she went down, not prow first, not upended, but as a stone sinks. The body of the boat sank; there was nothing of her left but the tops of her masts and sails and the upper stories of her two castles, fore and aft. Then they too went down. Down into the dark water. They slid out of sight.

Bertie clutched my wrist, and I kept swallowing and my mouth was so dry. Our sailors and oarsmen went silent. Without a word they pulled us towards the *Violetta.* Our rowlocks and oar-holes groaned.

Hundreds of men were floating facedown in the water, and many hundreds more must have died below deck. Just a few wretches were clinging to the sides of waterlogged skiffs, oak planks, oarsmen's benches.

Our oarsmen were very skillful. We drifted up alongside one of the skiffs, then held firm, and the sailors threw out four lines, and the survivors grabbed them. Then we lowered a rope ladder, and one by one, they heaved themselves up and flopped aboard.

At least, the first three did. The last of them had only the strength to climb halfway up.

"Come on!" shouted Bertie.

"Now or not!" the oarsmen yelled. "Not?"

"Wait!" I called out. I can't swim but I climbed up onto the gunwale and then . . . then I just stepped off.

The water was freezing, but when I surfaced, choking, I was very close to the rope ladder. I clawed the water and grabbed the ladder, and began to climb, pushing my head hard into the buttocks of the man halfway up.

"Come on!" urged Bertie. "You're doing it! Come on!"

He reached right out and down, grabbed one hand, grabbed both, and hauled the wretch up.

I dragged myself up the last few steps and collapsed over the gunwale right on top of him.

Such small hands. Sandy-pink.

"Simona!" I cried. "Simona!" I put my arms right round her.

Simona was like a sodden sack. Unable to support herself.

"Help me carry her," I said.

"Who is it?" Bertie asked. "How do you know her?"

Bertie and I lifted Simona away from the gunwale and laid her out on the deck. She looked up at us with her dark Venetian eyes, and her teeth began to chatter.

"Who is she?" Bertie asked me again. "What's her name?"

"Simona. The Master Shipwright's daughter."

Simona began to cough. Then she turned on one side, and spewed up. I knelt beside her and gently held her head.

Behind me, I could hear several of the oarsmen muttering.

"Woman."

"Witch!"

"Bad worse."

"Ship-woman no."

Simona gazed up at me.

"I'll look after you," I said.

"I will too," said Bertie forcefully.

"I didn't even know you were coming," I said. "You're alive! At least you're alive!"

Simona sighed feebly. "My father," she said, and her voice was quite expressionless. "Where is my father?" Then she sighed again, and closed her eyes.

Silvano! He must have drowned.

It wasn't because of the periwinkle, was it? The one I gave Simona? *Violette des sorciers.*

Bleeding by Night and Day

"WHY SHOULD YOU THINK YOU'RE ANY BETTER than the others?" Nascien asks.

"I don't."

"Why should you succeed when they have failed?"

"I've fought in Christ's name against howling heathens," Sir Lancelot says. "I've escaped from a city under siege and blazing; I've fought demons in a graveyard. I am resolved to achieve the Holy Grail."

"Do you repent of all your sins?" the hermit asks.

Sir Lancelot bows his head. "All of them," he says.

"All of them?"

"Except one," says Sir Lancelot.

"Which one?" asks Nascien.

"How can such sweetness be a sin?"

"All sins taste sweet," the hermit replies, "but their rewards taste as bitter as gall."

"My sin is love," Sir Lancelot says. "I love a woman, and she is a queen. She's married to a king."

"Foul lust!" says the hermit.

"No!" Lancelot quietly replies. "Our love is pure. I love her more than my own life, and whatever I do, I do in her name."

"You deceive yourself, Lancelot," the hermit replies. "You are Judas! You betray Jesus — you crucify Him."

"I've never told anyone," says Sir Lancelot. "I've never boasted of it, never betrayed it. I've never been disloyal to my king."

"Repent here and now!" Nascien orders him. "Lust is a deadly sin."

"How can I?" Sir Lancelot protests. "Whatever good I've done is because of our love."

"You're deaf," the hermit says. "Your ears are thick with wax. You're so blind, you wouldn't be able to see the Holy Grail if it appeared in this cave. But Lancelot! It's not too late. Once you were the greatest of all knights. You had no rival. You knew what was right, and you did what was right."

Sir Lancelot listens to the ring dove singing at the entrance to the cave. His whole life filters past him.

"Satan himself was racked with pain because he saw the Holy Ghost burning in you," the hermit says. "He longed to ruin you, and he knew his best chance was with a woman."

Sir Lancelot shakes his head.

"He entered into Queen Guinevere," continues the hermit, "and looked out at you through her eyes. The queen has blinded you to your deadly sin. You're lost to Our Lord."

Sir Lancelot sits in the cave, his arms wrapped round his knees, turning the hermit's words over and over.

"I've never been untrue to Guinevere," he says at last, "and she's never been untrue to me. Our love is honorable. I can never repent of it."

The hermit purses his lips. "But you will forgo it."

Sir Lancelot closes his eyes. When he opens them again, they're full of tears. "I will forgo it," he says heavily.

"Unless your thoughts and feelings and actions match your words," the hermit warns him, "you will never succeed."

Now Sir Lancelot leaves the cave, and canters up to the gates of the great marble castle, Corbenic. He is welcomed, as Sir Gawain was, and the same two knights lead him into the castle cloister.

I can see the Guardian of the Grail again. Sir Lancelot walks across the dead grass to the foot of his bed.

"Lancelot," the king whispers, "you have come to Corbenic, and I cannot even raise myself to greet you."

"Sire," says Sir Lancelot, "that's why I have come. I will not fail you."

A young woman enters the cloister. She's wearing a wimple. She comes over to King Pellam and begins to dress his wounds, shaking and sobbing.

And now she starts to sing . . . her long eyelashes are trembling.

"Lulli, lullay, lulli, lullay.
The falcon has carried my love away.

He carries him up, he carries him down,
He carries him into an orchard brown.

In that orchard, there is a bed,
Hung with gold shining red,

And in that bed there lies a knight,
His wounds bleeding day and night.

Beside that bed a young woman stays,
And she sobs by night and day.

And beside that bed there stands a stone,
CORPUS CHRISTI carved thereon."

It's true! There are words now on the block of stone at the foot of the king's bed, and there weren't when I saw it before. *Corpus Christi.* The body of Christ. Does that mean we fail Christ Himself in failing King Pellam?

The words of the lullaby are simple, but they're not easy to understand. Why does the falcon carry off the man the young woman loves? I think the young woman beside the bed is the one who rode into Camelot on a mule, and asked King Arthur whether there was no knight at the Round Table who could achieve the Holy Grail. And maybe the knight in the song is the Guardian of the Grail.

Now the two knights return to the cloister and lead Sir Lancelot to the gloomy hall where twelve white-haired knights are waiting. He sits, he eats with them, he talks to them.

A door opens. Two young women glide in, and the room fills with light. One woman is carrying the Holy Grail, covered with thick white silk, and a dazzling sunbeam rises from it.

But Sir Lancelot cannot even see it. He has come to Corbenic but he cannot ask the question. I can tell by his face, by my own heart, he's thinking about Queen Guinevere.

He's longing to see her again, longing to hold her to him. Cool and clean. How can he possibly forgo this?

After supper, the old knights proceed from the hall and Sir Lancelot is so utterly worn out, he cannot stay awake. . . . He lies on a couch and sleeps.

Now a horn blast echoes through Corbenic. A voice without a body booms through the hall: "The man who does not belong here: Let him be gone."

In my stone sound fades and shapes fade. Colors fade. Sir Lancelot fails.

SO MANY TONGUES

44

SIR LANCELOT IS A KNIGHT OF THE HEART AS WELL as the body. He is the knight of knights. King Arthur says he's won the greatest name of any knight in the world.

But if even Sir Lancelot cannot achieve his quest, how can we? How will we ever reach Jerusalem? Already we are foundering. We have lost almost one thousand men.

We speak with so many tongues, not only the tongues of English and Normans and Picardians and Angevins and Germans and Italians and everyone else, but the tongues of highborn and lowborn, of faith and zeal and ambition and self-interest and ruthless greed.

Mother Church herself speaks with many tongues, and some of them forked.

Why do churchmen preach love but despise women? Why do they turn a blind eye to injustice and suffering? Their thoughts and feelings and actions don't match their words.

Two Balls

ONE OF THE MEN WE RESCUED IS ONLY TWENTY. HE'S called Odd, which is a very odd name for a Venetian. He says it's because his grandfather was a Norwegian.

Odd told me that after the Doge had taken the Cross he announced that he wanted half the able-bodied men living on the Rialto to join him.

Some men were glad, but a great many more were not. They'd spent the last five hundred days boat-building, and hadn't been properly paid, and needed to attend to their own trades.

So the Doge and his councillors decided every man in Venice should draw lots.

First, candlemakers made pairs of wax balls, and inside one ball in each pair they put a little slip of paper. They gave these balls to all the priests, and the priests blessed the balls. Then they summoned their parishioners and put the balls into the hands of all the able-bodied men, two by two. Each man who found a slip of paper inside his wax ball had to take the Cross.

"Were you chosen?" I asked Odd.

"Yes," Odd replied. "Chosen to half-starve and half-drown. Chosen to leave my sweetheart wife. Me and her, we only married last year, and Venice is packed with wolves."

Lacrimae Rerum

46

For a long time last night I lay on deck, under the mainmast, swaddled in skins.

I stared at the glittering stars, so beautiful, so merciless, and thought how night swallows almost everything.

Then I thought of my hopes and sorrows and how I used to write them down. . . .

I want to please God. I want to be a knight of the heart, and I'm eager to enter Jerusalem, but sometimes I have night terrors. I want a magic fish to toss back my gold ring; I long to meet my poor mother. For Gatty I want all she's worthy of, and more. I want Bertie to live for years and years, and Simona's father to spit the ocean out of his blue mouth and come back to her. I want my father to praise me. I want him to die. I want Lord Stephen to know I know how well he has fathered me. I want to marry Winnie. And couldn't Serle marry Tanwen? My namesake, Arthur-in-the-stone, has enemies inside Camelot. His fellowship has gone with the four winds, and I'm fearful for him. . . . My heart would sing if I could see Merlin again. . . .

Tears were streaming down my cheeks, hot and icy cold, and she was on her knees, bending over me, and for a moment I thought she was my mother.

"Arthur!" she whispered.

"It's nothing," I said, rubbing my eyes.

"Everything."

"This cold! It makes my eyes weep and my nose run."

Simona looked down at me. *"Sunt lacrimae rerum,"* she said gravely.

"What's that?"

"The tears of things," said Simona. "All human sorrow, all our longings. That's what you were weeping for."

Then Simona flopped down beside me. She wriggled under my sheepskin. We slept like that.

more dead than alive

O YOU KNOW ABOUT SAINT PLACID?" LORD STEPHEN asked.

Turold shook his head and grunted.

"What about Maurus?"

"No, sir."

"Novices. Both of them. When he was seven, Placid almost drowned in a lake, but Maurus walked on the water without realizing it, and saved him."

Turold crossed himself.

"For martyrdom," Lord Stephen added grimly. "Sicilian pirates cooked him in a pot."

"They think the English all have tails," I told Turold.

Lord Stephen and Turold and I watched as our oarsmen eased us into the port of Pirano, just southwest of the city of Trieste. I'm going to be able to disembark Bonamy tomorrow and exercise him here.

"Saint Placid and Saint Maurus share the same day — the fifth of October — the day the *Violetta* sank," Lord Stephen said. "Our saints are so untrustworthy. Sometimes they hear our cries and help us, sometimes their ears are stopped with wax."

"Like Sir Lancelot," I said.

"Who?" Lord Stephen asked.

"This whole ship's sopping," Turold observed. "It's as well your armor is well wrapped."

"As well for you," Lord Stephen said tersely.

Lord Stephen isn't often tetchy or downcast, and I could tell he must be worried. I don't think it's anything to do with me. Maybe it's Simona, alone now and far from home. Or maybe he started thinking of Holt and Lady Judith, and Welsh raiders. But he doesn't usually worry over things he can do nothing about.

There's a long deepwater jetty at Pirano, so we didn't have to use the skiffs. When I stepped ashore, it took me some time to find my land legs. I tottered around like a two-year-old, and felt light-headed.

My father couldn't stay on his feet at all. He just plumped down on the quay in everyone's way. He protested he had bone disease, but for all that he looked cherub-cheeked and kept crowing and telling everyone today is his sixty-eighth birthday. Now the crusade is actually underway, he has somehow come into his true kingdom. He's all impulse and appetite and argument and action.

Many crusaders whooped as they came ashore. I could hear some of the Norman foot soldiers shouting, "Glory to God! There is no God but God. Lord of the Universe!"

That sounded strange because those are the same words the Saracen traders used.

Bertie and I followed three of them as they lurched up the street. At the far end, it widened and there were a number of stalls. One was decorated with patterned rugs and burned orange hangings. It was a Saracen stall.

The Normans swore and made coarse jokes, then they rushed at it and started kicking at the supports.

The stall collapsed and when two grey-haired men struggled out from under the hangings, the foot soldiers leaped forward. They punched the Saracens' noses.

"No!" I yelled. "Don't! They're traders!"

The Normans took no notice at all. They kicked them in the testicles.

"Don't!" I cried. "Leave them alone!"

One man rounded on me. "What's wrong with you?" he snarled. "You want a kicking too?"

"You can't say that," Bertie protested. "He's a knight!"

After this the three Normans cursed and spat on the groveling traders, and then they lurched on up the street.

I bent down and took one of the traders' arms. He was gasping and blowing bubbles of blood. But then some of the other traders left their stalls and began to shout angrily at Bertie and me. One woman came right up to me and screamed. She pushed me.

"They don't understand," I said.

"And you can't explain," Bertie replied. "Come on!"

He grabbed my arm and pulled me away, and we slowly walked back down the street.

Is this how things are going to be? Dishonorable and lawless and vile? We've come to fight the Saracens, army against army, not to attack traders who can't defend themselves. They were just old men.

On the quay, men were talking about the *Violetta,* and who was to blame. One knight from Champagne said it was the caulkers, and too little goat hair had been mixed with the pitch; and another man thought there wasn't enough ballast, and the huge siege engines made the boat top-heavy; a third man said she was holed on a reef, and another told us there's a huge Adriatic sea-beast and this isn't the first time it has seized a ship in its jaws.

"It's because a girl was aboard," Serle told us. "That's what all our oarsmen think."

"Well, Arthur," said my father, "at least you threw away that blasted flower. Otherwise, we'd be at the bottom too."

Some crusaders, the French especially, think we took a great risk in rescuing people from the water. They say that when the sea's hungry she's hungry, and if you rescue someone, she'll drown you instead. You or someone else. The sea's entitled, and we're her lawful prey.

When we were on our own, I asked Lord Stephen whether he believed this.

Lord Stephen blinked. "It didn't seem to bother our oarsmen," he said. "And a good many other boats tried to pick up survivors. I don't know. I don't think I could leave people to drown, if that's what you're asking."

"Neither could I," I said.

"So if there is a risk, it's a risk worth running."

"Yes, sir."

After this, Lord Stephen told me about the Seven Whistlers.

"Except there are six," he said. "They're lapwings. Six spirits of drowned men whistling and searching for the seventh. And long may they search!"

"Why, sir?"

Lord Stephen laced his fingers over his stomach. "Because when they find him, this world of ours will end."

Our horse carrier didn't dock until it was almost dark, so I won't be able to see Bonamy until tomorrow. I did want to write about a very unpleasant rumor I heard, but I'm running out of ink, and it's too late to mix more. Anyhow, everyone else aboard is already asleep, and I keep yawning.

the poisoned apple 48

THE RUMOR IS UNTRUE. AT LEAST IT DOESN'T MEAN what I thought it did.

Last night, some of the Venetians were saying our fleet was going to turn back, and I thought that meant right back to Venice because I know many of the Doge's sailors are grumbling and asking exactly what will happen if the Christians in Zara refuse to renew their pledge of loyalty to the Republic of Venice.

As it is, though, we're only going back to Trieste, about twelve or thirteen miles northeast from here. This is so their councillors can swear new oaths, and I expect there'll be a ceremony with priests and candles and trumpets and handbells, just as there was this afternoon when the Doge finally disembarked and walked along a strip of vermilion carpet on the quay, and the councillors of the city knelt on cushions and affirmed Pirano's loyalty to Venice.

The Doge required the councillors to provide one hundred sailors and the same number of oarsmen. That amounts to two more men on each vessel.

When Serle and I went aboard our horse carrier early this morning, Rhys met us, smiling. There was a great deal of whinnying and stamping and snorting, and it can't do any horse much good to be cooped up for so long, but neither Bonamy nor Shortneck had come to any harm.

Rhys backed them out of their stalls and led them down the plank; then he saddled them, and Serle and I exercised them until the sun was well up and we were very hungry.

They worked up a sweat more quickly than usual, like people when they have winter colds, and once they pulled us over towards standing water and slurped for so long, I thought they'd burst.

"Your boots are splitting," Serle said.

"I know. I must get them mended."

While Bonamy and Shortneck drank, Serle began to chant and I asked him what the words were.

"Part of an old poem:

> Then those brave warriors spurred their warhorses,
> their chestnut mounts renowned for speed and stamina.
> They raced each other where the track was even . . ."

Serle looked at me, and his eyes shone. He spurred Shortneck and I spurred Bonamy. First we galloped side by side, and then he pulled ahead.

"You won!" I gasped.

Or else we both won. Serle is often supercilious, but this morning he was companionable, and treated me as an equal, and once he even praised me.

"I like how you stand up for Simona," he said.

Sir William, spirited; Lord Stephen, tetchy; and now Serle, friendly: This crusade seems to be changing everyone. I wonder how it is changing me.

It isn't easy to find anywhere on board where I can be on my own but late this afternoon, as everything turned blue, I climbed down from the poop deck into the small skiff hanging over the water. For a while I stared out across the sea, so calm again now; I became calm myself, and then I unrolled my trusty, filthy, saffron cloth.

Sir Lancelot has come back to Camelot, and he and Queen Guinevere are alone. They're standing on a little drawbridge.

"You were so passionate," the queen says. "So wild. That's how you were. But now?"

"My lady," Sir Lancelot says, "I quested for the Holy Grail in your name and failed because of my love for you. Because in my heart I knew I would come back to you."

"And now?" the queen repeats.

"Now I fear for your reputation," Sir Lancelot replies. "People are talking."

"Who?" demands Guinevere.

"Sir Agravain. Sir Mordred."

"Vermin!" exclaims Guinevere.

"And many, many others," Sir Lancelot says. "I can come and go; you cannot. I can fight them; you cannot."

"Are you avoiding me?" asks the queen.

"I will not have your name dragged through mud," Sir Lancelot protests.

Guinevere narrows her chestnut eyes. "You don't love me, not as you did. That's the truth."

"It is not," Sir Lancelot says.

"How dare anyone slander us?" the queen demands. "And why are you listening to them? If that's how little you love me, I'd rather not see you at all. Half-love's worse than no love." Queen Guinevere starts to sob, and dabs her eyes with a little white kerchief.

"Lady," Sir Lancelot begins gently.

"Leave Camelot!" Guinevere commands him. "I don't want to see you."

In my stone places can change, and hours can pass, in no more than an eyeblink.

Now Queen Guinevere is sitting at a long table with the very knights who gossip about her and malign her, Sir Agravain, Sir Mordred, Sir Gawain and Sir Bors and twenty more. But not Sir Lancelot. "Welcome to this feast," she says. "No woman is as fortunate as I, with such knights for company."

Many of the knights look at one another. They know how bitterly the queen resents them; they suspect her intentions.

"Gawain," says Guinevere, "you always like to eat apples at each meal. Here!" She picks up a rosy apple and playfully throws it to Sir Gawain.

"And for you," the queen calls out, and she throws Sir Agravain a pear.

Sir Gawain and Sir Agravain grin; they toss their fruit to one another. Quickly all the other knights join in. Soon the hall is full of shouts and laughter, and the air is thick with flying apples, pears, oranges from Spain, cucumbers, greengages . . .

But all at once Sir Patrise clutches his stomach. His body is blowing up, like a bladder-ball. His face is purple.

He tries to stand up. He struggles, knocks over the whole bench, and falls backwards. Sir Patrise is dead. Dead as a boiled lobster. And in his right hand there's a half-eaten apple.

The knights stare down at the dead man. They glance at each other. They do not look at the queen.

"He was my cousin," Sir Mador says, "and I will avenge his death."

"Lady," says Sir Gawain, frowning, "your good name is in jeopardy."

Queen Guinevere just stands there, eyes lowered. She says not a word.

"Lady!" Sir Mador says loudly. "You have no love for any of us. I accuse you of poisoning that apple, and causing Sir Patrise's death."

When King Arthur hears Sir Mador's accusation, he tells him not to be so hasty.

"I do not believe it," he says. "Some knight will defend the queen. Some man will risk his own body rather than see hers burn. If I were not your king and judge, I would gladly do so myself."

"Not one knight who sat at that dinner is prepared to defend her," Sir Mador replies. "We know how she hates us."

"I give the queen fifteen days to find a knight to fight for her," King Arthur says. "If no one comes forward by then, she will burn. Be ready, Sir Mador, to fight on that day, here in the water-meadows."

Now all the queen's accusers leave, and she and the king stand alone.

"I am innocent," she says. "In the name of God, I swear I didn't poison that apple and I don't know who did."

"Where is Sir Lancelot?" asks King Arthur. "He'll fight for you."

"He has left court," Guinevere says in a low voice. "He did not say where he was going."

"What is wrong with Sir Lancelot?" King Arthur says. "No sooner has he returned to court than he's away again. Ask Sir Bors to defend you — for Sir Lancelot's sake."

Again, time and place change in my stone.

"I cannot, my lady," says Sir Bors. "I was at that dinner and if I fight for you it will look as if I'm in league with you. You've driven away the man who never fails you, the man I love most, and now you're shameless enough to ask me to help you."

Queen Guinevere gets down on both knees. "You are right and I am wrong," she says, "and I'll make amends. But unless you defend me, I'll be put to death. Is that what I deserve?"

Now King Arthur walks into the stone again. "Guinevere is wrongly accused," he says. "I am certain of it. Promise you'll fight for her."

"You could not ask anything more difficult," Sir Bors replies. "If I do that, my fellow knights will turn against me."

"Swear it!" the king says.

"In the name of God, then," says Sir Bors, "I swear to fight for Queen Guinevere unless a better knight comes forward."

Somewhere below me, there was a great flapping and yapping. A sailor must have thrown something overboard — a slimy bone, a piece of gristle — and hungry gulls were competing for it. It was almost dark. . . .

When I looked into my stone again, Sir Bors was standing at the mouth of a cave, talking to Sir Lancelot.

"They're saying she destroys knights," Sir Bors says.

"Destroys?" retorts Sir Lancelot. "She praises them. She gives them gifts. She never fails her king. What more do they want?"

"Her blood," Sir Bors replies.

"They're mean-minded," says Sir Lancelot, "and they're jealous. I will fight for the queen. You prepare, and ready yourself, and at the last moment, I will ride into the meadows."

Sir Bors does exactly as Sir Lancelot says. He rides to the water-meadows, and he and Sir Mador go to their tents and arm themselves. Sir Mador rides out, yelling, "Where are you, then? Knight of the false queen! Why are you keeping me waiting?"

Sir Bors delays as long as he can. But at last he slowly trots out of his tent.

At this very moment, a knight on a large white horse gallops into the water-meadows, bearing a red shield.

This knight rides straight up to Sir Bors, Sir Mador, and the king.

"This fight is mine," he tells Sir Bors.

"Who is he?" asks the king.

"That I cannot tell," Sir Bors replies, "but this knight will fight for your queen today."

"I've come here," the Red Knight declares, "because I cannot allow this noble queen to be shamed. You knights of the Round Table dishonor yourselves by dishonoring her."

"Enough talk!" Sir Mador says. "I'll shame you."

At once the Red Knight and Sir Mador ride to opposite ends of the list, couch their lances, and gallop towards one another. Neither swerves one inch.

As it strikes the Red Knight's shield, Sir Mador's spear splinters, and he is thrown backwards over his horse's rump.

At this, the Red Knight dismounts, and he and Sir Mador unsheathe their swords. They step forward, step back, feint, thrust, parry, whirl, swipe, and now the Red Knight cracks Sir Mador on the side of his helmet, and Sir Mador drops to his knees.

The Red Knight steps forward and reaches towards Sir Mador's helmet. But his opponent lunges with his sword, and gashes his right thigh.

The Red Knight smacks Sir Mador on the side of the head again, and Sir Mador begs for his life.

"On one condition," the Red Knight replies. "Withdraw your accusations and end your quarrel with the queen."

"I swear it," Sir Mador says.

The Red Knight helps Sir Mador to his feet, and the two men lumber over to Arthur and Guinevere.

"You are wounded," the queen says, taking the Red Knight's arm.

"Both of us," he replies. "Nothing that will not mend."

"I owe you lasting gratitude," the king says. "But whom am I thanking?"

The Red Knight pulls off his helmet.

It is Sir Lancelot.

"It is I who should thank you," Sir Lancelot tells the king. "You knighted me, and the queen belted on my sword. That's why I am her knight, and whoever quarrels with you quarrels with me as well."

The king sighs and smiles. "Sir Lancelot!" he says. "I will repay you."

Guinevere is weeping. Weeping without making a sound. She keeps looking at Sir Lancelot through her tears.

I know Queen Guinevere is innocent. She did not poison that apple. So who did?

Accusations

INCE HER FATHER DROWNED, SIMONA HAS BEEN LISTless and sad; she's nervous too because the sailors say a woman aboard means bad luck. When we reached Trieste, Lord Stephen suggested Serle and I should try to lift her spirits, so we took her with us when we exercised our horses.

We rode west towards Aquileia because Simona wanted to see the mosaics in the basilica there. They're almost one thousand years old and show all kinds of animals and birds. One of the priests in Trieste told us we'd get there well before the sun crowned the sky, but that wasn't true.

"He was only telling us what we wanted to hear," Serle said.

At midday we decided to turn back. The sun shone, steady and warm on our backs. Serle was quite friendly and for several miles he and Simona ambled along well behind me. Simona sat in front of Serle, and now and then I could hear them laughing. I was glad to be almost alone. Since Lord Stephen and I reached Venice on Saint John's Eve, I've been surrounded by other people, hundreds of them, thousands, for each hour of every day.

For a while we lay on the stony hillside set well back from the dunes. Simona and Serle both drowsed, but I listened to all the far sounds of the sea, and remembered telling Grace about the whispering spirits in the trees on Tumber Hill, and sitting with her for hours in my climbing-tree. . . .

I didn't see the old man coming down the hillside until he walked right up to us.

We all scrambled to our feet.

The old man glared, and his withered lips quivered. Then he began to shout. And he chanted something.

"What's he saying?" I asked.

Simona shrugged her shoulders. "Not Italian," she replied.

The old man pointed out at the ground and stamped. He stamped seven times.

"He's cursing us," I exclaimed.

"That's obvious," said Serle.

I spread my hands in front of the old man, and smiled, but he just spat on the ground.

"Come on!" said Serle. "Let's go."

"I wish I knew what he was saying," I said.

In silence the three of us walked Bonamy and Shortneck away. When we got back to our galley, though, several sailors blocked the gangway, and wouldn't allow Simona on board.

They began to shout at her, and then many more sailors and oarsmen crowded along the gunwale and looked down at us.

"Basta!" yelled Simona.

"What's wrong?" I asked her.

"They are liars!"

"Why?"

"I never slandered the *Violetta*'s captain. I never said he's the bad worse captain in the fleet."

"You didn't?"

"No!" said Simona loudly, and her breath was hot on my face.

"Well, was he?"

"I know nothing!" cried Simona. "I said nothing. I swear by God."

"I believe you, Simona," Serle said, and he moved a step closer to her.

"They say my father told me that," protested Simona. "Not! They're making it up. Liars!"

"I believe you as well," I said, "but I don't know what we're going to do about it."

Simona and Serle and I looked up at all the oarsmen lining the gunwale and jeering, and they looked down at us.

And then, of all things, Serle spoke up. I've known him for as long as I can remember, and he's the one who swims with the tide, and never stands up to be counted. Serle took Simona's hand and walked up the gangplank, and I followed them.

"Who speaks English here?" he demanded.

There was a good deal of jostling; then a sailor with a pitted face and eyes pale as olive stones was pushed to the top of the gangplank.

"You speak evil of the dead," Serle said in a loud, clear voice. "Silvano never found fault with the captain of the *Violetta,* and you know it." He pointed at the sailor. "Translate that!" he snapped.

Some men muttered and crossed themselves.

"You're using the father to attack the daughter," Serle continued. "Why? Because you're afraid of women? Why do you believe everything people say? Silvano was an honorable man, and you can see for yourselves that Simona's innocent. Her father loved her. He chose to bring her with him. And now she has lost him and she's far away from home; she needs your protection."

I listened openmouthed, and in my heart I cheered.

I can tell Serle really likes Simona, and that must be what made him so bold. But what about Simona? She likes Englishmen, and I could see she liked riding with Serle today. Shortneck did more than his fair share!

Serle is strong, but he looks so sour, and he's not at all courteous. He can never marry Tanwen, and he won't even see her again for the next two years, so maybe he and Simona can be good for each other.

"Simona, Silvano's daughter, is under my protection and she's coming aboard with us." That's what Serle proclaimed. "Lord Stephen will be very glad to protect her. So will Sir William de Gortanore."

"And me," I said indignantly.

Serle turned round. "And so will Arthur," he said. "Sir Arthur de Gortanore!"

"Yes!" I said loudly. "I will!"

"We're coming aboard," said Serle. "Make room! I'm going to speak to our captain."

A BAG OF WINDS

WHEN I LIVED AT CALDICOT, I LOVED ROARING days. I used to climb Tumber Hill and lean right into the wind. I thought I might be able to fly like Merlin.

But sea winds are more chancy. After we left Trieste I asked Piero, our steersman, whether the bora was likely to open its mouth again before we reached Zara, and he said, "You never know what blows out of Ulysses's bag!" He spread his arms. "Maybe solano. That makes you giddy, dust gets into your eyes and blocks your nostrils, and you can't steer straight. Or the harmattan . . ."

"What's that?"

"It flies out of Africa, carrying fog on its back, and it's so dry, it withers grass, and your skin peels off. Or the sirocco, maybe. That wears you out, then turns you mad. Like a bad wife!"

"There must be friendly winds as well," I said.

"The etesian," replied Piero. "Volturnus. Simoom."

"I like the sound of that."

"Sì," said Piero, "you need to know what wind if you want to sail before it."

I'm going to ask him whether I can visit his little latticed chamber and hold the tiller that steers our galley.

heels over head

To begin with, I was leaning over the gunwale with an old crusader.

"It will be like this all the way to the Kingdom of Jerusalem," he told me. "This light." He squinted and his eyes glimmered like Venetian sequins. "And the land. All the way. Arid!"

It grew dark, and we could see the bow lanterns of all the galleys in our fleet. Gently swinging, and yet seeming not to. Night-floaters. Adriatic fireflies!

Then our galley began to sink. And around us the entire crusader fleet began to go down, quietly. Down into the dark bowl of the sea. Our lanterns lit the underwater, and made it beautiful.

Lord Stephen and I and Bertie and everyone else swam in a tight shoal, and Milon led us. Wido and Giff and Godard kept darting in front of me, mouths gaping. Bertie was so happy. First he rolled over and over, then he dived away into the dark, and I knew I'd never see him again.

Many other shoals crossed our water-path and got in our way: Norman louts, and those German sausage-squires who half-drowned Bertie and me, a huddle of monkfish, the bloodthirsty Picardians who chopped each other's fingers off, and the angry knights Queen Guinevere entertained to dinner, the Flemings who looted the food-barge, the graveyard demons Sir Lancelot fought.

Rhys swam up beside me. "We should make our boats of horse hides," he said. "Sew them like coracles, see? You tell Simona that."

"I see," I said.

"You sew," replied Rhys. "You're clever, sir. You know what this is?

> "Some people carry their horses
> to the battleground on their backs.
> They leap on their steeds to catch
> their prey, then carry their horses
> home again on their shoulders."

A dusty wind began to blow through the water, and it snuffed out all our lanterns. We were in the dark.

Then shoals of fish began to rush at us and attack us. Their eyes were wicked — silver, bloodshot, periwinkle — and they arched their backs, and lashed us with the curved blades of their tails.

Their voices were shrill.

"Ours!"

"Not yours."

"We'll slit your throats."

"And sip your blood."

"And pick your bones."

"Ours!"

"Out!"

Fish of all kinds, with furious eyes, surrounded us and crowded us. They lashed us and spiked us, they grinned and stung us, they coiled round us, bit us.

I yelled. I flailed with my arms. That's when I woke up.

I lay under my skin and watched the breasting sails; I listened to each comfortable groan and creak and the rush and sluice of water.

Those angry fish, pike and swordfish, dogfish, octopus. Who were they? Were they Saracens?

If only Merlin were here. Or Johanna, the wisewoman, with her lobster whiskers. She'd be able to tell me everything my dream means. I wonder whether Simona can explain dreams.

OLD WOUNDS

O HENRI'S NOSE WAS LEFT DANGLING."

"Bloody Saracen!"

"He was! That's exactly what he was by the time I'd done with him."

"Still! I'd give my nose to win honor like Henri's."

"Honor! That's right. Let the bastards know they can always count on second helpings."

"You've heard about when he was lowered into the cavern?"

"Arthur!" said a voice in my ear.

"Sir!"

"I've been wondering where you were."

"Here, sir."

"So I see. And in a cavern."

I turned my back on the two knights from Champagne, and Lord Stephen and I walked across the forum to the other gunwale.

"Don't believe everything you hear," Lord Stephen said. The skin at the corners of his eyes crinkled. "Your face. Your poor troubled face. I know you."

"Yes, sir," I said, and all I wanted to do was bury my head on Lord Stephen's shoulder.

"Come on, now," Lord Stephen said. "Serle's been telling me how you and he faced down our sailors in Trieste, and insisted they let Simona come aboard. Is that right?"

"Yes, sir. Well, Serle did."

"Quite right!" said Lord Stephen crisply. "Poor girl! I'll be glad to protect her. Now you know I was gloomy a couple of days ago?"

"Yes, sir."

"Well, why now and not long ago I can't imagine, but your dear father suddenly accused me of working against him."

"Against him?"

"By trying to arrange a meeting with your mother."

The back of my neck tingled, and I shivered. "How did he know, sir?"

"There's only one way, isn't there? Do you remember when I warned Thomas that if he wasn't ready to help us, we'd make other arrangements? He must have run straight as a rat to his master."

"What did you tell Sir William, sir?"

"Nothing. I advised him not to be so unwise as to open old wounds. Listen, Arthur! I know you're trying to be dutiful to your father. That's proper, and I wish you godspeed, but don't lower your guard." Lord Stephen grasped the gunwale with both hands. "I do wish we could trust the man, but I'm sorry to say I fear Sir William. He's like a force of nature, one moment harmless, the next vengeful and very dangerous."

I thought immediately of Mordred.

Mordred. Mordant. Morbid. Mordor. Murdered. His name-companions are vile.

Mordred knows his father did not want him, just as I know my father did not want me.

Mordred and King Arthur: son and father. They too must feel so torn.

SIR URRY

FOR TWO DAYS AND TWO NIGHTS NOW WE'VE BEEN lurching and walloping south, and around us the waves have bristled. Short seas are what Piero calls them.

Most of us have been sick. I have a dozen times, and I can't even go down the hatchway without smelling vomit and feeling sick again, so I'm living on the deck, wearing two pairs of hose and two shirts, wrapped in my sheepskin.

I'm glad Winnie can't see me looking like this.

As if the smell below were not bad enough, Bertie had to pump the stinking water out of the bilge-well because he was discourteous to Milon yesterday. He was pretending to be a mad sheep, and to begin with, Milon was quite amused, but then he went too far and baahed in Milon's face and bit his right arm.

Bertie scowled at me. "Tell me other things that stink," he said.

"Shit."

"Worse than that."

"Rotten fish. So rotten they glow in the dark."

"What else?"

"I don't know. Vomit. Yes, vomit! And fear."

"Fear doesn't smell."

"It certainly does."

"What else?"

"Bad eggs. Sir William's breath. Stink-horn. A bitch in heat. Wild garlic."

"Farts," said Bertie.

"And goats," I said. "And a skin that hasn't been cured properly."

"And a corpse!" declared Bertie enthusiastically. "Add all those together and that's what bilge-water smells like."

When we sailed out of Venice, with all that chanting and cheering, I supposed we'd reach Zara in four or five days. I didn't realize that the Doge planned to disembark at Pirano and Trieste, and have all their city councillors swear new oaths. He likes to keep people waiting so they can see how powerful he is, and anyhow he's ancient, and never does anything quickly.

The day we left Saint Nicholas was the hundredth after we left Holt, and twenty-nine more days have passed since then. Last night Milon came up for air and sat with me. He told me it's too late in the year now to sail south from Zara. The winds and water are too unchristian; we'll have to winter there and sail in the spring.

For the Holy Land? Or Egypt? At this rate, we'll never get to Jerusalem at all.

I told Gatty once I would try to send her a message when I reached Jerusalem. How did I think I was going to do that?

Last night I unwrapped my seeing stone.

It looked like sea waves when they glow in the dark. Then I could see King Arthur standing beside his throne, speaking to his queen and ladies and knights.

"Sir Lancelot proved the queen was innocent when he defeated Sir Mador, and Nimue has confirmed it. She did not poison the apple. She did not cause the death of Sir Patrise."

The queen holds up her head.

"Nimue, Merlin's apprentice, most loyal to me, says she can tell by her magic the apples were poisoned by Sir Pinel le Savage. Sir Pinel. He wanted to kill you, Gawain, because you killed his cousin."

"I did," says Sir Gawain.

"But now Sir Pinel has fled," the king says.

While Arthur-in-the-stone is speaking, the far door swings open, and in walk two ladies, one the age of Lady Alice, the other twice as old, followed by two pages carrying a litter. A knight is lying on it.

"Come forward!" King Arthur calls out.

"I live close to Trieste," the older lady tells Arthur. "My name is Agatha. This is my daughter, Fyleloly."

Fyleloly curtsies to the king. She has black hair and high cheekbones, and her skin's sallow.

"And this is my son," says Lady Agatha. "Urry. Sir Urry of the Mount. He fought in a tournament and killed Sir Alphegus. But Sir Alphegus wounded him seven times. Three head wounds, three on his body, and one on his left hand."

"Lady," says Arthur-in-the-stone, "my people are courtiers, not surgeons or healers."

"Sire," the lady replies, "Alphegus's mother was a sorceress. She cast a spell on Urry. His wounds can never heal until the greatest knight in the world touches them. Fyleloly and I have traveled through every Christian country searching for him."

"Lucky the man with so loving a mother," King Arthur says.

"And sister," the lady adds.

"So loyal," says the king. "So persistent."

"For seven years we've searched," Lady Agatha continues.

"If any man can heal your son, it will be a knight of the Round Table," King Arthur says. "I wish only that they were all here, but forty of them are questing for the Holy Grail. I will try myself, not because I think I'll succeed, but if the king leads, others follow. Meet me in the castle meadow in the morning."

How easily my stone slips through time.

Sir Urry is kneeling on a gold cushion in the meadow, surrounded by all the kings and queens and dukes and duchesses and earls and countesses, all the knights and ladies and squires and pages at King Arthur's court.

Sir Urry doesn't look like the men I saw in Trieste and Pirano. He has no moustache, his hair is neatly cut, and he's as slight as a slender girl. His wounds are eating at him, and he's wasting away.

"May I lay my hands on your wounds?" asks the king.

"I am yours to command," Sir Urry whispers.

Gently the king lays his left hand over the ugly gash on Sir Urry's neck and cheek, and his right hand over Sir Urry's wrist.

At once both wounds open. They weep blood.

Seeing this, one man after another steps forward. King Uriens of Gore. Duke Galahaut. Earl Aristause. Sir Kay. Sir Melion of the Mountain and Sir Dodinas le Savage. The Knight of the Black Anvil, and the copper-colored knight and the spade-faced knight. Sir Grummor Grummorson. Sir Arrok, Sir Marrok, whose wife turned him into a werewolf for seven years, Sir Griflet, Sir Piflet, little Sir Gumret.

But they all fail. Brave men and bullies, loyal men, liars, they're no more able to cure Sir Urry's wounds than any knight could pull the sword out of the stone.

Sir Tor steps forward now. I like him. He's the son of a knight and a poor woman — the cowherd's wife. That's what I am too.

Sir Tor bends over, and carefully places both his big, flat hands on Sir Urry's back.

Sir Urry moans. Blood kicks out of his wound and drenches his linen shirt.

"Where's Sir Lancelot?" the king asks. "Why is he never here when we need him?"

"Look!" cries Queen Guinevere.

Sir Lancelot gallops into the meadow and dismounts.

"And how does he always know when he is needed?" asks the king.

"My heart," Fyleloly whispers to her brother, "my heart tells me this is the man."

"Do as we've all done," King Arthur instructs Sir Lancelot. "Lay your hands on Sir Urry's wounds."

"If you cannot heal him," Sir Lancelot replies, "I cannot."

"Try," says the king.

"I cannot disobey you," Sir Lancelot replies, "but I've no wish to try to do what other knights cannot."

"You misunderstand me," the king says. "The knights of the Round Table are equals. We are one fellowship."

If only that were true. When the Holy Grail floated into Camelot and circled the Round Table, and so many knights swore to quest for it, King Arthur knew his ring of honor was breached.

"On earth everything changes," that's what the king said then.

"But knowing you must die on your quests, many of you, is it wrong to grieve?"

Sir Urry looks up at Sir Lancelot. "Honor me, Sir Lancelot," he says.

Most of the knights get down onto their knees. Not all of them, though. Some are too old. Some are eaten by jealousy.

Sir Lancelot kneels beside Sir Urry. He raises his eyes. He mouths a prayer.

Now gently and firmly, he presses his fingers into Sir Urry's three head wounds, the three wounds on his body, the wound on his left wrist.

The open wounds close. Seven scars seal Sir Urry's torn flesh. The spell is broken.

Sir Urry gets to his feet and stretches. "I've never felt such joy," he exclaims. "I've never felt this strong."

"Strong enough to joust?" the king asks. "Strong enough to quest?"

"Tomorrow!" shouts Sir Urry. "And tomorrow!"

But Sir Lancelot? He sobs. Like a weeping wound.

Night-lights

IERO ALLOWED ME TO TAKE THE TILLER FOR THE FIRST night watch. "Aim for that cloud," he said.

"But clouds move."

"That's been sitting there all evening," Piero replied.

"How much longer?" I asked.

Piero pushed out his lower lip. "Ask the wind," he said. "Tonight and half a day?"

I whooped. "At last!" I shouted.

After a while, Piero pointed at something on the dark coast. "See that?" he said. "Follow my finger."

At once I leaned hard into the tiller.

Piero yelped and wrenched it back again. *"Sei pazzo?"* he barked. "With your eyes! Not with the tiller!"

I made out the contour of a little building with candles shining in its four windows.

"Church," said Piero. "Little castle church."

"Candles?" I said. "Why candles at this time of night?"

"Not," said Piero.

"There are!" I exclaimed. "Look!"

"I've seen it before," Piero replied. "Not candles."

"What do you mean?"

The steersman shrugged. *"Magia!"* he said.

The tiller throbbed under my right hand, and I stared into the dark. The church windows were flashing and flickering as if they were lit by hundreds of will-o'-the-wykes, or by specters.

"Leopard in there," said Piero.

"Where?"

"He jumps out of the window and kills crusaders. Three times." Piero pressed the tip of his right forefinger against his forehead. "Leopard fighting in Holy War," he said.

ZARA

OU HEAR HER NAME. YOU WONDER. YOU IMAGINE. You're so impatient. Afraid. You set sail towards her.

And then . . . there she is. Dream and body meet. For a little time there is no time.

That's how it was as we closed with Zara; as we dropped anchor, and rocked in the sparkling water.

I haven't seen much of this middle-earth yet, but I have looked up at the gap-toothed grey walls of London and the walls and towers of Ludlow Castle and Count Thibaud's castle in Champagne and the Doge's palace in Venice and they're nothing like as high or long or smooth-skinned as the Roman walls of Zara. You can only see the tops of the spires and bell towers behind them. Rubbing shoulders. Reaching for heaven.

We were all up on deck. Some men were kneeling and talking to God, many were leaning over the gunwales; some were silent, some were conversing in low voices and gesturing.

I overheard two men from Champagne.

"Impossible."

"All things are possible."

"Not with walls that thick."

"With God's help."

"They're as safe in there as hill-warriors."

Which warriors? Not the ones Nain told us about, guarding the Sleeping King?

I was about to ask them when Sir William strode towards me, singing loudly and badly out of tune:

"Water leaps from rock,
Manna snows on earth,
In the burning bush
The flame still flickers. . . .

"Sing, boy! Sing!" Sir William bawled.

"We'll root out the serpent,
Stone him out, smoke him out,
Starve him and dig him out
From behind his walls."

He grimaced, and I could see all his black teeth. "That's what we'll do, won't we?"

"But I thought . . . ," I began.

"You think too much," Sir William boomed. "You tie yourself in bloody knots."

"But Lord Stephen said we wouldn't have to attack," I said. "They're Christians. He said we'd talk and reach an agreement."

"And I said when they saw the size of our fleet they'd mess themselves. God's teeth, Arthur! They're in our way." Sir William sniffed loudly. "I know what I'd do," he said, and he strode off towards the stern, singing:

"We'll root out the serpent,
Stone him out, smoke him out,
Starve him and dig him out
From behind his walls."

At noon, the Doge came alongside in his vermilion galley. He dropped anchor and sent over a messenger to say we should await all the other boats, the transports and horse carriers.

"And then," said the Doge's messenger, "as the sun rises tomorrow, we will proceed."

"Thanks be to God! *Deo gratias!* Thanks be to God!"

I could hear myself shouting along with everyone else on board, but I don't know what will happen when we do proceed.

The sun's setting now, and the water is fretful, slopping and sobbing.

All the towers and spires are on fire. Zara! Her high walls are ashen already.

Tact and Tactics

56

OT LONG AFTER SUNRISE, THE *PARADISE* LED US ALL up the channel on the landward side of Zara. Our galley was one of three immediately following her. I could see the shadows of our masts gliding along the city walls.

The first I knew about the huge iron chain stretched across the channel was when the *Paradise* rammed into it, screeching and screaming. The chain sheared through the bow, and the iron bollards sunk into the stone moles on either bank were ripped out of their sockets. The two ends of the massive sea-plait sprang into the air before they fell back and lashed the water.

The oarsmen kept their heads, though, and brought the transport in to the first dock, only another two hundred paces up the channel.

Lord Stephen and I heard that two Venetian cooks hidden in a small chamber under the hold-planks were sawn in half, and they were naked as needles.

"God's own punishment," Lord Stephen said grimly.

The Doge ordered half the fleet to wait offshore, to discourage Zarans from escaping, but even so the harbor was packed with our galleys.

Everyone seemed in a hurry to go ashore after being aboard for three days and three nights, and the confusion on the quay was all the greater because so many people wanted to see the damage to the *Paradise* for themselves. But before we had time to disembark, a Venetian councillor came aboard. It was Gennaro, whom we met at the sea-feast, and he advised us to wait until we were assigned a campsite.

He was just about to leave when he saw Simona and Serle, and Simona saw him. First they stared at each other, then they both caterwauled. Such a storm of relief and delight and sorrow! They fell into one another's arms.

Simona told us Gennaro was her father's first cousin, and she didn't even know he was on our crusade, and he didn't know she was, and he is a good man, and has three daughters, and he's sailing on the Doge's own galley, and he will protect her. . . .

"We're protecting you," said Serle. "I am."

"I am!" said Bertie.

"Tutti! Tutti!" Simona cried gaily. "Everybody!" Then she engulfed Bertie in an embrace. *"Tu!"* cried Simona. *"Tu specialmente!"*

Gennaro winked at me. "*Signor* Artù!" he said. "Cows' eyes! Sea snails!"

When Gennaro went ashore, he took Simona with him. She didn't come back yesterday, but this afternoon she hurried into our camp, and told Serle and Lord Stephen and me what had happened.

The Doge's servants had scarcely hammered home the last peg of his vermilion tent before the councillors of Zara rode out of the city to speak to him.

"They offered him the city," Simona said. "They offered him everything in it. Everything! One condition only." Simona wagged her pudgy right forefinger. "He spare their lives."

"God be praised!" I exclaimed.

"What did the Doge say?" Lord Stephen asked.

"He said he must ask the French crusaders," Simona told us. "He told the Zara councillors to wait. In his tent."

"I see," said Lord Stephen.

"Surely Milon will be pleased," I said. "And Villehardouin."

"Of course!" said Lord Stephen. "The last thing we want is trouble here."

"So why did he ask them?" said Serle.

Lord Stephen's eyes gleamed. "Tact," he said. "And tactics. If he consults the French now, aren't they more likely to consult him later? And maybe the Doge thinks it won't harm the Zarans to simmer in the stewpot for a while. They've been troublesome for more than twenty years."

Then Simona told us Count Simon de Montfort and Enguerrand de Boves visited the Doge's camp while he was away, talking to all the other French leaders.

Simona cupped her left ear and leaned against the canvas. "Count Simon and Enguerrand talked alone to the Zarans," she said.

Lord Stephen never took his eyes off Simona for one moment.

"They said the French pilgrims are Christians and the Zarans are Christians. They said the French would never attack Zara. They told the Zarans not to surrender their city. Their beautiful city! So long as the Zarans can defend themselves against the Venetians, they have nothing to worry about."

"How dare they?" Lord Stephen said, very quietly.

"I don't understand," I said. "The Zarans have already surrendered. Doesn't Count Simon want them to?"

"Aha!" said Lord Stephen. "He feels slighted because he wasn't asked about who should build our ships, and he objects to a Lombardian and a Venetian leading French crusaders. But even so!"

"And Robert de Boves," Simona said. "Enguerrand's brother. He rode up to the walls and shouted the French pilgrims are friends, Christian friends."

"Outrageous!" Lord Stephen said angrily. "So what did the Zaran councillors do?"

"They thanked Count Simon and Enguerrand for telling them God's truth and for their Christian friendship. Then they left."

"Dear God!" said Lord Stephen. "Does the Doge know?"

Simona shook her head. "I go back now," she said.

"We'll come with you," said Lord Stephen. "Sooner or later actions have consequences, and I very much doubt whether Count Simon's actions will prevent bloodshed, as he supposes."

Behind Our Backs

When we reached the Doge's camp, the vermilion tent and the smaller pavilions surrounding it and the slimy steps down to the water were seething with servants and cooks and monks and vintners and falconers and blacksmiths and people hoping for an audience with the Doge, and I don't know whom else. I listened to a man practicing the wheedling bagpipes; then two Black Monks told me about the Rule of Saint Benedict, and I told them I knew about how Saint Maurus walked on the water. Simona and I talked to a surgeon called Taddeo, who told me the gut of a cat stretches for one hundred paces, and the worst way of dying is to be hanged and drawn and quartered, and once he trepanned a man whose blood was blue.

"I don't want bone cut out of my skull," I said.

The surgeon's mouth twisted. "Few people do," he said. "I please the Doge most when I'm doing least!"

We waited, but the Doge and his councillors still didn't come back.

"Come on!" said Lord Stephen. "We're wasting our time here."

We weren't, though. I found out about all kinds of things.

Early this morning I hurried back to the Doge's camp, taking Bertie with me. It was already packed. We had to elbow our way through the crowd, but Bertie used his head and feet as well.

"Sometimes you're a squire and sometimes a beast."

"A leucrota!" said Bertie, grinning.

"What's that?"

"Me!" exclaimed Bertie. "The body of a donkey, buttocks like a deer's, a lion's chest, a mouth that opens right back to its ears. And it talks like a human. You'd still be one as well if you weren't a knight. Your boots are splitting."

In the middle of the tent, a square space had been cordoned off, and a guard with a spear stood at each corner. On one side sat the Doge, wearing his cotton cap with the scarlet cross. His face was quite bloodless, except for his angry cheek-blotches.

Gennaro and the other councillors were standing behind the Doge, and so were the French leaders. I caught Milon's eye, and he nodded firmly. I think he was pleased that Bertie and I were witnesses.

On the other side stood Count Simon de Montfort, Enguerrand and Robert de Boves, and an abbot.

"In the name of God!" began the Doge in his high, light voice. "While all your fellow leaders begged me, yes, they begged me, to accept the surrender, you went behind our backs, telling the Zarans not to surrender. I was ready to spare limb and life. What do you want? The blood of Christian Zara?"

The count shook his head, but the Doge wasn't finished.

"Do you want to split our army? To wreck our great crusade? You are traitors to God!"

Count Simon turned to the abbot and the abbot stepped forward.

"I am Guy de Vaux," he said. "I have a letter. A letter from the Holy Father."

Around me, everyone gasped.

"Yes, from Rome. From Pope Innocent himself. My lords, in the name of the Pope, I forbid you to attack this city. The people here are Christians, and you have all taken the Cross."

The abbot shuffled across the space and put the piece of parchment into the Doge's hands.

"If you ignore the Holy Father's warning," he continued, "he will cut you off from the grace of God. He will excommunicate you!"

Some people began to cross themselves and get down on their knees. But others shouted insults at the abbot.

The Doge waited, then raised his right hand. He turned round to face the French leaders.

"My lords," he said, "you have encouraged and authorized me to accept the surrender. But your own fellow Frenchmen have gone behind our backs, and the Zarans believed them. So there is no surrender to accept." The Doge paused. He raised his blue, shining, blind eyes to heaven. "My lords," he said, "in Saint Mark's we made a solemn agreement. You swore to help me recapture this city, and now you will keep your word."

At this, yelling and hissing and jeering began, and there was cheering as well. Count Simon and the brothers and the abbot angrily barged out of one door of the tent, the French leaders bowed to the Doge and left by another, and Bertie and I ran back to our camps not knowing what was going to happen. . . .

This evening, Milon and Bertie walked in while we were all eating supper. Milon came straight to the point, as he always does.

"Against Pope or against agreement with Doge? Rome or Venice?"

"Well, which?" asked Sir William.

"If we go against Rome," said Milon, "ex . . . ex . . ."

"Excommunication," I said.

Milon winced. "If against Venice, we lose ships. Finish!"

Bertie kicked at his right heel with his left toecap.

"We are God's pilgrims," Milon said. "The Pope promise us pardons for all our sins."

"To hell with pardons!" muttered Sir William.

Lord Stephen wiped his mouth, and kept blinking.

"But we will not allow de Montfort and de Vaux to wreck our crusade," Milon said. He spat on the ground. "We send four envoys to the Pope to explain. We help the Doge to recapture Zara."

58 feet first

I TOLD YOU," SAID SERLE. "YOU SHOULD HAVE GOT THEM mended before we left Venice."

"They were all right then," I said. "They only need a few stitches."

But all morning I had to trail from camp to camp, searching for a shoemaker, and I was barefoot because my hose stops at my ankles.

The man in the Doge's camp was the first to turn me away. He was lining a pair of boots with some kind of cherry-red material and told me he had far too much to do.

It was the same wherever I went.

"You see this pile?"

"I've no time at all. I can't even look at them."

"It takes time, son. Lining. Punching the holes. Lacing the sides. Folding over the caps."

You might have thought I wanted shoes inset with precious stones and threaded with gold, or magic shoes to climb a glass mountain. "They only need a few stitches," I said.

"So you can trample all God's enemies under your feet? Well, boy, you'll just have to wait."

Eventually, though, I did find a shoemaker in one of the Italian camps who was willing to help me. He spoke some English and had his own little pavilion.

"Picardians and Venetians and Poitevins and Angevins," he said, "they're just cobblers. I'm a shoemaker. I'm a cordwainer. Look!"

Stacked in the corner of the pavilion were rolls of skin, dyed olive green and mustard and chestnut.

"Goat," said the shoemaker.

"Doesn't it tear?" I asked. "Goatskin used for parchment is so thin, it always tears."

"You wouldn't want it for marching," the shoemaker replied. "Goatskin for ladies' shoes."

"On the crusade?"

The shoemaker smiled a leathery smile. "I'll sell along the way. Embroidered shoes. Scorpion-tailed shoes. Boots edged with fur. And if there are any left when I get home, the ladies of Milan won't disappoint me." He pointed at another, much thicker roll, the color of old beech-mast. "Cow," he said. "Cow for soles."

"You could make up a riddle about shoes," I said. "They've got souls, and tongues. They've got eyes. . . ."

In another corner there were half a dozen lasts, all over the floor were little snips of leather, and seven pairs of beautiful new boots stood ankle to ankle on a trestle bench.

"Let's have a look, then," the shoemaker said.

I handed him my boots.

The shoemaker made a sucking sound. "Dreadful!" he said. "You're doing your feet a mischief, you are. And if you don't care for your feet, what kind of man are you?"

"What about monks who wear hair shirts?" I said. "And crusaders who scorch their own bodies?"

"I don't know about that," the shoemaker said. "You squires, you all think you're clever and you all wreck your boots."

"I'm not a squire. I'm a knight," I said.

"You? A knight? What's your name?"

"Arthur. Sir Arthur de Gortanore."

"Well, your boots are a disgrace."

"I know."

The shoemaker picked up a pair of handsome calf-length boots and smiled. "*Signor* Artù," he said. "You buy these."

"No, I can't. I've only got three farthings."

"When you buy," the shoemaker said, "always ask three questions. How long they last? How comfortable? And how elegant?"

"I wish I could buy them," I said. "My brother has boots like that. Can you mend mine, though?"

The shoemaker stared at me. "Feet first?"

"What do you mean?"

"Were you born feet first?"

"I don't know," I said. "I know I was born left-handed. I can write with my left hand and my right hand."

"You ask your mother, *Signor* Artù."

"My mother! Yes! Yes, I will, then."

The shoemaker started to stitch the seam of my right boot. "Feet first means magic. You can heal people."

"No," I said. "I can't do that."

"How do you know?" he asked me.

Then the shoemaker opened his tinderbox, and blew the spark

into a flame, and held a strip of leather over it until it began to smolder. It smelled disgusting.

"What are you doing that for?" I asked.

"You know nothing," said the shoemaker. "To keep away demons."

Gossip-Wind

It's strange. Last night, I tried to remember all the songs I've made up, and they're always about strong feelings, like love-fever and fighting-fever. Feelings are running high here now. Last night, Lord Stephen and Sir William had another argument, I don't know what about, and Serle told Simona she was a sow, and Rhys accused Serle and me of caring more about our boots than our horses. The French are building siege engines, and everyone's waiting for orders, and wherever you go you hear gossip and terrible new rumors:

Nobody's sure what so-and-so really said
But everyone knows someone who knows,
Roundabout it goes, and we all suppose.

A says the abbot says that, boiled and lightly salted, a Saracen's like rabbit, and you should wash him down with sherbet. . . . B says the count's a reckling, a runt, and rides out at night, and grows a snout and fangs. . . .

Round and round, round again it goes,
And somewhere between word and word and word,
Everything worsens as the gossip-wind blows.

What about the Doge? C says he'll stop at nothing, gouge out eyes, drown men in sludge, scourge them with flames. . . . D says if only the marquis were here, then something I don't understand about a black girl, a chalice, a pear. . . .

Nobody's quite sure, though we all know each word,
But no one cares and no one counts the cost
When roundabout it goes, and we all suppose,

And truth and honor and trust lie lost.

Ready to Die

HEN I STEPPED OUT OF CAMP THIS AFTERNOON, and sat with my back against a weather-beaten stanchion beside the canal, and unwrapped my stone, I saw jealousy and scheming and treachery as bad as Count Simon de Montfort's.

"Disgraceful!" exclaims Sir Agravain.

Many knights turn their heads and listen.

"It's disgraceful that day after day and night after night Sir Lancelot beds the queen, and we do nothing about it, and allow the king to be shamed."

"Enough!" says Sir Gawain, Sir Agravain's brother. "I want to hear no more of it."

"Neither do we," say their brothers, Sir Gaheris and Sir Gareth.

"But I do," says Sir Mordred quietly.

Sir Gawain's mouth tightens. "I can well believe it," he says. "You always make bad worse."

"Whatever becomes of it," Sir Agravain says, "I mean to tell the king."

"And cause conflict? Many knights will side with Sir Lancelot." Sir Gawain puts his right hand on his brother's shoulder. "Don't forget Sir Lancelot has often come to the king's rescue. He rescued me from King Carados; he rescued you and Mordred from Sir Turquine. Do his kindness and courage count for nothing?"

"Sir Lancelot knighted me," says Sir Gareth. "I won't hear another word against him."

"Here comes the king!" Sir Gaheris says. "Keep your voices down."

"I will not," says Sir Agravain.

"Neither will I," Sir Mordred says.

"Then because of you and Mordred," Sir Gawain tells his brother, "not because of the queen and Sir Lancelot, our great gathering of knights will splinter and split."

King Arthur approaches them. "What a hubbub!" he says.

At once Sir Gawain, Sir Gareth, and Sir Gaheris bow and walk away.

"What are you arguing about?" asks the king.

"Mordred and I," Sir Agravain says, "we're the sons of your own sister, and we can hide it from you no longer. Sir Lancelot and your queen are lovers. He is a traitor."

Arthur-in-the-stone lowers his eyes. Is he thinking of Merlin's warnings? "Love can be blind. . . . Don't say I haven't warned you."

"If what you say is true," the king replies gravely, "then yes, Sir Lancelot is a traitor. But if he is accused, he'll fight and prove his innocence. No one can match him."

"Sire," says Sir Mordred, "it is true."

"I must have proof," the king insists. "Sir Lancelot's my knight of knights. He has honored me by serving me."

"When you go hunting tomorrow," Sir Agravain says, "send word you'll stay overnight in one of your lodges. I'll catch the rat. I'll bring him to you alive or dead. Mordred and I will have twelve knights with us."

"That may not be enough," the king says grimly.

Sir Lancelot and Queen Guinevere: Their sin is hot — it is the strength of their love and the weakness of being unable to resist it. But Sir Agravain and Sir Mordred? Their sin is hate, not love. It is cold. They don't care about protecting their king. They want to ruin Sir Lancelot. What Sir Gawain said is true: Because of them, the Round Table will be shattered.

I can see a small chamber hung with chains of flowers. A bed. Sir Lancelot and Guinevere lying on it. Sir Lancelot's sword is on the floor beside him.

There's a loud knocking at the door.

"Sir Lancelot!"

"You traitor!"

"Come out or we'll come in!"

"We're lost!" cries the queen.

Sir Lancelot sits up. "My lady," he says, "is there any armor in here?"

"None!" the queen cries.

Guinevere is shaking, and Sir Lancelot wraps his arms around her. "There's nothing to fear," he said.

"There is everything!" says the queen.

Sir Lancelot holds Guinevere close.

"You cannot fight them all," Guinevere whispers. "You'll be killed. I will be burned."

"And all because I'm not wearing armor," Sir Lancelot replies.

Now the knocking and shouting begin again.

"Come out!"

"You scum!"

"Dear Jesus," says Sir Lancelot. He draws Guinevere to her feet. "My lady, my queen," he says, "I have loved you from the day I first saw you. Can you remember what I said when you belted on this sword?"

Guinevere trembles.

"'Who can fully live unless he's ready to die?'"

"No!" whispers Guinevere.

"Guinevere! Guinevere, you will not be burned. My nephew, Sir Bors, Sir Lavaine or Sir Urry, one of them will rescue you."

"If you die," the queen whispers, "I will be ready to die."

With his arms still wrapped around the queen, Sir Lancelot leans back and looks at Guinevere. "I'll sell my life dearly. But I'd rather have a suit of armor now than be ruler of Christendom."

"My love and my life," Guinevere whispers.

"Jesus, be my shield!" Sir Lancelot says. "Jesus, be my armor."

"Let us in!"

"We'll spare your life."

"And take you to the king."

Sir Lancelot wraps his cloak around him; he picks up his sword, and unbars the little door, and a large knight bends his head and steps in. His sword is drawn.

"Sir Colgrevaunce de Gorse," says Sir Lancelot. "Welcome!"

At once Sir Lancelot slams the door and bars it again.

Sir Colgrevaunce jabs at him, but Sir Lancelot steps sideways and thwacks the side of his helmet. The knight falls over sideways.

With Guinevere's help, he puts on the dead man's armor.

Sir Lancelot looks longingly at Queen Guinevere. He swings round to the door, unbars it again, and steps out.

Sir Lancelot roars and, with his first stroke, he kills Sir Agravain. With eleven more savage blows, he fells eleven men. Only Sir Mordred is able to escape.

Slowly Sir Lancelot turns. He stoops and steps into the queen's chamber. He is breathing deeply.

"It is true," he says. "This is the end."

Guinevere bows her head.

"I have given my king cause to become my deadly enemy. We must leave, here and now, and I'll protect you. That is best."

"That is not best," replies the queen. "You've done harm enough. Go now to your own chamber."

Sir Lancelot sighs.

"But if, tomorrow," Guinevere says, "you see they mean to burn me —"

"I will rescue you," says Sir Lancelot. "With all my heart, I swear it. For as long as I draw breath, I am your knight."

They breathe; they gaze at one another. There is nothing more to say.

A little, flailing, biting, whimpering thing

LEASE!" I PANTED. "DON'T!"

Wido and Giff and Godard took no notice.

The boy yelled at the top of his voice. His yell rose into a scream.

"Don't!" I pleaded. Then I heard myself shouting, "Let him go!"

Giff glanced at me. He was grinning.

"Milon," I said. "Wait! Let me find Milon."

"Hear that, boys? Sir Arthur's going to ask Milon."

Now the boy was whimpering.

"Don't you start that wailing," bawled Giff. "Like a bloody Saracen."

"Come on!" Godard urged them. "For God's sake! Knees up, right under his chin. Tighter!"

"No!" I cried. "He's only small."

What happened was this.

Early this morning Milon and the other French leaders instructed their men to wheel their mangonels and tormenta and other siege engines into place, facing the city walls.

Giff and his gang were positioned right at the head of the channel, nearest to the Land Gate.

While they were heaping up stuff to hurl at the Zarans — a whole cartload of horse manure, a dead dog, hundreds of stones the size of heads — many of the Zarans stood on the walls waving and cheering, and several times they started to sing, and burst out laughing.

They still believed what Count Simon and Enguerrand had told them. They must have. They didn't think the French were really going to use their siege engines.

Then a bunch of young boys jostled out through the Land Gate. At least twenty of them. They ran towards us. They yelled at us. They came even nearer, and arched their backs, and hurled stones at us. Then they sprinted away and back again through the city gate.

To begin with, Wido and Giff and Godard ignored them. But each time the boys came out, they got more daring.

"Get lost!" yelled Giff.

"Pests!" shouted Godard.

"Bloody wasps!" bawled Wido, mopping his brow.

The boys chanted and jeered and chucked stones, and then one of them hit Godard on his left shoulder.

Godard wiped his big, wet mouth with the back of his hand. "Right!" he said. And he started to run. Huge, heavy, lumbering steps.

The boys saw him and hared away again, but one of them tripped over a pothole and fell. He scrambled to his feet, but Godard grabbed him.

He scooped up the little, yelling, flailing, biting thing and carried him back.

Godard and Wido and Giff just looked at one another.

Then Godard threw the boy onto the ground, groveling at his feet. He kicked him in the groin, and the boy gasped and sobbed.

Wido picked up a coil of rope and he and Giff wound it round the boy's body, pinioning his arms. Then they brought his knees up under his chin, and wound more rope round his back and shins.

"This'll surprise them," said Godard.

That's when I knew for sure. I lost my breath. My heart began to hammer. But before I could say another word, Wido gave me an almighty shove.

"Out of the way!" he growled.

I staggered sideways and fell onto the pile of stones. At once I got up, but Wido jammed his elbow into my face.

They dumped him in the cup. He was silent now, his eyes shut, eyelids tight.

Then they released the engine's arm, and the torsion rope howled. They hurled him high. They hurled him right back over the wall.

62 THROWN

I WAS SO DAZED, I CAN'T EVEN REMEMBER GETTING BACK to our camp. But I did, and the only person there was Sir William.

"What do you think this is, Arthur?" he demanded. "A birthday celebration? It's a crusade. The only mincemeat and jelly here will be human flesh and blood."

"A little boy!" I said. "Only eight or nine."

Sir William sniffed. "It'll wake the Zarans up," he said. "The sooner they see sense, the better for everyone."

"But there must be . . . well, a code. A code, isn't there?"

"What do you mean?"

"Rules."

Sir William snorted. "Rules!" he exclaimed. He stepped towards me, and punched me on the shoulder. "You'll soon get used to it."

I don't want to get used to it. Used to the killing of children. Sir Lancelot said war is to protect children and women and other innocent people. I know we're going to fight and I'm ready to fight. Well, I thought I was. But not if it means killing children and attacking defenseless old men. There's no honor in that.

That boy's mother. His father. They must know by now.

Giff and Wido and Godard are vile. I hate them. I hate myself for not being able to stop them.

I'm going to talk to Milon. He is an honorable man. I know he'll be angry. Very angry . . .

Then Rhys told me my moping was troubling everyone, and even if I was no use to other men, I could be of use to my beast, and I should exercise him.

That's what I did, and I was glad of Bonamy's spirit and strength and large damson eyes and warm neck. Riding him away from Zara, I could still hear shouts and banging and jeering. I pushed my forefingers into my ears and buried my face in Bonamy's mane.

Bonamy and I have been friends since the day I brought him back to Holt. My hoof-weaver! My trailblazer! I think he must have sensed how upset and angry I was. First he kept whisking his tail, then he kicked his back hooves and snorted.

"Steady!" I said. "Steady!"

But Bonamy writhed and shrugged; he started to buck; and then he galloped as if he were being goaded by an invisible enemy.

"Steady!" I yelled. "Bonamy!"

Bonamy dug in his hooves. He shuddered and reared up, neighing wildly. I tried to stay in the saddle, but he threw me.

I could hear all the bones in my body crunching. Stars burst! I saw them bursting inside my head.

The next thing I knew, I was wandering around in the almost-dark, wondering where I was and what had happened. My neck and shoulders ached; my arms ached; my legs ached; my eyes ached.

Without my hearing him, Bonamy came up behind me and gently butted me.

"Bonamy," I groaned. "You've never done that before."

He licked my chin with his rough tongue, and I yelped. I stared at my raw elbows, my oozing knees. I thought of everything that had happened, and of how desperate and useless I felt, and I groaned again.

"I've never hurt like this before," I whispered.

Grim and Ugly and Vile

A KNIGHT NEEDS TO KNOW WHAT LIFE IS LIKE FOR HIS people," Lord Stephen said. "For the men and women and children living on his manor."

"Sir William doesn't care," I said.

"I do," Lord Stephen replied. "Sir John does. So does Sir Walter de Verdon. And so will you. Have you been biting your nails?"

"No, sir. Only this thumb."

"Don't!" said Lord Stephen sharply. "Now it's just the same here as at home. We need to understand warfare for all it is."

"Killing children," I said bitterly.

"I don't condone that for one moment," Lord Stephen said. "What they did was utterly wrong. Depraved. That's not what we're here for. But warfare isn't glorious, Arthur. It's not only parading on horseback and listening to trumpets. No, it is grim and ugly and vile. Someday you'll lead others, and may have to make difficult decisions, so it's essential you know the truth about it."

"Yes, sir."

"It's not easy, I know. Not for me either. But we must face up to whatever happens."

"Yes, sir."

"So I want you to go over with the miners and help them begin to dig the trenches. Milon agrees. You and Bertie can go together. I know it's not a knight's work, and not a squire's work either, but we must understand."

There were fourteen of us. Bertie and I and twelve diggers from Provins. Their foreman was Chrétien.

"First things first," said Chrétien. "These hides and stakes. The tin sheet. All the stuff for the shelter. The sledgehammers. You two, Sir Arthur and Bertie, you link your shields, and hold them over you like a roof. Head for that crucifix hanging on the wall there!" Chrétien clapped his hands. "Come on, then! What are you waiting for?"

The Zarans saw us as we lumbered past the Land Gate and under the high walls. But Wido and Giff and Godard provided us with cover.

I could see they were only hurling head-sized stones, but the moment I heard their torsion rope howling, I felt ill and began to shake.

"Seen a ghost?" yelled Chrétien. "For Christ's sake, sir, get a move on!"

We hammered the stakes into the hard ground; we stretched the hides over them, and the tin sheet.

"Right!" shouted Chrétien. "Back for the picks and axes and spades. You, Bertie! You and Sir Arthur bring over one of the props. Ready?"

We all made a run for it, but this time the Zarans were waiting for us. They pushed lumps of rock over the wall, and one smacked into the tin sheet. We all got away unscathed, though.

While we were digging a trench at the foot of the wall, Wido and Giff and Godard kept their mangonel busy, but that didn't stop the Zarans from tipping all kinds of stuff onto us. Stones. Buckets of dung. Bones.

One of the mangonel's cup-loads fell short. I heard it spitting and cracking against the wall, and then the hide right above me was pierced by the silver-tipped crucifix. Jesus's nailed feet were dangling beside my right ear.

Chrétien opened his eyes wide and crossed himself, but another man guffawed. "Near thing, sir!" he exclaimed. "Nearly skewered by our Savior!"

I know now what a rabbit trapped in its burrow feels like. Quivering. Helpless. Overhead are humans, shouting and stamping, and stinking ferrets. In a siege like this, there's no chivalry, no courtesy.

"This'll take us days," said Bertie. "The ground's so hard and dry."

"Get a move on, then!" Chrétien snapped.

"Have we got to dig right under this wall?" Bertie said.

"And then up again?" I asked.

"Not up again!" said Chrétien. "Just far enough to bring the whole thing down."

"What? On us?" Bertie exclaimed.

"That's the trick, boy," said another miner. "That's what the props are for."

"The wall starts to move," said Chrétien. "It sags a bit. It sinks."

"And you put the props in," Bertie said.

"Got it!" said Chrétien. "Then you dig a bit more. That's what the Angevins are doing down there. And beyond them, the Gascons."

"And then what?" I asked.

"Fire!" Chrétien said. "We build a fire beside the props and scarper. You'll see."

The men showed us little respect. They told Bertie and me we were lily-livered and scrawny chickens and they complained we kept getting in their way. But all the same, they were quite friendly.

When it was quiet overhead, Chrétien told two men, Gaston and Giscard, to remove some of the rocks and bones and stuff from the sagging hides.

No sooner had they started than Giscard was hit on the head by a huge block of dressed stone. We hauled him back under our shelter, feet first, but the top of his skull was completely crushed. One moment he was alive, the next dead. Stone dead.

Four of the miners picked him up and, leaving our picks and axes and spades behind, we hurried back to the other side of the channel. We laid out Giscard's body beside the mangonel.

"Poor sod!" said Chrétien. "Who's going to dig the grave?"

No one replied, and Chrétien nodded at Bertie and me.

"Where?" asked Bertie.

"Holy ground," I said.

"Wherever Giscard lies will be holy ground," Chrétien growled. "Any man who falls in a siege will find a place in heaven." He stared at Giscard's mangled skull and scuffed the ground. "Poor sod!" he said again. "If we'd had that cat . . ."

"What's that?" Bertie asked.

"A shelter," said Chrétien. "On wheels. It creeps up to the walls, and it's got a roof with a steep pitch so nothing can lie on it. The Normans are building them but they took too long. If we'd had that cat . . ."

"Did you know Giscard before?" I asked.

"All my life," said Chrétien. "And his wife. Six children, and another in the oven."

Five days have passed since I wrote about Giscard and digging under the wall, and each day Lord Stephen and Milon have given Bertie and me new duties. One day I helped the Norman carpenters build the cats — they call them sows — but Bertie actually had to help saw lengths of wood; one day we rowed round to the western side of Zara, and Bertie had to take an oar, and we both helped the Venetian sailors stretch long ladders from the docked ships onto the city walls while the Zarans hooted and tried to stop us by pouring hot oil and steaming water over us; and one day I had to work with Turold, checking all the nails in our armor, and polishing it, but Bertie's job was worse: He had to pull out all the stinking fustian pads and clean the inside of each piece.

This afternoon, the same three Zaran councillors who came to see the Doge on the day we disembarked rode out through the Land Gate again. They were unarmed, and each was holding up a large crucifix.

They rode straight to the Doge's camp and offered to surrender the city and everything in it on exactly the same terms as before.

"Well," said Lord Stephen, "he can scarcely do less than spare their lives."

"He can," said Sir William.

Lord Stephen's mouth twitched. "Not with any honor," he said.

"You shall not leave any creature alive," Sir William rasped. "You shall annihilate them. The Book of Deuteronomy."

"The Zarans are Christians, and sparing life is the least the Doge can do," Lord Stephen insisted. "Otherwise the Pope will never forgive him."

"If that's all they're asking, they've got no bargaining power."

"Couldn't they provide men for the crusade?" I asked.

"They will!" replied Sir William. "The Doge will see to that."

"So what have the Zarans got out of all this?" Lord Stephen asked.

"They're in deep water," Sir William said darkly. "The Doge is extremely angry. They've held out against him for twenty years."

"What did I say?" Lord Stephen asked.

"You always know best!" Sir William barked.

Lord Stephen drew himself up like an offended peacock, but the top of his head still only comes up just above my shoulders.

"I said Count Simon's — "

"Treachery!" barked Sir William.

". . . Count Simon's action would not have the effect he supposed. He wanted to stop Christians from fighting Christians. But look what has happened!"

Sir William sniffed.

Lord Stephen wagged his right forefinger. "They've caused exactly what they tried to prevent," he said.

into the flames

WHY ARE YOU ALL ARMED?" ASKS SIR LANCELOT.

"Each of us woke from his own dream," Sir Bors replies, "and in each of our dreams you were in danger of your life."

Sir Lancelot gazes at his nephew, and at all the others. Twenty-two faces white in the candlelight.

"Now I know who are my friends and who is against me," he says.

"Lancelot, we will do as you do." One by one, they all swear it.

"But what am I to do?" Sir Lancelot asks. "What if the king sentences Guinevere to death?"

"If that's her sentence, it's because of you."

"And so you must rescue her."

"If the king can lay his hands on you, he'll have you burned as well."

"Or hanged and drawn and quartered."

Sir Lancelot listens to his friends' advice. The candles tremble.

"But if I rescue her," he says, "there will be more bloodshed. In all the confusion, I may kill more of my own friends. And where would I take her?"

"That's the least of your problems," Sir Bors replies. "Ride her to Joyous Gard, your own castle."

"You must rescue her."

"We will do as you do."

"We'll ride beside you."

Now Sir Mordred is kneeling to King Arthur. His father.

"Blood!" the king exclaims. "You're caked in it."

"We trapped him in the queen's chamber," Mordred tells him. "He was unarmed. But he slew Sir Colgrevaunce and put on his armor. He killed thirteen of us."

"Thirteen!" King Arthur cries.

"Knights of the Round Table," Mordred says, very deliberately. "Only I escaped."

Arthur-in-the-stone holds his head in his hands. He groans.

Mordred backs away into the shadows, into the deep darkness, and Sir Gawain steps into my stone.

"Lancelot was found in the queen's chamber," the king says. "The queen is guilty of treason. Guinevere must burn."

"Sire," Sir Gawain says, "be wise and wait." He looks so grave. So troubled.

"Lancelot has killed thirteen knights."

"My king," Sir Gawain says, "you don't know why Lancelot went to the queen's chamber. I don't know. We only know what other people say. Lancelot has fought for her; he has saved her life. For all we know, she summoned him so she could reward him in secret."

King Arthur stares at Sir Gawain. "Is that possible?" he asks.

"So as to avoid gossip," Sir Gawain continues. "And maybe that was unwise. But we often do things we believe for the best, and then they turn out to be for the worst. I trust Queen Guinevere. She is honorable. And I know Lancelot will take on anyone who openly accuses him."

"He may be stronger than any other knight," King Arthur replies, "but that doesn't mean he's innocent."

"Or guilty," says Sir Gawain. "We must be knights of the heart as well as the body. That's what Lancelot says."

"Damn Lancelot!" shouts the king. "Guinevere will burn and he'll never fight for her again."

Sir Gawain shakes his head.

"How can you?" cries the king. "He has killed Agravain, your own brother. He has killed your two sons, Florence and Lovel."

Sir Gawain lowers his eyes and three times he crosses himself. "I warned them," he says quietly. "My brother. My own dear sons. I mourn them and I always will, but they've caused their own deaths."

"Gawain," says the king, "put on your best armor. Tell your young brothers, Gaheris and Gareth, to do the same. In one hour go to the queen's chamber and bring her to the fire."

"Never!" says Sir Gawain. "Guinevere is good and true. I cannot bear to see her die. My heart would burst."

"Instruct your brothers, then," the king says hoarsely.

"They'll feel the same as I do," Gawain replies, "but they're so young, they will not dare refuse you. They've no quarrel with Lancelot. I will tell them to come unarmed."

Sir Gawain's eyes are brimming with tears. My seeing stone is brimming with his tears. Like black ice thawing, the whole world of it is weeping.

◆ ◆ ◆

I can see her.

She is tied to a stake, wearing a simple white smock. Heaped all around her are branches, dead branches that were once alive, reaching arms of beech and oak that lived and breathed in the greenwood.

And around the pyre stand lords and knights and ladies, hundreds of them, weeping, clenching their fists. But not one of them raises a hand to save the queen.

Now King Arthur nods, and his hooded executioner thrusts a flaming brand under the branches. . . .

Smoke. Smoke in my stone.

Now there's a thrumming, a thunder of hooves. Horsemen crowd into the courtyard and whirl their swords. Heaven help all those unable to avoid them.

In the drifting smoke, Sir Lancelot jabs and lunges and beats and lashes and thrashes his way through the crowd to the pyre.

Without knowing whom he is striking, he kills his own knight, Sir Gareth.

He kills Sir Gaheris.

They are buried beneath Sir Griflet and Sir Tor, Sir Gauter, Sir Gilmere, Sir Driant, Sir Priamus . . . a pile of his own friends.

Sir Lancelot spurs his horse right into the licking flames. With his dagger, he cuts the queen loose. He throws his cloak round her, and she grasps his hands and clambers up behind him. She puts her bare arms around his waist.

Now Sir Lancelot wheels round. He shouts to high heaven.

Across the courtyard, across the width of this middle-earth,

King Arthur and his knight of knights gaze for all time at one another.

So proud. So desolate.

Away they gallop! Away they stream, out and away, Sir Lancelot and Guinevere and all their followers, leaving in their wake the quick and the dead.

65 the dark-eyed doll

"ER-NUH-DA HOOPLITH SITT!" LORD STEPHEN announced.

The eye-slit in my glistening helmet is so narrow that I couldn't see him without turning right round to face him.

"What, sir?" I called out.

"ER-NUH-DA . . . ," Lord Stephen bellowed, and then he opened his mouthpiece. "Sorry!" he said. "I forgot! Speaking in here is like trying to talk underwater."

"What were you saying, sir?"

"Another!" Lord Stephen replied. "Another hopeless saint!"

"Who, sir?"

"Chrysogonus. Today's his feast day, his bones are buried in this city, and he still can't save it!"

The Doge has agreed to spare everyone's lives, but he's forcing them all to leave the city at once so that the crusaders can use their houses.

The Zarans are not allowed to remove anything valuable from the city. They've had to leave behind all their church plate and decorated manuscripts, their necklaces and armbands, their gold and silver coins, all their cows and goats and chickens and other livestock.

We rode towards the Land Gate, creaking and clanking, followed by Rhys and Turold with our chests and saddlebags, and I was filled with relief that Zara had surrendered without more bloodshed. A band of Venetian pipers and drummers greeted us; I felt a surge of hope. This is why I took the Cross. Onward to Jerusalem!

But then we met a long line of Zarans on their way out of the city. . . .

Some of them turned their faces away and flattened themselves against the inside of the Gate; some crossed themselves, and one man spat on the ground in front of us. But most people just stared at us with their dark, sad eyes.

I kept looking into their faces. You? Or you? Each looked like the mother or the father or the brother or sister of the boy in the mangonel.

Gennaro and Piero say crops and vegetables and fruits of all kinds grow along this coast, but today there's a freezing wind from the north, and not a stitch of green in the fields. So where will everyone find food? Where will they sleep tonight?

Just inside the Gate, four sergeants were checking no one was disobeying orders. I saw one of them put his arms round a woman, then tug her linen shirt. She was wearing a glittering waistband inside it. The sergeant cursed her and tore it off.

"That's what they're like, these people," he said. "They'll swallow precious stones and dig them out of their own excrement."

One of the Zaran men had a woollen bag slung over his back. When a sergeant jabbed at it with his knife, the bag squawked and shuddered.

The sergeant smacked his lips. *"Poulet Zara!"* he exclaimed. "Very nice too." He pulled the bag off the man's back. "Chickenbrain!" he bawled, and kicked the man on his way.

Behind us, someone yelled, and I saw dozens of mounted knights and squires waiting to come through the Gate. We were blocking the way.

"English!" the sergeant called out, and he flapped his hands helplessly.

"I'm Welsh," Rhys objected. "Welsh, not *Sais*!"

"Clots!" added the sergeant.

"And you?" demanded Sir William. "French slime! Slick as fresh snot!"

The Doge and the French leaders have agreed we should spend the winter here because we can't be sure of supplies if we sail on south, and anyhow, the weather will be against us. They have divided the city, and we have been given a stone tower-house.

But who lived here until this morning? In one corner of my room, which is right at the top, I found a little dark-eyed rag doll lying on straw, tucked up under a scrap of cloth.

The Doge has kept all the houses on the east side of the island, nearest to the ships, for his own councillors and sea captains. That's where Simona will be billeted, but she says she'll come and find us.

Simona fusses over Serle and keeps ruffling his hair and bumping into him and laughing. I feel glad for them but sorry for Tanwen. Poor Tanwen!

I wish Winnie were here. Or Gatty.

Turold helped me to unarm. "Well?" he asked. "How was it?"

"I have worn it before," I said.

"Only for practice."

"You can't call this action," I said. "Turning defenseless people out of their homes."

"Amans, amens!" Simona told Serle, laughing, as she unarmed him.

"What's that?" asked Serle.

"You," giggled Simona. "Lover, lunatic! You're mad, Serle."

"That's what's wrong, Turold," I said. "There's nothing to laugh at anymore."

Turold removed my skullcap. "Your ears are red, sir," he said.

"And my tongue is blue," I replied. "Simona! How do you know so much Latin?"

"Not much!" Simona replied. "My best brother is a monk. He teaches me sayings."

Zara is about two and half miles long but only five hundred paces across. If we were gulls, wheeling above it, it would look like a giant's thumb, pointing north.

Once we'd stabled our horses in an undercroft beneath the house, Serle and I walked out to look around. I felt so strange — curious and guilty at the same time. Most of the streets are very narrow and the walls are so high, you can't see over them, but a little way north and east from our tower-house, there's a marketplace.

"A forum," said Serle. "The same as on deck."

"How do you know?"

"Simona."

"Si-mo-na!" I moaned. "You're love-struck and moonstruck."

"Moonshine!" said Serle. He looked quite pleased, though.

The forum was deserted, and on the far side of it there's a very strange, large church. Circular, with three apses bulging out, like a huge, misshapen loaf. It was locked, though, and the windows were out of reach.

"Come on!" said Serle. "On my shoulders! Let's see if we can climb in."

"We can't," I said.

"We can," Serle replied. "Zara's ours now."

"This is a church, though."

"There may be things in it."

"What do you mean?"

"The chalice. The paten. I don't know."

"We can't take them."

"Stop being so high and mighty, Arthur! If we don't, someone else will."

"It's wrong whoever does it."

What put an end to our argument was meeting Simona and Gennaro with two other Venetians.

"Have you seen this?" Gennaro asked me, and he pointed with his left foot.

A block of white marble built into the foundations had lettering on it. IOVI AVGVSTO.

"And this," Gennaro said.

IVNONI AVGVSTAE.

"Jove and Juno," Simona translated. "God and goddess."

"Roman gods," Gennaro explained. "Church builders took stone from the old Roman temple. Altar stones. Blood sacrifices."

"Really!" I exclaimed. "What did they sacrifice?"

Gennaro shrugged.

"But this is a Christian church," said Serle.

"Et nova et vetera," Simona observed. "New and old. Both."

Oliver wouldn't like the way this marble has been used a second time. He thinks things are either Christian or unchristian, but Merlin told me that Yule and Easter were once both heathen feasts.

While we were talking, we heard shouting, and I saw two men chasing a woman across the forum. They had green crosses stitched on their chests, so they must have been Flemings.

The woman screamed and headed towards us, but the men grabbed her and brought her to the ground.

"Serle!" I exclaimed. "Come on!"

Gennaro put a hand on my right shoulder. "No."

"We must. We can't just let them."

"Serle!" Simona cried. "Yes, Arthur!"

"Come on!" I yelled.

I ran towards the screaming woman. The Flemings were on their knees, ripping her clothes.

I grabbed one of the man's shoulders, and drew my knife. "Stop!" I yelled.

The Flemings looked up.

They saw Serle and Gennaro and the Venetians.

And then Simona ran up, howling, and started to kick them.

The Flemings scrambled to their feet, and stumbled away. "Eunuchs!" they yelled. "Plenty where she came from!"

The woman got to her feet and straightened her clothes.

"You shouldn't have done that!" Serle said angrily. "I'm not even armed. They both had knives!"

"We couldn't just leave her!" I shouted.

Simona stepped towards the woman and put an arm round her.

“She shouldn’t be here anyhow,” Serle said. “The Zarans are meant to have left.”

“Many still here,” Gennaro replied. “All the women . . . holy women . . . all the nuns in Saint Mary monastery.”

“They’re asking for trouble,” said Serle darkly. “From what I’ve heard, the ordinary crusaders will use every woman and girl they can find.”

Serle may be right. This evening thousands of men have crushed into Zara. Crossbowmen, foot soldiers with pikes and staffs and slingers, grubby miners, all the men who work the siege engines, sailors, oarsmen . . .

The streets are heaving. Men are pitching tents wherever they can squeeze them in.

They’re thirsty.

They’re hungry.

Heaven help any Zaran left in the city.

When Milon came to inspect our tower-house, he told us the Doge had seven Zaran councillors arrested as they tried to leave the city. They were decapitated outside the Land Gate.

“He promised to spare everyone’s lives,” I cried.

“These men were enemies for twenty years,” said Milon. “Their pirate ships attack Venice boats.”

“But if the Doge doesn’t keep his word, why should anyone else?” I asked.

“Without leaders,” Milon said, “the Zarans will not attack Venice again. They go to hills. To monasteries.”

I am sitting in my high room, and the dark-eyed doll is sitting on my saddlebag, looking at me.

There are ninety-four steps up, and I can see right over the walls. I can see an island, west and a little north. It's called Molat.

Catmole! My mother . . . Not this year . . .

Since I began writing, it has got death-dark. I heard a group of men running down the street, hooting. Then there was far-off slamming and cheering. And just now I heard someone screaming right down below this tower. A woman. A girl.

Divided in itself

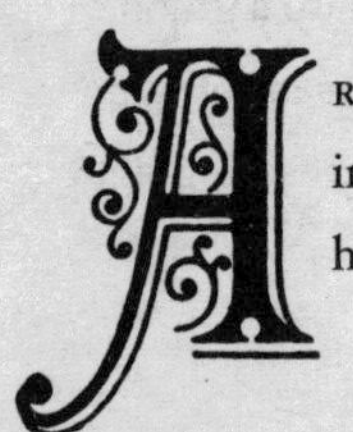

RTHUR-IN-THE-STONE GAZES AT THE RUINS OF NAMES inscribed on the Round Table. So much of the gold leaf has flaked away.

G HE IS He is — whom? G

ARE Are? Are what?

Gaheris . . . Gareth . . .

Letters. No more than a litter of characters, half-gone, wholly gone.

O NCE

LOVE

Florence . . . Lovel . . .

Yes, they loved once, Sir Gawain's sons, and they were well loved. But their eager faces and shining eyes have turned to dust.

The king leans over the Round Table. He spreads his hands over its face. Moving now as an old man moves.

This sphere. This whole world of rock crystal.

The air of it still gleams. Planet-eyes, seething stars, leaping golden comets. The sea of it still twirls its whirligig holes, and spins its silver threads. The fire of it shoots arrow-rays. But the earth of it is splitting — one crack is widening into a chasm. A ravening dark mouth.

King Arthur closes his eyes. His body looks slack as a sack full of slops.

"Divided in itself," he says. "The Round Table is wrecked."

The finest fellowship . . . All that was, and almost was . . . All that now cannot be.

this is going to hurt

I CARRIED BERTIE LIKE A BABY ALL THE WAY TO THE HOUSE where the Doge is staying, and from there to his surgeon, Taddeo.

"You again!" he said. "Well, you're in luck. By the sound of things, I'm going to be busy tonight."

I gently laid Bertie on the table, on his left side, and Taddeo took hold of his right forearm.

Bertie yelped. "I never saw it," he sobbed.

"So," said the surgeon thoughtfully, "in here . . . grazing your collarbone. Down! Right through." He sighed. "The tip's just sticking out of your back."

Bertie moaned.

"Take hold of Arthur's hands," Taddeo told him. "Try to crack each bone in them. What's your name?"

"Bertie."

While he was talking, Taddeo was examining Bertie, and then he turned to his brazier, and pushed the iron deeper into it.

"What's in that pan?" I asked.

"Elder oil," the surgeon replied. He placed the pan on the open coals. "Seethe it. Don't let it start popping. Now, Bertie! This is going to hurt."

Taddeo put his left arm under Bertie's neck and grasped the arrow shaft and drove it in deeper.

Bertie screamed. He cracked my hands. Then, all at once, his own hands went as limp as dead sparrows. His whole body went limp.

"Now the pliers," the surgeon said. "Why do things always hide when you need them?"

I was panting and shaking.

Taddeo rummaged in the straw on the floor until he found the pliers, and he gave them to me.

"Good lad!" he said to Bertie. "Some men writhe and scream, and however terrible the pain, they still stay awake."

The surgeon put his left arm under Bertie's neck again, and cradled him.

"Now, Arthur!" he said. "Got the pliers? Snap off the point. Quickly!"

As soon as I had, Taddeo pulled the shaft back out. Bright red blood flowed from the wound and dripped from the table onto the floor.

Taddeo pulled the iron out of the brazier. The tip was red hot. He just touched it to Bertie's wounds, front and back. "To seal the blood vessels," he said. "Now! The oil. Tip some onto his neck and his back."

Taddeo rubbed in the oil, then wiped his own hands on a bloodstained shaggy towel.

"A very near thing," he said. "An inch away from his windpipe. He may be all right, but I'm no Avicenna."

"Who, sir?"

"Avicenna. A Saracen. He wrote a book about medicine. Yes, he should be all right."

"Coeur-de-Lion wasn't," I said. "An arrow went in through his shoulder and stuck out of his back."

The surgeon's mouth twisted. "He will be rather sore," he said, "when he wakes up."

I didn't even realize it was Bertie to begin with. I just rounded a corner and saw two Venetians dragging a boy down the street by his legs.

You can't run in armor, but I waded after them.

That's when the arrow struck him. Some Venetian shot it from a window or up on a roof.

They let go of his legs, and he screamed and clutched his neck, and I clanked up to him, and that's when I saw it was Bertie.

The two Venetians faced me. One had a glittering knife, the other a staff.

I unsheathed my sword. The dazzling blade Milon gave me. I grasped the pommel in my left hand.

The man with the staff leveled it at my chest, but as he lunged at me I sidestepped. Then the other man raised his right arm. The knife flashed. It glanced off my cheek guard.

I swung my sword. I missed. The blade clashed against the stone wall, and struck sparks.

The man with the knife threw himself at me. I heard the blade grating against my mail-shirt. Then the other man drove his staff at my groin, and grabbed me.

I don't know how I worked myself loose. I must have raised and swung my sword, but I don't even remember hitting him — the man with the glittering knife. All I can see is his nose. His nose. Lying in front of my feet.

I can see them running.

I can hear the man howling.

I can hear Bertie choking and moaning.

It's a good thing Lord Stephen had told me to put my armor on.

Frenchmen were chasing Venetians; Venetians were chasing Frenchmen. They were knifing each other. Hacking. Jabbing. Slinging stones. Loosing arrows.

Lord Stephen and I tried to stop them, and so did many other knights and squires — Milon, even Sir William — but it was almost impossible. There were so many of them, rushing along the narrow streets, searching, killing.

It was dark, and Lord Stephen and I were soon separated. I didn't know where to go. I was cold and sweating and trembling. My mouth was dry. I was afraid of dying. And that's when I rounded the corner and saw them dragging Bertie away.

It started around Vespers and went on all last night. It didn't stop until midday.

As soon as it was quiet in one street, there was fighting in another. Like fire in Pike Forest you can't put out. But the French were the stronger, or the braver. They swept the Venetians back into their own half of the city. They almost pushed them back to the channel and their ships.

Some say the French began it, but no one agrees. We all visited Milon's quarters this evening, and Bertie was sleeping deeply in one corner. Milon told us his men were angry because they're not allowed to keep plunder for themselves — gold and silver and stones and spices and silks and carpets and things like that — but the Venetians are.

"Certainly not!" Milon said. "I say who and what. First we pay the Venetians for their ships."

Sir William says the French dislike being led by a Venetian, Serle says if only the marquis were here, this would never have happened and he only hopes Simona is safe, and Lord Stephen says the French object to staying here.

"It suits the Doge," he said, "because he needs to secure Zara, but it doesn't suit the French. They've already been away from home for three seasons, as we have, and now we've all got to wait here until Easter."

In any case, everyone agrees the Venetians were asking for it, but I keep thinking of that man. His blood leaped over my boots and stained them. His nose! I didn't mean to. I was just trying to protect myself.

Milon thrust out his jaw. "One hundred and one men dead," he announced.

"It's going to take a lot of time and skill to calm things down," said Lord Stephen.

"Sir Gilles de Landas. Dead!" Milon said fiercely.

"How?" asked Sir William.

"They arrowed his eye."

Sir William grunted. "Not so lucky as your squire, then."

"Except for Arthur," Milon went on, "Arthur and surgeon, Bertie is dead."

Lord Stephen looked down at Bertie. "Poor pumpkin!" he said.

In his sleep, Bertie said something. Well, he made a noise like someone talking. Like a leucrota. Then he began to pant.

The upper part of his body is covered with a marjoram poultice, but I could see it's almost twice its normal size. His face is so white, and shining with cold sweat. His hands and feet are cold too. I know that's a sign someone may die.

Not Bertie!

Surely Death won't dance for him tonight. He'll kick and yell and tell Death to go away. . . .

jihad

IS ALL WAR UNHOLY?

When armies fight, do they always both claim that God is on their side?

Does Mother Church have to speak with a tongue of fire?

Do innocent and helpless people always get caught up in it?

My eyelids are drooping. Five times I have vomited, and my throat's so sore. My head's reeling.

Merlin told me once that if only I could ask the right questions . . .

From my room in the tower-house, I watched a boat little larger than our landing skiff skimming between us and the island that is called Ugli and looks so pretty. She had two masts, one about twenty-five feet tall and one in the stern much shorter, and she was skipping and bouncing over the waves. The very strong west wind was blowing a gale and pushing her onshore.

The helmsman swung the boat round to face me; she came racing in, and I doubled down the ninety-four steps and ran to the water to meet her.

The moment she crunched into the gravel, her two sails were like huge white birds struggling in an invisible net; her rigging whipped and cracked; at the top of the mainmast, the little wind-pennant whirred.

There were only seven people aboard: the helmsman and his mate, and two bearded men and three women wearing strange crimson wimples that reached below their waists, and walnut-colored skirts down to their ankles.

The older man called out to me. I couldn't understand him.

"Greetings in God!" I said, and steadied the bow.

The man frowned.

"Do you speak English?" I asked. *"Français?"*

"Français. Oui, oui."

"Moi aussi. Un peu."

The man shook his head and spoke to his companion. "Allah go with you!" he said to me.

The same words the dying man in Coucy said, and the traders in Venice. They were Saracens.

The older man disembarked, and the younger one followed him, carrying a long box like a coffin. They left the three women to look after themselves, and they all got the bottoms of their skirts wet. They chirruped like springtime finches.

Leaving the helmsman and his mate to haul down the sails, I led the Saracens up to our tower-house, but no one was there, so I took them to Milon's house. Milon had gone off to discuss rules of conduct with Villehardouin, but his priest, Pagan, was in the hall. So were at least a dozen knights and their squires, and Bertie was still lying in the corner on a heap of straw.

At first, the Saracens thought we were Zarans. The older man looked like thunder and his eyebrows twitched when Pagan explained who we are and how we've recaptured Zara, and told him we are sailing to Jerusalem.

To begin with, though, he was quite courteous and so was Pagan.

He said his name was Nasir, and he was a singing teacher.

"Like Ziryab!" I cried. "I've learned about him."

Nasir stroked his black beard. He told us the young man was his disciple and was called Zangi. He told us the women were his two wives and his daughter.

"Two wives!" I exclaimed.

"The other two are at home," Nasir replied. "Allah has spared them."

Four wives! No Englishwoman would agree to that!

"You filthy swine!" growled one of Milon's knights.

"What are your names?" I asked the women.

"They have names for me," Nasir rasped. "Not for you."

"Who do you think you are?" another knight demanded, and he stepped towards Nasir. "This is our place, not yours."

"You hypocrites!" snapped Nasir. "What do you care about your holy places? You use your tents as churches. All you want is our wealth. Our gold and silks and spices . . ."

Pagan and Milon's men looked at each other. They've exchanged insults with Saracens before.

"Keep your stinking thoughts to yourself!" said the first knight.

"Or I'll cut your tongue out," said the other.

"You're pests!" said Nasir. "Swarms of flies without wings. You infidels! You attack people of your own faith."

The Frenchmen started to mutter then. They grew restless.

"You're pigs!" said Nasir. "Leprous pigs. The sons of sows!"

At this, Pagan pointed at the Saracen women. "They've stolen their color from night," he jeered. "They've stolen their breath from old latrines."

"You yellow-faced Christian," Nasir snarled. "The nation of the Cross will fall."

Pagan raised both hands. "In the name of God . . . ," he yelled.

Nasir stood up. He looked like one of the angry Old Testament prophets.

"In the name of Allah!" he retorted, and his voice was trembling. "We have a gift for you."

He stepped over to Zangi, then beckoned the three women. They huddled over the coffin-box. Then there was a terrible clatter and they sprang apart, all five of them brandishing scimitars and howling.

"Allah! Hand of Allah! Allah!" they howled.

Everyone ducked and dived and scrambled. We all drew our short knives.

"Jihad!" roared the singing teacher. "The vengeance of God has come down on you!"

They killed three of us and wounded four more. They tried to cut Bertie in half, but Pagan threw himself over his body, and so they killed him instead.

But there were more of us. Milon's knights overpowered Nasir and then Zangi, and slit their throats, and disarmed the women.

The women clutched their own throats and wailed.

I couldn't watch anymore. Not as the men began to rip off their clothes.

I ran out.

Anywhere.

But there's nowhere. Nowhere in this dark world to hide.

Milon's men slung their five bodies into the salt water.

They won't go away, though . . . I don't know how to stop myself thinking.

I don't want to talk to Lord Stephen. I want to be alone.

Wounding, killing . . .

When is it wrong and can it ever be right?

The boy in the mangonel. Giscard. The Zaran councillors whose heads were cut off. Rampaging Frenchmen and Venetians. That man, the one I wounded. Nasir and Zangi and the women with no names. Pagan. Milon's men. All the knights in my seeing stone . . .

What am I to do when I cannot even tell who is innocent and helpless, and who is not?

Women killers!

How deeply the Saracens hate us.

All this hatred and suffering. How can one person make any difference at all?

miserere mei

THE CHURCH OPENED HER ARMS.

There was nobody inside. When I walked across the marble floor I could hear my own footsteps.

All the church plate must have been looted, but high up on the north wall, beside a wind-eye, there was a bronze crucifix.

I stared up at Him and He stared down at me.

His face was so drawn. His cheekbones were almost sticking through His stretched skin.

He died for me. He died for us all. Our Savior.

Why didn't He save the Zarans? Why does He allow us to wound and kill one another? Why has He chosen to set us free?

When we hurt each other, do we also hurt Him?

Have mercy on me, O Lord. Have mercy on me.

Standing at the door, I turned back. A ray of sunlight was shining through the wind-eye. It lanced the crucifix. One moment it was flashing, the next bleeding.

the spirit-garden

70

A NUN PEERED ROUND THE RIBBED OAK DOOR.

She opened it a little, and I stepped in.

She didn't ask me anything. She just laid her calm hands on my aching shoulders and gazed at me. Then, without moving her head at all, she raised her eyes to heaven and very slightly smiled. I thought she looked like Mary.

She led me to a little fountain, its water plashing into a stone basin. Oh! I sank my face into it. My whole head. I tried to wash away everything.

"Thank you," I said. "God go with you!"

The nun looked puzzled. ***"Govorite li engleski?"***

"What? Is that . . ."

"Slavonic, yes. You speak English?"

"I am English," I said eagerly.

She gazed at me, eyes shining; then she raised her eyes to heaven again, and smiled blissfully.

"I never meet English," she said. "I study English. You know Oxford."

"Well, I know about Oxford," I replied. "Schoolmen."

The nun clapped her hands, then took my right arm, and we walked through the cloister into a little garden protected by high walls.

"In the name of the gardener," she said, "greetings! You know? The Gospel of John."

Her voice was quite light, and reminded me of Lady Alice's, but the way she talked was spare and rather hesitant.

"This is the garden of spiritual love," she told me. She shook her head. "Not in bloom yet. Not in December. Look!" she said, stooping to a plant with white-spotted leaves. "Jerusalem Cowslips. Or you say Mary's Milkdrops?"

"I don't know," I said. "Lady Alice would. She's my stepmother. In England."

"Here is a passion dock," the nun said. "Yellow Archangel. Ladder to Heaven."

"This is Saint John's Wort," I said. "We pick it on Saint John's Eve and put it outside each door. And under our pillows. . . ."

The nun laughed. "Nuns no!" she said. "This is Aaron's Rod. And here spikenard: Steps of Christ."

"Where do they all come from, these holy flowers?"

"I grow them. I send for them."

"Send?"

"From other *samostan*." She screwed up her eyes and smiled. "Slavonic!" she said. "Monastery! I send for them from other monastery and nunnery. Other country."

"How can you send plants? They'd arrive more dead than alive."

"Like you," said the nun.

I groaned. "It's so peaceful here. My head!"

The nun smiled like the sun in the earliest spring.

"I could stay here forever," I said.

"You wrap them in waxed cloth, and sew the cloth and smear it with honey," the nun said in her light, bright voice. "Then powder it with flour. You can send plants wherever you like."

We sat side by side on a little bench. The December sun winked and warmed my back. How much time seeped away, I do not know.

Then the monastery bell began to toll, and the nun stood up and smoothed down her habit and straightened her white wimple. Her skin was unblemished as a baby's.

I began to shiver again.

"You stay until you are ready," she said. *"Da?"*

"Yes," I replied. "But . . ."

"Sshh!"

For just a moment one of her hands alighted on my head, light as a butterfly's wing. "I am Sister Cika," she said. "You?"

"Arthur."

"Arthur?"

"Well, Sir Arthur de Gortanore."

"Let Jesus be born in the cradle of your heart," she said gently. "We expect you."

And then, like a summer stream, she glided away.

I walked for hours and hours before I came to that ribbed oak door, I'm sure I did. I don't know why I knocked on it. I didn't know it was a nunnery.

But when, later, I let myself out, I saw I was only a very little way from our tower-house. I must have gone round in circles.

lady, we thank you

NE OF GOD'S GREATEST GIFTS IS MEMORY," LORD Stephen said.

Christmas Day. We were sitting right up on the wall. Zara was at our feet.

"When things are going poorly," he said, "memory consoles us. We remember better days."

"Writing is partly remembering too," I said. "My grandmother thinks unless you can remember something it's not worth knowing, but there's too much knowledge for that."

The bells of the round church, the one that looks like a misshapen loaf, began to ring. Its patron saint is Donat, but

I know not
    who or what
        Donat was.

"Christmas has taken us by surprise," Lord Stephen said. "We've scarcely prepared for it."

"Christmas is like a fold," I said. "That's what I wrote once. And we're all inside it, eating and drinking and keeping warm and singing . . ."

"Not this year."

". . . but we know the year's hunger and terrors and anxieties and opportunities and sorrows are still there on the outside. We know they're all waiting for us."

Lord Stephen nodded. "They are," he said. "Shall we pray for Lady Judith? Shall we pray for everyone at Holt?"

"And Caldicot," I said. "When I think of Christmas, I'll always think of Caldicot. Everyone hauling Yule logs up to the manor house, and calling out to each other. The white bags of their breath. Wat Harelip disguised as a gabbling wild man, and Lady Helen pretending not to recognize him. And Merlin's salmon-leap."

"What was that?"

"You know Merlin."

"No one does," Lord Stephen said with a faint smile.

"We had a leaping contest, and Merlin jumped forty-seven feet!"

Lord Stephen looked at me, and very slowly he shook his head.

"The songs and the tabor and the boar's head," I said, "and the holly and yew and ivy and mistletoe, and the riddles . . ."

Lord Stephen gently lifted his right hand.

"I'm sorry, sir."

"No, no. It's all right." He lowered his head, and swallowed. "Even memory is a double-edged sword," he said. "Consolation and melancholy."

"We used to sing this carol," I told him.

> "Lady, we thank you
> With hearts meek and mild
> For the good you have given us
> With your sweet child."

"Yes," said Lord Stephen. "There are several things to give thanks for. I never expected it, but Bertie is going to live, and it seems he'll make a full recovery."

"Taddeo thought he might," I said.

"And you're looking a bit more like yourself," Lord Stephen added. "And let us give thanks Marquis Boniface has rejoined us."

"These weeks have been terrible," I said.

"Well, we'll soon find out whether it was worth his going to Rome," Lord Stephen said. "Anyhow, the Doge won't get his way so easily now, and there'll be better discipline."

"The bells are quickening," I said.

"How does that song end?" Lord Stephen asked. "The one you were singing."

> "Mother, look down on me
> With your sweet eyes,
> Give me peace and give me bliss,
> My Lady, when I die."

"That's it," Lord Stephen said.

the heart-in-waiting

YULETIDE IN ZARA HAS BEEN BLEAK, AND SO MUCH HAS already gone wrong that people are afraid about what will happen in the new year.

But whatever happens begins in our hearts, doesn't it? I've made this song about Jesus before He was born.

Jesus listened in whispering wood:
"I am pale blossom, I am blood berry,
I am rough bark, I am sharp thorn.
This is the place where you will be born."

Jesus went down to the skirl of the sea:
"I am long reach, I am fierce comber,
I am keen saltspray, I am spring tide."
He pushed the cup of the sea aside

And heard the sky which breathed and blew:
"I am the firmament, I am shape-changer,
I cradle and carry and kiss and roar,
I am infinite roof and floor."

All day He walked, He walked all night,
Then Jesus came to the heart at dawn.
"Here and now," said the heart-in-waiting,
"This is the place where you must be born."

Ivory and Gold and Obsidian

KING ARTHUR IS SITTING AT ONE END OF THE GREAT hall in Camelot, talking to his foster brother, Sir Kay.

"More than forty men are questing for the Grail," he says. "But Sir Gawain has failed. Sir Lancelot has failed. How can anyone succeed?"

"I doubt anyone will," Sir Kay replies.

"Sir Galahad?" says the king. "Sir Bors?"

Sir Kay raises his eyebrows, and smiles a twisted smile. "Not even Sir Perceval is perfect," he says. "But what about you?"

Arthur-in-the-stone shakes his head. "Lady Fortune would prevent me," he said. "And my own failings."

Now a young woman wearing a wimple and riding a white mule — the woman who came to Camelot before — rides straight into the hall again.

"Dismount!" yells Sir Kay.

The young woman ignores him.

"I said dismount!" Sir Kay shouts rudely.

"Forgive me," says the woman, "but I will not dismount until a knight comes to Corbenic and wins the Grail. The shield I left here is still hanging on that pillar. Is there not a single knight here fit to claim it?"

"Many of my knights have made the Grail their dream and

cause," King Arthur replies. "More than forty of them are in the field now, riding through forests, crossing seas . . ."

"They'd do better to look into their own hearts," the young woman says.

Now she raises her right hand, and sweeps off her wimple.

The king and Sir Kay lower their eyes.

She is still bald.

"Not a hair will grow on my head," she says in a low voice. "Nothing will grow until a knight comes to Corbenic and asks the question."

"What is your message?" asks the king.

"Sire," says the young woman, "King Pellam, Guardian of the Grail, greets you, the greatest king on this middle-earth. He implores you to urge all your knights still here at Camelot to quest for the Grail. The world is a wasteland."

"I will," the king replies.

The young woman takes off the little pouch hanging round her neck.

"King Pellam has sent you this gift," she says.

Arthur-in-the-stone unties the pouch. He draws out a reading-pointer, quite long and slightly curved, like a bone hairpin. One end is tapered, the other flat and triangular.

"Ivory," the young woman says. "Gold bands."

"And this little triangle?" the king asks.

"A precious stone, made of ice and fire."

"I have never seen anything more beautiful," says the king.

"King Pellam lies in agony," the young woman tells him. "But he used to mark and follow words with this pointer when he read the scriptures."

"As I will mark King Pellam's words, and act on them," King Arthur says. "Thank him and assure him I will urge all my knights to quest for the Grail. Tell him I will use this pointer when I read the scripture."

NOTHING BUT PAWNS

74

I DIDN'T WANT TO GO. NOT AFTER WHAT HAPPENED THERE. But I had no choice. Lord Stephen and Sir William and Serle and I all went to Milon's hall as soon as we'd finished supper, and Simona came with us.

Milon told us German envoys from the court of King Philip of Swabia arrived here last night. The first day of this new year. They met the Doge and Marquis Boniface and the French leaders this morning, and there was a second meeting this afternoon.

"First," said Milon, "they tell us our duty."

"We know our duty," said Serle.

"They say we march for God, we march to right what is wrong, and now our duty is to help people who have been robbed."

"Who has been robbed?" Lord Stephen asked suspiciously.

"We have," said Serle. "We've been robbed of Jerusalem."

Milon stuck out his jaw and pursed his mouth. "Me first!" he said. "Then you. The envoys come from King Philip and his wife's brother, Alexius Angelus. Crown Prince of Constantinople. His throne has been robbed. He is the true Emperor, not his uncle." Milon turned to Serle. "You how old?" he asked.

"Me? Nineteen."

"Very good. Alexius Angelus nineteen. He and King Philip say if the crusaders lay siege to Constantinople and help him, he help us.

He give us food when Venetians, Venetians . . ." Milon tossed his head and turned to Simona.

"The Venetians are providing all the crusaders with food for one year," Simona explained. "Until Saint John's Eve. After that, Alexius Angelus will."

"Sì," said Milon. "Also he give us two hundred thousand silver marks. Two hundred thousand! And also he raise crusader army of ten thousand men."

"Moonshine!" said Sir William. "Supplies, silver, men . . . they don't come as cheaply as words."

"Let's hear the terms," Lord Stephen said irritably.

"Lickspittle promises!" grumbled Sir William.

"And Alexius Angelus offer to send five hundred knights to the Kingdom of Jerusalem," continued Milon, "and keep them there."

"Blether!" exclaimed Sir William.

"And," said Milon, spreading his arms, "Alexius Angelus say his empire — Byzantine Empire — will swear obedience to Rome." Slowly he shook his head as if he could scarcely believe what he was saying.

"It does sound generous," I said.

"Why doesn't this pretender offer us paradise?" Sir William demanded.

"What do you think, sir?" I asked Milon.

"Doge reminds crusaders we still owe Venice thirty-four thousand silver marks," Milon replied.

"And with the money Alexius Angelus promises, we could pay our debt," Lord Stephen said.

"Sì," said Milon.

"I know what I think," Sir William said. "If you Frenchmen and the Doge accept this offer, our crusade will be doomed. It will be a disaster."

No one replied.

"People make mistakes and survive them," Sir William said. "God knows, I've made mistakes. But this would be monstrous! We're pilgrims, aren't we? Soldiers of Christ."

Sir William was speaking louder and louder, and I thought of Pagan and Milon's men and the Saracens, and suddenly felt afraid.

"No!" my father exclaimed. "We're just pawns. Pawns in the hands of leaders using our crusade for their own purposes."

"The Abbot de Vaux say we must go straight to Jerusalem," Milon said. "Count de Montfort say so."

"Sir William de Gortanore agrees," my father announced. "What about you, Serle? As if I can't guess!"

"I'm not sure," said Serle.

"You never are," Sir William retorted.

"I mean, it's not up to me."

"It is," said my father. "You, Arthur?"

"I don't know enough, sir. Is it true Alexius Angelus should be Emperor? Will we have to attack Constantinople? It's a Christian city. How long will all this take?"

"Quite right, Arthur," Lord Stephen said. "Hasty choices are usually wrong ones."

"I do know what I want, though," I added. "I want to enter the Kingdom of Jerusalem."

"This German offer may sound simple," Lord Stephen said, "but the consequences will be enormous."

“I’m surprised you two haven’t died of a surfeit of your own words,” Sir William remarked.

“On the whole, though, Sir William,” Lord Stephen continued, “I think I incline to agree with you.”

On our way back to our tower-house, Sir William fell into step with me. At least he tried to. But his bones ache, and he quickly runs out of breath.

“I’m sixty-eight,” he said.

“Yes, sir.”

“Slow down, can’t you! We’re not sailing until Easter.”

“Sorry, sir.”

“Easter . . . and then what? Constantinople! I tell you, Arthur, if things go on like this, I’ll not see Gortanore again.” Sir William was panting. “Tom will have Gortanore and the manor in Champagne. I’ve told you that.”

“Yes, sir.”

“That’s where Lady Cécile lives.” Then, to my astonishment, my father slung his left arm round my shoulders, and whether it was in kinship or to slow me down, I’ll never be sure. “And you know I’ve named you heir to Catmole.”

“Thank you, sir.”

“It’s your right,” gasped Sir William. “For God’s sake, what’s the hurry? I’ve told you about it, have I?”

“One foot in England and one foot in Wales,” I replied.

“The river in loops,” Sir William said. “The shapely mound, yes, the manor-mound, and the greenness of the green in the water-meadows. I’d be glad to ride there again, boy.”

An Olive Branch

Y LORD BISHOP ROCHESTER," SAYS SIR LANCELOT. "Have you ridden far?"

The bishop looks his cloak up and down. Covered with spots of mud.

"From King Arthur's court at Carlisle," he says. "I have here a letter from Rome. The Holy Father charges King Arthur to take Guinevere as his queen again, and make peace with you. He warns the king he will excommunicate everyone living in Britain if he fails to do so."

"What does the king say?" Sir Lancelot asks.

"Here is his Great Seal — his assurance of safe conduct when you bring the queen back to court — and his letter undertaking to bury what's past."

"I never wanted to separate the queen from the king, but simply to save her life," Sir Lancelot says. "God be praised the Pope has intervened. I'll be a thousand times happier to ride Guinevere back to Carlisle than I was to take her away. But if anyone —"

The Bishop of Rochester waves his hand. "Fear nothing!" he says. "The Pope's word is divine law. It's not his intention, or mine, to see the queen shamed or you angered."

"And will the king also make peace with me?" Sir Lancelot asks.

"That's what he longs for. He says there has been enough suffering already. But Sir Gawain will not hear of it. You slew Gareth, the brother he loved best. He says he'll hound and harry you until one of you has killed the other."

Sir Lancelot sighs. "Tell King Arthur," he says, "that eight days hence I will bring Queen Guinevere to him."

Queen Guinevere and Sir Lancelot ride their horses into the great courtyard at Carlisle, where Guinevere was tied to the stake and scorching flames lapped around her ankles.

One hundred knights and twenty-four ladies follow them, each holding an olive branch. They're all wearing green velvet and gold chains, and so are their horses, right down to their fetlocks. But the queen and Sir Lancelot are both dressed in cloth of gold.

Sir Lancelot and the queen dismount. He takes her right arm, and they walk up to the king.

Arthur-in-the-stone glares at them. He doesn't move. Not one muscle. He says nothing.

"My king," Sir Lancelot says loudly, "as the Pope requires and as you command me, I've brought back your queen. Queen Guinevere is loyal. But you've listened to libelers and slanderers; you've believed jealous liars. It's they who are disloyal, not your queen. Not I."

"You're a traitor!" Sir Gawain shouts.

"Where is Sir Mordred?" Sir Lancelot demands.

"Away!" replies Sir Gawain. "At Camelot."

"The only survivor," Sir Lancelot says. "If God were not on my side, how could I have fought fourteen armed knights?"

"Sir Lancelot," says the king. "You have been my knight of knights. I've always praised you and honored you. I've given you no cause, no reason whatsoever, to do as you have done."

Sir Lancelot turns to Sir Gawain. "The king well knows how I've served him," he tells him, "and you should remember it too. You should remember our close friendship. If I had your good will, I would have his as well."

"The king can do as he likes," Sir Gawain says. "You and I will never make peace. You have killed three of my brothers, and my two sons."

"I loved Gareth and he loved me," Sir Lancelot says, shaking his head. "I knighted him: He was noble and courteous. But he was unarmed. Gaheris and Florence and Lovel were unarmed. I never meant to kill them."

Sir Gawain says nothing.

The king says nothing.

"Even so," Sir Lancelot tells the king and Sir Gawain, "I'll do penance. I'll walk barefoot from Sandwich to Carlisle, and each ten miles I'll found a friary or a convent where monks and nuns pray for Sir Gareth and Sir Gaheris and your sons. I will have them built, and fund them."

Still King Arthur and Sir Gawain say nothing.

"Surely this will be a better memorial than conflict between us," says Sir Lancelot.

The cheeks of many of the knights and ladies in the courtyard are glistening.

"I've heard you, and all your offers," Sir Gawain replies, "and I've heard enough. The king will do as he wishes, but I'll never forgive you for killing Sir Gareth. If the king forgives you, I'll leave court. I'll no longer serve him."

"Gawain . . . ," Sir Lancelot begins.

"No!" says Sir Gawain. "The time for words is past. You have safe conduct here, but you must leave England within fifteen days. You must go to your estates in France. You've betrayed the king; you've betrayed me. Fifteen days, and then I will come after you."

"I wish I had never come to the court of King Arthur," Sir Lancelot says, "if I'm now to be banished — in disgrace. But the Wheel of Fortune that raises us also hurls us down." Sir Lancelot steps towards the king. "I have been your knight of knights," he says. "Not least because of me our Round Table has been honored and feared throughout this middle-earth."

"There'll be nowhere for you to hide," Sir Gawain says.

"Hide?" retorts Sir Lancelot. "I'll be waiting for you in France."

"Enough!" growls Sir Gawain. "Set the queen free! Leave this court!"

Sir Lancelot turns to face Queen Guinevere, and she turns to him. I can see her chestnut eyes. The little yellow flecks in them. The quills of her eyebrows. Proud and unblinking, she returns her knight's gaze.

"My lady," Sir Lancelot says so that everyone can hear. "Now I must leave you and this fine fellowship forever." He comes close to the queen and lowers his voice. "Pray for me. Speak well of me. And if any false tongues threaten you, send for me at once. I'll rescue you."

Sir Lancelot kisses the queen.

Her eyes are brimming now. She clutches his right wrist. She mouths words for him alone.

Sir Lancelot lifts his voice again. "Is there anyone here who accuses the queen of being untrue to King Arthur? Let's see who dares speak."

No one speaks.

Sir Lancelot takes Queen Guinevere's right arm and ushers her towards her king. He inclines his head; he turns away.

The king is weeping. Everyone in the courtyard is in tears. Everyone except Sir Gawain.

76 the pope's letter

THREE OF THE FRENCH ENVOYS WHO WENT TO SEE the Pope to explain why we laid siege to Zara have returned safely. But the fourth, Robert de Boves, broke his oath. He disappeared in Venice, and went aboard a merchant ship and sailed for Syria.

At midday all the church bells in Zara began to ring, and criers walked through the city announcing that the Holy Father greets each of us, and well understands we only laid siege to Zara to hold our great army together. He lifts his sentence of excommunication and absolves us all.

Everyone was so joyful. The same French and Venetians who tried to kill each other embraced and wept. People cheered. The streets bubbled.

But what the criers were shouting out wasn't true! Not even almost true. Lord Stephen has told me on the strict understanding that I don't tell anyone else.

"Milon has shown me the Holy Father's letter," Lord Stephen said grimly. "Firstly, the Pope says he can scarcely believe his ears. How can we have attacked a Christian city with crucifixes hanging from the walls? He accepts, however, that we did so with great reluctance and only because it was the lesser of two evils."

"That's true, isn't it?" I asked. "Otherwise, the Doge would have stopped us from using his ships."

"But the Holy Father is angry that the Doge and his councillors have not asked for his forgiveness."

"In Saint Mark's," I said, "the Doge told us it was his right to recapture Zara."

"The Pope says he has no wish at all to damage our crusade and so he will absolve us —"

"God be praised!" I cried.

"— subject to certain conditions and undertakings," Lord Stephen continued. "But he will not absolve the Venetians."

"But that's not what the criers said," I exclaimed.

"No," Lord Stephen replied. "Not only have our leaders chosen to suppress the Pope's letter. They've invented a new one."

"But why?"

"Fear, I suppose. If people knew the truth, they'd be even more discontent. This gives them hope. But there's another thing," Lord Stephen told me. "In his letter, the Holy Father also said he had received a letter from the Emperor in Constantinople, and he strictly warns the crusaders against becoming involved. He knows we'll need supplies and has written to the Emperor requiring him in the name of Christ to provide them for us."

"What's going to happen?" I asked.

"Heaven knows!" Lord Stephen replied. "The envoys have been waiting for more than three weeks, and we still haven't made up our minds. Why should our leaders bother to heed the Pope's warning, unless it happens to suit them? They've ignored his letter about the siege of Zara."

"It's all so muddy," I said.

"It is," Lord Stephen replied. "Each day that passes, this crusade is getting into deeper water."

In the blue hour, Lord Stephen and I walked along the walls, and he began to talk about Holt again. The peacocks. And Wilf clutching and catching the harvest ewe, and falling over backwards. And whether he should have brought in more men from Wigmore to protect the castle while we are away.

I didn't say much at all. I don't think he really wanted me to. He just wanted my company.

But then Lord Stephen turned to me and asked me what I thought I'd learned from him. . . .

He's more thoughtful, more troubled than he was on Saint Nicholas. He keeps looking back.

BYZANTINE EYES

OU CAN'T TELL WHAT PEOPLE ARE LIKE BY LOOKING AT their noses or their ears. Or what they're feeling by looking at their hands. But when you look into their eyes . . .

Bertie's eyes, darting and daring, and Ygerna's eyes, patient and gazing; Queen Guinevere's, burning, freezing; Tom's, easy and friendly and amused; Sir William's eyes, one bloodshot, one glittering.

I can see that long line of Zarans straggling out through the Land Gate, leaving their homes, and the boy Godard caught, and that woman the Flemish louts assaulted in the forum, and the five Saracens — before their eyes became flames of fire.

I think eyes tell the weather of the spirit.

In the churches here, there are small paintings called icons, and in them Mary and Jesus and the saints and martyrs and patriarchs and virgins all have much larger eyes than in paintings in England or France:

> dark almonds lit with inner light,
> doe-wide, sometimes wistful,
> watchful and designing,
> full of longings and long-suffering,
> darkling, somehow smudged,

old-young and see-in-the-dark,
secretive, inward.

Byzantine eyes! They're mysterious. Look into them, down deep, and you begin to wonder whether you can understand them at all.

COMBAT

"I TOO HAVE MY ALPHABET OF KNIGHTS," SAYS SIR LANCELOT.

He looks to left and right at all the men gathered in the hall.

"Earl Armagnac, Sir Bors, Sir Blamore and Sir Bleoberis, Sir Clegis and Sir Clarrus, Sir Dinas, Earl Estrake, Earl Foix, Sir Galihodin and Sir Galahantine . . . From my heart, I thank you all for your loyalty, and for sailing with me to France."

Many of the knights tap the tops of the long tables or slap their thighs as a sign of their support.

"You've heard how King Arthur and Sir Gawain set sail from Cardiff and landed here in Beaune with sixty thousand men," Sir Lancelot says. "You've heard how the king has appointed Sir Mordred as Regent of England in his absence, and put Queen Guinevere in his care."

"He will regret that," says Sir Bors.

"Now today I've been told the king and Sir Gawain have set fire to seven of my manor houses, and burned them to the ground. What are we to do?"

"The longer we delay, the worse things will become," Sir Bors replies at once.

"This is what I think," Sir Lionel says. "All our towns have strong walls. Let's have all our country people shelter inside them and wait until the king's men grow hungry and impatient and start to blow on their fingertips. Then we'll fall on them like wolves on a flock of sheep."

"In the name of Christ," says Sir Bors, "let's get amongst them."

"I'm loath to do that," Sir Lancelot replies. "They are Christians, and I will not willingly shed Christian blood. War is always evil; it should always be the last resort. I'll send a messenger to my king."

War is always evil. . . .

Cardinal Capuano said, "War is violent, war is cruel, war is bloody, but it is natural. It is natural, and peace is unnatural."

"What," demands Sir Gawain, "do you propose to do?"

"I cannot think any man has ever been so restrained, so considerate, so honorable," the king replies quietly.

"Have you come all this way to turn back now? Do that, and everyone on earth will say you're weak. Weak or unwise."

Arthur-in-the-stone nods. His eyes are wounds. "I will follow your advice," he says. "I will not make peace with Sir Lancelot. You speak to the messenger; I cannot force my tongue to say the words."

At once Sir Gawain strides over to the messenger.

"Tell Sir Lancelot it's a waste of time to send offers to my uncle and he's left it too late to make peace. And tell him I, Sir Gawain, will not rest now until I've slain him, or he has slain me."

Sir Gawain is at the town gate, mounted on Kincaled, fully armed and holding a huge lance.

Sir Lancelot is standing high above him, on the wall, with many of his knights.

"Can you hear me, you traitor?" Sir Gawain shouts. "Why are you hiding like a rabbit in its burrow? For day after day, I've fought one of your men. I've wounded Sir Bors. I've wounded Sir Lionel. Are you afraid of me?"

All around him, Sir Lancelot hears voices.

"Sir Lancelot! Now! . . . He's mad with fury. . . . Stop his mouth with mud. . . . Defend your honor. . . ."

"Come down, you traitor!" Sir Gawain shouts. "Pay with your blood for killing my brothers!"

Now King Arthur trots up alongside Sir Gawain.

"My king!" Sir Lancelot calls down. "My king! I could have fought you long since. For six months I've been patient. But now Sir Gawain is accusing me of treason. I've no wish to fight you, but he keeps goading me like a beast at bay."

"Babble!" Sir Gawain shouts. "If you dare fight me, come down now."

I can see Sir Lancelot and many of his men riding through the town gate. Sir Lancelot and Sir Gawain say nothing. Side by side they lead the way to a common not far outside the walls, and trot to opposite ends of it.

They couch their lances. They raise their shields. They shout and spur their horses, and loosen their reins.

Their armor rattles; leather groans and creaks; the hooves of the horses pound the ground.

These two men the king loves more than any others. These men who once were dearest friends.

Sir Lancelot and Sir Gawain both drive their lances into the middle of the other's shield. They draw their swords. They land such heavy blows that the legs of their horses give way, and they collapse.

Each hour before noon, Sir Gawain grows as strong as a giant, and Sir Lancelot can do nothing but shield himself. Sir Gawain slices his shield into pieces; he cuts notches in Sir Lancelot's sword until it's as jagged as Bertie's teeth, and dents his helmet and bruises his brains. . . .

But at noon Sir Gawain's strength begins to ebb. He's no more than himself again.

"Now!" gasps Sir Lancelot. "Now it's my turn."

At once Sir Lancelot gives Sir Gawain such a swipe on the side of his head that he reels sideways and falls over. Blood streams over his face. Sir Lancelot stands motionless.

"Kill me and have done with it!" pants Sir Gawain. "You traitor! If you spare me, I'll fight you again."

"You're wounded," Sir Lancelot replies. "I'll never kill a man who cannot defend himself."

Slowly he turns away from Sir Gawain and stumbles towards his horse.

Sir Gawain wipes the blood from his eyes. He tries to get to his feet. . . .

Sir Gawain is at the town gate again, mounted on Kincaled, fully armed and holding a huge lance.

"Can you hear me, you traitor?" he shouts. "I am Sir Gawain. Come out! Come and fight!"

"Jesus help me if ever I'm at your mercy as you were at mine," Sir Lancelot calls down. "That would be the end of me."

Sir Lancelot and Sir Gawain ride towards one another in a roll of thunder.

Sir Gawain's lance shatters into one hundred pieces, but Sir Lancelot hits the middle of the shield with such force that Kincaled rears up and throws Sir Gawain.

Sir Gawain jumps back to avoid Kincaled, and draws his sword eagerly.

"Dismount!" he yells. "My mare may have failed me, but this son of a king and queen will not fail you."

Again, Sir Gawain grows as strong as a giant. Sir Lancelot weaves and crouches and ducks and leans sideways and backwards. He saves his wind; he saves his skin. And each time he fends off a stroke, Sir Gawain becomes a little more discouraged.

"It's noon!" shouts Sir Lancelot. "You are strong, Sir Gawain. But you've done your best, and now I'll do mine."

Sir Lancelot's sword pricks and caresses Sir Gawain's armor. It whispers to it. It shaves and slices it. Sir Gawain does all he can to guard himself, but now Sir Lancelot whirls his sword and smacks Sir Gawain on the side of his head, right on the place where he was wounded before.

Sir Gawain's knees buckle and look in opposite directions. He staggers and sinks to the ground, unconscious. When at last he opens his eyes again, and blinks the blood out of them, he sees Sir Lancelot standing right over him.

"You traitor!" Sir Gawain mumbles. "You haven't killed me yet. Come on! Have done with it."

"I'll fight you when you're able to stand on your feet, and your wound has healed," Sir Lancelot replies, "but I'll never strike a man who is already wounded. God save me from such shame. There are ways a knight may fight, and ways he must never fight."

Slowly Sir Lancelot turns away and stumbles towards his horse.

"You traitor!" Sir Gawain calls after him. "As soon as I can, I'll fight you again. I will never rest until one of us lies slain."

Deserters

HE FRENCH FOOT SOLDIERS MAY BELIEVE THE POPE has lifted his sentence of excommunication, but they're still discontent: They're complaining half the food supplied by the Venetians has gone rotten, and they object to hanging around here for another ten weeks.

But worse, some of them have actually deserted. Simona bundled into the tower-house this morning and told us that in the middle of the night a number of men from Poitiers — enough to subdue the crew — crept aboard a Venetian galley and untied her moorings.

There was nothing the crew could do because they were outnumbered and unarmed, and although some Venetians onshore were woken by the shouting, there was nothing they could do either. They stood on the quay and watched the dark shape drifting down the channel, and listened to the Frenchmen yelling, "Row! Row, damn you! Row or drown!"

Three Venetian sailors did end up in the water, and they couldn't swim. No one knows whether they were pushed, or tripped in the dark, or jumped and hoped someone would rescue them.

Simona says there may have been as many as one hundred Poitevins. But where will they go? Will they ever get there? In any case, they've got away. And one of our ships is gone.

The news about the deserters has troubled us all. Lord Stephen keeps blinking and clucking and Turold is leathery and Rhys is restless and Serle's in a temper.

"Poitevins!" Sir William proclaimed. "Cowards from the cradle! This crusade's got a curse on it."

I keep thinking our tower is about to topple. Before long, there's going to be a storm.

half a horse blanket

80

I WENT TO SEE SISTER CIKA THIS AFTERNOON, AND WE SAT IN the spirit-garden, and she said I look less like a scarecrow than a month ago, and quite handsome considering I'm English, and the only true strength is inner strength. . . . She is witty, sometimes, and very calm, and visiting the nunnery is the only good thing that has happened today.

Downstairs, everyone is still so irritable and argumentative. That's why I asked Lord Stephen to excuse me after supper. At least I can write up here in my room.

Not long before we ate, Bertie came round for the first time since he was arrow-shot.

"Milon says you'll want to know what's been decided," he began. "This afternoon, the French leaders and Marquis Boniface and the Doge accepted the offer of Prince Alexius Angelus and — "

"The fools!" shouted Sir William. "Disastrous!" And he hurled his beaker of wine at the wall.

"Milon says if you break your fast with us — "

"I'll break his head," snarled Sir William. "What's wrong with them all?"

Long after Bertie had left, Sir William went on cursing and complaining, and Lord Stephen told Serle that if we have to go to Constantinople, he didn't see how we could get home for at least three more years, and Rhys reported there's something wrong with all our horses, and one moment they're restless, the next listless. . . .

At supper we began to talk about Holt, and Rhys told us he wondered whether after three years he'd have anything to come back to.

"Why ever not?" Lord Stephen asked.

"Like that story," Rhys said, "about the man who gave his son his croft and strip of land, and then his son threw him out with nothing but half a horse blanket."

"He threw out his own father?" exclaimed Serle.

"My son's got my cottage and croft," said Rhys.

"Disgraceful!" snorted Sir William. "You stablemen and cowherds, you're bloody animals!" He slurped down a whole beaker of wine, and turned to me. "Well, I'm not leaving anything to chance," he announced loudly. "You needn't think you or Tom are getting anything from me. I'm not giving you a penny or an acre before I die. . . ."

BLOOD=BLADE

I HEARD SHOUTING IN THE HALL.

I dropped my quill and picked up my candle and ran down. My soles slapped the stone steps.

Just before I reached the gallery there was a huge thump, then a crash.

The refectory table was lying on its side, and Sir William and Lord Stephen were facing one another across it. Jugs and beakers and spoons and knives were lying on the floor, and red wine was oozing across the stone slabs.

My father was sodden with wine, blind with anger.

"You worm!" he bawled. "You lump of filth! How dare you? Behind my back."

Lord Stephen didn't reply, but Sir William's anger was fueling itself.

"She's worthless! Just a Welsh drudge. You grub! You meddlesome dwarf! What's it got to do with you? Or Arthur?"

My father kicked at a broken jug and advanced to the near end of the table. I could see his right eye glittering. Then he saw me.

"Talk of the devil!" he snapped, and he lurched towards me, waving. "When people start digging," he said, and his voice grew cold as steel, "they may find their own bones. Isn't that what I told you, Arthur? Their own bones."

My father belched, then he turned towards Lord Stephen again, and spat in his face. "Black bubbles!" he muttered.

Lord Stephen drew himself up a little. "No, Sir William," he said. His voice was quiet and firm. "Not their own bones. The bones of a dead man."

Sir William growled.

"I believe you threatened Arthur's mother. You forced her to bed with you, then you murdered her husband."

My father drew his knife from his belt.

I clenched my fists.

My father stepped forward.

"No!" I yelled. "No!"

Sir William lumbered towards Lord Stephen and pulled back his right arm.

Lord Stephen just stood there, blinking. "Dear God!" he said in a surprised voice. He didn't even move.

I leaped down from the gallery.

I was too late.

Sir William stabbed him. I think he aimed for Lord Stephen's heart, but the blade went into his left shoulder, right up to the hilt, and then Sir William drew it out, dripping.

For a moment Lord Stephen still stood upright. Then he turned whey-pale and toppled backwards. His head cracked against the stone floor.

I threw myself at my father, howling. I grabbed him from behind and wrapped my arms around him.

We wrestled.

With my left hand I seized his right wrist. I squeezed it.

He bit my knuckle.

I tried to make him drop the knife. I could hear myself gasping.

"You bastard!" he panted. "You runt! I'll have you too."

I squeezed, I squeezed. He filled his lungs with air. His whole body expanded and he heaven-bellowed. He roared.

My father leaned back, grunting. I still had his right wrist. He wrenched himself forward, and almost threw me over his head.

He reeled. He fell. He'll always be falling . . .

My father fell forward and I fell with him, still clutching his wrist; the stone floor smacked against his arm, and crushed it, and he drove his blood-blade deep into his body.

He buried the knife in his own heart.

a little we die

82

I DIDN'T KILL HIM.

But I keep feeling as if I did. I hated him and once wrote that I wished he were dead.

But he was my father. I am his son.

I rushed to find Milon, and he came with me immediately.

Milon closed my father's eyes and made the sign of the cross over him. "May God welcome him!" he said hoarsely.

Then Milon told me to fetch Taddeo, the Doge's surgeon, as quickly as I could. I did, and by then Rhys and Turold had returned, and they carried my father down to the undercroft to prepare his body for burial. Taddeo bled Lord Stephen at once, and I sat beside him all night in his small chamber. I thought. I prayed. Sometimes I held his hand. I listened to his breathing. I didn't sleep at all.

Serle didn't come back until early this morning. He had been with Simona.

He found me with Lord Stephen and I told him what had happened. Serle looked stunned, and afraid, and he got onto his knees.

"I've been here all night," I said.

"You get some rest," he said. "I'll take over."

I couldn't rest, though. I walked out, and as soon as I knocked on the ribbed door, Sister Cika was there, and she led me at once to the spirit-garden.

"I was expecting you," she said. "Is it your father?"

My heart began to hammer.

"How did you know?" I asked.

"Things you've said and have not said," replied Sister Cika. "Your eyes! By thinking, by looking, by — how do you say it? — intuition. There are many ways of knowing."

She put both my hands between hers.

I began to sob then. Hot tears streamed down my cheeks. They kept dripping into my lap. I told her everything.

"Let them flow!" Sister Cika said warmly. "Wash away your pain, and your grief."

We sat side by side for a long time.

I remember the nunnery doves singing their sweet, gulping songs.

"If I hadn't tried to find my mother," I said, "Lord Stephen would never have become involved. And if I hadn't gone up to my room . . ."

"No," said Sister Cika. "You've done nothing wrong."

"But I held his wrist."

Somehow Sister Cika knew what I was thinking. "It's not your fault," she told me.

"He was my father, but he didn't care about me. He wanted to kill me."

"But you were one blood," Sister Cika said gently. "Who can see his father die and not die a little?"

"It's Lord Stephen who feels like my father," I said. "I feel so lost."

Sister Cika squeezed my hand softly. "Arthur," she said, "you care and think and feel, you are awake to the world; and the more awake we are, the more we hurt when those we love lie ill, or leave us. This is how God's children are. But He never allows us to hurt more than we can bear."

Around us, the almond-blossom blinked and fluttered.

"I will pray for Lord Stephen. All will be well and all manner of things will be well," said Sister Cika, almost as if she were bidding me farewell. "Take my words on your way. Living we die, but dying we live, Arthur."

Sister Cika half-smiled at me, and she lifted her eyes.

When I got back to our tower-house, I found Taddeo bleeding Lord Stephen again to balance his fluids. He says he can do nothing more for him.

His knife wound is a clean one, but the lump where he cracked his skull is as large as my kneecap, and still oozing puce and purple. I have shaved the hair on the back of his head and am to apply a marjoram poultice twice each day. He has been asleep now for three days, and that's even longer than Bertie.

Lord Stephen. He is my almost-father. My heart will break if he dies.

Hundreds and Hundreds of Miles

NO, GOD DID NOT WELCOME MY FATHER.

Heaven spat into his grave, and a fierce wind blew from the northeast. It ripped off my rabbitskin cap, and skipped it across the graveyard, and I only just caught it before it rolled into the water.

We buried him right next to the grave Bertie and I dug for Giscard, the miner from Provins. I squeezed a clod of gritty earth in my left hand, and crumbled it, and trickled it into the grave. We all did. The earth whispered, it chuckled.

I didn't feel anything. Not sad, like I was when we buried little Luke. Not relieved. I mean, I just felt numb. I still do. I know I should care. Perhaps I will later.

After the burial, Serle embraced me and so did Simona and Gennaro and Bertie. Turold clasped my hands, and a number of Milon's knights and men bowed to me and expressed their sympathies. Not Wido and Giff and Godard, though — they weren't there, and Rhys was sitting with Lord Stephen. Then Milon grasped my right elbow, and led me out of the graveyard; we walked back through the Land Gate, and climbed up onto the walls.

The wind was pulling the clouds to pieces. They looked like wool before it has been carded.

"This is where I used to come with Lord Stephen," I said.

"Quite often. He told me that one of God's greatest gifts to us is memory. Because it can console us."

"You are a knight," Milon began. "My knight."

"Yes, sir."

"And a good young knight."

"I don't think I am."

"Very good," Milon said. He tapped his head and then his heart. "I watch you. You hope; you care . . ."

"Too much, sometimes," I said.

"And you bravee," said Milon. "You save Bertie. And in Soissons . . ." Milon tapped my arm. "You are a knight," he repeated, "but you still have duties to Lord Stephen. Yes?"

"Oh yes!" I said.

"He will not fight no more."

"What do you mean?" The nape of my neck tingled.

"He will not fight no more. Maybe not stand up no more."

"No!" I said. "That's not right. I'm sure it's not."

Milon said nothing.

"I've been sitting beside him the whole time, almost. Yesterday he moved his lips. He's starting to suck water from a sponge. And his eyelids flickered. They didn't before."

Milon laid a hand on my left shoulder. "Maybe he die," he said in a firm, warm voice.

"No!" I said. "He won't. I'm sure he won't."

"Maybe he live," said Milon. "But he will not heal for a long time." He paused. "Your duty to Lord Stephen is to help him . . . home."

"Home!"

Milon looked at me.

"But I can't! How can I? I've taken the Cross. I can't break my vow."

For a while Milon waited. The wind was driving all the cloud-shreds out to sea. He rubbed his nose.

"This crusade is bad and worse," he said, and he sucked his right forefinger and held it up.

"But if we go home we'll never see the Holy Land. Sir William has wrecked our dream of journeying to Jerusalem."

Milon blew on his forefinger. "Jerusalem and Saracens? No! Constantinople and Christians? Yes! *Désastre!*"

"That's what Sir William thought."

"What is your dream, you?" Milon asked me. "To be young crusader knight? To fight? Or lead your people in your own manor?"

"Well . . . ," I said. "Both!"

Milon shook his head and smiled. "Which more difficult?" he said. "Not easy for you. Not easy for me without you! But I tell you, your duty is to care for Lord Stephen. You go home. Lord Stephen's wife . . . Lady Judith. Good woman. Strong woman."

"Yes," I said.

"You explain her. And Sir William's wife . . ."

"Lady Alice."

"Yes, you talk to her." Milon shook his head. "No way is easy way. But now you find Mair, your mother, yes?"

I drew in my breath. "You did know about her," I said. "That's why you had that ring engraved on my sword."

Milon smiled. "Lord Stephen," he said. "He told me secret."

“It’s all because he helped me,” I began miserably, “because he tried to . . .”

For a while we sat on the wall, and questions began to race and chase each other in my head.

Alone? How? How do I find a boat to take us back across the Adriatic? And there’ll still be snow in the Alps, won’t there? In March? How long will I have to wait before we can cross them? I know Lord Stephen’s going to get better, but what if he gets worse? If he dies . . . What are all the other questions I haven’t thought of?

Milon smiled and nodded. He said of course I couldn’t take Lord Stephen on my own.

“Rhys and Turold are Lord Stephen’s men,” he said. “They go with you. Not good for me, but . . .” Milon shrugged.

“Thank you,” I said.

“And Simona,” Milon added. “Crusade bad for Simona. She go to Venice with you.”

“Does she know?” I asked.

“Gennaro tell her now.”

“What about Serle?”

“Serle? He come with me.”

“But he and Simona . . .”

Milon shrugged again. “Love-sorrows,” he said. “Many as seashells.”

After this, Milon told me that a merchant galley from Split docked here only last night and if the bora has blown itself out by then, she’ll leave the day after tomorrow morning, and make a run straight across the Adriatic to Venice. “No pirates in winter,” Milon informed me.

"But that's too soon," I said. "I can't get ready by then."

"Must," said Milon curtly.

"But I can't. Packing everything. I've got to talk to Serle and Bertie. And what about Bonamy? Rhys and I will both have to exercise him tomorrow, before such a long sea journey."

"No horse on merchant ship," Milon said slowly, not taking his eyes off me for a moment.

"What do you mean?"

Milon shook his head.

"But I must take Bonamy!" I cried. "I must!"

"Horse transports take horses," Milon said, "not merchant galleys. No horse transports now to Venice."

"I'll ride there, then," I said fiercely. But even as I said it, I saw how impossible that would be.

"You, Turold, and Rhys buy horses in Venice," Milon said. "I give you money, much money. Money to go home."

"Poor Bonamy!" I cried.

But really, I meant poor me.

"Simona help you in Venice," Milon said. "After crusade, Bertie and I come to England. Yes?"

"Yes, sir."

It all seems so far away.

Milon punched me lightly on my chest. "We bring Bonamy," he said.

I sniffed.

"Bertie . . .," I began, "he's so . . ."

"I know," Milon said warily. "My sister's son."

"Sir, please take care of him."

"You, Arthur. You take care Lord Stephen."

"I will. I will," I said.

I've sailed hundreds and hundreds of miles in my head and my heart today. In different directions.

Down into the dark earth with my father, Sir William de Gortanore.

And now this. This long journey . . .

Nothing Lasts

84

THE BORA RAN OUT OF BREATH YESTERDAY, AND THEN the warm sirocco began to blow from the southeast, and the captain was in a great hurry to set sail. We had to come aboard last night so we could leave at dawn. Everything has happened so quickly.

Yesterday morning I got more marjoram and linseed and wormwood from the surgeon, and then I ran down to the nunnery to see Sister Cika one more time. I knocked loudly on the ribbed door, but no one answered it; perhaps they were all at Terce. After that, it took me quite some time to find Bertie. He wasn't in Milon's house or exercising his horse, and in the end I found him in my own tower room, just staring out of the window.

"I've been looking for you everywhere," I said.

Bertie punched the wall.

"That's how I feel too," I said. "Angry and worse than that."

"Tell Milon you're going to stay."

"I can't!" I exclaimed. "I must take care of Lord Stephen. Milon's right. I must get him home."

"But . . ."

"I know."

"Nothing lasts," said Bertie. "When those German sausages gave me a chin-pie, and we went to the *campo* together and met the

Saracens, and I told you I was a leucrota, and when the arrow got me and you saved me . . ."

"I know," I said.

Bertie shook his head furiously.

"I'll miss you too," I said. "You make me laugh. And worry."

"Why?"

"Why do you think?"

Bertie screwed up his face.

"Don't be such a miserable wood louse," I said. "And don't believe everything other people tell you."

Bertie and I caught one another's eyes, and the next thing was we were embracing each other.

"At least you've completely recovered," I said huskily. "Milon has promised he'll come to England, and he says he'll bring you."

"And Bonamy."

"You'd better!" I said. "Bertrand de Sully!"

I heard someone calling me, so Bertie and I raced each other down the steps, and he won.

Serle was standing at the bottom. "That's where you are!" he said. "I'm going to exercise Shortneck. Do you want to come?"

"Of course!" I said.

Bertie and I embraced each other again, and he ran across the hall.

All at once, I remembered my Saracen-fish dream, and our galleys sinking; I remembered Bertie laughing and rolling over and over and diving away into the dark. And I knew I'd never see him again.

Give them hope

ONCE WE WERE OUTSIDE THE WALLS, SERLE AND I rode Shortneck and Bonamy hard. We must have galloped for at least two miles, and then we reined in.

I rubbed Bonamy's fiery neck. "Rhys made up a song about the color of horse coats once," I said.

Serle answered my feelings, not my words.

"I'll look after him," he said. "I'll do my best."

"Do you want to send Sir John and Lady Helen a letter?" I asked.

"You know I can't write."

"I'll write it for you."

"What shall I say?"

"What do you want to say?"

"I don't know," said Serle. "What they want to hear."

"Say three things, then. About you."

"About me. I am well. I am healthy. Say that."

"Three special things, I mean. How you saved a Venetian girl from angry sailors . . . I don't know. About Zara. How when you close your eyes you see Caldicot and the winter wheat growing . . ."

Serle shook his head. "You're better at words than I am."

My mouth went dry. "Or about Sir William," I said slowly. "Something. He was your uncle. Sir John's brother."

“You must feel terrible,” said Serle.

“I do,” I replied in a low voice.

“What you did.”

“You’re not saying — ”

“I’m not saying anything,” said Serle in his thin, cutting voice. “Why? Should I?”

“If you’d been there and not with Simona,” I exclaimed, “it wouldn’t have happened.”

“I see!” said Serle. “You’re passing the blame.”

“I didn’t kill him!” I cried. “You know I didn’t! He wanted to kill me.”

When I lived at Caldicot, Serle was always so unfair, and he’s still mean and insinuating sometimes.

For a while we drew apart. I trotted Bonamy and buried my face in his warm neck. Then we began to talk again.

“You and Simona.”

“What about it?” Serle bit his upper lip. He made it bleed.

“I won’t tell Tanwen,” I said. “I’ll tell her you talked about her and Kester, and often think about her.”

Serle gave me an odd look — suspicious and grateful at the same time.

“I do,” he said forlornly. “I wanted to ask you something.”

“What?”

“That rag doll. The one with the dark eyes. Can I give it to Kester?”

I lowered my eyes, then I slowly shook my head. “She’s too sad,” I said.

When we got back to the undercroft and dismounted, Serle said, "You'll know what to tell them. My mother and father. Everyone. Greet them all in God. Give them — "

"What?"

Serle shook his head unhappily.

"Hope?"

"Yes. Give them hope."

"I will," I said.

"And this," said Serle, twisting and twisting one of the shiny brass buttons decorating Shortneck's bridle until it came off. "Give this to Kester!"

"I will!"

"If I don't come back . . . you know . . . can you watch over him?"

I smiled. I wanted to cry. I embraced Serle. I know Milon will welcome him, but it will be difficult for him here without Lord Stephen or Sir William or any of us. To begin with, anyhow.

"Say a prayer for me," I told him. "In Jerusalem. God bring you back home!"

When Serle left me alone with Bonamy, I couldn't help myself — I began to sob. And through my tears, I could see Bonamy frowning and flicking his eyelashes; then he gently nuzzled me.

"Oh Bonamy!" I sobbed. "Bonamy!"

I wanted to tell him everything: how I'd chosen him, and trained him, and trusted him, and relied on him, and loved him.

My thoughts and feelings about people are sometimes so complicated. My love for Bonamy is so simple. So blessed.

I threw my arms round his neck.

Alive!

HERE AM I?” MURMURED LORD STEPHEN.

“On a boat, sir.”

“I thought so.”

He didn’t seem surprised; he just accepted it.

After a while, he said, “You’re smiling.”

“Because you’re alive. Hearing your voice.”

Lord Stephen yawned.

I held the water sponge to his lips. “Suck this!” I said.

“On a boat,” Lord Stephen said, and he yawned again.

“I’ll explain. Let me heat some pottage first. You haven’t eaten anything for five days.”

Lord Stephen just looked up at me. His eyes were misty.

“You were wounded,” I said. “I’m taking you home.”

He frowned slightly, as if he were trying to work out what my words meant, and then he yawned for a third time. “Peacocks,” he said. He closed his purple eyelids and drifted into sleep.

Rhys and Turold are both asleep on a pile of Persian carpets. Simona’s sitting on the steps that lead up to the deck, and she keeps dabbing her eyes. . . .

We’re both so raw, with all our good-byes. We’ll talk tomorrow.

Early this morning, the sun rose right behind Zara. It dazzled me, and I couldn’t make out any of the towers or spires.

Slowly the city shrank.

Across the water, nothing but a dark tear.

BY FAIR MEANS OR FOUL

MY STONE, IT IS MY FIXED NORTHERN STAR. EVEN when it shows me suffering and sorrow, it still eases me.

I can see Sir Mordred, Regent of England, standing on a dais, and in front of him are hundreds of knights, all wearing surcoats stitched with their shields. Dukes and earls and lords and knights. All the great men of the land.

Sir Mordred holds up a sheet of parchment. He waves it.

"My lords," he says, and he clears his throat. "This letter comes from Sir Gawain." Sir Mordred crosses himself. "King Arthur is dead!" he calls out in a loud voice. "Your king is dead."

For a moment, there's silence — the silence of disbelief — and then huge commotion in the hall.

"May God preserve his soul," Sir Mordred calls out, but only the knights standing nearest to him can hear him. "He has been killed in battle by Sir Lancelot."

The way thunder claps and heaven shakes, and the sound rolls round the sky's rim: That's how it is in the hall.

Sir Mordred waits, head bowed.

"He was my father," he calls out, and his voice is level and somber. "I am his son." He pauses. "His time came; his time has gone. For as long as he lived, he led us by serving us and served us by leading us. May God save his soul!"

Around Sir Mordred, men begin to call out.

"The king is dead! Long live the king!"

"Mordred!"

"Crown Mordred!"

"Vivat!"

"May Christ the Lord guide you!"

"Mordred the king!"

How can King Arthur be dead? If it were true, my seeing stone would have shown me. And how can they think Mordred would be a just king?

Now I can see Sir Mordred and Queen Guinevere at Winchester. Her silk dress is black, threaded with spears of silver.

This man who hates Sir Lancelot, her own husband's scheming son: Guinevere can scarcely bear to look at him.

"I won't mince my words," Sir Mordred says. "For the good of this kingdom, you and I must be of one mind. One heart . . . and one body."

The queen stiffens. She is very still.

"I desire you. . . . For the good of this kingdom, I will marry you."

His father's wife.

The queen raises her eyes and looks her stepson full in the face. "You are right," she says. "Quite right! I lament the death of the king. I lament the cause of it."

"You are wise," says Sir Mordred. His voice is like a newly sharpened knife.

"If we are to marry," the queen says, "I must go to London. I must buy samite. I must talk to my dressmakers. My jewelers. A hundred things."

Sir Mordred nods slightly.

"And linen. Cornflower blue," says Guinevere eagerly. "A new beginning!"

"Let us fix a day," says Sir Mordred.

Now I understand!

Now I see why Queen Guinevere told Sir Mordred he was right.

She didn't dare tell him otherwise. She wanted to win his trust, win time, escape . . . anywhere.

No. Not anywhere. The Tower of London. I recognize it.

Sir Mordred is standing outside the walls, and speaking to the captains of his tormenta, his ballistae and petraries and mangonels.

"I don't care what you throw at them," he yells. "Throw everything! Dead dogs, boulders, buckets of dung, sodden logs, river mud, rotten fish, scraps of metal, paving-stones. Flatten these walls!"

A knight stands in one of the towers, and Sir Mordred's men howl at him. They're a parliament of black dogs and mongrels and curs.

"Queen Guinevere says this," the knight calls down. "She will kill herself. Rather than marry Sir Mordred, she will plunge a knife into her own heart."

Sir Mordred's dog-knights growl and bay and bark and howl.

Now I can see the old archbishop — the man who crowned King Arthur at Canterbury — with his golden staff and three priests.

"How dare you?" the archbishop demands. "How dare you pretend King Arthur is dead? You concocted that letter; you tricked all the knights. Today I have received a letter from the king. . . ." The archbishop reaches inside his cloak. "How dare you force yourself on your father's wife?"

"Enough!" snaps Sir Mordred.

"You have angered God," the old archbishop says. "You have shamed yourself. You have disgraced the whole order of knighthood."

"Enough, I said!" Sir Mordred shouts.

"Raise this siege or I'll curse you with book, bell, and candle."

"Do your worst!" says Sir Mordred in a biting voice. "Whatever you do, I'll defy you."

"I'll do what's right," the old archbishop replies. "You're a traitor."

"You . . . turbulent priest!" Sir Mordred snarls. "One more word and I'll strike off your head."

The archbishop gathers his cloak. He turns away.

"You old fool!" Sir Mordred calls after him. "The men of England are my men. They're of one mind. With Arthur there was nothing but war. War on the heels of war. Argument! Anger! Now, there's hope. I give them hope!"

"Traitor!" the archbishop says again.

Sir Mordred whirls round to face the high walls. He looks up and bawls, "Can you hear me? I'll have Guinevere, by fair means or foul! When Arthur comes back, I'll be waiting for him."

TODAY IS THE FEAST OF SAINT DAVID WHO WENT ON A pilgrimage to Jerusalem, and that means it's my birthday.

"Do you know how old you are?" Simona asked me.

"Of course. Seventeen."

"What day of the week were you born?"

"I don't know that," I said, "but it was the first day of the month."

"That's a good day," Simona told me. "You'll win fame, and be clever and wise; and you love books and reading and writing."

"The last part's true, anyhow," I said.

"Be careful of water," Simona warned me. "It may drown you."

"How do you know?" I asked.

Simona's eyes widened. "Everyone knows," she said. "My father. He was born on the first day of September."

"How old are you, then?" I asked Simona.

"I don't know exactly. Maybe twenty-one, and I was born on a Tuesday. I will tell you a birthday secret."

"What?"

"I have six older brothers, and my parents prayed for one daughter. But when I was born I was a boy."

"A boy?"

"They prayed so much, they wept so much, I became a girl," Simona said.

"You don't believe that?"

Simona smiled. "My father told me that's how much he wanted me."

MY OWN SON

"I FELT MY BRAINS SOMERSAULT," SIR GAWAIN TELLS KING Arthur. "For four weeks I've been unable to see straight. To think straight."

They're sitting on soft deerskins in a spatter of primrose-and-violet light. Beside the king lies his Bible, open, and on it rests the beautiful reading-pointer given to him by King Pellam, Guardian of the Grail. Ivory and gold and obsidian . . . Above them, the poplar trembles and whirrs.

"That's how hard Sir Lancelot clouted me," Sir Gawain says, nursing the side of his head. "But now! Spring in the air! Spring in my blood! In three days I'll be able to fight the traitor again."

Now a horseman gallops up to them, and both men stiffen and scramble to their feet.

"Arthur, King of Britain!"

"Take your time, man," says Arthur-in-the-stone. "Words need breath."

"From the Archbishop of Canterbury, sire. Sir Mordred has concocted a letter — a letter, he says, from Sir Gawain — announcing you are dead."

"The traitor!" shouts Sir Gawain.

"He has seized your throne, sire! He says he'll marry your queen."

The king clenches both his hands.

"She's taken refuge in the Tower of London, and Sir Mordred's laying siege to it. He threatens to cut off the archbishop's head."

A gust of wind shakes the poplar and the primrose-and-violet spots shudder and dance.

"Half the men left in England have rallied to him, sire," the messenger pants.

"I see," the king says quietly. "This is how he repays his father's trust."

Slowly he walks away. He paces around the poplar tree; Sir Gawain and the messenger watch him.

"My son," he says to himself. "My own son. A monster." He pauses, then strides back to the waiting men.

"Each day you're out of England, sire . . . ," the messenger begins.

King Arthur looks him in the eye. "When I need advice," he says, "I'll ask for it. Raise the siege, Gawain!"

"But —"

"First things come first. My kingdom. My poor people. My suffering wife. We'll sail home and pursue Mordred. Then and only then will we fight Sir Lancelot."

"Yes, sire," says Gawain in obedience.

"Ah!" says the king. "But if only Sir Lancelot were to sail with us now."

head-line and heart-line

SIMONA AND I BOTH HAVE TO DO THE SAME THING: WE have to bring home the news about our fathers. She has to tell her mother that Silvano was drowned when the *Violetta* sank — the ship he named after her. I have to tell Lady Alice about Sir William, and how he attacked Lord Stephen.

At least Simona loved her father and he loved her.

"What about Lady Alice?" Simona asked me. "Will she be sad?"

"Sir William beat her."

Simona shrugged. "My father beat my mother," she said.

"And he was away half the time, with Lady Cécile. So she had to manage two manors, and do the accounts, and it made her weep. He was twice as old as she was. But maybe . . . maybe she will miss him."

"First yes, then no," Simona said.

When we sailed in through the Porto early yesterday morning, the water became less rough. Gently it rocked us, and the oarsmen cheered. Each man raised one hand from his oar and waved.

I stared at Saint Nicholas. We passed so close to our camp. There was no one there.

Once, Serle and I rode to a hill where there had been a battle between the Welsh and the Saxons hundreds of years ago, and the Welsh won. There was nothing to see. Nothing to touch or hear. And yet somehow there was.

I think it will be the same on Saint Nicholas. A hundred years from now, our huge, restless army will still be in the air.

Yesterday, Simona and I talked to the captain. He's called Hamadat. His mother's a Christian, but his father's a Saracen.

"I've never heard of that before," I said.

Hamadat's eyes were deepset; his skin was cracked and dark as a date.

"In Aleppo, yes," he said. "And Nablus. Saracens and infidel women, Saracen women and infidel men."

"But how do they meet?"

Hamadat shrugged. "Trade. Crusade. Pilgrimage."

"What do their families think?"

"My mother's father," the captain said, "he would not pay dowry."

"The more I find out," I said, "the more I realize how little I know."

When I told Hamadat we were going to cross the Alps, he threw up his hands. *"Stupido!"* he exclaimed. "May the prophet preserve you!"

He said that if I take Lord Stephen overland all the way to England, I must be intending to kill him, because he'd be jolted to death. Besides, he said, unless we joined a larger group, we'd certainly be attacked by robbers. And he told us in any case Mont Cénis and the other mountain passes will be snowbound for at least another six weeks.

"It's safer and quicker to go by ship," Hamadat said, "and for Lord Stephen more comfortable. Genoa! Take horses and cross to Genoa. It's a good road. It's Roman."

"How far is that?"

"Hmm!" Hamadat grunted, and he pursed his dry lips. "Twenty days. No more. You go with my merchants. They take cargo to Genoa. Silks, perfumes, carpets, pearls!"

"I must talk to Turold and Rhys," I told Hamadat.

"Thank Allah!" said Hamadat.

"After Genoa," I asked, "where then?"

"Easy! You find merchant ship to France . . . England . . ."

While I was talking to Hamadat, I kept thinking that I have to choose which way we are to go, and it made me excited and nervous. I must decide. It is up to me.

Hamadat's right: Crossing the Alps would be much more uncomfortable for Lord Stephen, and less safe. So even if it's not as easy to find a ship as he says, even if we have to wait there for several weeks, it must be better to cross to Genoa.

So that's what we're going to try to do.

As soon as we had docked on the Rialto, quite close to Saint Mark's, Simona went off to find us accommodation, and before long she came back smiling and saying she'd found us places in a Benedictine monastery. We carried Lord Stephen there, and the monks welcomed us and took Lord Stephen to the infirmary, and then Simona hurried off again to find her mother and brothers. We didn't see any more of her until this morning.

Lord Stephen hasn't spoken another word since he asked me where we were, and I told him we were aboard a boat. He's like a baby again, except he doesn't howl. He sleeps and sleeps, he wakes to drink and eat a little, he passes water and messes himself, and then he goes to sleep again. I wish he would stay awake. I wish he'd start to ask questions, and complain a little, and cluck, and blink.

"The trouble with you, Arthur," Turold told me, "is you always want things to happen now. Or yesterday. Lord Stephen's asleep because he needs to sleep."

Yesterday afternoon, the two monks in the infirmary stripped Lord Stephen, and washed him from head to toe, and changed his poultices. They fed him boiled breast of chicken, minced and mixed with well-baked apples.

"As soon as he's a little stronger," said one monk, "we'll give him milk-soaked venison. That will clean out the wound-filth and wound-slime inside him."

"Here!" said another. "Chew on this."

"What is it?"

"Fennel. To sweeten your breath."

"Your whole body," the first monk said. And he smiled.

Since leaving Zara, we've taken it in turns to sit beside Lord Stephen, but here two monks are always on duty in the infirmary.

So when Simona came this morning, I went with her to find the Saracen traders in the *campo*.

They were sitting in their rug-tent, and recognized me at once. One of them called out.

"What's he saying?" I asked Simona.

"Ostrich-head!" Simona exclaimed.

I laughed, and clasped the hands of the two men, and bowed to the woman.

The woman frowned, and pointed to the creature on one of their rugs, half-bird, half-beast.

"She says where is your blue-white friend?" Simona said.

"Bertie?"

"Not dead?" the woman asked.

"Oh no!" I said. "He's . . . on the crusade."

"Yach!" exclaimed both men in disgust.

"She says why aren't you there too?" Simona asked me.

"My lord has been wounded."

I felt so glad to see them again. I know they're Saracens, but they're open and warm.

"I want to buy some spices," I said.

All three narrowed their eyes and drew in their breath, as if I were asking for slices of the moon.

"Ginger, cumin, things like that."

The woman laid out little bags of ginger and cumin and cinnamon and mace and coriander.

"You must bargain with them," said Simona. "They like word-jousting."

Simona was right. It was like Ludlow Fair.

"Ten marks," said one of the men.

"Ten!"

"Cheap. Cheap for ostrich-head!"

"I can't afford ten," I said. "That's as much as it costs to feed two horses for a year."

"Nine. Cheapest."

"No! They're not for me, you know. They're for a lady. Lady Judith, in England."

"Ah! Spices for lady. Eight!"

"Eight marks. Last price," the other man said.

"What do you think?" I asked Simona.

Simona smiled. "I think . . . less than the cost of feeding one horse," she said carefully.

In the end, I agreed to pay six marks, and the two men grinned and we clasped hands again.

"Word-jousting," I said. "Yes. If only we'd word-jousted with the Saracens . . . with everyone in Zara."

The Saracen woman reached out and took my right hand, and murmured.

"She says it's your turn," Simona translated. "They'll tell your hand."

"Oh no!" I said. "Well . . ."

At once the man who told Bertie's palm stared at mine.

"I'm left-handed," I said.

The trader took my left wrist, and at once he whistled.

"What is it?"

The man shook his head, and began to talk very fast.

"What's he saying?" I demanded. "It's my hand, not his."

"He says he's never seen this before," Simona replied. "Your head-line and your heart-line are not separate. They are one. One line . . ."

"What does that mean?"

"He says you'll live many years. Sixty, even. And you'll have three children. Maybe sons, maybe daughters. He can't tell."

"And my head-line and heart-line?"

Simona talked for a while to the trader. "He says you will never have a thought in your head without your heart feeling it — joy or hope or fear or sorrow. And you will never feel emotion in your heart without your head seeking to understand it."

"I hope that's true," I said.

"He says this can be a great weakness or a great strength," said Simona. "That's up to you."

Great Beds, and Other Wonders

'VE HEARD ABOUT GREAT BEDS. NOT SIR JOHN'S AND LADY Helen's, that's just their name for it. The one in Chester sleeps thirteen people, and the one in Canterbury fourteen. But the Great Bed here holds sixteen!

I can't get back to sleep, so I've put on some clothes and come across the courtyard to sit with Lord Stephen and write.

What with buying the horses, and having them shod, and hiring a man to make a litter with straps for Lord Stephen, so he can lie between two horses and it's not too bumpy for him, we stayed five nights in Venice.

When it was time to leave, Simona and I had very little to say. I don't suppose we'll ever see each other again, and without hope, words soon run out of breath.

"What's England like?" she asked.

All at once, I saw Tumber Hill. Green and growing. Wild raspberries. The new beech leaves, soft as fingertips . . .

I swallowed. "Well, it's home!" I said. "An ostrich's head!"

"Why did the trader say that?"

"Because England looks like that on a map. That's what he told me before."

We sat side by side, staring at the dancing water.

"You made Serle happy," I said.

Simona didn't say anything.

"That's what I'll remember most," I said. "Yes, and you knowing about love and being betrothed to an Englishman, and being a boy-girl, and teasing Lord Stephen, and that periwinkle, and looking like an apricot!"

"Oh Arthur!" cried Simona. She crowded against me, then she hugged me. "You!" she said. "You saved my life."

"Sometimes the full moon looks like an apricot," I said.

"Sometimes like an ostrich-head!" Simona replied. She was laughing and sobbing.

"I know!" I said. "Let's think of each other at each full moon."

"And send a blessing," said Simona. "I'll send you a blessing and say a prayer for Lord Stephen."

As soon as we left Venice, we saw wonders. First a trembling rainbow encased us, and painted us orange and green and blue and violet.

Merlin told me rainbows are spirit-bridges between earth and heaven. Lying in the quivering light, Lord Stephen kept smiling and nodding; he looked quite blissful, as if the rainbow were all his idea.

Between Padua and Vicenza, we saw a tree throbbing with gold-crests, hundreds of them, all twittering; and then in a forest glade on the way to Verona, we met a wandering scholar with his back against a tree, reading a little book of poems. He had a pointed black beard, and was wearing a dirty old sheepskin.

"Rus habet in silva patruus meus," he said.

"What does that mean?"

"My father's brother has a farm in the middle of a forest."

"So does mine," I said. "Sir John de Caldicot. In England."

"Huc mihi saepe . . . ," the scholar went on. "I often go there to get

away from ugly, unhappy things." He looked up. "Do you go to quiet places?" he asked me.

"Yes, a glade like this," I said. "And my climbing-tree."

"Go there again," the scholar told me earnestly, *". . . et me mihi reddunt*. These places give us back ourselves."

"I will," I said.

Between Verona and Cremona, we met a knight out hunting with his hawks. His falconer was carrying a muzzled animal. Its coat was fawn with dark brown spots.

"I've never seen a beast like that before," I said in English, then in French. "What is it called, sir?"

"Pard," the knight replied. "Some people say Leo-Pard."

"Leopard!" I exclaimed, and I remembered our steersman Piero telling me about the beast in the church north of Zara that leaps out and attacks crusaders. "He's very beautiful."

"She," said the knight.

"Did you catch her?"

The knight laughed. "Here in Lombardy? No, she comes from Tartary. Far east. Beyond the Saracen lands."

"Do you hunt with her?"

"One leap," said the knight, "and she kills a deer or a goat — meat for me and my hawks."

I gave the leopard a long, wary look. And with her burning eyes, she gazed at me.

The knight smiled and rubbed the leopard's white belly. "Like Italian girl, yes?"

"Well . . . yes," I said.

All this, and then in Piacenza I started talking to a trader in the market, and ended by buying a glass wand with a curved handle. It's full of thousands of tiny, colored seeds and the trader told me that if I put it in Lord Stephen's bed it will protect him from night demons. He said as soon as a demon sees the wand, he has to count all the seeds, and that keeps him busy all night.

Why did I half-believe him?

Because I'll do anything to help Lord Stephen to get well again, I suppose.

Yes, and now this Great Bed.

The straw mattress is covered with several layers of dried bracken, and the men sleep on one side, the women on the other, separated by a long bolster.

Until I got up, there were thirteen of us mother-naked under the men's bedcover — the six merchants we're traveling with, and Turold and Rhys and me, and two pilgrims and a trader and a messenger — and I've never heard so much belching and farting and snorting and gurgling.

There were three women on the other side: a mother with a squashed nose, and her pretty daughter, and a French nun.

"If two or three lie together, then they have heat," the nun said, "but how can one be warm alone?" She peeled off her habit and crossed herself, and then the mother and her daughter made a tent of their bedcover and took off their clothes too.

"Amen," said the woman with the squashed nose. "May God save us from the dangers of this night."

Then the three women snuggled into one another, and scarcely made another sound.

For a long while the men sang songs, and told jokes, and

guffawed, and snatched the bedcover off each other. But at long last, it grew more quiet, and I couldn't stop yawning. I must have fallen asleep. . . .

What woke me up were the women's squeals.

Turold had got up in the dark and pissed in the pot outside the door, and then he carefully felt his way back into the wrong side of the bed.

"Let go!"

"Wooh!"

"You hairy warthog!"

It was only when I heard Turold harrumphing and groaning that I knew for sure it was him.

"Go on!"

"Get off me!"

Turold rolled over the bolster and right onto me, and of course by then most of the men were awake.

"You over there!"

"Squash nose!"

"What about me?"

"Have pity on a poor pilgrim!"

The women giggled a little, and I could hear them whispering, but they didn't reply, and after a while it grew quiet again.

I couldn't get back to sleep, though.

Lord Stephen is making little sipping and sucking sounds.

wail as you will

HAMADAT WAS RIGHT!

It was easy to find a merchant ship in Genoa. We have been extremely fortunate. This boat's carrying a cargo of marble and wine all the way to Cardiff.

Cardiff! That's where King Arthur and Sir Gawain embarked on their way to Beaune. And from there, Rhys says, it's only four days' ride to the Middle March. We're running before the wind. We've already passed through the Pillars of Hercules!

Dear God! Let Lord Stephen see Holt again. Around us the ocean swirls, but I will bring him home. I will!

I have made this determined song:

You ghost-waves and furious crests,
Wail as you will, foam!

Blue eyelids and bloodred chest:
I mean to bring my dear lord home.

You opening graves and sweeping scythes,
You cannot drown this burden.

I love a girl so lithe and blithe,
Winnie de Verdon.

You dark-dream roamers, swirl, advance!
Wake all you will, and wring!

Where Wales and England twine and dance,
Soon it will be spring.

You wild wastes! Salt-wilderness!

93

in my blood and bone

"ATTENZIONE!" YELLED ONE OF THE OARSMEN.

I ducked behind the gunwale. Just in time! A huge wave smacked into our boat, and almost upended us, and water sluiced around the deck.

If I hadn't taken cover, the wave would have knocked me off my feet. As it was, I was completely soaked, and my seeing stone flashed and glittered like glass in sunlight.

I held it tight, and stared into it.

King Arthur is standing on the beach at Dover, under the white chalk cliffs. He's up to his knees in water, and around him pairs of men are locking, arrows are whirring, pikes are jabbing, swords are swinging, soldiers are lurching, landing skiffs are bobbing, blood is staining, words are cursing and praying, ordering, threatening, begging . . .

"Pursue Mordred!" Arthur-in-the-stone shouts. "Catch him! Take him alive!"

Now one of Sir Mordred's men runs straight at the king. The king stops his lance with his shield and drives the man backwards.

"Take him prisoner!" the king shouts.

"Arthur," shouts Sir Kay, staggering through the water, "Sir Gawain is wounded. Come to him!"

At once the king hurries along the beach. He splashes through the shallows and places both hands on the stern of a skiff.

"Hold it firm!" he instructs the men standing around him, and he clambers into the skiff.

The king can see Sir Gawain is half-dead. He sits down on the stern bench and draws his nephew to him; he lays his head on his lap. Around them the wavelets suck.

"Gawain," he says gently.

Slowly Sir Gawain opens his eyes.

"My sister's son," the king says. "The man in this world I love most. I've placed more trust in you and Lancelot than any other knights, and you and Lancelot have given me the greatest pride, the greatest joy. Now I have lost you both."

"Uncle," says Sir Gawain, in a weak voice. "My head wound has opened again, the one Sir Lancelot gave me. In my blood and bone, I feel I will die today."

Softly the boat sways. The little waves keep lifting it.

"If Sir Lancelot were with us and not against us," Sir Gawain says, "this would never have happened."

The king cradles Sir Gawain in his arms.

"But I would not make peace with him," Sir Gawain says. "I have brought about the conflict." Now he struggles to sit up.

"Uncle," he says, "have parchment and pen and ink brought to me here. I will write to Sir Lancelot before I die."

To Sir Lancelot, knight of knights

Greetings!

The wound you inflicted on me at Beaune has opened again. I know in my blood and bone I will soon die.

I want the whole world to know that I, Sir Gawain, King Arthur's sister's son, son of King Lot of Orkney, knight of the Round Table, have brought about my own death. Not you but I am the cause of it.

Lancelot, pray for my soul. Kneel at my tomb. Come back to this kingdom.

In the name of our old friendship, come at once! Sail with your knights over the sea and rescue King Arthur. He's in mortal danger. The traitor Sir Mordred has had himself crowned. He has tried to force Queen Guinevere to marry him, but she has taken refuge in the Tower of London.

Today King Arthur and I have fought Sir Mordred and his men at Dover. We've put them to flight. But my old head wound has opened again.

This sheet is speckled with my lifeblood

Now tears slip from Sir Gawain's eyes but he makes not a sound. He leans a little sideways against the king, and the king holds him.

Time drifts.

Gently the boat sways and swings.

AT SEA

ORD STEPHEN! DOZING AGAIN. HIS SHOULDER WOUND is healing, but he gave his skull such a crack that he injured the inside of his head. He smiles; he's serene. But where are all his sharp questions and opinions and dry jokes? Will they ever come back?

"He will not fight no more. Maybe not stand up no more." That's what Milon said. He said, "Maybe he die."

Sir William has wrecked Lord Stephen's life.

His angry heart and drunken body ignored his head, and acted without the least regard for the consequences. The same as when he took advantage of my mother. And when he did away with her husband. When he threw my ring into the waves.

Yes, my father has wrecked Lord Stephen's life; he has wrecked our dream of journeying to Jerusalem.

But one thing he and Lord Stephen and Milon did agree was that the crusade is going badly. Sir William said it was launched under a dark star, and Lord Stephen thought the Doge has been using us for his own purposes, and Milon said the decision to go to Constantinople is a disaster.

In Zara, I scarcely had time to think, or maybe I just didn't dare think. I was so shocked and scared.

But now I can't stop myself thinking, and remembering. . . .

Sometimes I wake up sweating and trembling. I've seen things I wish I'd never seen.

In my stone, warfare is glorious. It is quick and clean, almost painless, not foul and excruciating. Right fights against wrong. But really it's nothing like as simple as that.

Even my father knew that. He admired Saladin. . . . And Sir John said Saladin was an honorable man, and he and Coeur-de-Lion were both fighting a holy war.

The Pope says by killing infidels I will win salvation. But how can that be true? How can Count Thibaud and the cardinal and the knight with the cross branded on his forehead and even Lord Stephen be right? Jesus redeemed us by laying down His own life, not by slaying others.

What the Holy Father says troubles my head. It troubles my heart.

So maybe it's best after all that I've had to leave our crusade. But it's still difficult and disappointing to have to turn back.

On deck, saltspray stings my eyes, and my sight blurs; the roaring wind deafens me and the ocean-reach chills me.

Please God, let me always keep asking questions. Let me say what I believe.

hiraeth

WELLING HILLS! HEAVEN-HILLS! THEIR CURVE AND RISE and swoop.

As our boat plunged towards them through the heavy, flint-grey water, my heart felt as if it might burst. I was choked with longing.

Hiraeth! That's what Rhys calls it, and I don't think there's any one English word that describes it — a longing for each thing: each smile and creaking stile, each green hidden place, each stone. Such tearing, fierce longing for home.

The Middle March: Its manors have one eye on heaven, one on the ground. As we plunged and climbed, I began to list all the dear places around Caldicot and Gortanore and Holt, and to recall their stories:

Clee and Neen Savage and Upper Millichop,
Greete and Hope Bagot, Hilluppencott,
Cleobury Mortimer and Middleton Scriven,
Quabbs and Glog Hill, Arscott, Duffryn,
Snitton, Aston Aer, Llanfair Waterdine,
And Catmole, Catmole
Where Wales and England twine . . .

At noon, we landed safely at Cardiff. God be praised!

Rhys soon found a Welsh farmer ready to loan us five horses, and he and his daughter will ride with us all the way to the Middle March so they can bring their horses back again.

Neither of them can speak one word of English, and I could see how happy Rhys was to have his mouth crammed with Welsh words again. His face was wreathed in smiles all afternoon.

Lord Stephen is alive and crowing, and we'll leave at dawn! Cardiff and Chepstow, then north through the Forest of Dean. Ross . . . Hereford . . . If it's God's will, we'll ride into Holt on the fourth afternoon.

The day after Jesus died for us; the day before He rose again.

A Path of Feathers

WE WERE STILL IN THE WOOD, BUT I KNEW WE WERE almost there because I heard them screaming.

"My lord!" I cried. "Can you hear them?"

Lord Stephen looked up from his litter and smiled sweetly.

"Lady Judith's peacocks!" I exclaimed.

I thought of the turquoise peacocks spreading their feathers on the tent of the Saracen traders, and the mosaics in Saint Mark's, and Simona telling us they promise everlasting life.

Lord Stephen looked up at me. "A path of feathers . . . ," he said wonderingly.

"Sir?"

"Are you deaf?"

"Oh sir!" I gasped. "You're talking! A path of feathers, yes. With Lady Judith's peacocks, a path of feathers from earth to heaven."

Lord Stephen smiled again, and closed his eyes.

He is going to get well. I know it! He is!

Then our horses picked their way out of the wood, and there it was! The seven-sided castle capping the small, steep hill. The curtain walls. The drawbridge. All yellow in the gentle, late afternoon sunlight.

Robert was the first to see us — he was working on his croft.

Then Agnes, the wisewoman, came limping down the track from the castle. The hounds started barking, and Sayer strode up from the kennels to see what was going on.

This was when Rhys saw his wife at the door of their cottage in East Yard.

"Bronwen!" he yelled. "Bronwen!" He dismounted and leaped towards her, crying *"Gogoniant! Gogoniant!"*

Then, as I looked across the Yard towards the stables, I thought I saw Pip. His shape. His color. The way he pricks up his ears and holds his head slightly to one side. I wasn't quite sure.

He saw me. He gazed. He went completely still.

Then all at once he trumpeted and I shouted. I swung down out of my saddle. I raced across the Yard and reached up and threw my arms around his neck.

He shifted and stamped, he almost knocked me off my feet.

"Pip!" I cried. "Pip!"

By now Donnet and Piers and Abel had come up from Clunside and were standing quietly beside Lord Stephen's litter. I greeted them, and then I took my horse's bridle and led everyone up the track and across the drawbridge. As we entered the courtyard, Rowena and Izzie stepped out of the castle with two men I haven't seen before.

As soon as she realized it was me, silly Izzie screamed and threw herself at me, and I had to hold on to her to stop myself from falling backwards.

"Izzie!" I exclaimed. "You're as bad as Pip!"

The men were two of the soldiers from Wigmore hired to guard Holt. Izzie wants to marry one of them.

Then I saw Lady Judith standing in the doorway.

Everyone grew silent.

Lady Judith looked at me. She gazed at the litter slung between the two horses. She lowered her eyes.

I stepped towards her. My head felt as if it were ten feet up in the air.

I bowed. "My lady," I said.

"Arthur! Greetings in God!" She looked over my shoulder. "Is he dead?"

"Oh no! Not dead! He'll get better. I know he will."

Lady Judith and I crossed the courtyard. She bent over Lord Stephen. He was sleeping. She grasped the side of the litter and got down on her knees, and prayed.

Lord Stephen opened his eyes.

"My lord," she said gently. "My husband." She laid her right hand over his heart.

Lord Stephen smiled at her.

"He was wounded in the shoulder," I said, "and he's hurt inside his head."

Lady Judith got to her feet, and looked at the whole group of us.

"Turold! Welcome home!"

Turold took both her hands between his, and dumbly nodded.

"Rhys!" said Lady Judith. "Welcome to you!"

"My lady," said Rhys, gently shaking his head. He too was almost dumb.

After this, Lady Judith greeted the Welsh farmer and his daughter and thanked them for their help, and Rhys translated what she said. Most people are quick to show their feelings, but not Lady

Judith. She always minds her manners, and you can't tell what she's thinking. I've never seen her weep; I could feel her anxiety, though.

"He can't walk?" Lady Judith asked.

"He hasn't," I replied. "Not since . . ."

"No. Well, one step at a time."

She asked Turold and Rhys to unhook the litter and carry Lord Stephen straight up to the solar, and told Agnes and Rowena and Izzie to go up with them. Then she turned to me again and walked me to the drawbridge.

"He was attacked," I told her, "and he cracked the back of his head against a stone floor."

Lady Judith took my arm.

"I wouldn't," I said. "I'm dressed in mud."

"So I can see."

"And worse. I haven't washed for days."

"You brought him all the way?"

"Yes."

"From Venice?"

"From Zara, across the Adriatic Sea. Milon said I should. He said it was my duty to care for him and help him home."

Lady Judith nodded and sighed.

"We did go to Venice, though," I said.

"I know. That girl told me."

"Tanwen, you mean?"

Lady Judith sniffed.

"She did get home, then! It's so far."

"I'm sure it is . . . And you, on your own."

"Not on my own! I couldn't possibly have done it without Turold and Rhys."

Lady Judith turned to me. Her eyes were dark and shining. "You're dirty and you stink and you're exhausted," she said. "Oh! Arthur." Then she buried me in her arms, the same as she buried Winnie when her cloak got scorched. She smoothed my hair.

Tears welled up into my eyes. I couldn't help myself. I felt so happy and sad and relieved and tired.

"You've done your duty," she said warmly. "More than your duty."

"He's my father, really," I said.

"Yes," said Lady Judith, pushing me away, but still keeping her hands on my shoulders. "I want to hear more, much more, but first I must wash and dress Lord Stephen, and lay him in a clean bed. Rowena and Izzie can help me, and then I want Agnes to search his wounds. And you . . ."

I yawned!

"Exactly. You should wash and get Gubert to give you something to eat, and sleep."

"Once," I said, "when I was like this before, Lady Helen made me swim in the moat."

"Quite right! Go down to the flat stone and swim in the river."

"In the water's womb, whirligig!" I said, and I yawned again.

"I've no idea what you mean," Lady Judith said sharply, "and I don't think I want to."

I grinned. "It's where Rowena and Izzie used to sit and cast their spells," I told her.

"Tomorrow's the feast of Easter," Lady Judith continued, "and it's important to do what we always do. That's what Lord Stephen would say."

"You mean . . ."

"I mean celebrate the Eucharist, and climb Swansback together, all of us here in the manor, and eat hare pie."

"And search for the Easter Hare's nest."

"The old ways," Lady Judith said. "They're right, and comforting."

"There's so much to tell you," I said. "And ask you."

"Lady Alice has promised to ride over," Lady Judith said. "Arthur, what's wrong?"

"Nothing!"

Lady Judith fixed me with an eagle's eye.

"They haven't come back as well, have they?"

"Who?"

"Sir William. Serle."

"Oh no!" I said. "No, they haven't."

"Well then," Lady Judith continued, "you can tell me and Lady Alice everything. And of course there are things you should know."

I yawned once more.

"His shoulder, you said?"

"And his head," I replied. "The back of his head. Inside his head."

"Sometimes it takes a long, long time for a wound to heal," Lady Judith said. "I've only to look at you, Arthur, to see what horrors you've faced."

vessels of the spirit

SOMETIMES I WAKE NOT BLINKING OR YAWNING BUT alert, thinking I've just heard my stone calling me. At once I pull on my shirt and hose and then I unwrap my stone. With my right hand I grasp and warm it; I become part of it again.

It was like that early on this pale green Easter morning. I woke in my little room at the top of the castle before all the villagers began to gather in the courtyard, sniffing and coughing, talking in low voices, ready to climb Swansback and stare into the rising sun.

I remember doing that, and Haket crying out, "The Lamb! Can you see his banner burning white, and its blood cross?"

Rowena said the sun looked bloodred, and Izzie saw it black as a cormorant's wing, and I thought it was gold, then purple and green, and spinning, but Lord Stephen said it was burning white, and told me that each man who takes the Cross has seen the Lamb.

My stone glistened. . . .

Three knights are kneeling in an arbor beside the Guardian of the Grail. The wounded king. Shining blood is still seeping from the gash between his ribs.

The arbor with its shriveled vines and parched grass swells with light more dazzling than the rising sun.

"You have come to Corbenic at last," the king whispers. He's in such pain. "Sir Perceval and Sir Galahad and Sir Bors, you are one in three, three in one. You have mended Solomon's sword and voyaged to the Island of Elephants and stopped the spinning of the Turning Castle and fought with Joseph of Arimathea's shield against the demon Knight of the Dragon, and many other wonders. But more than that, far more, you are true knights-of-the-head-and-heart."

The three knights bow their heads.

"You are the chosen ones," the Grail King says in a hoarse voice. "You know a man is never worthy to become a knight simply because of his prowess. Strengths and skills are only means; they're not ambitions or ideals. A knight always has duties. . . ."

Yes, to have one heart hard as diamond, one heart soft as hot wax. To be open-minded, openhanded, and generous.

"You are the chosen ones," King Pellam says again. "Sir Perceval, Sir Galahad, Sir Bors, you have given yourselves to God. Rise now and go to the Grail chapel. Go now and ask the question."

My seeing stone flashed; it half-blinded me.

The Holy Grail is uncovered. It is made of light. A pillar of sunlight flows upwards out of it.

Sir Perceval and Sir Galahad and Sir Bors kneel in front of it. I see their faces reflected in it.

The air is thick with frankincense and myrrh.

Out of the Grail a man rises. He rises, with dark eyes. Except for His loincloth, He's naked, and His feet and hands and ribs are all bleeding.

"My sons!" Jesus says. "My sons! I will hide Myself from you no longer."

The cheeks of the three knights are wet and shining.

"So many knights have quested," Jesus says. "Many have come close. Each man and woman and child in this world can cure the wounded king and heal the wasteland."

Sir Perceval and Sir Galahad and Sir Bors: three men, speaking as one.

"Whom does the Grail serve?" they ask.

"The Grail serves Me," Jesus replies. "The Grail serves you." Jesus lifts His voice. "My body and blood lie within you and each of you becomes the living Grail. You are knights-of-the-head-and-heart. Vessels of the spirit."

The three knights bow their heads, and raise them.

Above the Grail, within the pillar of light, Jesus rises. He rises again!

For a long time my stone shone. It sat in the palm of my hand, and shone.

The young woman wearing a wimple — the one who rode into Camelot on a mule — kneels beside King Pellam's bed with Sir Perceval, Sir Galahad and Sir Bors, and many other ladies and knights. She begins to sing the lullaby I heard her sing before:

> "In that orchard, there is a bed,
> Hung with gold shining red,
>
> "And in that bed there lies a knight
> His wounds bleeding day and night . . ."

King Pellam's terrible wound, the gash in his ribs, stops bleeding. It closes. All his wounds close.

His skin looks unblemished again.

Around the king, all the knights and ladies weep and pray. The young woman reaches up; she pushes back her wimple. Already her hair is beginning to grow, corn-gold.

The trees gently shake their heads, shoots of green grass begin to grow again, finches twitter and carol. On the arbor vines the grapes swell, misty-skinned.

King Pellam sighs. At last he's able to die in peace. He closes his eyes.

The earth itself sighs and begins to breathe.

The wasteland lies waste no more.

"But our world still waits and suffers," Sir Galahad says. He's holding the shield the young woman left hanging on the pillar at Camelot: the snow-white shield on which Joseph of Arimathea painted a cross with blood. "I have work to do," he says. "I will sail to Sarras, near Jerusalem, and fight Estorause, the pagan king."

"For as long as I live, my quest will not end," says Sir Bors. "I will go on a crusade."

Sir Galahad leans over the Grail King and gently takes off his scarlet hat emblazoned with a gold cross. He places it on Sir Perceval's head.

"Guardian of the Grail," he says.

"So many of us have quested," Sir Perceval says. "Many have come close. Each of us must have a dream."

Below me, in the courtyard, everyone is gathering. A peacock swaggers across the drawbridge. It screams the resurrection.

In Your Green Care

ADY ALICE WAS WEARING HER OLD BURNT-ORANGE cloak. She lifted her reins in greeting as she always does, and I was filled with such a rush of joy that as soon as she had dismounted, I threw my arms around her and crushed her.

"Arthur!" she cried in her light voice. She kissed me on both cheeks and shook out her gown, and tucked her sandy curls under her wimple. "Squeezing me like that!" she said reprovingly. She put her head on one side and inspected me. "Can it be you? Where is everyone? We didn't think you'd come home this year!"

"Come up to the solar," I said. "Lady Judith's there. And . . ."

How long did we sit in the solar, the three of us, under the wall hanging, with Lord Stephen sleeping in the inner room?

The sun was not long past its zenith when Lady Alice rode in. It was bleeding and dying when we stood up.

I told them everything.

Backwards.

I mean I told them first about how Sir William attacked Lord Stephen. They both stiffened and sat up straight. They didn't look at each other to begin with, and their breasts heaved, and then they both began to weep and sob, and Lady Judith crossed over to Lady Alice and raised her and held her in her arms for a long time.

Sometimes, even words just get in the way.

After a while, they asked me questions, hesitant at first, as if they didn't really want to know.

I answered. I answered them all. I told them about the horrors, the Saracen singing teacher and his wives and their slashing scimitars, the boy, the dark-eyed Zarans, the old Saracen traders being beaten, crusaders attacking each other and Bertie being wounded, the rag doll. I told them there was so much bloodshed and cruelty that it began to seem normal — as normal as courtesy and kindness feel here.

Sometimes I had to stop because one of them began to weep again, and that made the other weep, but I told them many other things too. About Simona, and the *Violetta* sinking, and how Lord Stephen and I often talked and he counseled me, and the wonderful day when Milon knighted me and gave me a superb sword, and how Sir William was the oldest knight and I was the youngest in the entire army and how we met the Doge. . . . Sometimes they were listening; sometimes they seemed to be far away, inside their own heads and hearts.

But when I told them about my mother's gold ring! About her sending it and Thomas giving it to me, and Sir William ripping it off my finger and throwing it into the sea! They both listened then, and Lady Alice's whole body jerked as if she had convulsions.

"God forgive him!" she sobbed. "God forgive him! I cannot."

Lady Judith had Catrin bring us up little honey-cakes and juice pressed from pears. We sat quietly together. Talking about little things. How my boots need stitching again, and Lady Alice saw a red kite on her way over this morning, and how at Gortanore Grace found the Easter Hare's nest this year.

"Gubert made hare pie for us," Lady Judith said. "And Arthur said the words."

"What words?" asked Lady Alice.

"The ones Lord Stephen says each Easter before we eat dinner," Lady Judith replied. "He shows the hare the palms of both his hands and says, 'Eostre, Eostre, this is your hare. Keep us all in your green care.'"

"Who is Eostre?" Lady Alice asked. "Easter?"

Lady Judith shook her head.

"In Zara," I said, "there's a church and the builders used marble from the old Roman temple with the names of old gods on it. Eostre could be a name like that."

Then Lady Judith stood up, and asked Lady Alice to go with her to Lord Stephen's bedside and pray. She turned me round to look at the wall hanging.

"As you can see," she said, "Rowena and I have been busy. This panel shows the two of you taking the Cross in Soissons. But when people are looking at the life of Lord Stephen de Holt one hundred years from now, what else should they know? This linen and silk, Arthur: What are they to tell? Your crusade may have been curtailed, but it has still been the greatest adventure of Lord Stephen's life. I think we should sew four or even five panels, don't you?"

"There are so many things," I said. "One panel could show the Saracen traders and all their spices."

"You must choose."

"Lord Stephen reminded me about buying them," I said, "and I got them for you in Venice on the way home. Lots of different kinds."

When Lady Judith and Lady Alice came back from the inner room again, I told them I didn't know what to say to Tom and Grace.

"I mean," I said, "do they have to know everything?"

"Yes," Lady Alice said at once. "It will hurt them. No one wants to hear evil of their own father. But in the end it's better to tell the whole truth. You know that, Arthur."

Lady Judith sipped some pear juice, and cleared her throat. "What you've told us, Arthur, has been very painful," she said. "Painful and difficult. For you too I know. You've been very careful. . . ."

"And fair," Lady Alice added. She looked at Lady Judith, and I saw her give a slight nod. "We have something to tell you as well," she said.

The moment she did so, I thought of the way Sir John told me he and Lady Helen were not my blood-parents.

"Why?" I said. "What is it?" My heart rose up, protesting, inside my chest. "It's not my mother?"

Lady Alice gently shook her head. "No," she said.

"What is it then?"

"Winnie."

"What?"

"She's only fourteen. Not even fifteen. You're betrothed, of course, but . . ."

"Is it Tom? Is that it?"

"You know how impatient and impulsive she is. She blows this way and that way."

"And my brother's not firm enough with her," Lady Judith said.

"She hasn't seen you for a year," Lady Alice said, "and, really, she didn't think she'd be seeing you for at least another year. None of us did."

"Then what . . . ," I began. I wasn't sure what to ask.

"You must go to Verdon," Lady Judith said.

"Nothing's decided," Lady Alice said. "Nothing at all. It's just that it's not as clear as it should be."

"I almost knew," I said. I looked at my rough knuckles. I thought of the poem I wrote for Winnie: "Why am I anxious that you'll be true?"

"You must go to Verdon," Lady Judith said, again.

"And then things will become clearer," Lady Alice said. "We will help you, all of us, but you and Winnie and Tom must decide for yourselves."

99 the voice of an angel

"THAT FRIEND OF YOURS," SAID RAHERE.

He looked at me with his sky-blue eye, then with his green eye.

"Who?"

"Who walked here from Caldicot just to see you."

"Gatty."

Rahere raised his eyebrows, then lifted his pipe and played a trill. "You may be a knight now, but you could learn a thing or two from her," he said.

"I have."

"You rascal!"

"No! I don't mean that."

"That potbellied priest brought her over."

"Oliver. I hoped he might!"

"So I could listen to her voice. *Ut, re, mi* . . . out of her nose and head. The very top of her head."

"She's never had any lessons."

Rahere shrugged. "Her voice is the voice of an angel," he said. "Do you remember I told you about the Saracen? Ziryab, the singing master?"

I remembered Nasir and lowered my eyes. "I do," I said.

"If he'd heard your Gatty . . . mmm . . . I don't know what. If all the Christians and Saracens could hear Gatty, I don't think they'd want to fight any longer."

"Rahere!" I exclaimed. "That's wonderful!"

"She should go into a nunnery and have singing lessons, and put her voice to good use. That's what I told Oliver."

"What did he say?"

"It costs money to enter a nunnery, lots of it, and Gatty hasn't got any. Or anyone to pay for her. What's so funny?"

"The thought of Gatty being a nun," I said, grinning.

"Well, she's wasted out in the fields all day," Rahere said. "That's what I think."

I can't wait to see Gatty. When I tell her everything that's happened! She'll be more interested and understand better than anyone else.

I want Gatty to sing to me.

Knowledge of Good and Evil

IT WAS AS IF I WERE LOOKING INTO THE GARDEN OF EDEN, except that Winnie and Tom weren't naked, of course.

They were wearing long-sleeved white linen shirts, and hoses tucked into their boots, and gloves, and white veils. Close together they stood beside the covered hive, so caught up with each other and what they were doing that they didn't see me, in the middle of the orchard. I leaned into the apple-tree trunk and watched them.

The eighth day of April in the year of Our Lord 1203. Lady Anne's orchard was humming and whirring, unfolding in the sunlight. Everything looked new, each grass blade, each leaf. Around me were clumps of primroses, white violets, and I could smell the damp scent of young horsemint.

All at once Winnie giggled and pushed Tom, and ran off. Around the orchard they gamboled, Winnie squealing, Tom yelling, and then he caught her, and they threw back their heads and laughed, and he marched her back to the hive.

They were so free. So . . . at ease. They don't know how people tear each other to pieces. They haven't smelled death. They don't have nightmares that ride you when you sleep.

Winnie and Tom: They looked so young!

I wished I could be like them.

I wished I could just go away.

Tom was Adam and Winnie was Eve and I was the apple of the knowledge of good and evil, and I thought if only I could go away, and not trouble them with love and pain and guilt, they could stay in the orchard blind and innocent and delighted, and live forever.

"Come on, then!" said Winnie. "Let's open it!"

She and Tom pulled and lifted the hive's weather-beaten old canvas cover and at once the air around them grew hot and blurred with indignant bees.

Winnie and Tom raised their arms, pulled their veils over their faces, and stumbled towards me.

I didn't even notice the bee until I felt it sting me. On my right wrist.

I yelped, and Winnie and Tom heard me and pulled back their veils and stared at me, amazed.

"I've been stung!" I said.

Neither of them was sure it was really me. They floated around me.

"I'm not a ghost," I said. "It's you who look like ghosts."

"Arthur!" cried Winnie.

"Arthur!" said Tom, and he came and hugged me, and then Winnie put her arms round us both.

"I didn't know you were coming back," Winnie said, breathless and accusing, as if it were my fault. "I thought . . ."

"This hurts," I said.

"I'll pop it out!" said Winnie. "Have you got a knife, Tom?"

"I'll do it," I said.

Winnie grasped my wrist. "I can see the black point," she said. "Tom!"

"I'll do it myself," I told her. I unsheathed my jackknife and scraped the blade towards the sting. The third time, it popped out.

"Sore," said Tom.

The Most Bitter Day

101

King Arthur is sitting on a platform in a large pavilion, surrounded by hundreds of knights and bishops. Sir Kay, Sir Lucan, Sir Bedivere, Sir Dinadan, Sir Grummor Grummorson, the Bishop of Rochester, the Archbishop of Canterbury. All the great men of the kingdom loyal to him except for the three knights of the Holy Grail.

"In my dream," he calls out, "I was dressed in cloth of gold, and all around me and under me was deep water; black as the devil's tongue, seething with serpents and slimy beasts, sea creatures with snouts and fangs.

"I woke up, crying for help, and when I slept again, I saw Gawain with many beautiful ladies and young women.

"'I was with you when you died,' I told him. 'But now I see you're very much alive! Who are all these ladies and young women?'

"'All the ones I fought for while I was alive,' Sir Gawain replied. 'They begged God to let me warn you, and they've led me to you. Don't fight Sir Mordred tomorrow, or you will be killed. You, and all your followers.'

"'What shall I do, then?' I asked.

"'Make a treaty with Mordred, and be as generous as you have to be,' Sir Gawain told me. 'Offer him Cornwall here and now. If need be, offer him Kent. Offer him all England, after your death.

Buy yourself time! Within one month Sir Lancelot and his army will sail home; he will fight and kill Sir Mordred and whomsoever is loyal to him.'

"Then Sir Gawain vanished," the king tells his knights and bishops. "I have always loved and trusted him, and I will do as Gawain says. I name Sir Bedivere and Sir Lucan to ride over to Sir Mordred and offer him terms."

King Arthur's knights and bishops remain silent.

"Tell him I will meet him on that hilltop at noon tomorrow, each of us with fourteen men, and I'll sign a treaty with him. And you, all of you, keep watch!" the king calls out. "Mordred's as slippery as a snake. He's a traitor! If you see a sword blade flash, sound the horns and trumpets, and gallop up the hill as fast as you can. Kill Sir Mordred!"

"I don't trust my father," Sir Mordred tells his men. "Why this sudden change of heart?"

Many of his knights murmur in agreement.

Sir Mordred looks round his pavilion. "I don't trust him!" he snaps. "He'll try to take revenge. I'll talk to him, but you keep watch, each one of you. If you see a sword blade flash, storm up the hill. Kill my father!"

Now Sir Mordred mounts his black horse, and he and fourteen of his knights canter up the sandy ridge to the top of the hill.

King Arthur and his men are waiting. They have brought a low table, and set it in the shelter of a gorse bush, and laid out beakers and jugs of wine.

Sir Mordred dismounts. He stalks towards his father. They do not embrace, or clasp hands, or touch each other at all. Both men nod.

King Arthur repeats his offer; Sir Mordred agrees to it.

"In this way," says the king, "each of us wins. Innocent lives will not be lost. There will be peace in England."

"Give peace in our time, O Lord," Mordred replies.

"Then let us both put our hands to this, and sign a treaty," King Arthur says.

Now Sir Bedivere and Sir Lucan pour wine, and knights who once were friends and rode out from Camelot on adventures together begin to talk, and smile again.

Something winks in the gorse bush. An eye.

An adder writhes out of the bush, I can see the diamonds on its back; it shrithes across the sandy soil, and bites the right foot of one of the knights.

The knight yelps. He snatches at his pommel and draws his sword to cut the adder in half. The blade flashes in the sunlight.

Down below, horns and trumpets blow. Short, sharp blasts.

I can hear thousands of men grim and shouting.

"Alas for England!" the king calls out. "Because of an adder! There's no stopping this battle now."

Now Arthur-in-the-stone and Sir Mordred turn their backs on each other. They mount, and ride down to meet their armies, two dark breaking waves surging and scrambling and howling and heaving, seething up the hill.

My stone is grave-silent.

I can see shapes in the gloom. Mounds of arms and legs and torsos and heads. Eyes bloodshot and bulging.

Dear God! Two huge armies, one hundred thousand men, all the best men of England, and there's not one man left standing.

No! I can see King Arthur, masked in blood, standing over Sir Bedivere and Sir Lucan.

"Jesus forgive me!" mutters the king. "My friends . . . my knights of the Round Table . . . my brother, Kay . . . all the good men of the shires of England. There has never been so bitter a day."

Sir Bedivere and Sir Lucan groan, too drained to reply.

"I wish I knew where that traitor was," the king says. "I wish I knew for sure Sir Mordred was dead."

King Arthur sighs. He rubs the blood out of his eyes and looks around him.

"There!" he says. "Can you see him, leaning on his sword? Beside that heap of dead men!"

"Sire," groans Sir Lucan, "leave him."

"Give me my spear," says the king.

"He's no threat now," Sir Lucan says. "He stands alone, and there are three of us. Sire, remember your dream."

"My own son," growls King Arthur, "he is evil. I have to put an end to him. Whether I die or whether I live, Sir Mordred will not escape me now."

"God save you!" cries Sir Bedivere.

The king grasps his spear with both hands and runs straight at his son. "Traitor! You traitor!" he howls.

Sir Mordred runs at his father, his sword poised.

King Arthur drives his spear right through Sir Mordred's body, just under his shield.

Sir Mordred still comes on. He thrusts his body right up to the bur of King Arthur's spear. Gasping, he swings his sword, and the blade shears through his father's helmet.

Sir Mordred falls sideways. Spitted on his father's spear. His mouth gaping like the gateway to hell.

King Arthur collapses onto a bed of grit and mud and blood.

I Just Don't Know!

E KNIFED LORD STEPHEN FIRST!" I SAID. "I TRIED TO stop him, but then he turned on me, and we started wrestling, and he tripped and stabbed himself. I didn't kill him, but I kept feeling I did."

Around us the finches twittered and caroled, singing that everything changes, and yet stays the same.

"We buried him in sacred ground," I said. "The wind howled."

Tom closed his eyes. "May God receive his soul!" he said in a solemn voice.

For a while we sat in silence on the fallen pear tree. It was quite springy. Each time one of us moved the other bounced.

"As he lived, so he died," said Tom.

"What do you mean?"

"Impulsive and angry."

"And violent and selfish," I added.

"He was," agreed Tom.

"It's still very strange without him, though," I said. "Our father."

"He was never much of a father to me," Tom said. "Most of the time he ignored me. And as for you!"

"You can imagine how I felt when he appeared in Venice," I said.

"I scarcely knew him," said Tom. "Half the time he was away in France."

"I met his mistress," I said.

"You did?"

"Lady Cécile."

Tom whistled.

"I'll tell you later. Go on!"

"Yes, half the time he was in France," Tom continued, "and then he often stayed for days at Catmole."

Catmole! My heart lurched.

"That manor's yours now," said Tom.

"Yes."

"We'll have to talk to Lady Alice, and sort things out." Tom smiled, but his eyes were serious.

"And Winnie?"

Tom knotted his forehead and sighed. "I know," he said. "I mean, I don't know."

Tom. My half-brother; my friend; my rival . . .

He turned round and looked at me with his bright blue eyes.

"Tom!" I said. "I wish it wasn't like this. I wish you'd come with us. On the day I was knighted, I wished you were there, you more than anybody."

Tom nodded. "Go and talk to her now," he said. "I know you want to, and she's so impatient that if you don't, she'll probably burst."

"Why were you so long?" Winnie demanded.

She had exchanged her white clothing for a linen dress, forget-me-not blue, and tied her rash of red-gold hair behind her neck.

"What was so important?"

But then, without waiting for me to reply, Winnie came close.

She put her arms around me and tightened herself against me, and I could feel her shoulders and her breasts and . . . her whole body. She gave a long, deep sigh. Then she put one hand on each side of my head, and for a moment gazed at me with her leopard eyes. . . .

Her mouth was so soft. Her breath so warm. I closed my eyes. I felt like crying. Then she pulled away from me, grinning.

I realized I was out of breath. Shaking.

"There!" said Winnie in a definite voice.

"But I thought . . ."

"What?"

"You and Tom."

Winnie shook her head, and her hair lashed from side to side.

"I don't know!" she cried. "I just don't know!"

"But —"

"I know!" She reached over and tugged at the betrothal coin hanging round my neck. "I didn't mean to."

"No!" I said loudly. "And I didn't mean Sir William to die."

"No!" shrieked Winnie, and she clapped her hands over her ears.

"And I didn't mean Lord Stephen to be wounded, and I didn't mean to leave the crusade and come back so soon, but we're betrothed, we've exchanged vows and I never thought —"

"Oh Arthur! Don't!" cried Winnie. "It's so awful! Can't I love you both?"

The hall at Verdon is always decorated with flowers and leaves. It's only the second week in April, but Lady Anne has already colored it with branches of furry yellow catkins and sprays of hawthorn blossom, and little pots of primroses and violets.

The five of us sat at the refectory table: Sir Walter and Lady Anne on one side, and Winnie between Tom and me on the other.

"Welcome back, Arthur!" Sir Walter began.

"Yes! Welcome! Welcome!" Lady Anne said.

"Twelve months ago . . . ," Sir Walter mused. "Here in this hall. We all joined hands around you, and you and Winnie broke the coin."

"We all know that," Winnie said rudely.

"That's quite enough!" said Lady Anne.

Sir Walter sighed.

"And you, Tom," Sir Walter continued. "I remember you said that if Arthur didn't come back from the crusade, you'd gladly marry Winnie instead."

"I wasn't serious, sir."

"Half-serious," Sir Walter replied. "Now this is a difficult situation. For you, Arthur, because you and Winnie have plighted your troth, and I know how you care for her. She said your poem to us."

"Winnie!" I muttered.

"I wanted to," said Winnie.

"It's difficult for you, Tom," Sir Walter went on, "because you and Arthur are brothers and friends, and the last thing you wanted is to be disloyal to him."

"That's right," agreed Tom.

"And for you, Winifred, it's doubly difficult because you've exchanged vows with Arthur but realize now how much you care for Tom too . . . and because the decision isn't yours."

"It is," said Winnie. "Partly."

"What's certain," said Sir Walter, "is that we can't possibly decide here and now what to do. These things take time."

Winnie groaned.

"You two boys have a great deal to do. Your father is dead. You have to divide all his possessions, and his manors at Gortanore and Catmole, and in Champagne. You have to console Lady Alice, and provide for her. It's most important you work together."

"We're on the same side," I said.

"I can always work with Arthur," Tom said, smiling.

"Good!" said Sir Walter. "Well, first you must attend to all this. As you know, I suppose, your father and I never reached a full and final agreement."

"You would have done, though," I said. "If he'd come back."

Sir Walter sighed.

"Who's to tell?" Lady Anne said lightly. "Who's to tell? One moment he spoke of your marrying Winnie, and the next of Winnie marrying Tom!"

"You never told me that!" cried Winnie.

"And my father never told me," I said.

But now I remember Sir William did say something while we were on Saint Nicholas. He told me it wasn't at all certain I'd marry Winnie; he said it might be better if I married Sian instead!

So was my father tricking me? Did he allow me to exchange vows with Winnie without meaning me to marry her?

"Muddy waters!" said Sir Walter. He smiled consolingly at all three of us. "I promise you, we'll find out what's best for each of you, and best for both our families."

Best for me . . .

I remember when King Arthur fell in love with Guinevere,

Merlin warned him that love can be blind. He told Arthur he could find him a wife not only beautiful but loyal.

It will only be best for me to marry Winnie if she is loyal, and loves me alone.

Like Guinevere, she's willful and impatient; and first she blows one way, then the other.

But she's still only fourteen.

"That first day we met, that first hour, we both knew . . ."

Before I went on our crusade, I would have been exactly like Winnie now. Impatient and feverish and anxious. I would have thought any decision far better than none.

Have I changed, then?

I know I must try to be patient even though it's painful. I must find out. My head, my heart: I'll keep asking them questions.

DOWN TO THE WATER

THEY CANNOT WALK IN A STRAIGHT LINE. THEY'RE LIKE blind men. Or drunkards.

Sir Bedivere has a hand under King Arthur's left arm, and Sir Lucan under the king's right arm, and the three of them keep staggering sideways. They cannot go much farther.

Now Sir Lucan gasps and lets go of the king; he totters. He's made such an effort that he's forced part of his gut through the wound in his stomach. Sir Lucan moans and falls.

"My brother!" cries Sir Bedivere.

"His need was greater than mine," the king says, "but he was so brave, he still tried to support me. May Jesus open His arms and welcome him."

"Amen!" Sir Bedivere says.

"I cannot stand," says the king. "My head is spinning."

Sir Bedivere helps Arthur-in-the-stone to sit on a sheep-run. The greatest of kings in the dirt and dust.

"Bedivere," says the king, "take my sword. Take Excalibur down to the shore and throw it into the water. Then come back here at once and tell me what you saw."

"My lord," Sir Bedivere says.

"Be quick!" the king tells him. "There's so little time."

Sir Bedivere takes Excalibur, and as he limps down to the shore, he looks at it closely.

"The pommel and the grip: inlaid with precious stones," he says. "Nothing good can come of throwing this sword into the water — only waste, only loss."

Sir Bedivere hides Excalibur under a twisted hawthorn tree and wearily walks back to the king.

"What did you see?" asks the king.

"See? Nothing, sire. Nothing but waves and wind."

"You're lying, man," the king says. "You didn't throw the sword into the water. Go down again, be quick. If you care for me, throw it in!"

Sir Bedivere walks down to the hawthorn tree. He pulls out Excalibur, and stares at it.

"I cannot!" he says. "No! I cannot. It would be a sin to throw away this noble sword."

Sir Bedivere hides the sword again, and toils back to the king.

"Have you thrown it in?" the king demands.

"I have, sire."

"What did you see?"

"Sire, nothing but water lapping, and overlapping, waves darkening."

"You traitor!" gasps the king. "You've betrayed me twice. Who would have thought the man, the noble knight who has been so loyal to me, would betray me for a few precious stones? Go down again, be quick."

"Sire."

"You've endangered my life; my head wound has gone cold. Unless you do as I order you, here and now, I'll wring your neck with my own hands."

Sir Bedivere hobbles down to the hawthorn tree, and pulls out Excalibur. He crosses the foreshore, and stands on the shingle-bank, and now he hurls the sword as far as he can into the water. . . .

"What did you see?" asks the king.

"A hand rose from the water, a hand and then an arm dressed in white samite," Sir Bedivere replies, "and the hand reached for the sword, and caught it by the crossguards, and shook it three times, and brandished it. Then the arm and the hand and the sword vanished into the water."

"Help me now!" King Arthur whispers. "Down to the water! I fear I may have delayed too long."

home

RTHUR!" YELLED SIAN.

She rushed across the hall, and threw herself at me, and hugged me.

Tempest and Storm followed on her heels. They jumped up, barking, and Tempest licked my face.

"Father!" cried Sian. "It's Arthur!"

"Are you quite sure?" Sir John said, smiling.

I bowed slightly. Then we too embraced.

"We've been expecting you," he said. "Lady Alice sent a message."

"She's told you," I said.

"Verdon first. Quite right."

"No, sir."

"Oh! About my brother, you mean."

"Yes."

"Yes! Yes, she did." Sir John frowned. "Come on, now! You've scarcely crossed the threshold, and Lady Helen will never forgive me if I don't tell her you've arrived. We thought you'd ride over today."

"Is this the sword Milon gave you?" Sian asked.

"How did you know?"

"Tanwen told us," said Sian.

"Tanwen! Is she here?"

Sir John nodded. "Where she began," he said.

"Lady Judith's still angry with her."

"So I should think," said Sir John. "Walking out without a word."

"Can I see the blade?" asked Sian.

"Anyhow," said Sir John, "it suits Lady Helen, having Kester here. She sings him Welsh songs, and trots him on her knee and tells him he's on his way to Ludlow Fair. I can't think why but she likes the grubby beast."

"He's so little," said Sian.

"Exactly!" Sir John replied.

"Where is Lady Helen, sir?" I asked.

"Sian!"

Sian groaned. "Do I have to?" she asked.

"Go on!" said Sir John. "Go and find your mother."

"I won't be long, Arthur," Sian called out. "Can I cut something with it?"

I prowled around the hall. . . .

Gatty's face when she tasted blood-pudding . . . Oliver sticking our snails to the wall, and saying their slime would tell us who we're going to marry . . . my new bow shining in the candlelight . . . and King John's messenger, the one who kept moaning and clutching his stomach and saying "God's guts!" . . . and the fiddler's daughter singing in a piercing voice:

> "Love without heartache, love without fear
> Is day without sunlight, hive without honey.
> *Dulcis amor!*"

When Lady Helen hurried in, she embraced me and rubbed my cheeks, and told off Sian and Tempest and Storm for getting in our way, and railed at Sir John for not offering me almond-milk or ale, and stamped on a beetle — all at the same time!

"Can I see the blade?" said Sian.

"Not inside the hall," Sir John said. "Not bare steel. You know that."

"You wait your turn, young lady," Lady Helen said.

"I have," said Sian.

"Here's Arthur," said Lady Helen, "and you want to take him away again."

We sat around the dozy fire on handsome new blocks of wood, rounded at the corners, shaved along the edges.

"One of the oaks came down," Sir John said. "Right across the Lark. Brian and Macsen took a whole month to chop it up."

"I walked along the trunk," Sian said.

Lady Helen clicked her tongue. "Kester fell off. He caught his toe in a woodpecker's hole. I keep telling that girl, she should look after him."

"I got right across the stream," said Sian.

"Across, yes," Sir John said slowly. "Between life and death. Now we want to hear everything, Arthur. Especially about Serle. But first —"

"Nain!" Lady Helen said. "She died last October."

I crossed myself. "God will welcome her," I said. "He'll be glad of her!"

"Amen," said Sir John.

"She was seventy-three," Lady Helen told me.

"Maybe," said Sir John. "Sometimes she added years and sometimes took them away. She didn't really know."

"I know she was married to the dragon," I said, grinning, "and I once made a song about Nain wearing armor:

"And her mail-shirt's strapped to her neck flap,
And her neck flap's fastened to her helmet,
And her helmet's bolted to her nasal . . ."

Lady Helen looked at me, bright-eyed.

". . . and she told us wonderful stories, like the one about poor Gweno being thwacked by the dead man, and the great king sleeping inside the hill. . . . I'll never forget that one. Nain asked me what the wind said, and told me to honor the power in each and every thing, and I wish I could remember every word she said."

"God bless you, Arthur!" cried Lady Helen.

"Nain, and now my brother," Sir John said in a somber voice. "May God grant him peace! You'd better tell us what happened."

So I did. I told them everything. It wasn't quite as difficult as telling Lady Alice and Lady Judith.

"He didn't expect to come back," Sir John said. "He wasn't as old as Nain, but he —"

"He was the oldest in the whole army," I interrupted.

"But!" Sir John said firmly. "As I was about to say, he was creaking and aching. He told me this would be his last journey."

"In that case," I said, "I wish he'd agreed everything with Sir Walter first."

"I think he wanted to," Sir John said.

"I don't," I said.

Sir John gave me a long look. "I see," he said slowly. "Well, we can't pretend Sir William led a godly life. Far from it. We know all about that."

"About what?" demanded Sian.

"But whatever he did or didn't do can't be changed now. And you, Arthur, you inherit Catmole."

"Tell us about Serle," Lady Helen said.

"Well!" I said, and I took a deep breath. "He's healthy. He wanted me to tell you that. He was very brave and stood up for a Venetian girl against dozens of angry sailors. He asked me to tell you he keeps thinking of home, and when he closes his eyes he often sees the winter wheat growing."

"He said that?" Lady Helen exclaimed.

"Yes."

"Gogoniant!"

"Milon de Provins has taken him into his camp," I told them. "Serle really likes the crusade."

"But you didn't," said Sir John.

"I liked the riding, the sea journeys, the companionship," I said. "Warfare numbs people and sets comrades at each other's throats but it also brings them together. Serle's happy. Well, almost!"

Sir John nodded and smiled.

"He's going to look after Bonamy for me."

"Ah yes!" said Sir John. "Bonamy."

"Your gift to me," I said. "My heaven-leaper! My loyal, lasting friend. Milon's promised to bring him back."

"What about Tanwen and Kester?" Lady Helen asked.

"Serle often thought and talked about them," I said. "He's sent Kester a present."

"Serle!" cried Lady Helen.

"I think he wants you to be hopeful," I said carefully. "That's what he is himself."

"How long will he be away?" Sir John asked.

"There are so many difficulties. I don't know. It could be three years."

"Three whole years!" exclaimed Sian.

"There's so much I want to ask you," I said. "And I want to see everyone. Everyone!"

Lady Helen gave a little cry. "Arthur!" she sang in her lilting Welsh voice. "You haven't changed."

I have, though.

"We'll ask everyone to come up here tomorrow and break their fast with us," Sir John said, smiling. "Most irregular! It's not even a feast day."

"It is!" protested Lady Helen. "The feast of Saint Gwyddelan."

"Ah yes!" said Sir John.

"And Saint Llwchaiarn!"

"Ha! You're in luck, Arthur. Two dismal Welsh saints with unpronounceable names!"

Lady Helen waved her right fist in front of Sir John's face. "You . . . Englishman!" she cried. "The dragon dropped a cursing-pebble into Saint Llwchaiarn's well."

"And he drank the blood of Englishmen," said Sir John, smiling.

"Drink!" cried Lady Helen, leaping up. "You never offered

Arthur anything, and now I haven't either. Come on, Sian! Come and get something. We must ask Slim to bake for tomorrow morning, and carve collops."

"With Arthur's sword," Sian said enthusiastically.

Lady Helen was already at the door. "Sian!" she demanded. "Are you coming?"

I grinned at Sir John. It felt so comfortable to be sitting in the hall. Home at Caldicot, where I know everyone and everyone knows me.

Sir John read my thoughts. "Away from home," he said. "Always on duty. Facing horrors. Facing yourself. So much depending on you. You must be very tired."

I yawned.

"What the French say is ***reculer pour mieux sauter,***" Sir John told me. "To draw back so as to jump farther. That's what you need to do. Rest!"

"Do you remember Merlin jumping farther?" I asked.

"Who could forget it? The most extraordinary thing I've ever seen."

"I do wish we could see Merlin again," I said.

"So do I," said Sir John. "It's almost three years now since he went away." He shook his head. "I can't understand it."

"And I still can't believe I won't see him again," I replied.

"Ah yes!" Sir John said. "There is one thing you should know."

"Sir?"

"Gatty."

"What about her, sir?"

"You know Hum died?"

"Tanwen told us."

"And not long after that, Gatty's grandmother died."

"Poor Gatty!"

"Mmm!" Sir John said. He pursed his lips. "There's something about that girl."

"Sir?"

"You know Oliver took her over to Holt, and Lord Stephen's musician listened to her voice."

"Yes, Rahere! He told me."

"What did he say?"

"If all the Christians and Saracens in the world could hear her, they wouldn't want to fight any longer."

"I know about you two. When she was in trouble, you spoke up for her; and she walked over to Holt to see you, and got lost, and slept in a tree; and then you sneaked off to Ludlow Fair. You're right, of course. Gatty's brave, and resourceful . . . and helpless."

"Sir?"

"So I decided to help her."

"How, sir?"

"It's unusual, I know. Each of us has our own place and duty. However, a good knight should never be unbending; he must respond to circumstance."

"Yes, sir."

"I did think of putting Gatty into a nunnery," Sir John said. "After all, she can never marry Jankin — not after Lankin wrecked her father's funeral."

"But you didn't?" I asked.

"Too expensive!" Sir John replied. "The holy women ask an

unholy price. I was disappointed, because Gatty could have given her voice to God. But then Dame Fortune winked at us!"

"Sir?"

"Lady Helen has a cousin up near Chester, Lady Gwyneth of Ewloe. The daughter of one of the dragon's sisters." Sir John rubbed his nose. "She's a widow. Helen rode up to see her and discovered she was looking for a new chamber-servant."

"Not Gatty!"

"That's what I thought. But then I asked myself: Why not? Gatty can learn."

"You mean she's not here?"

Sir John sniffed. "Don't look so alarmed. I thought you'd be glad. Think, Arthur! Think what an opportunity this is for her."

"Gatty's not here?" I said again.

"I've never done anything like this for anyone else," Sir John told me. "But . . . Gatty's a most unusual creature."

"I'll go and see her," I said.

Sir John drew in his breath. "I don't know about that."

"I must."

"I understand," Sir John said, "but Lady Gwyneth has left on a pilgrimage. She's taken Gatty with her."

"Where to?"

Sir John looked me straight in the eye. "Jerusalem," he said.

The fire fell into itself, and a wisp of grey smoke curled out of it. I felt so tired.

"You must go and talk to Oliver," Sir John said. "Gatty had no idea when you'd be coming back, of course, but I believe she left some kind of message for you."

where are you today i keep wondering

Y DEAR BOY," SAID OLIVER, "I WANT TO HEAR ABOUT the Saracens! And that cardinal — Capuano. The sword of the Spirit and the helmet of salvation! Jerusalem!" Oliver waved his arms as wide as the world. "Yes, and about Venice, and your reading, your writing. I want to hear about holy men and heathens and the way to heaven, but you — all you want to do is ask about Gatty!"

"I'll tell you!" I replied. "Everything! I promise I will."

"But . . . ," said Oliver. "I know you."

"Sir John said she left me a message. Can't you tell me that first?"

"Tell you?" said Oliver. He levered himself up from the bench and lurched across to the chest. He turned the key. "I can do better than that, Arthur. I'll show you."

Oliver triumphantly held up a little roll of parchment, as if it were the king's Great Seal.

"Did you write it?"

Oliver puffed out his chest. "And Oliver the priest and scribe . . . ," he said very grandly.

"The Book of Nehemiah!" I cried. "It wasn't Oliver, though! *And Ezra the priest and scribe . . .*"

"Excellent, Arthur! All's not lost, I see." He handed me the parchment. "Your missive," he said.

I saw at once that it was bound with violet ribbon.

The ribbon I bought for her, with my last farthing, when we went to Ludlow Fair. "To tie up your hair . . . or wind round your field hat . . . or wear like a belt . . ."

I began to shake.

"She bit it in half," said Oliver, screwing up his face. "Half for you and half for her, she said."

I unrolled the parchment.

"And she wound hers round her wrist," Oliver said. "Her left wrist." I knew he was watching me closely.

"Your characters are all so neat and small," I said.

Oliver sniffed. "Oliver the scribe," he said. "Not, I fear, Oliver the grammarian. I did offer."

Gatty to Arthur on any day

Where are you today I keep wondering. I often talk to you and see you easy. You got the sky on your shoulders. You remember when I said let's go to Jerusalem? I can't explain but somehow I thought it, I believed it, and now I'm going. You and your singing will keep us all safe, Lady Gwyneth says. Arthur, when are you coming back? I haven't forgot going upstream. You promised. Or can you ride to Ewloe. Them bulls, and me wearing Sir John's armor, and rescuing Sian from the fishpond and going to Ludlow Fair, and everything . . . It's true! It is. Best things don't never get lost.

BY YOUR TRUE GATTY

I don't know how many times I read her words.

"Jerusalem!" I said. "Gatty! She'll enter Jerusalem."

"As we all hope to do," Oliver said. "And I saw the Holy City, the new Jerusalem, coming down out of heaven from God, prepared as a bride adorned for her husband . . . Well, Arthur? Which book?"

"I can't remember."

Oliver tutted. "The Book of Revelation," he said.

I should have been happy, I know — happy for Gatty, and her escape from fieldwork and hunger, happy for her new life, her singing, her pilgrimage.

"Come on now!" Oliver said in a warm voice. "Head before heart."

"It's . . . it's just that . . ."

Oliver patted my back. "Thank God for His great mercy. He has brought you safely home."

"And sent Gatty away," I said.

Mother Slim and Sister Grace

106

SLIM WOBBLED INTO THE HALL, FOLLOWED BY RUTH, each of them bearing a huge platter heaped with dough-cakes and collops and slices of cheese. Everyone cheered.

Then Robbie, the new kitchen-boy, came in, holding up a little pot as if it were a chalice.

"Cowslop syrup," he said in a small, squeaky voice.

Everyone laughed, and Robbie turned pink.

"For Arthur to pour over his dough-cake," he added.

"You need cowslop," said Slim.

"Why?" I asked.

Slim drew himself up and laid his hands over his huge stomach:

"Sip this spring's cowslop,
Then whisper her name.
Wherever she is
She'll be able to hear you.
It works like a charm.

And if you dream cowslop
You'll come to no harm
Wherever you are.

It will protect you
And ease your heart's pain."

I was so happy to see everyone. Ruth is pregnant, but she won't give up working in the kitchen just because of that — she says she can put the baby in a bucket — and Dutton says we got more blood from poor Stupid than any pig before or since, and Joan has been in trouble again for letting her cow trespass on Sir John's pasture, and Johanna's got pains in her gut. . . .

Tanwen! The last time I saw her was when she was rowed away from Saint Nicholas. The oars creaked and bumped in the oar-holes; they made such a hollow sound.

We understand and trust each other, because of being together on the crusade. I can depend on Tanwen and, somehow, I feel responsible for her. Maybe she and Kester can come to Catmole for a while.

Kester yelled when he saw me. I lifted him and whirled him around. Then I told Tanwen how Serle thinks of her and talks of her, and I gave Kester the shiny brass button.

"From your father," I told him. "From him and Shortneck. It's one of Shortneck's bridle buttons. You can think you're riding together."

Kester closed his damp little fist over the button.

"Let me see," said Tanwen.

But Kester hid his fist behind his back.

Everyone in Caldicot — almost sixty of us — stood in the hall, talking and teasing each other and laughing, and then Sir John led me up to the little balcony and rang his handbell.

"April!" he called out.

No one said a word.

"Wake up!" said Sir John. "April!"

Still not a word.

"All right!" Sir John struck his bell. "January!"

"By this fire we warm our hands," everyone shouted.

"February!"

"And with our spades we dig our land."

"March!"

"The seeds we sow grow into spring."

"April!"

"And now we hear the cuckoo sing."

"We do," said Sir John. "We hear the cuckoo sing and we see our own fledgling fly back home."

Everyone cheered again. My eyes felt hot.

"Each night has its own dangers and perils," Sir John said. "Wolves in the fold, foxes in the coop, night demons, nightmares. To go on a crusade is more dangerous than all that. We should all get on our kneebones and thank God for bringing Arthur safely home."

For a moment, it was quiet in the hall, almost quiet. Just Joan muttering, and Brian sneezing . . .

"All right! You can get to your feet!" Sir John said. "Now if you go on a long journey, homecoming is bittersweet. Nain has died. Hum has died. Hum's mother has died. Lankin has died. The wisewoman we need to cure us is very sick herself. Not only this. Merlin seems to have left us. Gatty has gone away. And yet —" Sir John paused. "The seeds we sow . . . in the dark they grow . . . green blades rising. Ruth is pregnant. Martha's pregnant."

"So am I!" Slim shouted out.

Everyone howled with laughter.

Sir John waited until there was order again, flicking his handbell with his forefinger.

"Well, Slim!" he said. "Pilgrims will be soon coming to Caldicot instead of leaving Caldicot. You're a miracle!"

Everyone laughed again.

"Each ending is a beginning," Sir John called out. "Leaves fall and die, a tree sticks its black fingers into the sky and rattles them, and the next moment its buds are sticky and rosy and then it bursts into leaf again. So Arthur's return — I should say, Sir Arthur . . ."

Everyone gasped.

"Yes," said Sir John. "Arthur was knighted in Venice! Sir Arthur de Gortanore! His return is a beginning. He's to take over his father's manor at Catmole, down near Knighton. He has work to do. New duties! High hopes! Isn't that right, Arthur?"

"Yes, sir," I said.

"Welcome home!"

Just as Sir John and I were coming down from the balcony, Lady Alice arrived from Gortanore with Grace and Thomas and Maggot.

"Grace and I both want you for ourselves," Lady Alice told me, smiling, "but I'm your stepmother, so you must honor me. Grace, you can talk to Arthur after that — all day, if you want."

Lady Alice and I strolled out to the herb garden.

"I rode over to Holt again yesterday," she said. "Guess what? Lord Stephen was sitting up."

"That's wonderful!" I cried.

"He knows he's back home, but he can't remember anything

about the journey. I do believe he's going to make a complete recovery."

"I'll go and see him," I said. "As soon as I can."

We sat down on the same bench where, four years ago, Lady Alice told me she'd heard rumors Sir William was a murderer, and I swore by Saint Edmund not to tell anyone.

"I have to talk to Thomas and Maggot," I said. "You know how Thomas gave me my mother's ring?"

"I do now," Lady Alice replied. "But I didn't until you told me and Lady Judith. They promised to help you find your mother too."

"Yes, and in return they made me promise to give them positions at Catmole after Sir William died."

"They had no right to ask you that," said Lady Alice.

"But I agreed."

"They were desperate to find somewhere safe," Lady Alice told me. "While Sir William was alive, people at Gortanore were afraid to accuse them, but they'll speak up now. Several villagers have told me that Thomas and Maggot buried Emrys's body. You need to confront them."

"What do you mean?"

"Tell them they broke their promise. Tell them they didn't help you."

"They'll say they tried everything. They did before."

"What they did," said Lady Alice, "was use you."

"They threatened Lord Stephen too," I said. "When he warned them he'd make other arrangements so I could meet my mother, they threatened to tell Sir William."

"You see," said Lady Alice, "they're two worms. Tell them they didn't keep their part of the bargain and you have no intention of bringing them to Catmole." Lady Alice's eyes softened. "Catmole!" she exclaimed, and she smiled. "Anyhow, I know exactly what Thomas and Maggot are like. They can stay at Gortanore, whether they like it or not, and I'll keep an eye on them."

The last time Grace and I saw each other at Caldicot was before we found out we had the same father, and still believed we might be betrothed. I remember we sat in my climbing-tree for hours. Then we stood on top of Tumber Hill but we couldn't see Wales because it was too dark, and Grace said that didn't mean it wasn't there, and Wales was a matter of faith. She said she knew we couldn't often meet, but she and I could be like that for one another. A matter of faith.

She was so angry when we couldn't be betrothed; she accused me of not really caring but just saying I did.

But the daggers have disappeared from Grace's eyes now. She's tall and willowy, and quite pale.

We walked down to the churchyard to visit Nain and little Luke, and I picked a few wan, starry primroses and placed them at the foot of each grave.

"When little Luke died," I said, "he took Lady Helen's happiness with him. But now she's found it again."

"I hope Winnie won't take away your and Tom's happiness," Grace said. "Or your friendship."

We walked over to the wall overlooking the pond, and hoisted ourselves onto it.

"You need each other more than either of you needs her," she said in a thin voice.

"We'll be all right," I said. "I think we will."

Grace put her arm through mine. "Boys do have strong feelings," she said. "You were right."

"You remember!"

"I'm sorry for you and Tom. I love you both."

For a while we sat side by side. I picked up a pebble lying on top of the wall and lobbed it into the water. Slowly the ripples spread, until the whole pond gently swayed.

Grace leaned forward and put her face between her hands. "I have chosen," she said, "to become a nun."

"Grace!"

"Well, a novice. I told our father."

"He never told me."

Grace winced.

"What did he say?" I asked.

"It wouldn't cost him as much as paying a dowry!"

"Tom didn't tell me either."

"Quite right," said Grace. "He knows I wanted to tell you myself. I've thought about it for three years."

"Since . . ."

"I want to wear white robes and black," Grace said. "I want to learn to read and write, like you. I want to sing and pray seven times each day. I want to be a bride of Christ."

"I couldn't do that," I said. "Be a monk, I mean."

And neither could Gatty, I thought. Better a pilgrimage than a nunnery.

"Actually," said Grace, "I think you could. Part of you, anyhow."

"In Zara," I said, "on our crusade, there was a nun. Sister Cika."

"That's a strange name. I'm entering White Ladies as soon as the prioress sends for me! You know, beyond Wenlock."

"I saw terrors," I said. "A singing teacher cut to pieces. Women used and murdered."

"Were they Saracens?"

"What does that matter? A little Christian boy trussed and catapulted over the city wall."

"Oh Arthur!"

"Sister Cika took me to her spirit-garden. Each flower and plant there was holy. Aaron's Rod, Yellow Archangel . . . I wanted to stay forever."

Grace nodded. "But your way's through the world," she said. "I do know that." She gazed at me, and then her eyes filled with light. "Arthur!"

Sitting on the wall, we embraced.

"I'm so happy you've come back," sighed Grace. "I've been able to see you again. It's a gift from God!"

DIGGING

OU PROMISED," SAID MAGGOT. "YOU GAVE US YOUR word."

"And you broke yours," I said.

"We did all we could, sir," Thomas protested.

"More than," sniffed Maggot.

"More than, yes. Your mother, she said she couldn't no more. Drizzling and sobbing the whole time."

"Did you tell her how much I wanted to meet her?" I demanded.

Maggot gizzened, and put her face in mine. "And we gave you her ring and all," she said. "Didn't we, sir?"

"You only helped me when there was something in it for you," I said. "My own mother! And you wouldn't tell me anything."

"That's not true, is it, Maggot? We was helping you."

"What? By threatening me — me and Lord Stephen — that you'd tell Sir William?"

"Yes, well, it's we what did the hard work, isn't it?"

"The going between," said Maggot. She wiped her dripping nose on the back of her hand.

"Doing you favors," grumbled Thomas.

Maggot put her face in mine again so I couldn't even see her straight. "Hard work!" she repeated.

"Digging!" I said loudly.

I didn't mean to, but that's what I said.

Maggot took a step back, and avoided my eye; Thomas peered at me sideways.

"You murdered Emrys," I said.

"We never," Thomas said.

"You buried him, then."

Thomas clucked and shook his head.

"Sir William murdered him in the cellar . . . ," I said.

"Who told you that?" snapped Thomas.

"The thick walls did," I said. "No one upstairs would have heard anything."

"You can't prove that," said Thomas.

"And I know where you buried him," I said in a steady voice.

Thomas gave a sudden jerk.

"Near that shelter. On the edge of the wood."

"No!" shrieked Maggot. "Only because . . ."

Thomas rounded on Maggot, snarling.

"I know enough to have you both hanged."

Actually, I knew far less than I was pretending. But it worked. Thomas and Maggot had proved their own guilt.

"How could you?" I asked them. "Emrys was crippled by a wild boar, wasn't he? He couldn't even fight back."

"We don't know nothing about that," Thomas muttered.

"I'll give you a choice," I said. "Find Emrys's bones before I do. Bring them to me. He must be buried in sacred ground. Either that, or I'll accuse you both in court."

the king who was and will be

108

THIS LITTLE ROOM, UP HERE UNDER THE THATCH.

This is where I looked out through the wind-eye and spied the world. Where I looked into my stone, and saw King Arthur born. Where I looked into my own head and heart, and prepared parchment and mixed ink, and tried to find the fitting words.

And this is the slice of the old apple tree Gatty and I carried up here, so I could perch my inkwell on it.

Gatty! Yes, we'll go upstream when you come home. If you want, I'll bring you to Catmole.

Four years have gone by since Merlin gave me my obsidian on the top of Tumber Hill. My seeing stone. This is where I used to hide it, in this gap between these two blocks of stone.

Up here, it seems so quiet. I can hear my own breathing. If I rub my forefinger against the soft wall, I can hear the tiny white flakes fluttering to the floor.

But there was something scratching under the floorboards until I stamped on them. Now it's listening, as I am. April puts her mouth to the wind-eye and blows very gently. In the thatch, I can hear soft purring: the house-martins, maybe, home again and nesting.

Is there anything on this middle-earth better than waking in this little room on a chill April morning, and lying warm under my sheepskin, and listening to one uncertain whistler, then ten, then a thousand, the whole parliament of birds singing to high heaven?

That's what I did this morning.

Slowly I unrolled the filthy cloth. You can still see it was once saffron.

Ice and fire. With my fingers I pressed the stone against my palm. I looked into its eye.

"The stone's not what I say it is. It's what you see in it." That's what Merlin told me.

Sir Bedivere is carrying King Arthur on his back.

As if he were a little child.

He plows across the foreshore to the very place where he hurled Excalibur into the waves. Below the shingle-bank, a barge is waiting. Many women wearing black hoods are sitting in it, and as soon as they see the king, they wail and shriek.

"Put me in the barge," King Arthur says.

Sir Bedivere slithers down the shingle-bank with King Arthur on his back.

The women reach out for him. A crowd of white hands. A cradle of arms. They wrap King Arthur in scarlet and gold cloth and lay his head in the lap of one lady.

"Arthur," she whispers. "Why have you taken so long? My dear son!"

Her son?

Ygerna! It's Ygerna! I saw her place her hands over her unborn baby, and embrace the whole world. Arthur was taken away from her when he was two days old, and at last he has returned to her.

"Your head wound is so cold," Ygerna murmurs.

"My lord Arthur!" cries Sir Bedivere. "My king! Without you, what will become of me?"

The king gazes at Sir Bedivere. His eyes are dim.

"Here and alone?"

"I can no longer help you," the king says quietly. "You must trust in yourself."

Again, all the women in the boat keen. With their fingernails they shred their gowns.

"If Sir Lancelot sails home, tell him of my need of him when I fought Sir Mordred. Tell him I always loved him."

Sir Bedivere grips the gunwale. He cannot let the king go.

"I will cross the water, and go into the hill," says Arthur-in-the-stone. "I will sleep a long sleep, and many knights will sleep there with me. I will sleep and heal. I will heal and wake, and march out of the hill, and drive all my enemies back into the sea. I am Arthur, son of Uther and Ygerna. The king who was and will be."

Now the oarsmen lean forward. They pull. . . .

Sir Bedivere's fingers loosen their grip.

Away across the stabbing silver wavelets the barge glides.

Ahead of it now, a hill begins to rise. First grey-blue and misty, like something in the mind long forgotten. Now green, grass-green and growing.

It humps its back. High!

Tumber Hill!

such high happiness

I NEVER REALIZED! I NEVER SUPPOSED ARTHUR WAS THE Sleeping King.

Now I know he's not in Caer Caradoc. Or Weston. Or Panpunton. He's here in Tumber Hill.

Where he and Guinevere held their wedding feast.

In the hall everyone was still asleep. Sian and Grace, Slim, Tanwen and Kester, Ruth, Robbie. I snapped my fingers and Tempest and Storm jumped up.

It was so light outside. So bright.

First I walked right round the bottom of the hill, keeping my eyes open for any sign of an opening. That took a long time. Maybe it's higher up. There must have been a lake here once. I'll go on searching. . . .

Then I hurried to the little green glade and my climbing-tree. I remembered the wandering scholar reading in the glade near Verona. I sat in my high perch amongst all the beech leaves just bursting out of their wrappings.

I ran up to the crown of the hill. I stood and stared out across the whole world of our Middle March. The row of beehives. The shining stream. Our scarlet flag dancing. Gatty's cottage, empty now. Pike Forest, the shadowy hills. The way to Catmole.

The hounds chased round in giddy circles, barking themselves hoarse.

Somehow I left all my fears and sorrows at the bottom of the hill. My head and my heart swelled with such high happiness. I opened my whole self, and shouted.

Lady Alice met me as I came down.

"Leaping like a deer! How do you do it?"

"Yard-skills!" I gasped.

"Now, Arthur! I want you to come to Gortanore as soon as you can."

"I will!"

"But before that, I've arranged for you to meet your mother."

"My mother!"

Lady Alice nodded. "Mair," she said gently. "You've waited so long."

"When?" I panted.

"Tomorrow."

"Tomorrow! Where?"

"Where do you suppose?"

"The Green Trunk?"

Lady Alice smiled.

my mother

HE WAS THERE ALREADY.

Sitting on the Green Trunk.

She was wearing a straw hat, and her head was bowed. Her hands were joined. They lay in her lap like a white dove.

I had this thought: that she had always been there, only before I'd been unable to see her.

Very quietly I dismounted. I didn't take my eyes off her but, out of the corner of my eye, I thought I saw someone else slipping away between the trees into the green gloom. Lady Alice?

She sat as still and patient as Mary on my ring.

I let go of Pip's reins and stepped up to her. . . .

All the way from Caldicot to the Green Trunk, I kept thinking how long it's taken to meet my mother but how I would have gone on forever, because nothing mattered so much.

Pip's cantering hooves drummed my own heartbeat; it sang out the words that have driven me on: Winnie announcing, "Everyone needs to know who their own mother is," and Gatty saying she'd search just the same as me, and Lord Stephen saying, "Your mother is your mother and you should find her."

. . . and very slowly she looked up.

Her violet eyes.

Wide and waiting.

Her Ygerna-eyes deep as the little wood-violets that grow round the fringes of Pike Forest. Her almond-shaped face.

I gasped. "I've seen you before."

She gazed at me, unblinking.

"In my stone. I can't explain it. Well, I will!"

She swallowed. Her breasts heaved.

"You are . . . I mean, you are my mother?"

Slowly, gently, she nodded.

Her eyes were filling with tears.

"I've thought and thought of all the things I'd say, and what I'd say first, and what I wanted to say most, and now I can't think of one thing."

"I've seen you every day," she whispered.

"Every day?"

"Looking like you did on my ring. Giving me that apple."

We both wept then. I drew her up and pulled her to me, and by mistake I knocked off her straw hat, and we sobbed and howled. I never knew there was such pain.

I kept screwing up my eyes. Trying to stop.

She was so small. So slight. Just a scrap.

"They . . . they . . ."

She couldn't say the words. Her sobbing and gasping kept getting in the way.

"They . . . they said you were sickly and died."

My mother's whole body was shuddering.

"I . . . I thought they murdered you," she said.

"I'm here," I said. "I'm here. I'm here."

"They wouldn't let me see you," my mother said, and I could hear the lovely Welsh lilt in her voice.

"Who?" I asked.

"They wouldn't tell me anything about you."

She trembled, as if she had caught a fever.

I sniffed, and somehow inside me I began to feel more calm again; the calm spread right through my heart, then my head. I held my mother to me, warm and quivering.

"It's all right," I said. "Sir William's dead. You do know that. Don't you?"

"It's them," she gulped.

"Who? You mean Thomas and Maggot?"

My mother pressed her head against my chest.

"They can't hurt you. Not any longer." I could hear my voice was hoarse.

Suddenly my mother jerked away from me. Her face was cracked and glistening.

"I loved you!" she cried. "I loved you so much! I never wanted Sir William! I didn't. But that doesn't mean I didn't want you." She grabbed my shoulders. "You never thought that?"

"I . . . I wasn't sure," I said.

"I wanted you! I loved you!" my mother cried. "I didn't want you to be taken away. I couldn't bear it!"

"I think I've been waiting all my life to hear that," I said huskily.

Mair. My own blood-mother. Her own son. We were inside-out somersaulters. Dreamers, red-eyed and waking.

"I thought you might be like Sir William," she said in a low voice.

Fiercely I shook my head. "I've kept trying to find you," I said. "From the day Sir John — Sir William's brother — told me about you. I came here before to meet you, you know."

I rubbed my sore eyes and my mother looked at me.

"Your ears stick out like mine," she said, wonderingly. "I've longed to know what you looked like."

"Once I thought I was growing a tail," I said. "I was afraid."

My mother laughed and sobbed, both at the same time. "You're so handsome," she said.

"You live at Catmole?" I asked her.

My mother nodded.

"Lord Stephen told me," I said. "He was my lord, and he wanted me to meet you. He and Lady Alice. You do know Catmole's . . . well . . . you know it will be mine now?"

My mother looked anxious.

"I can go away," she said in a low voice.

"Go away?"

"I will. If it's difficult."

"Away? Never!"

My mother stared at me.

"Not now! Not ever!" I shouted.

She smiled the ghost of a smile. "You'll scare the birds away!" she said.

"Listen to them!" I cried. "Each one of them! That lark! Singing its heart out!"

each one of us

RIDING TO THE GREEN TRUNK, I WAS SO EAGER AND anxious: It felt as if I were making the whole journey while holding my breath.

But after I promised my mother I'd come to Catmole soon, very soon; after she reassured me she'd be waiting for me, and stepped away into the gloom so lightly . . .

I felt very strong as I rode to Gortanore. And very tired too. I didn't want any more to happen! Twice, I almost fell asleep in the saddle.

Haket, Lord Stephen's priest, was right when he told me many people behave like animals. I've seen that for myself. But surely he was wrong in saying none of us can enter Jerusalem until everyone is truly Christian in word and deed.

Jesus was merciful. He died on the cross to redeem my sins.

And Sir Perceval, Sir Galahad, and Sir Bors: They quested in the wilderness, and suffered, and achieved the Holy Grail not for themselves but for each of us.

Sister Cika told me Saracens and Jews believe a person who saves the life of another saves the whole world. I believe that too.

I believe each of us can make a difference.

It's people like Wido and Godard and Giff, following each other like cattle, never questioning, never thinking for themselves, becoming numb to bloodshed and other people's pain, who turn our world into a wasteland.

Sir John's right. Each person does have his own position, her own duties — in a family, a manor, a kingdom. But what I want at Catmole is one fellowship. One ring of trust. I want everyone in the manor to know we all need each other and each one of us makes a difference.

That doesn't mean there won't be cheating and complaints and arguments and rivalries and anger. Of course there will.

But there are all kinds of ways of preventing and punishing without spilling blood, aren't there?

That boy in the mangonel, and the Venetian whose nose I sheared off, and Nasir and Zangi and the women with no names: Not one day passes without my seeing them.

I think I was wrong to threaten Thomas and Maggot with hanging. I knew it the moment I said it. After Sir John struck off Lankin's left hand, all Caldicot suffered and festered for a long time.

Sometimes I think how Saladin could easily have killed the Christian pilgrims who journeyed to the Holy Land, but he chose what was honorable and much more difficult: He gave them safe passage.

My stone! My seeing stone!

I've seen in it my own thoughts and feelings. All I hope to be; all I must never be.

I've seen my mother in it. And Tom, and Winnie, and Serle, and Merlin . . .

But the last time I looked, I couldn't see anything in my stone at all.

King Arthur has gone into the hill.

"Without you, what will become of me?" Sir Bedivere cried.

What will become of him?

And Sir Lancelot! Will he sail back from France after he hears Sir Gawain's letter?

What will happen to the half-moon, lying on her back — the shining rock crystal with the names of all the knights cut round the rim?

What will happen to Queen Guinevere?

There's so much to discuss now with Tom and Lady Alice.

About Winnie, of course, but before that we have to divide Sir William's land and livestock and belongings. Tom hasn't seen the manor in Champagne; he has never left the Middle March. And I've never seen Catmole.

"Why don't you ride over there first?" Lady Alice said. "Before we bloat our heads with arrangements and numbers and duties and everything."

"On my own?"

"You're ready, aren't you? You've proved yourself." Lady Alice smiled. "They're waiting to welcome you."

"Do you know," I said, "just before he died he slung an arm round my shoulders?"

"Who?" Tom asked.

"Sir William. It's the only time he ever did anything like that." I shook my head. "Even then, it may just have been because I was walking too fast!"

"Oh Arthur!" said Lady Alice. She touched my right cheek. "Only you would say that."

"Anyhow, he was complaining about all the delays and arguments in Zara, and about being sixty-eight, and maybe not . . . not seeing you again. And then he began to talk about Catmole. I can remember exactly what he said:

" 'The river in loops. The shapely mound, yes, the manor-mound, and the greenness of the green in the water-meadows. I'd be glad to ride there again, boy.' "

The three of us leaned forward a little and looked steadily at one another. Then Tom laid his right hand over Lady Alice's hand, and I laid my left hand over Tom's.

We drew ourselves up and smiled.

"It's a strange name," said Tom. "Catmole."

"Not really," I replied.

I remembered how I said "Catmole, Catmole" to myself over and again, almost three years ago now, and how all the letters began to seethe: catmole, catmole . . . cometale . . . mot . . . malecot . . . elmcoat . . . comelat . . . camelot . . .

Camelot!

"Good!" Lady Alice said. "It's decided, then. I'll send a messenger."

"Not Thomas," I said.

"Certainly not!" Lady Alice exclaimed. "I've told Thomas and Maggot not to go anywhere near the place, and they know what will happen if they do."

Tom drew his forefinger across his throat, and grinned.

"They've got work to do for you here, haven't they?" Lady Alice asked.

"Did they tell you?" I asked.

"What work?" asked Tom.

"I told them to find Emrys's bones," I said. "Before I do."

"They asked me to tell you they can help you . . . ," Lady Alice began.

"That's what they always say."

". . . and give you what you wanted."

"Oh!"

"Yes," Lady Alice said very brightly. "A messenger. I'll send myself! I'll ride over to Catmole early, and tell everyone you're coming."

the king in yourself

112

PIP AND I WERE UNABLE TO KEEP UP WITH THE CLOUDS. Opening their fingers and closing them, stretching them again, like huge sky-women kneading dough.

There were pockets of blue. Little muzzy promises.

Around us, rabbits scurried and sprinted — they never touched the ground. Arrogant cock pheasants prinked and stalked, allowing us to come close, but never closer.

Each silly, tender leaf. Each petal of hawthorn blossom.

But as soon as we came over the ridge, we ducked right under the wind.

And there it was.

Catmole.

The manor house ensconced on its shapely mound, almost growing out of it; its walls, mossy and oaten, buttermilk in the sunlight; the little flag, scarlet and white, thrilling to the wind.

First you cross a sloping field thick with sandy, sloppy cattle. Pip splashed straight through a pool of first-day dung.

You come down to a curling river, and that's where England ends and Wales begins.

Someone was standing on the wooden bridge. He was wearing a dark hood, but as I rode up to him, he swept it back.

"Merlin!" I shouted.

At once I dismounted.

"Is it really you?" I exclaimed. "Where have you been?"

Merlin inspected me and smiled. "I am where I'm needed," he replied.

"Here and now!" I said firmly. "I need you."

"Young kings often do."

"I'm no king."

"But you've discovered the king in yourself," Merlin said. "Haven't you? And isn't this Catmole your . . . Camelot?"

"I know! It is!"

Merlin smiled an inward smile. "You have grown into your name," he said, "as each of us must. You've understood the stone's meaning."

"Wonderful. Terrible."

Merlin sighed. "Just like life," he said. "Well! You know its story now."

"But there's so much I don't know."

Merlin looked at me with his mysterious silver-grey eyes. "There always will be," he told me. "But it's time to give the stone back."

"Give it back!"

My seeing stone has been my day-and-night companion for the last four years.

"The king has gone into the hill," Merlin said gently. "The stone has nothing more to show or say to you."

"I thought it was mine," I said.

I delved into my saddlebag and pulled out the obsidian in its dusty saffron cloth. I cradled it between my hands and squeezed it as hard as I could. Then I handed it to Merlin.

"It is yours," said Merlin. "Its story will never end in you, will it? But there's always someone else just ready for this stone."

"You will stay here?"

Merlin nodded. "For a while," he said. "Provided you treat me just as well as Sir John did! And you, Arthur, you'll keep asking? Asking the right questions?"

First you cross a sloping field.

You come down to a curling river.

You pass over the wooden bridge and step into a little water-meadow so impossibly bright green, everything seems possible. . . .

And there she was, my mother, as she said she would be, standing by her croft, wearing a white cloth cap, holding a hoe.

I strode, then I half-ran towards her.

I held her to me, and in a low voice I said-and-sang:

"That lark! It was singing its heart out.
And we were clinging, winging, half-wild.
Ring-giving mother unending you are.
King of the Middle March I will be."

All around us the people of Catmole — forty-three souls, Lady Alice says — were leaving their strips and crofts and cottages, and walking towards us. They came from the stables, the sty and the sheepfold, the fishnets stretched from bank to bank; they came from the hives and the herb garden, the orchard, the headlands and open fields.

I greeted them. Each one of them.

◆ ◆ ◆

Across a sloping field and down to a river, silver, sizzling in the sunlight . . . over the wooden bridge and into a water-meadow . . . you come to three huge oaks sinking their claws into the ground. You follow a track along the foot of the mound, and now it doubles back, rising to the courtyard and the manor house.

My mother and I led the way, and everyone fell in behind us.

The ribbed oak door was wide open.

"Welcome-wide," my mother whispered. That ghost of a smile again.

I took a deep breath and walked in.

Around me, spacious whitewashed walls; above my head, the cruck-roof, soaring; beneath my feet, rushes strewn with cowslops, primroses, rosemary, violets.

There was a long table. Something lay on it, shining.

Obsidian and gold. Ivory . . .

I caught my breath.

King Arthur's own reading-pointer!

"Merlin!" I called out. "Where are you?"

Merlin appeared in the doorway. A dark icon framed in sunlight.

"Well!" he said in his deep voice. "Do you see?"

I picked up the shining pointer. The little triangle of ice and fire grew warm in my left palm.

I planted it between my thumb and king-finger, and drew a loop around my people.

I waved it like a wand. I made words out of air.

word list

Aeolus in Greek mythology, the god of the winds

aketon a quilted garment of buckram worn under a mail-shirt and reaching to the knees

alum mineral salt used as a fixative by cloth manufacturers

argent in heraldry, the color silver or white

azure in heraldry, the color blue

ballista (plural: ballistae) a kind of huge crossbow, used for shooting missiles

Barb breed of horse that originated in Morocco, and was the mount of the Muslim Berber horsemen

bracer a leather guard for the wrist, used in archery

braies baggy linen drawers

bur a small, round plate on a spear to protect the hand

Byzantine (adjective) of Byzantium or Constantinople

caltrops iron balls with four sharp prongs (strewn on the ground to wound foot soldiers and horses)

the categories The Greek philosopher Aristotle argued that meaningful language consists of ten categories (*substance, quantity, quality, relationship, place, time, position, equipment,* and the active and passive tenses). *Substance* stands on its own; the other nine belong to *substance* and depend on it for their meaning.

chausses leggings made of mail

chin-pie rubbing the chin (usually someone else's) with the hand until it feels hot

citole a stringed instrument, similar to a lyre

collops small slices of meat

costrel a large bottle with an ear so it can hang from a waist-belt

cowslop Middle March name for *cowslip*

CRUCK-ROOF a roof with a framework made of pairs of curved and arched timbers

CUISSES thigh-guards made of quilted linen, worn over the chausses

DAMSON a small plum with a dark purple or black skin

DESTRIER a warhorse

EXCOMMUNICATION a sentence of exclusion from the communion of the Church, including the sacraments

FARRIER a man who shoes horses

FARTHING a coin valued at one quarter of a penny

FIRST NIGHT WATCH a period of duty aboard ship lasting from 8 P.M. until midnight

FLEUR DE SOUVENANCE (FRENCH) a flower, sometimes made of jewels, to serve as a reminder or keepsake; used here to mean a kiss

FONTANEL a membrane-covered space between two bones, especially the spaces between the bones of the skull

FORUM an open space on deck around a ship's mainmast where people can assemble

FUSTIAN a coarse cloth woven from cotton and flax, first made in Fustat (a suburb of Cairo) in Egypt

GALINGALE the aromatic root of an East Indian plant, used in medicine and cookery

GALL a bitter excrescence on trees produced by the action of insects

GIZZEN to grin audibly

GOGONIANT! (WELSH) Glory be!

GOLDCREST a golden wren

GRAIN OF PARADISE a West African plant used as a spice

GULES in heraldry, the color red

JOUST a war game in which two mounted men try to unseat one another, using lances

KEEN to wail or mourn bitterly

LANCET-WINDOW a tall and narrow window, pointed at the top

THE LAND OVERSEA the name for the territory, including Palestine and the Nile Delta, over which Christians and Muslims fought during the Crusades

LAST a wooden model of the foot, used by shoemakers

LATEEN SAIL a triangular sail suspended at 45 degrees to the mast

LEUCROTA a fabulous beast, which combines elements of a donkey, stag, lion, and horse, and makes a noise resembling human speech

MANGONEL an engine of war designed like a huge catapult, used for throwing stones

MARK two-thirds of the pound sterling

MAST nuts that have fallen to the forest floor

MOLE a stone pier or breakwater

NAKER a kettle-drum

NOVICE in religious orders, a person (often a child) under probation, prior to taking monastic vows

OBSIDIAN volcanic glass, usually black, believed by some cultures to have magical powers

PATEN a shallow dish used for bread at the celebration of the Eucharist

PEL a wooden post against which squires practiced swordplay

PETRARY much the same as a mangonel

PILLARS OF HERCULES the huge rocks standing at the entrance to the Mediterranean, one in Spain, the other in Morocco

PYX a box or vessel in which bread consecrated at the Eucharist is kept

QUINTAIN a post, or the object attached to it, used for practice at jousting with a lance

READING-POINTER a little rod, like a pencil, with which to follow text word by word

REBEC a stringed instrument played with a bow

RECKLING the smallest or weakest animal in the litter

ROUNSEY a strong horse without special breeding used mainly by knights and travelers

SAIS (WELSH) Saxon, or Englishman; sometimes used as a term of abuse

SAMITE heavy silk, sometimes threaded with gold

SHAWM a kind of oboe, with a double reed in the mouthpiece

SHEEP-RUN a track made by sheep

SHRITHE to move in a supple, sinewy, threatening way

SOLAR a withdrawing room, where one can be alone or talk to people in private

STINK-HORN a foul-smelling fungus

Straits of Morocco Straits of Gibraltar

Terce a set of prayers said or sung at 9 A.M. In all, nuns and monks attended seven services during each twenty-four hours: Matins/Lauds, Prime, Terce, Sext, None, Vespers, and Compline.

tinctures, the seven a term used in heraldry to describe colors, metals, and furs, each of which have their own names: *azure* (blue), *gules* (red), *purpure* (purple), *vert* (green), *argent* (silver/white), *or* (gold/yellow), and *sable* (black)

tormentum (plural: tormenta) a stone-throwing machine, worked by making a spring out of twisted ropes

tournament a magnificent sporting and social occasion at which knights engaged in a series of contests

undercroft an arched space under the ground floor of a building

vellum the best kind of parchment, made from the skin of calf, lamb, or kid

verjuice the acid juice of unripe grapes and other sour fruit, used in cooking

vermilion bright red or scarlet

water-meadow a pasture periodically flooded with water from a stream or river

CALENDAR

406–7 The Romans withdraw from Britain.

c. 500 The legendary Arthur defeats the Anglo-Saxons at the Battle of Mount Badon.

c. 597 The missionary Augustine, sent by Pope Gregory I, lands in Britain.

1076 Jerusalem is captured by the Turks.

1095 Pope Urban II proclaims the First Crusade; Usamah ibn-Munqidh, friend of Saladin and author of *Memoirs*, is born.

1096–1102 The First Crusade

1099 The crusaders capture Jerusalem.

c. 1118 Enrico Dandolo, Doge of Venice, is born.

1122 Eleanor of Aquitaine is born.

1134 Sir William de Gortanore is born.

1136 Geoffrey of Monmouth completes his *History of the Kings of Britain*.

1138 Saladin is born.

1147–9 The Second Crusade

c. 1150 Geoffrey de Villehardouin, Marshal of Champagne and author of *Conquest of Constantinople*, is born.

1154 Henry II is crowned.

1158 Richard I (Coeur-de-Lion) is born.

1170s Chrétien de Troyes, author of *Erec and Enide*, begins to write his Arthurian romances.

1180s Marie de France writes her *lais* or short story poems.

1183 Saladin unites Syria and Egypt; ibn Jubayr chronicles his pilgrimage to Mecca (1183–5); Serle de Caldicot is born.

1185 Tom de Gortanore is born.

1186 Arthur de Caldicot is born on March 1.

1187 The Sultan Saladin captures Acre and Jerusalem; Gatty is born; Lady Tilda de Gortanore dies in giving birth to Grace de Gortanore.

1188 The Saladin Tithe (tax) is levied to help finance the Third Crusade; Gerald, author of *The Journey Through Wales* and *The Description of Wales,* travels with Baldwin, Archbishop of Canterbury; Sir William de Gortanore marries Lady Alice; Winifred de Verdon is born.

1189 Henry II dies, and Richard I (Coeur-de-Lion) is crowned.

1189–92 The Third Crusade, led by Frederick Barbarossa of Germany, Philip Augustus of France, and Richard Coeur-de-Lion of England

1191 Sian de Caldicot is born.

1192 Richard Coeur-de-Lion leaves the Holy Land and is imprisoned by Leopold of Austria until 1194.

1193 Saladin dies, aged 54.

1199 Richard Coeur-de-Lion is wounded at Chalus and dies; his brother John (b. 1167) is crowned; Pope Innocent III proclaims the Fourth Crusade, and Fulk de Neuilly preaches it.

1200 Lord Stephen de Holt chooses Arthur de Caldicot as his squire, and they take the Cross at Soissons.

1201 The Venetians agree to build the crusader fleet, and Arthur de Caldicot and Lord Stephen return from Venice in April; Thibaud de Champagne dies, and Boniface de Montferrat is chosen to lead the Fourth Crusade.

1202 Arthur de Caldicot and Winifred de Verdon are betrothed in April; the crusaders muster in Venice; on July 27, Arthur de Caldicot is knighted Sir Arthur de Gortanore; the crusaders sail for Zara early in October. Zara falls on November 24.

1203 Sir Arthur de Gortanore returns to the Middle March.

1204 Christian Constantinople is wrecked and looted by the crusaders; Eleanor of Aquitaine dies.

1205 The crusaders return home without reaching Jerusalem.

About the Author

KEVIN CROSSLEY-HOLLAND GREW UP IN THE ENGLISH countryside at the foot of a high hill. While an undergraduate at Oxford University, he fell in love with the Middle Ages and Anglo-Saxon poetry — a passion now reflected in his many highly praised collections and retellings of medieval stories and myths. In 1985, he received the Carnegie Medal for his novel *Storm,* while *The Seeing Stone,* the first book in his Arthur trilogy, won the Guardian Children's Fiction Prize and was shortlisted for the Whitbread Award and the *Los Angeles Times* Book Prize. It was also named an ALA Notable Book for Older Readers. The Arthur trilogy has won worldwide acclaim and is being published in twenty-one languages. It has already sold more than a million copies.

Kevin writes: "Writers, painters, composers, filmmakers, artists of all kinds have been visitors to Camelot for more than eight hundred years. If you, too, want to spend more time with some of the characters Arthur de Caldicot sees in his stone, there are dozens of ways of doing so. Some of the better Arthurian novels written during my lifetime are *The Sword in the Stone* by T. H. White (adapted by Lerner and Loewe for *Camelot* and by Walt Disney); *The Lantern Bearers* and *Sword at Sunset* by Rosemary Sutcliff; *The Dark Is Rising* (set in modern Britain) and other novels by Susan Cooper; *Merlin Dreams* by Peter Dickinson; and *Corbenic* by Catherine Fisher. When I taught in an American university, my students particularly enjoyed *The Mists of Avalon* by Marion Zimmer Bradley and Donald

Barthelme's *The King*. Or how about Tennyson's wonderful poems, *Idylls of the King*, and the paintings of the Pre-Raphaelites, and the film *Excalibur*? All these works were inspired by the great medieval Arthurian romance writers; like mine, they're new leaves on an old tree."

Kevin and his wife, Linda, live on the coast of the North Sea in Norfolk, England.

Journey to worlds of adventure and danger

The Keys to the Kingdom

by Garth Nix

Seven days. Seven keys. One boy ventures through the doorway to a mysterious and fantastical world.

DELTORA

by Emily Rodda

Enter the realm of monsters, mayhem, and magic.

GUARDIANS of GA'HOOLE

BY KATHRYN LASKY

A thrilling series about an owl world where unknown evil lurks, friends band together, and heroism reigns supreme.

Available wherever books are sold.

SCHOLASTIC

www.scholastic.com

FILLFAN1